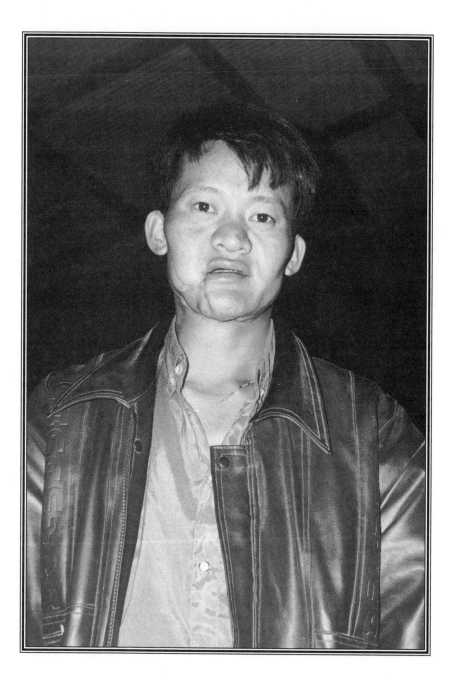

THE ATLAS

ALSO BY WILLIAM T. VOLLMANN

You Bright and Risen Angels
The Rainbow Stories
The Ice-Shirt
Thirteen Stories and Thirteen Epitaphs
Whores for Gloria
Fathers and Crows
Butterfly Stories
The Rifles
An Afghanistan Picture Show

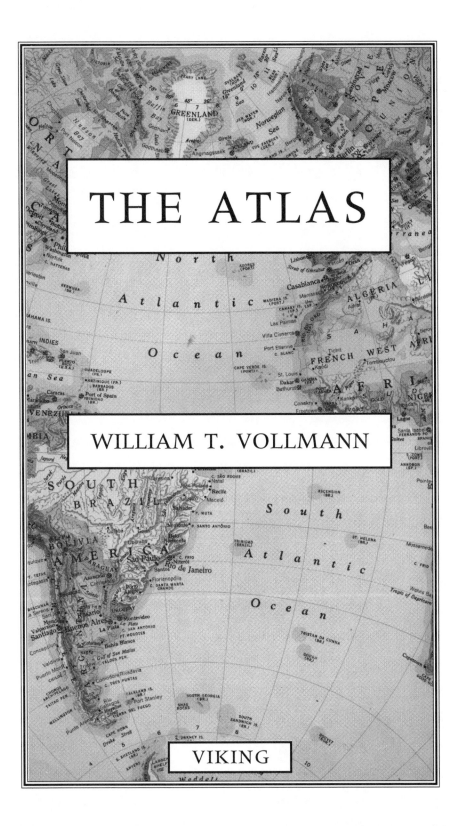

THE ATLAS

WILLIAM T. VOLLMANN

VIKING

VIKING
Published by the Penguin Group
Penguin Books USA Inc., 375 Hudson Street,
New York, New York 10014, U.S.A.
Penguin Books Ltd, 27 Wrights Lane,
London W8 5TZ, England
Penguin Books Australia Ltd, Ringwood,
Victoria, Australia
Penguin Books Canada Ltd, 10 Alcorn Avenue,
Toronto, Ontario, Canada M4V 3B2
Penguin Books (N.Z.) Ltd, 182–190 Wairau Road,
Auckland 10, New Zealand

Penguin Books Ltd, Registered Offices:
Harmondsworth, Middlesex, England

First published in 1996 by Viking Penguin,
a division of Penguin Books USA Inc.

1   3   5   7   9   10   8   6   4   2

Copyright © William T. Vollmann, 1996
All rights reserved

Page 468 constitutes an extension of this copyright page.

LIBRARY OF CONGRESS CATALOGING IN PUBLICATION DATA
Vollmann, William T.
The atlas / William T. Vollmann.
p.   cm.
Includes bibliographical references (p.   ).
ISBN 0–670–86578–8 (alk. paper)
I. Title.
PS3572.O395A85   1996
813'.54—dc20   95–39987

This book is printed on acid-free paper.
∞

Printed in the United States of America
Set in Bembo
Designed by James Sinclair

For some fine people who've helped me travel:
    Will Blythe of *Esquire* magazine.
    Elizabeth Mitchell and Bob Guccione, Jr., of *Spin* magazine.
    Paul Slovak of Viking Penguin.
Without you, friends, I would have seen much less.

                                                                W.T.V.

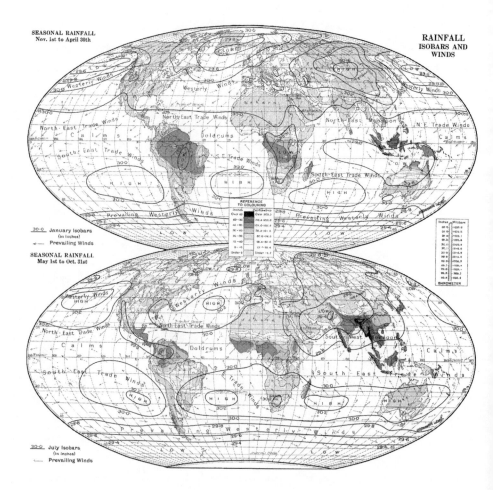

SEASONAL RAINFALL
Nov. 1st to April 30th

RAINFALL
ISOBARS AND
WINDS

SEASONAL RAINFALL
May 1st to Oct. 31st

30·0   January Isobars
       (in inches)
───   Prevailing Winds

30·0   July Isobars
       (in inches)
····· Prevailing Winds

COMPILER'S NOTE

This book was inspired by Yasunari Kawabata's "palm-of-the-hand stories," which I enjoy rereading at bedtime, in the five minutes between lying down and turning off the light. It is equally pleasurable for me to page through a certain great atlas that I have, idling over unknown countries while I wait for my companion of the evening to finish brushing her teeth. The writing of these stories has given me the same sort of desultory joy. As James Branch Cabell remarked, "Toward no one of those pre-eminent topics of my era do I feel incited to direct an intelligent and broad-minded concern." What you hold, then, is but a piecemeal atlas of the world I think in. I hope that you like it, in spite of its omission of a continent or two. And if you were to keep it by you as a pillow-book, reading through it in no particular order, skipping the tales you find tedious, dozing amidst my somniferous paragraphs, I'd feel that at last I'd done as much good in the world as the manufacturers of our drowsiest codeine syrups. Slide it under your buttocks when commencing the night's revels. Slay the nightmarish flies of sleep with its hard covers. Lay it across your eyes to guard yourself from light. And may your soul flit freely across this world! For, despite the opinion of a certain Transcendentalist, who informed us that "traveling is a fool's paradise," other philosophers reverence the salubriousness of a change of clime. Consider the school essay of a second grader of Cambodian origin. The children were asked to expound upon the topic "The Future." This boy wrote:

> IN the Future I would like the world to be a WAR zone IN CHINA. I hope I will be in the NAVY to help the USA NAVY to Kill ALLIES. I will Kill polpot and his men and famliy. I will come back as a heor. I will be the only CAMBOADIAO on the ship.

May we all kill our best allies before they kill us. And so, reader, good night.★

W.T.V.

★ For those who require games and calculations in order to drowse, I should state that this collection is arranged palindromically: the motif in the first story is taken up again in the last; the second story finds its echo in the second to last, and so on. In addition, certain tales have titles in common with books I have previously written; they are thematic reductions in the manner of Kawabata's short "Snow Country," derived from his novel *Snow Country*. (However, while Kawabata's metonym contains material present in the parent tale, my own attempts use new material, because we Americans like new things.) As for the title story, that contains a little something from each of the others.

GAZETTEER

Mount Aetna, Sicily   37.45 N, 15.00 E

Afghanistan

Agra, Division of Uttar Pradesh, India   27.09 N, 78.00 E

Algonquin Provincial Park, Ontario, Canada   45.50 N, 78.20 W

Allan Water, Ontario, Canada   50.15 N, 90.14 W

Antananarivo, Madagascar   18.52 S, 47.30 E

Avignon, Départment Vaucluse, Provence, France   43.56 N, 4.48 E

Bangkok
(Krungthepmahanakhornbowornrattamakosinmahintarayuthayama-
hadlikokpopnopparatratchathaniburiromudomratchaniwetmahasathan),
Phrah Nakhon-Thonburi Province, Thailand (Prathet Thai)
13.44 N, 100.30 E

Ban Rak Tai, Mae Hong Song Province, Thailand

Battambang City, Province Battambang, Cambodia   13.06 N, 103.13 E

Battle Rock, Oregon, U.S.A.

Beograd, Serbia, Yugoslavia   44.50 N, 20.30 E

Berkeley, California, U.S.A.   37.52 N, 122.17 W

Berlin, Germany   52.32 N, 13.25 E

Big Bend, California, U.S.A.   39.16 N, 120.39 W

Bologna, Emilia Romagna, Italia   44.30 N, 11.20 E

Boot Hill, Nebraska, U.S.A.

Boston, Massachusetts, U.S.A.   42.20 N, 71.05 W

Budapest, Hungary   47.30 N, 19.03 E

Cairo, Egypt   30.00 N, 31.15 E

California, U.S.A.

Capri, Campania, Italia   40.33 N, 14.15 E

Charlevoix, Québec, Canada

Chiang Mai, Chiang Mai Province, Thailand   18.48 N, 98.59 E

Churchill, Manitoba, Canada   58.45 N, 94.00 W

Coral Harbour, Southampton Island, Northwest Territories, Canada 64.10 N, 83.15 W

Cornwall, Ontario, Canada   45.02 N, 74.45 W

Delhi, India   28.40 N, 77.14 E

Diesel Bend, Utah, U.S.A.

Elma, Manitoba, Canada   45.50 N, 95.56 W

Eureka, Ellesmere Island, Northwest Territories, Canada   80.00 N, 85.40 W

Frankfurt am Main, Germany   50.06 N, 8.41 E

Goa, Goa, India   15.31 N, 73.56 E

Grand Central Station, New York City, U.S.A.   40.40 N, 73.58 W

Great Western Desert, Northern Territory, Australia

Guildwood, Ontario, Canada

Hanover, New Hampshire, U.S.A.   43.42 N, 72.17 W

Herculaneum, near Napoli, Campania, Italia   40.50 N, 14.15 E

Highway 88, California, U.S.A.

Highway 395, California, U.S.A.

Ho Mong, Shan State, Burma (Myanmar)

Home

Hong Kong, territory of United Kingdom, Southeast Asia   22.20 N,
114.15 E

Interstate 80, California, U.S.A.

Inukjuak, Québec, Canada   58.25 N, 78.15 W

Jaipur Province, India

Japan

Jerusalem, Israel/Jordan   31.47 N, 35.13 E

Joshua Tree National Monument, California, U.S.A.   34.09 N, 116.20 W

Karenni State, Burma (Myanmar)

Key West, Florida, U.S.A.   24.34 N, 81.48 W

La Loma, near Mexico City, Distrito Federal, Mexico   19.25 N, 99.10 W

Limbo

Los Angeles, California, U.S.A.   34.00 N, 118.15 W

Lutton, Oklahoma, U.S.A.

Madagascar

Mae Hong Song, Mae Hong Song Province, Thailand   19.18 N, 98.01 E

Mahebourg, Mauritius   20.24 S, 57.42 E

Malachi, Ontario, Canada   49.56 N, 94.58 W

Marakooper Cave, Tasmania, Australia

Masada, Territory of Judea, Israel   31.19 N, 35.21 E

Mendocino, California, U.S.A.   39.20 N, 123.46 W

Mexicali, Estado de Baja California, Mexico   32.28 N, 115.29 W

Mexico

Mexico City, Distrito Federal, Mexico   19.25 N, 99.10 W

Mission-Sainte-Marie, Midland, Ontario, Canada   44.45 N, 79.53 W

Mobile, Alabama, U.S.A.   30.40 N, 88.05 W

Mogadishu, Somalia   2.02 N, 25.21 E

Mont-Pellerin, Canton Vaudois, Switzerland

Montréal, Québec, Canada   45.36 N, 73.38 W

Nairobi, Kenya   1.17 S, 36.50 E

Napoli, Campania, Italia   40.50 N, 14.15 E

Nevada, U.S.A.

New Orleans, Louisana, U.S.A.   30.00 N, 90.03 W

New South Wales, Australia

New York City and State, U.S.A.

The Nile River, Egypt

North America

Omaha, Nebraska, U.S.A.   41.15 N, 96.00 W

Orillia, Ontario, Canada   44.36 N, 79.26 W

Ottermere, Ontario, Canada

Pacific Palisades, California, U.S.A.

Paris, Département Paris, Région Parisienne, France   48.52 N, 2.20 E

Philadephia, Pennsylvania, U.S.A.   40.00 N, 75.10 W

Phnom Penh, Cambodia   11.35 N, 104.55 E

Pickering, Ontario, Canada

Poland

Pompeii, Campania, Italia   40.45 N, 14.27 E

Pond Inlet, Baffin Island, Northwest Territories, Canada   72.40 N, 77.59 W

Port Hope, Ontario, Canada   43.58 N, 78.18 W

Puako Bay, Hawaii, U.S.A.   19.58 N, 155.49 W

Reddit, Ontario, Canada

Redfern, Sydney, New South Wales, Australia   33.55 S, 151.10 E

Resolute Bay, Cornwallis Island, Northwest Territories, Canada
74.40 N, 95.00 W

Rice Lake, Manitoba, Canada   47.44 N, 82.08 W

Roberts Camp, Wyman Creek, Deep Springs Valley, California, U.S.A.
37.21 N, 117.59 W

Roma, Italia   41.53 N, 12.30 E

Sacramento, California, U.S.A.   38.33 N, 121.30 W

Samuel H. Boardman State Park, Oregon, U.S.A.

San Bruno, California, U.S.A.   37.37 N, 122.24 W

San Diego, California, U.S.A.   32.45 N, 117.10 W

San Francisco, California, U.S.A.   37.45 N, 122.27 W

San Ignacio, Belize   17.14 N, 89.03 W

Sarajevo, Bosnia-Herzegovina   43.52 N, 18.26 E

Savant Lake, Ontario, Canada   50.16 N, 90.44 W

Sioux Lookout, Ontario, Canada   50.05 N, 91.55 W

The Slidre River, Ellesmere Island, Northwest Territories, Canada
80.00 N, 85.39 W

The Sphere of Stars

Split, Dalmatia, Republika Hrvatska (Croatia)   43.31 N, 16.28 E

State of Vatican City (Città del Vaticano)   41.54 N, 12.27 E

Sudbury, Ontario, Canada   46.30 N, 81.01 W

Sydney, New South Wales, Australia   33.55 S, 151.10 E

Tamatave, Madagascar   181.05 S, 49.23 E

Taxco, Guerrero, Mexico   18.32 N, 99.36 W

Thailand

The Pas, Manitoba, Canada   53.50 N, 101.15 W

Tokyo to Osaka, Japan

Toronto, Ontario, Canada   43.42 N, 79.25 W

Virginia Beach, Virginia, U.S.A.   36.51 N, 75.59 W

Wailea, Maui, Hawaii, U.S.A.   19.52 N, 155.08 W

Washago, Ontario, Canada   44.45 N, 79.20 W

Winnipeg, Manitoba, Canada   49.53 N, 97.10 W

Winnitoba, Manitoba, Canada

Yangon (Rangoon), Myanmar (Burma)   16.47 N, 96.10 E

Yukon Territory, Canada

Zagreb, Republika Hrvatska (Croatia)   45.48 N, 15.58 E

CONTENTS

THE ATLAS

THE ATLAS

I always liked books that contained some fine thoughts, but books that one could read without stopping, for they aroused ideas in me which I could follow at my fancy and pursue as I pleased. This also prevented me from reading geometry books with care, and I must admit that I have not yet brought myself to read Euclid in any other way than one commonly reads novels.

LEIBNITZ, letter to Foucher (1675)

OPENING THE BOOK

Grand Central Station, New York City, U.S.A. (1991)

Scissoring legs and shadows scudding like clouds across the marble proved destiny in action, for the people who rushed through this concourse came from the rim of everywhere to be ejaculated everywhere, redistributing themselves without reference to each other. A few, like the small girl who sat on the stairs holding her bald baby doll, or the lady who stopped, shifted the strap of her handbag, and gazed at the departure times for the New Haven Line, delayed judgment (and an executive paused in his descent of the steps, snorted at the girl's doll, and said: I thought that baby was real!). But no one *stayed* here, except the souls without homes. Above the information kiosk, the hands of the illuminated clock circled all the directions, tranquilly, while the stone-muffled murmurs of the multitude rose up and condensed into meaningless animal sounds. There was a circle, and its spokes were their trajectories. But the circle turned! They did not understand the strangeness of that. Creased black trousers, naked brown legs, merciless knees, skirts and jeans, overalls swollen tight with floating testicles, paisley handbags passing as smoothly as magic carpets, these made noise, had substance, but the place became more and more empty as I sat there, because none of it was *for* anything

3

but itself. The belt of brass flowers that crossed the ceiling's belly meant something, made the place more like a church; the sunken tunnels where the trains stretched themselves out, gleaming their lights, were the catacombs. One of those passageways went to the Montréaler, my favorite train. Canada's railroads continued north from Montréal, which was why when I peered into that tunnel (I'd ridden the Montréaler so many times, and wouldn't anymore), it was almost as if I could see all the way to Hudson Bay; one Canadian National sleeper did still go to Churchill—

A policeman came and told me to move on. So I went past the double green globes; I left the people who were going somewhere (a girl in high heels galloped by me, biting her lip with concentration, and one of her breasts struck my cheek); so I too went my way, obeying the same law that dispersed the others . . .

THE BACK OF MY HEAD

Sarajevo, Bosnia-Herzegovina (1992)

Sarajevo, Bosnia-Herzegovina (1992)

There came a sharp low snapping of the air, somewhat louder than before, and then another at a distance, which briefly and metallically rippled. But these variants were incidental to the main sound, the weighty unpleasant sound of earth falling on earth, as if for some burial. Granted, they were all different in their unhappy way, like a chain of sobs. Now somebody was dropping things, slowly, with a nasty kind of weariness. Something thudded down. White smoke rose diagonally and lethargically in the hot air. So it was not fuel or tires burning. Analyzing was the first step to not listening (at least to the more distant impacts). After three or four days I no longer felt a naked tenderness at the back of my head where I imagined a sniper taking aim. I could feel the nose of the bullet pointed at me just as you can feel eyes staring at your back. No matter which way I turned, the sniper who was going to kill me kept the back of my head in his sights. The spot of tenderness was small, round, localized. Why it was that particular place (the center of the occiput) I could only theorize. Perhaps it was because it was 180 degrees from my eyes, the farthest possible point from anyplace that I could ever see, the place where I used to shoot cows to be butchered. This absurd and useless sensitivity persisted until my visit to the morgue at Koševo Hospital. On that day as always I was in the back of the car, gripping the doorhandle as the militiaman shouted to the driver to move his

5

fucking ass because we were in a very dangerous open place and so we screeched around the corner and then the driver floored it; I saw the speedometer pass 120 kph and then we made another sharp turn. The back of my head itched. Not too far away, a sound came like a resinous twig bursting cozily in the fireplace. Then something ripped horribly. I remembered the UN observer at the airport coming to his feet at a similar sound, saying: That's bad. I don't know what that is. Sounds like a chain gun, but they're not supposed to have those. Maybe a rocket. — Last week's casualty list at the Holiday Inn, prepared by the Institute for Public Health, had figured up 218 killed and 1,406 wounded in Bosnia-Herzegovina, which worked out to 90 deaths and 540 injuries in Sarajevo, which became momentarily intelligible when, as I said, I smelled the day's harvest at the morgue and saw the dried blood on the floor. With no electricity and no water a morgue is not very nice. I saw the unidentified man whose legs had been blown off by a grenade. By law they had to keep him for twenty-four hours while he lay swelling and reeking on the table, a mass of shit and blood demarcating the end of his stomach. Next to him lay the twenty-five-year-old man with the bloody face (one wound was all that he had, a neat drilling from an antiaircraft gun); he was covered with flies and his hand was clenched and his naked body was reddish brown but blotched with a terrible white whose contrast with the extraordinary yellowness of the child's corpse (an antitank grenade had solved him) seemed almost planned, aesthetic, unlike the child's doll-face grinning, the eyes dark slits. From the child as from the others came the vinegar-vomit smell. It was unbearable to see how his head moved when the pathologist tried to unwrap the sheet, turning him round and round as his little skull shook; and in the end the pathologist could not do it because he'd been fossilized in his own dried blood, the sheet now hardened brown and crackly against his belly where the intestines had mushed out. Still the pathologist endeavored to remove the sheet in a professional manner, and the doll's head jerked rhythmically back and forth; so that I recollected a small Croatian girl I'd seen in a park in Zagreb; she had reddish-gold hair and was swinging. She moved almost like this doll. Sometimes she just seemed passive, with her legs locked out in front of her; at other times her knees hinged urgently until she made rapid arcs, but the creak of the swing was always the same. A man with a military crewcut sat smoking; his hair was the color of his smoke. After awhile he threw the cigarette down into the sand. It lay beside a boy's plastic spade and continued to smoke. Four boys came by and snatched it up. They passed it around from hand to hand and tried to make each other inhale. The one who'd actually found it kept his prize, watching the smoke rise from between his fingers as they all went off shouting together. The girl went on swinging. — This next one was killed several days before, said the pathologist. Perhaps you don't want to look. — The head, tiny and black, was a ball of swarming insects which for some reason had not yet attacked the yellow bloatings below. Beside him lay a woman, smiling, stained with blood.

Do you think these people died in great pain? I asked the pathologist. You look at them every day; maybe you know what they know . . .

He took me into another room. — This young boy lived three days, he said. See how his stomach is open? They say he screamed day and night. But I think he's an exception. My brother was wounded last month by a grenade. I asked him what he felt. He told me that he felt nothing. He was injured very seriously in his arm. He said it was not until later that the pain started. So I believe that most of these people felt nothing.

His words comforted me. When I left the morgue, returning to the not-yet-dead outside the hospital's dusty window-shards like gray scraps of cloth where a man sat flirting with the nurses, his hand-bandage sporting a blaze of autumn, and a smiling girl took the sun with her friends, offering to God her deep scars just under knee and eye; I got back into the car (the militiaman had refused to go in with me because last time when the pathologist raised the sheet on an unidentified body it turned out to be his friend's), I found that the tenderness at the back of my head had gone away. I wasn't afraid of being shot there anymore. I feared only getting my stomach blown open. In general, of course, I remained just as afraid. A week later, when I was standing outside one of the apartment buildings near the front, waiting for my friend Sami to buy vodka, I felt a sharp impact on the crown of my head. Reaching up to explore the wound, I felt wetness. I took a deep breath. I brought my hand down in front of my eyes, preparing myself to see blood. But the liquid was transparent. Eventually I realized that the projectile was merely a peach pit dropped from a fifteenth-floor window.

IT'S TOO DIFFICULT
TO EXPLAIN

Sarajevo, Bosnia-Herzegovina (1992)

Sarajevo, Bosnia-Herzegovina (1992)

S he sat next to me at the table, utterly trapped in silence while
the laughs burst around her like shells. Finally I asked her why
she was so unhappy.

It's too difficult to explain, she said.

Try.

You have only a few words. I have only a few words.

So it's not the war, then, I said. I think you were always unhappy.

She leaned toward me. — Yes, she said.

Me too, I said.

She smiled. She laid her pale hand down on my hand. I felt a
violent tenderness for her.

Come, she said. I must cook for these people. You can be
with me.

As we went out together, the others all shouted with glee at the
conquest they were sure I had made. The host, wounded twice since
he'd volunteered a month before, was very drunk. His was one of
those apartments still intact (or perhaps refurbished by means of that

8

special liquidity which property acquires in wartime), with carpets, glass cabinets and windows (astounding to see them unbroken), fur rugs, and all the Ballantines and vodka you could drink. He had pulled out his pistol in the middle of the party and announced that he would test my bulletproof vest, which I was wearing. His eyes gleamed with desperate laughter and the barrel wavered. — May I finish my drink first? I asked. — I *like* your style, James Bond! he shouted. He strode to the window and fired three times, roaring. Maybe he killed one of the neighbors and maybe the bullets went nowhere. And I remember how she shivered with sorrow and despair, trembling as the shots went off. — You know, I have a pathological fear, she said to me. I want to go with you, but I cannot. I have a fear of going anywhere. This street is in the center of town. It is one of the worst for snipers. And every morning I must go to work, and I must go to the doctor for my mother. I must always run. And I cannot sleep at night. The sounds of the artillery terrify me. — At that moment I would have died for her if doing that would have helped her, but nothing could help her. So we went to the door together, and the others laughed.

Outside the candle-lit apartment it was night-dark, of course. We felt our way down the two flights of stairs to the landing where the stove was, and she bent over it. — No good, she said. She put my hand on it, and I found that it was cold. Nothing would be cooked today.

So we came back to the party, and the others stared at us. They thought that we must have quarrelled.

She said to me: What I don't understand is why we have to live. Life is nothing but sadness.

But you said you liked music. Don't you have moments of happiness?

Happiness? Oh, yes, in brief flashes. And sadness for years and years.

What would make you happy?

Not to work. To live entirely alone. But I cannot, because I have no money. And I don't understand why there must be money to live.

How much money would you need to be happy?

I don't know. It's impossible anyway.

A hundred thousand deutsche marks a month?

No, no, that's too much.

How much?

Maybe two hundred.*

A month?

Yes.

So if I gave you two hundred deutsche marks you could be happy for one month?

She smiled for the second time. She thought I was joking, but she liked the joke. — Yes. You are a good man . . .

When it was time to go I got out the money and gave it to her. I had to kneel down in front of the single candle in the middle of the room to read the denominations, so everyone was watching me and I could hear their laughter hiss down eerily into nothingness. The shadow of my hand and of the bills trembled monstrous on the sniper curtain. It smeared their faces with darkness.

She wouldn't take it. — You understand nothing, she kept saying. Please, please.

So I understand nothing, I said. Take it. I can live without it.

No, no. Please.

Finally I gave up. But as I went out, preparing to descend with the other guests those cold and utterly dark flights of stairs, remembering the rotten bannister at the bottom and then the terrible danger when we had to open the front door and run out into the open street; as the militiaman shouted in rage and pain because he'd gotten drunk and done something to break open the wound in his arm where the bullet still lay grinding against the bone and which was now bleeding through his sleeve; as the host called to me, laughing: She wants to *kiss* you, James!; as the driver slipped a round into the chamber of his gun; as the women tucked up their dresses so that they could run, she came to me and squeezed my hand.

* In 1992, 200 DM would have been about U.S. $120.

ARE YOU ALL RIGHT?

Sarajevo, Bosnia-Herzegovina (1992)

Whenever I could find a phone that was working, I tried to call the woman who had said that things were too difficult to explain, but I never got through. Finally I reached her on the night before I was going to leave Sarajevo.

Are you all right? she said. That was how everyone seemed to greet each other.

A little shrapnel in my hand, but I wasn't hurt. And you?

A grenade came into our neighbor's house, she said quietly. It was dreadful.

But you, you're all right?

Yes.

We didn't say anything to each other for a moment, and then I said: I'm probably leaving tomorrow. The BBC said I could ride along in their armored car. I guess it depends on whether the road to Kisjeliak is safe.

I don't think there was a silence after I had said that, but my guilt about being free to leave has built a silence over time that drowned whatever she actually said. Every day I'd have liked to call her and ask: Are you still alive? Are you all right? But of course no one could call Sarajevo.

LOOK AT ME

Puako Bay, Hawaii, Hawaii, U.S.A. (1992)
Puako Bay, Hawaii, Hawaii, U.S.A. (1992)

Puako Bay, Hawaii, Hawaii, U.S.A. (1992)

Bleeding brackish droplets which his skin had borrowed from the artificial lagoon, he parted from his wife, she bound for sun, he for shade. They had not seen the giant turtles. He was almost dry now. His towel was stretched out beside the farthest boat. Before lying down he made certain that his watch had not been stolen. He had never had anything stolen at the beach but he continually expected something bad to happen. Coddling his little unhatched egg of anxiety, he could not see or think of anything else until he had done this. His wife had once bought him a very expensive watch which had been stolen in a hotel. The watch he had now was not expensive, so his vigilance must be some irrelevant suffix of guilt. Anyhow it had not been stolen. He lay comfortably alone. Then he noticed that a Japanese girl had pitched her chair next to him. She too was a subject of the shade kingdom, it seemed. Her husband lay on his belly in the sunny sand, twenty feet away. The girl wore a black bathing suit. She had long slender pale arms, thighs as slender as bones.

He looked into the distance, where his wife basked almost at the water's edge, reading the self-help book that promised to save their marriage.

12

The Japanese girl sat watching her husband with the utmost attention. Whenever he turned or stretched, she padded down to his claim of sand and knelt beside him, gazing into his face. Then she'd return to her chair in the grass by the rental boats and sit again, watching him patiently.

The long black locks of her hair twisted down her back and shoulders like beautiful roots. Later he would remember the sharp pelvic bone straining to break through her thigh-flesh, but for the moment he saw only her hair.

Her face was blurred as if in a dream. The way she sat, he could see only her profile, and the dark hair spun itself about her cheek like steam.

He waited for her to turn her head. He said to himself: If she turns her head, that means that she and I were born for each other. But if my wife turns her head, that means that my wife and I belong together.

He waited. Any moment now the girl would turn, and he'd see her face.

But without ever looking at him, she got up and went to her husband once more. Then she returned, slipped on her sundress and went away. Her husband lay still.

He looked at his wife, who at precisely that instant turned her head and smiled at him. He ached with dismay.

Puako Bay, Hawaii, Hawaii, U.S.A. (1992)

Fish-scales of light spread rapidly across the river. Trees shivered in their pots. The Japanese girl, shivering, tossed up her eyes in impatience, arms crossed as she stamped her feet. It was night at the lion-headed bench. Lanterns illuminated statues. Palm-fronds creaked like bedsprings. Glancing up at them, he forgot the girl at once, transfixed by the nodding of those sad and crazy shagheads, those spider-legs of darkness scuttling limp and sick, impaled on their own swaying trunks, caressing themselves evilly while curtains licked each other from lighted balconies.

Are you finished staring or do I have to go inside by myself? the girl said.

He saw a big coconut like a skull. High on a palm-pole, fronds blew back from the skull's forehead like hair or warfeathers.

I'm going inside, the girl said. I'm going in to my husband.

His gaze wandered down.

I thought you wanted me, the girl said, swallowing her tears. You followed me; you sneaked off from your wife—

But I never expected this wind! he cried. This wind blows everything away—

She had taken off her wedding ring and was squeezing it in her hand. Suddenly it escaped to the tiles by her feet, meeting them with a musical sound. Startled, he looked into her face. At once her expression changed. She glowed with a greedy ecstasy.

So you love me, she whispered. Now I know you love me. Just keep looking at me. That's all I need.

GOING BUBEYE

Sacramento, California, U.S.A. (1992)

S it back! Achilles, sit back! We're gittin' ready to go bubeye. I said jist wait a minute. Look around! Those are LIGHTS. That's fer the night time when people's readin'. Now sit back an' *enjoy it!* I said *enjoy it!* Isis, gimme the bag. Isis, I'm not playing. Isis, stop. Now eat your crunchies. That's it. That's a good girl.

When's the light gonna come on?

In a minute, okay? You don't want no more? Now *eat* 'em! Bus driver gonna come in a minute. Sit back in yer seat. He'll be there; now jist sit down. The man who took the ticket, the same one, he's the *driver*.

Can you smoke up here?

No.

Why?

'Cause it says don't smoke.

The bus driver didn't scare me, Mama. He didn't scare me.

Here we go.

How come the light don't come on?

They don't put the lights on.

Why?

That's at nighttime, hon.

Is this the freeway, Mama?

Uh huh.

Good morning, ladies and gentlemen, and welcome aboard Grey-

15

hound's Oakland–San Francisco service. I'd like to thank you for travelling Greyhound. Sit back, relax and enjoy the ride. Thank you.

Is this where we went before?

Shut up and eat. That's right. Have some more, hon.

What's this?

Just leave it. Leave it alone.

Why?

'Cause I said so.

Mama, what's that?

I assed you to sit back!

What's that boy and girl doing over there?

Sit back! Sit back and act like you don't see things!

Is he helping her go to the bafroom?

Shut up! Don't talk dirty.

That boy and girl sure are fidgety. How come they don't sit back? How come that boy keeps pulling up that girl's dress?

Uh huh.

I'm hot. I'm gonna pull up my dress, too.

You can't.

Why?

'Cause you're not supposed to. Pull down your dress. No more, now.

Mama, is they going to the bafroom?

Sit back! I'll *whack* you! Now REMEMBER that. Sit back. Just move yourself back. That's a boy. Sit back. I'm not telling you again. I'll knock you down.

Ow!

Leave 'em alone. That's a girl. There you go. What you got your hands up Achilles's pants for? Stop it right now.

They was doin' it over there.

I said take your hand out!

Ow! Ow!

You gonna remember now? Now shut up! I told you not to see things. What's over there?

They's . . . He's helping her go to the bafroom. — Ow!

Now you know what happens when you try to see things. What's over there?

I dunno, Mama. Nothing.

That's right. That's right. Don't you *ever* try to see things.

AN OLD MAN IN OLD GRAYISH KAMIKS

Coral Harbour, Southampton Island, Northwest Territories, Canada (1993)

Coral Harbour, Southampton Island, Northwest Territories, Canada (1993)

An old man in old grayish kamiks set out to hunt walrus on a morning of fresh sea-clouds. He owned a Peterhead which he had purchased down in Halifax many years before. He'd sailed her up through the Strait of Belle Isle and then northwest along the inclined coast of Labrador, careful of the treacherous Labrador Sea, and by degrees he'd come back into the country that is called Nunavik, which means *The Great Land*. Rounding the tip of the spearheaded peninsula, he sailed through the strait called Nuvummiut Tariunga until he made the town whose name means *Floating Ice*. He still had some distance left to go, but he was not tired. He went westward out of Nunavik, crossing Hudson Bay, whose mouth is narrow like the neck of a flask, and when he was almost entirely across he reached the large island that was his home.

This island we ourselves call Southampton, after the third Earl after that name who was Shakespeare's patron. The old man in old grayish kamiks had never read Shakespeare and never would. His was a low flat world of green, blue, yellow and gray, with blue sky and white ice-horizons. He owned a great deal of knowledge about ice, clouds, the Bible, motors and animals. On this island at certain seasons the people stand with their hands over their eyes and scan for polar bears before they sit down. The old man in old grayish kamiks still had very good vision, or maybe it was just that he never stopped paying attention, but he often saw polar bears before his grandchildren did. Perhaps it was because they did not get to hunt very much. First of all, many of the new generation worked at desk jobs in other towns; and secondly, fuel for the Peterhead was very expensive. The younger ones had never been walrus hunting. He was the one who told them how, when and where.

Two evenings before, the ice had been coming in and people were out shooting narwhals—rare to see any in Coral Harbour; the last time had been seven years ago. Now a whole pod of narwhals was here, which was strange with pleasing and ordinary strangeness, like the adventures of the three children who squatted, catching bigheaded green minnows in the puddles at low tide, exulting over each: Little big *big* one! — Their fingertips went cold. It had been overcast, but at around nine that night the sun came out and gilded the boats where a crowd was winding a net with fish in it. The sky tanged with salt like a single harpsichord string, a taut clean note of smell, sea-smell, no chord of rot or musk. Mosquitoes jumped and crouched. And the grandson who always got in trouble went to the old man and asked if they would be going out for walrus tomorrow, but the old man looked at the sky and shook his head.

The next evening three figures went poling very slowly out in an aluminum canoe, the nose tipping down almost to water level with every stroke of the tall one, and then they vanished behind a sailing ship in the middle of the harbor. A young woman rode a bike with her baby in the armauti of her parka. Her girlfriend came running after her, laughing. She swung off her bike and walked off beside her friend. Their footsteps were very crisp in the brown sand. That was when the youngest grandson went to the old man and the old man said: Tomorrow.

So it was that on that subsequent morning of excellent weather the old man in old grayish kamiks throttled his Peterhead slowly out of the harbor. The blocky blind-windowed houses grew small. There was one roof that had a rack of caribou antlers on it. These silhouetted themselves into the stalks of some strange weed, blended with the power wires behind them, and vanished. The two fuel towers retracted into the wide low land, and the town became the merest cluster of pastel-colored protrusions. The young boys with dogskin-ruffed parkas lay dozing on the cabin hatch, while the grandson who always got in trouble helped the old man string wire. The old man called him "the bad boy" because his parents had named him with a white man's name and the old man hated to speak English. The bad boy was not so very bad. He used to cut holes in beached boats and smash the windows of shacks, but he was still trying to finish high school and he loved his grandfather very much. He called the younger boys, in ascending order of age, One-Nut, Two-Nuts and Three-Nuts. He was Four-Nuts. He sat down among the bow's rusty chains that resembled guts.

The old man sat on top of the pilothouse, letting his legs hang down and steering with the sole of one foot inside an old grayish kamik. His kamiks were made of sealskin, which is waterproof footwear and not too warm for summer, and the duffel liners rose up above the tie and went almost to his knees. He sat, and you might have thought he was resting, but he was not. His foot was steering, and his eyes were watching for animals and ice, and his hands were busy taping wire with black electrical tape. The young men strung this wire up the mast cables. They saw a seal, but let it go because they were hunting walrus first.

Is this your seventeen magnum? one grandson called to another. — They were loading the rifles now. — Hey, what should I use, a softpoint or a hollowpoint?

Near the boat the sea was as flat as a blue-brown lake, and the sun's white reflection flapped along in it. It was breezeless, but cold, and the grandson who always got in trouble buttoned his collar up to the neck. One of the grown men stood in the hatchway, chewing a mouthful of bannock, working his gloved fingers. The boy who hated white people sat sullenly with his back turned toward me and sighted in his rifle. I was only allowed along because I had paid three hundred dollars. No one else had to pay anything. This boy had threatened to shoot the white construction foreman for no reason, and the foreman, who was big and wise and tough, just told him: Go

ahead. I'm ready for you anytime. — The boy who hated white
people was very angry at me because I had only paid three hundred
dollars and he thought that I should have paid five hundred. As for
the old man, he did not dislike me very much, but he never smiled
at me or said a word to me. I didn't care; I was used to it. The
grandson who always got in trouble liked me well enough and sometimes came to my tent to eat some of my dried meat.

Hey, let me see some of your seventeen bullets, said the grandson
who always got in trouble. Then he started to go to the hatchway.
He said to me: That's what we do, is sit with the old guy, take turns.
Been doin' that ever since we were old enough to know the guy.
Kind of a thrill to be sittin' next to him.

But later they were admiring each other's guns, and the old man
sat alone, watching ahead and steering with his feet in those old grayish kamiks.

They crossed the floe-edge quickly, sighting through their guns.
The old man had said that One-Nut could harpoon the walrus because he was the youngest. One-Nut looked proud and a little anxious, so the grandson who always got in trouble leaned toward him
and said: My big sister harpooned a seal herself up by Repulse Bay,
so she beat me! I was jealous, but so happy for her. Last time I tried,
but then when the seal's head came up I got scared. That's why I've
only shot them.

Then he winked at his own fear, and One-Nut giggled.

From a distance the edge of the ice was a series of black speckles
in a line like rocks. Presently these resolved into a long slab of turquoise with darker pyramids and trapezoids on it. The young boys
sat on the hatchcover, passing a scoped rifle from eye to eye.

Hey, little brother, you want one of my seven-six-twos? — This
was the grandson who always got in trouble, who owned a Yugo-
slavian rifle from which he'd taken the bayonet. One-Nut nodded.

Now they were at the place of sharp ice-islets where it was sunny
and cold. The old man sat smiling slightly, steering through them
with barely perceptible motions of his foot on the wheel.

In a place where the water was so shallow that they could see the
rocks and blackish algae on the green bottom, somebody pointed.
There was a piece of brown ice in the distance. A bearded seal might
have shed his winter coat there, or walruses might have shat there.

The old man said one word and throttled the motor down. Everyone was standing, looking. Hunters' faces swooped from side to side. They stepped up onto the gunwales and watched. Only the young children moved or talked, and these did so quietly.

Then the old man pulled the throttle open again, and they went on and on in that sunny world of ice-islands.

A seal came up for breath very close, and the grandson who always got in trouble chambered a round and went to the side. But the old man, who could kill a beluga whale in one shot, did not stop, and the seal disappeared.

The water kept getting deeper and shallower. Dripping white blue-shadowed ice-beasts hid their blue bulking underwater. Some ice was low and broad like a crab's back. Some was canted.

There were two grandsons sitting with the old man right then, and suddenly all three fired shots, then stood, rifle-points funning out.

Ee-yah! cried One-Nut.

Two-Nuts's spotted a walrus!

Black shapes sprawled on the ice. The boat ran quietly in the blue-gray water between the floes. Everyone gathered round the old man in old grayish kamiks, who just smiled faintly.

Three walrus!

Where's my seven-six-seven? Gotta start putting my hardpoints in this thing.

Bareheaded like the others, the grandson who always got in trouble fed the dull golden bullets in.

My grandpa don't think they're walrus, said One-Nut. He think they're nothing.

Seal, right there!

Better not shoot it, or the walrus will go underwater.

No. Those aren't walruses, said the grandson who always got in trouble. Just dirty ice. I should shoot it just for looking like that.

Just then a shot pealed over the ice. The boat almost stopped.

Fast bullet, eh?

Why don't you use two twenty-two?

Glaring ahead, they fired almost simultaneously, their barrels dark against the pale water. The boat moved slowly onward.

Get the bullets for my gun, Three-Nuts. In the box.

They fired again, the reports again almost simultaneous. The air smelled like gunpowder. There were three concentric ripples, very close, and the seal's head came up again, then ducked down too quickly, before the animal could draw breath. Again they shot, and the boat ghosted forward; again, and water leaped up around the seal's lurking-place. Suddenly the seal vanished. The boat slowed even more and everyone looked around on all sides.

Then the old man in old grayish kamiks called, and started the motor, and they went on. There were sky-blue eels of light in the gunmetal sea.

Well, that was fun for awhile, said the grandson who always got in trouble, but he wants to hunt walrus.

A hunter was sitting with the old man. They both looked straight ahead, without talking. The old man kept the sole of his kamik firmly on the wheel. The older boys were teaching the younger ones the finger-signals for seals that their grandfather had taught them. A finger straight up was a ring seal, because those creatures tended to peer out of the water. A finger which went up but then crooked out straight was a bearded seal; they were usually seen swimming. A finger that crooked downward was a harp seal; they were divers.

Indulging his grandsons, the old man stopped the boat and pointed one finger straight up. They looked, saw the ring seal's head, and shot.

Oh, look at this! cried One-Nut in delight, gathering hot black cartridges from the deck.

They shot again, just as the seal-head came up to breathe.

Fuck, gimme the twenty-two magnums!

Get ready, get ready!

They were very close to the seal now. For the fifth time it surfaced without being able to breathe. On the seventh time a bright red circle of blood marked its surfacing, and with a splashing sound they stabbed it under its dark head with the old man's harpoon, whose point was made of caribou antler. The black flipper moved feebly.

Grab it!

They pulled it in, stabbed it once in the neck, and it died, lying there whiskers up as bloody water ran out of its head. The grandson who always got in trouble pulled the harpoon out and licked the blood off his hand.

Ah, it must taste *good!* he cried. Wanna eat it right now!

All bent over it in gladness and admiration, and then Three-Nuts rolled it into the hold.

There's a bearded seal out on the ice, said One-Nut. My grandfather sees it.

No! Walrus! Walrus!

Hollowpoint!

They rushed and aimed.

There was a brown islet which turned out to be all walruses wriggling and crawling on each other on a piece of ice you couldn't even see. As the boat bore down they began to flee like a slow explosion of heaviness but the old man in old grayish kamiks had already shot the big one. He'd shot him in the right place, which was the bump behind the head. One-Nut cast the harpoon and they all smiled at him proudly. So much bright blood spread like paint under the boat and beyond.

Now it was the old man who did everything, going over the side to the dinghy for the butchering. It was a wonder how quickly he did it, from the very first moment when the brim of his cap pointed down like a beak as he squatted in the dinghy and leaned, his left hand resting on the side while his right arm and hand slanted down in parallel with his cap, extended by the long knife whose point gleamed sunstruck as it touched and dimpled a sunny place on the pink-mottled brown skin of the dying walrus which lay like a torpedo between the Peterhead's gunwale on which the other hunters crouched and the dinghy, in which Two-Nuts pulled tight the harpoon cable which the old man in old grayish kamiks had so carefully strung, and the cable passed through the boy's clenched fingers and then into the old man's left hand, which was not resting after all; every part of the old man's body was doing a job; and then the cable doubled back up toward the Peterhead and into the grip of the grandson who always got in trouble. In the bow of the dinghy, the boy who hated white people sat holding two lines to keep the vessels close together. And the knife went in. In seconds the old man had begun to lay bare the walrus's yellowish ribs and blue-green membranes behind. His head turned from side to side as quickly as his knife and he grinned a little with effort as his reddened wrist flowed with perfect skill and confidence through the flesh. He'd opened the creature up like a boat, and it lay so whiskery and ancient with its tusks pointing upward, reddish-yellow and lined with long grooves. Between the dinghy and the Peterhead, seawater sparkled and foamed red like fresh raspberry juice. The wrinkled gray hulk of the walrus still breathed, such was the old man's quickness, and even after the first quarter was winched up over the side (the dark meat reddish-purple and the light meat pinkish-orange), the heart still beat. Its wound-gash now clean and bloodless, the next quarter went up only a moment later, making the Peterhead heel a little under the weight. The grandson who always got in trouble guided each still-trembling walrus-chunk into the well at the bottom of the boat, bending one knee and grabbing high where the meat was hooked to swing it down. When the belly-chunk came, the intestines were still squirming and working. Slowly the rectum discharged a mound of custardy excrement and then it gaped open and still. And the Peterhead sat alone in the still sea, the center of a million concentric ripples which bore away with them the last marks of the animal's struggle.

The final quarter came aboard, and for a split second it seemed that the grandson who always got in trouble was embracing it so passionately with his head buried in the flesh just below the hook, but that was only for an instant; then the arms which had gathered the flesh in continued to push it laterally and down; and it was all done. The gray flesh, the black and reddish steaks filled the entire floorspace of the hold.

The walrus penis was given to the kids to use as a baseball bat. Then they turned around for home. There were many other walruses, but the old man said they only needed one. They motored back to their island where the houses of their village would rise up from the muddy bouldery land; they'd go back to the scarlet sunfooted days ahead like toadstools, to the sunny days of swatting mosquitoes, to the summer as huge, scarlet and mysterious as a walrus liver. And the old man sat on top of the pilothouse with One-Nut, whose walrus it was, steering with the sole of his kamik and not quite smiling.

BAD AIR

Los Angeles, California, U.S.A. (1992)
Los Angeles, California, U.S.A. (1992)

Los Angeles, California, U.S.A. (1992)

U p the glary gray roadstripe whose white and red truck-lights were the jewels on the necklace, up they went. He sat beside her, being nothing. The white dots in the passing lanes were other jewels. Effortlessly they ascended that black hill. They could see the drivers of the other cars and trucks pallidly entranced. Headlights glared on a comb of power wires. Headlights masturbated the wheeled blocks of trucks studded with hard lights. A car, a black die of death, came down the hill toward them bearing two red headlight-dots—a low roll. Then it was gone. Opening their palms like seashells, they reached the crest of the hill and began to descend into Los Angeles. He heard her clear her throat. The hot night air made his eyes water. His throat began to ache. He looked sidelong at her and saw her swallowing the bad air. For some reason he did not want her to know that he had seen her. She did not see; she stared ahead, her interest in him long since molded white like a mongrel pigeon's feathers. They passed a clean white truck which was a wall of perfect cream. Their headlights picked across the rivets of another truck. The sky was already glowing putridly ahead, just beyond the black ridge. He took another breath and willed it to be as clean as the light-sweat on white trucks, but it burned inside him. They went down the dashed white

25

line that dribbled into the night like an old man's urine. He took another breath and coughed. They passed a truck in the night, pleated like a dirty gray accordion. The air was getting murky; there were no white trucks anymore. They followed the curve down between black ridges, marked ahead by the pale lights of oncoming cars. He inhaled the stale smell of some chemical. Foolish rectangles of car-vision swept down across pavement and dead grass. Then at last he saw clearly the low horizon riddled with lights. The weariness of the air was something he could not win over; he could only deny it. Everything was such an effort! The dashed white line had become his only friend now, as long and straight and even as the row of screws in the window-moldings that ran the length of a Greyhound bus. — We'll be there soon, she said without looking at him, and he almost believed that he hadn't heard her. He was already forgetting that the air hurt. He was already saying to himself: I could get used to this. — He was already looking forward to being there.

Los Angeles, California, U.S.A. (1992)

To the ancient ones who lived behind horse-headed gates, people like him and her would have been appalling. Those two thought themselves at home everywhere, and so they had no home.

Long before Magic Mountain the greasy-gray air had begun to smell like burning tires. Three patrol cars sped past. Through his window he saw one of those skeletal-trailered trucks used to haul racks of new automobiles to the dealers' lots; it was carrying nothing but police cars. He and she both had sore throats by the time they passed the Pico Canyon exit. The air smeared itself more and more thickly over the mountains ahead. To the east, no mountains could even be seen. She drove rapidly. They continued to descend. His eyes began to water.

I've never seen it this bad, she said.

They passed another car. The driver was looking where the road led and shaking his head. Two men in the next car were gesturing to one another.

He had a terrible headache. Ahead, the air was a featureless curtain, opaque and purplish-gray. The hills nearby were paradoxically clear, their greenery standing out on the chalky eroded walls. It is always like that in a fog; the very clarity of one's immediate surroundings points up the obscurity ahead.

The sun was large, pale yellow and soft in the turbid sky.

She clenched the steering wheel. — Do you think they burned Uncle's store?

I don't know. I hope not. I like your uncle.

They were close enough to see the black smoke now. Another patrol car screamed past.

Later they were at a dinner in the expensive hills where the smell of burning was not so bad. A white woman said: You know, I was a student at Kent State. I was there when the National Guard shot Allison Krause and those other students. I saw it! I saw the blood! I breathed it all in . . .

Somebody was coughing.

And I—I *knew* the pigs were the enemy, the woman said. No question about it. They were the pigs. And tonight, well, tonight I'm thinking that the police are *protecting* me. Thank God the police are standing between me and the enemy! And I'm trying to understand what changed. Because I don't feel that I'm any different; the police sure aren't any different—

His throat ached. He said: Do you mean that the blacks are your enemy?

She put down her wineglass and he thought that she might cry. She said: Yes, they are. It's not fair that I have all the nice things I have and they have nothing. I understand that, I really do. Once I had black friends. But I'm afraid. And I hate them because they make me afraid. And that truck driver, the way they dragged him out and beat him half to death . . .

Another guest had come in quietly from the pool while they were talking, and he was black.

The black man said: So you've hated me for a week. I've hated you for half a thousand years. Nothing personal.

My friends, my *friends!* cried the host, waving his hands. Don't *listen* to what you're both saying; it's just the stress and this awful air . . .

WHAT'S YOUR NAME?

New York, New York, U.S.A. (1994)

New York, New York, U.S.A. (1994)

The long weary pushbroom whose dark bristles were as kinky as pubic hairs dragged itself attached to a man's arm and hand. It was very late. Two children sat drinking sodas and playing with straws and crying out: What's your name? — When the man's toil brought him near enough, they shouted their question at him in shrill excited voices. — Get Up Mess is my name, the man responded. That's what they call me. You make a mess and they call me get up mess. — The next man sat chewing gum and resting on the sides of his feet. — What's your name? called the little ones. — Sir, the man replied, his eyes shining like the cross on the chain around his neck.

Now it was ten-o'-clock in this tiled cave like an immense toilet, and the buses pulsed outside, and now it was eleven-o'-clock, and then it was midnight. The two children snored with their mouths open. Their mother's eyes closed slowly, and then a security guard came and shook her shoulder. The guard left the children alone. The buses all seemed to be either absent, gone, or out of sight. Half-asleep people queued or leaned. Only the escalators moved, winding remorselessly up and down like the treads of some monstrous tank turned turtle. A man fell asleep on the silver coast between escalators.

Not tonight, a ticket agent was saying to a sad man. Not unless you want to sleep in the terminal in Hartford.

Finally light burst out at the side of a bus outside, and it sped away. Then in the darkness another bus came speeding, and he who waited and watched knew that she was on it, but then it kept speeding and was gone. A man sagged against the wall, curling his fingers against the side of his head, and slept.

Then suddenly another long bus angled in and upflung its sidehatch to unchoke itself of suitcases which were taken like medicine into the hands of people who then gave themselves to the emptiness between escalator railings and were accordingly transfigured, decapitated, unbreasted, waistcut, kneesplit, anklesliced and then gone, leaving not even the soles of their shoes behind.

Another bus swam rapidly by, so that his heart rose and fell again.

He saw a sleeping woman who resembled her blurrily. The security guard shook her, and she woke and looked into his eyes.

What's your name? he said on impulse.

Sweetheart. You wanna date? What's *your* name?

Gonorrhea, he said.

You sound like my type, the woman laughed. Let's go.

The security guard was still there, so he said: And what's your name, sir?

Fuck You, said the security guard.

Oh, said the woman. I guess he's my type, too. At least that's what all the men do to me.

He took her hand and they went out. — What's your name? he said to the taxi driver.

Go To Hell, the driver said, and he stepped on the gas and sped them straight there . . .

NO REASON TO CRY

Bangkok, Phrah Nakhon-Thonburi Province, Thailand (1993)

Bangkok, Phrah Nakhon-Thonburi Province, Thailand (1993)

In that street the Thai criers wore suits and ties. They looked at me in contempt or else they said: Japanese only! or they shouted: Members only!

How can I become a member? I said. How can I become Japanese? But to this they had no answer.

At last I found a manager who led me upstairs personally. His place had been open for only two weeks. He could not afford to exclude me.

It was nothing but a long narrow lounge without windows. There were not even any girls at first, not until they brought in Ting.

She was dressed in a kimono and she spoke English like a Japanese. When she haltingly sang a karaoke love-song, she sang *wirging*.

Oh, are you a virgin? I said.

Nit noy. Little bit.

The woman on the other side of me, more experienced, probably sent to encourage and spy on Ting (who had been there only a week), laughed, patted her own rear and said: Me virgin here.

Every time I said something to Ting that she did not understand,

30

the manager interpreted for her because he sat right across from me in the darkness and devoured us. Now and then he'd announce: She want you to kiss her! and say something to Ting and then that beautifully expressionless face would approach mine, after which Ting would arise to bring a napkin with which to wipe her lipstick off my mouth. The manager asked what I would like to eat from the Japanese restaurant which he just happened to own upstairs, and by some fine serendipity he had a menu with him, so I asked Ting to order and with the manager's help she chose the most expensive foods to chopstick into my mouth. Betweenwhiles she sang solemnly into the microphone. I came to hate that dark place where the manager worked so hard at listening and Ting had to sing those country songs and love-songs over and over like hymns. The manager asked if I wanted another Johnnie Walker, and I said I'd finish the one I had first, so he motioned to Ting, and she picked up my glass and gulped it. — Good girl. — She still had sweetened colored water in her glass. I said I'd wait for her to finish that, so the manager gestured and she gulped it, too. Then the manager brought me another Johnnie Walker. I said to myself: This girl is so sad and trapped and needs my help; let me rescue her . . .

Bangkok Phrah Nakhon-Thonburi Province, Thailand (1993)

Ting sat sulkily in the front of the taxi as it navigated the red-reflected wetness of the night expressway past the pink and yellow light-strings of the New Excellency Club and the glare-spidered construction booms. She had believed that I would be a quick and easy customer, but here I was taking her past the airport. At the giant camera and soft drink signs the traffic closed around us and we stopped for an hour, and she began to seethe. All in all, it was not going to be a lucrative evening for Ting even though I'd spend a hundred and twenty dollars; a Japanese no doubt would have spent more.

The upraised helmeted faces of the motorcycle drivers swarmed about us when I rolled down the window at Donmuang to ask for directions. Ting was pale with rage. A dog on the sidewalk growled. People interflitted on the narrow sidewalks beneath hanging sausages and roasted birds. We were lost. Ting and the driver turned to me, pointed at street signs written in Thai, and shouted: *Binai?* which means: *Where?* I had given them the brochure for the place, which contained a detailed map in Thai; what's more, I even knew how to get there, but the driver had not turned where I told him to turn, and now we were lost. He would not go back to the turn until a motorcycle driver assured him that he had to. Then Ting stared wrathfully into my eyes and cried: *Whaiiiiieeeeeeeeee?* while the driver shook his head in disgust.

Forty minutes later we were on the proper road, rolling slowly, ever more slowly beyond the sickening black glint of night earth at a construction site. The place had been deliberately located on an unfrequented lane of trees. Although it was only a couple of miles from the airport road, the taxi driver made us take a quarter of an hour because he was so sure that I must be wrong, and Ting sat twisting and turning with vindictive rage, which gradually gave way to fear as she saw that there were no people, no houses, on this dismal way. We came to the turnoff at last, and then the gate. The watchman came out with his flashlight. Recognizing me, he pulled up the rusty stop and swung back that hinged barrier. I made the driver turn left, then take the second right, and we were at the guesthouse.

I told the receptionist to call the nurse.

Ting sat by the door, refusing to speak to me. She'd told the taxi driver to wait. *Short time!* she'd snarled. *No all night you! Only short time!*

When the nurse came the three of us went to the coffee shop, and the nurse explained why I had brought her here. She told Ting that the women who stayed here had all had that job before, Ting's job. They were learning to be seamstresses and beauticians now. She told Ting that she and I wanted to help her, that if she wanted to leave the bar she could stay here for free and learn to do something else.

Ting replied that she loved her job. She said that she liked to buy nice clothes, that she wanted to go to Japan someday, that her boyfriend was proud of her. Slowly she had calmed down; after an hour she liked the nurse, but when I asked her if she was still angry at me the nurse said: *Nit noy.* Little bit.

At the end, the nurse told her what AIDS was. I gave her a handful of condoms. Was it good or bad that when the nurse hugged her and she hugged the nurse back beside the waiting taxi (she scarcely touched my outstretched hand) she was crying? (She understand now AID, the nurse later told me, with weary satisfaction.) She was going back to work. A case can be made that if a girl is going to get AIDS there is no reason to cry while she is getting it.

THE PROPHET
OF THE ROAD

Yukon Territory, Canada (1983)

Yukon Territory, Canada (1983)

Pity the poor biologist who had to prove (I never found why) that caribou in the Canadian Barrenlands lose a pint of blood a week to the mosquitoes. Of course caribou have more blood to spare than we; perhaps it is not as bad as it sounds, to pay a pint a week for the privilege of living. I remember summer days in Alaska when I could hardly see the backs of my hands because they were so thick with mosquitoes. And a bush pilot told me how he once overflew a man on a hilltop who seemed to be signalling him with long black streamers; these too were mosquitoes in their thousands, using the man for a windbreak while they attacked him, rising and falling in eerie concordance with his frantic arms, veiling his face with whining hungry blackness. It is usually difficult to apprehend the concept of an ocean by analogy with a single drop of water, but in the case of these unpleasant creatures, one will fall upon you with sufficient vampirish alacrity to represent the whole swarm, unlike a dewdrop which lies so docile in the palm as to seem altogether alien to reef-tides and shipwrecks. The dewdrop is at rest anywhere. The mosquito seems fulfilled only when installed upon your skin, its six knees drawn tightly up above its wings, the forelegs stretched partly out like a basking dog's, antennae alertly cocked, head down, proboscis stabbed into you to drink a little more of your life. Even in this state of fulfillment the creature appears tense. It is ready to withdraw from the wound at any time (although as it swells up with blood it becomes less able to do so quickly); it gains, in short, a furtive and half-disengaged orgasm, which is all that natural law permits when a pygmy rapes a giant. The spectrum of feeling between lust and fear and satiation in mosquitoes must be very narrow. When they crouch restlessly on leaves or ceilings they do not seem so different from when they are feeding. This family Culicidae is a family of machines. Delicately tooled with bands and scales, equipped with near-infallible sensors to locate their victims, they've been adjusted by their maker to the behavior best suited to carry out their mission in a given place. In the tropics they are silently multitudinous. Knowing that if one doesn't get you another one will, they launch themselves directly, though by all means taking advantage of leaf-shade and darkness. Temperate latitudes do not hold so very many of them. As a result, they are cunning and wary there. On a black sticky night, a single mosquito in a room may succeed in biting you half a dozen times. When you finally turn on the light to search for it, you cannot find it. Farther north, and again they have less need for these subtleties. Kill one or ten, it makes no matter. A hundred more will come. Proof that the manufacturer is not concerned about the potential loss of a few automata is given by the noise they so often emit, which not only alerts the victim, but also annoys, as anyone who's endured the quavering whining of a mosquito lodged inside the ear would agree. This provocation, combined with the itching, would require a Brahmin's self-control not to avenge. Anyhow, kill them, shoo them away, or let them bite, it makes very little difference. They will win out. I remember how grateful I was when the days were cold enough to keep them sluggish; and even when they swarmed everything was so beautiful with flowers and red sphagnum moss that they didn't matter until I began to get tired; parting the river-brambles and river-trees I forded braids of rivers without minding the mosquitoes on my face; and then I climbed the tussock-hills to where the tundra was very thin, like the greening on a pool table, and had a nice view of rivers and snowdrifts, always the sound of a river to remind me that mosquito-songs were not all there was, and sometimes a bird sang, too. If I was lucky there might be a breeze to scatter the mosquitoes; and I could eat my lunch very quickly. But I'd often stop early on those days, not having been able to rest enough. (Doubtless if I'd been born there they would have affected me less.) Pitching my tent was unpleasant, because the time it took was more than sufficient for my guests to thicken about me and I could not fight them all off since that required constant use of both hands and I must use at least one to work. If I slapped a tickle on my cheek, I'd kill a dozen bloated mosquitoes, my palm wetted with my blood. I did have repellent, but it didn't stay on long, because the thick clothes which the mosquitoes compelled me to wear made me sweat. So by evening, when I was exhausted, I'd squeeze a few more drops of that bitterly toxic elixir onto my skin before shaking the tentpoles out of their stuffsack, but I'd always miss a few places: maybe my ankles that time (secure, I'd thought, behind the armor of my pants-cuff), or the inviting slice of flesh at the back of my neck, just behind my collar. I'd scarcely have one pole assembled before being seized by that maddening itching, which I was already tensed to expect, and as I forgot everything but slapping the pole would fall apart again, and I'd have to laugh, since swearing wouldn't have helped. At least I did have thick clothes on and could get the tent up in due time, then crawl inside and zip the door shut behind me, kill the twenty or thirty mosquitoes who'd ventured in (they were not good at hiding), rub some cold canteen-water over my burning lumps, scratch my swollen face and hands, and relax upon the top of my sleeping bag, listening to mosquitoes pelt against the fly of the tent like rain. The next day, more mosquitoes. Four miles up Inukpasugruk Creek was a waterfall climb. Surges of water made me uneasy. I didn't know whether it was runoff from rain over the ridge, or whether a glacier-finger waited for me. The mosquitoes weren't too bad. They only bit my eyelids, earlobes, cheeks, knees, buttocks, wrists, hands and ankles a few times. The worst thing, as I said, was that singing whine. It was not enough that they bit; they must also make that noise, louder as they got closer, always teasing, uneven so that I could never get used to it; and one note became a chord as more of them came singing around until I could think of nothing but where they would land next. I'd sweep the air and my arms would meet mosquitoes; I'd make a sudden fist anywhere and mosquitoes would be caught inside. — Of course it was a failure on my part to be so disturbed by them. There's a scene in Tolstoy (in "The Cossacks," I think) when mosquito-bites suddenly become glowing love-bites and the sportsman strides happily through the forest of his own self-reliance. — And what about the Inuit, who'd lived with mosquitoes for perhaps twenty centuries without repellent? An old lady from Pond Inlet once told me that she could remember living in a sod house. The mosquitoes had been very bad, but her family fanned themselves with feathers. They'd done that every summer for all their lives until the whalers came to stay.

And now I did not have to think about the mosquitoes too much, either because I was in my tent again looking at the bloodstains on the ceiling where I'd squashed the ones that had followed me in and bitten me and gotten away for a minute or two before I caught up with them, and I could see the shadows of so many others on the outside of the nylon, smelling the blood inside me but unable to get at me, waiting for me to go out, and then after I ran back inside scratching my new bites and killing the assault guard, the others would land on the fly again, waiting now for the sunny night to end so that I'd expose my flesh to another day; but meanwhile I was inside and they could not torture me; I did not have to slap the backs of my thighs every minute on general principles, or sweep my sleeve across my face to kill mosquito-crowds; and it was astounding how quickly I forgot them. They were all around me and had not forgotten about me, but I'd shut them out and they meant nothing. I cannot remember what I thought about. Most likely I did not have to think about anything, because I'd gained asylum into an embassy of the easy world that I was used to, enjoying it flapping round me in the sunlight like a boat, all blue and orange, with the shadow of the blowing fly bobbing up and down.

When I hitchhiked from San Francisco to Fairbanks, mosquitoes surrounded me with the hymning hum of a graduation—not right away, of course; not until I got to Canada. As soon as I was safely in a vehicle they could not affect me anymore and I rode the familiar thrill of speed and distance, lolling in the back of the truck, with a beautiful husky kissing my hands and cheeks, and we slowed to let a moose get out of the road and at once I heard them again. — A mosquito bit me. — I was on the Al-Can Highway now. I forgot the night I'd given up, not yet even in Oregon, and stayed at a motel, my face redburned and filthy, my eyes aching; and it had felt sinful to spend the sixteen dollars on the room but it was raining hard as it had been all day, so no one would pick me up. In hitchhiking as in so many other departments, the surest way not to get something is to need it. The more the world dirtied me, the less likely someone would be to take me in. — But the next morning was sunny and I had showered and shaved, which was why a van picked me up within half an hour and took me into Oregon, and as I rode so happily believing that I now progressed, I didn't even consider that the inside of the van was not so different from the inside of the motel; I was protected again. When I remember that summer, which now lies so far behind me, I must own myself still protected, in a fluctuating kind of way, and so a question hovers and bites me unencouraged: Which is worse, to be too often protected, and thereby forget the sufferings of others, or to suffer them oneself? There is, perhaps, a middle course: to be out in the world enough to be toughened, but to have a shelter sufficient to stave off callousness and wretchedness. Of course it might also be said that there is something depressing and even debasing about moderation—how telling that one synonym for *average* is *mean!*

On the long stretch of road between Fort St. John and Fort Nelson, where the mosquitoes were thickest, we came to where the Indian woman was dancing. It was almost dusk, round about maybe nine or ten-o'-clock. The country was full of rainbows, haze and yellow flowers. Every hour or so we had to stop to clean the windshield because so many mosquitoes had squished against it, playing connect-the-dots with the outlines of all things. We pulled over and went to work with ammonia and paper towels. They found us as soon as we got out. The driver's head was a big black sphere of mosquitoes. There were dozens of them in the space between my glasses and my eyes. When we got back into the camper, mosquitoes spilled in through the open windows. We jittered along at fifty miles an hour over the dirt road until the breeze of our passage had sucked them out. By then the windshield was already turning whitish-brown again from squashed mosquitoes. The driver did not want to stop again just yet, but I noticed that he was straining his eyes to see through the dead bugs, and I was just about to say that I didn't mind cleaning the windshield by myself this time (I was, after all, getting a free ride), when far ahead on that empty road (we hadn't met another vehicle for two hours) we saw her capering as if she were so happy, and then we began to get closer to her and saw the frantic despair in her leapings and writhings like some half-crushed thing's that could not die. Not long ago I thoughtlessly poured out a few drops of dilute solvent upon waste ground, and an earthworm erupted, stretched toward me accusingly, stiffened and died. But the convulsions of this woman went on and on. Just as her dance of supposed happiness had seemed to me entirely self-complete like masturbation, so this dance of torture struck me as long-gone mad, sealing her off from other human beings, as if she were some alcoholic mumbler who sheds incomprehensible tears. It was not until we were almost past that I understood behind our hermetic windows that she was screaming for help. I cannot tell you how terrifying her cries were in that wild place. The driver hesitated. He was a good soul, but he already had one hitchhiker. Did he have to save the world? Besides, she might be crazy or dangerous. Her yellings were fading and she was becoming trivial in the rearview mirror when he slowed to think about it, and it was only then that we both understood what we had seen, because protected brains work slowly: mosquitoes darkened her face like a cluster of blackberries, and her legs were black and bloody where the red shorts ended. The driver stopped. Mosquitoes began to pelt against the windows.

We had to help her get in. She embraced us with all her remaining strength, weeping like a little child. Her fearfully swollen face burned to my touch. She'd been bitten so much around the eyes that she could barely see. Her long black hair was smeared with blood and dead mosquitoes. Her cheeks had puffed up like tennis balls. She had bitten her lip very deeply, and blood ran down from it to her chin where a single mosquito still feasted. I crushed it.

That afternoon, no doubt, she'd been prettier, with sharp cheekbones that caught the light, a smooth dark oval face, dark lips still glistening and whole, black eyes whose mercurial glitter illuminated the world yet a little longer, shiny black hair waved slantwise across her forehead. That was why the man in Fort Nelson had decided to support her trade. Reservation bait, he thought. She got in his truck, and there were some other men, too; they used her services liberally.

But unlike slow mosquitoes, who pay the bill, if only with their lives, the men had their taste of flesh with impunity. They weren't entirely vile. They didn't beat her. They only left her to the mosquitoes. They let her put her clothes back on before they threw her out—

She'd tried to dig a hole in the gravelly earth, a grave to hide in, but she hadn't gone an inch before her fingers started bleeding and the mosquitoes had crawled inside her ears so that she couldn't think anymore, and she started running down the empty road; she ran until she had to stop, and then the mosquitoes descended like dark snow onto her eyelids. Two cars had passed her. She'd craved to kill herself, but the mosquitoes would not even give her sufficient peace to do that. I'll never forget how I felt when she squeezed me in her desperate arms—I'll never forget her dance.

That was the most horrible thing that I have ever seen. For awhile I thought about it every day. I know I thought about it when at the end of that summer I was hitchhiking home and had gotten as far as Oregon, where I slept entented in a tree-screened dimple on a field by a white house, hoping that no one in the white house would see and hurt me, and the next morning I ducked under the fence and was back on the shoulder of the freeway and it was already a very hot morning, so I was drinking from my canteen (which I'd filled at a gas station in Portland) when another hitchhiker came thumping down the road toward me. He was like a prophet from the old times. He wore a long robe and carried a great wooden staff which he slammed down at every step. He was not so old, and yet his beard was long and gray (possibly from dust), and his gray hair fell to his shoulders and his eyes were wild like a bull's. His face was caked with dust. He licked his lips as he came near me, and his eyes were on me unwaveringly, so I offered him water as he came closer and closer, continuing to stare into my eyes, and then he shook his head sternly and walked on. I did not live up to his ideals. There was another hitcher I'd met in Washington State who'd been crazy and called himself the Angel Michael and whispered to me that he didn't know anymore whether he was a boy or a girl and I believed him because he was so angelic: angels are undoubtedly hermaphrodites. In the same way, I believed in the prophet wholly. I could not but admire him for rejecting me. He went on and on down the freeway shoulder, with barbed wire at his right shoulder and cars at his left, growing smaller (though I could still distinctly hear the tapping of his stick) and I wondered what he would have done or said if it had been he and only he who came across the woman whom the mosquitoes were eating. I could almost see him there on the Al-Can, toiling on, mile after mile, his face black-veiled like that minister in Hawthorne's tale, black-veiled with mosquitoes; he'd walk on and stab the gravel with his staff and never deign to brush away a single mosquito; he'd glare terribly through eyes swollen almost shut by mosquito bites and go on, mile after mile, week after week; and maybe someday he'd come upon that woman shrieking in her crazed torment. Would he have stopped then; would the mosquitoes leave her for him in a single flicker of his divinity, after which he'd pass on in silence, followed by unimaginable clouds of humming blackness? Would she fall to her knees then and thank God and regain herself? — Or would he never have stopped at all, marching contemptuously on, ignoring her need as he ignored my gift, and dwindled just the same along that highway's inhuman straightness?

FIVE LONELY NIGHTS

San Francisco, California, U.S.A. (1984)
New York, New York, U.S.A. (1990)
Berlin, Germany (1992)
Antananarivo, Madagascar (1992)
Nairobi, Kenya (1993)

San Francisco, California, U.S.A. (1984)

In the River City Deli he was always happy, no doubt because inexperience remained his friend. Sometimes Brandi the whore went by and he could run out and kiss her. He felt loved then. That was at night. Sometimes he'd sit drinking a beer in the middle of a rainy Sunday afternoon, the only customer there, and his knees didn't hurt anymore. At that time they had beers from all over the world. From the ceiling hung flags of all beer-drinking countries, and beer labels and plaques. There were over a hundred imported beers in the fridge, so they said, though he never counted them. Later they cut back to fifty and then the sandwiches got smaller and then they fired John and turned into a soup place and he stopped going. John was the one who used to make the giant sandwiches.

He'd known John for two years. He wrote him notes about the excellent and doubly large sandwiches he made and John put them up on the bulletin board. Then John would get in trouble for making the sandwiches too big, but John didn't care. John had been a student forever, making films. John turned up the radio as he chopped onions, sang *I'm glad to be gay* along with Dire Straits. He felt that he could count on John, that John understood his neediness. Sometimes when John was off, he went there and got drunk. Although he hardly knew John, he didn't want him to see that.

There had been an aquarium a few years before John, but the fish died one by one. Now there was a jukebox instead.

The girl who stood in for John that night was thin and blonde and homely. He was drunk and so he loved her through his heart's arch-windows of phallic narrowness. He knew what love was because he always felt it. It was simple loneliness.

If he had a gun right now he'd probably go kill himself, but he'd be calm and very very happy.

He decided that he would drink two more beers and then one beer and then he'd be ready to ask her to go out with him. Having never seen her before, he loved her so much. Love notched his soul like the close-packed circular indentations on the trunk of an imperial philodendron. He loved listening to the jukebox and being drunk all alone with no one to bother him, and her not being bothered yet by knowing that he loved her. He loved the nice quiet careful way that she made sandwiches.

Seven-o'-clock. He'd been here for four hours.

The 7-Up machine buzzed fretfully—no, it was singing! It was happy; it too wanted to express itself . . .

A blonde in an army surplus outfit and a white headband came in and ordered a sandwich with melted cheese. He smiled at her. She smiled back. He was so happy that now he could die and no one would be bothered.

The thin girl came to take the empty beer bottles away. She smiled at him.

He loved to see her working so hard, cleaning the meat slicer. A few weeks ago, on a Saturday night, he'd been in here with his best friend, who'd now cut all ties. He'd talked about shooting his ex-wife, then himself, just for fun. He wondered if this waitress had been here then. He remembered a thin one, who'd been so patient behind the counter. He'd given her a ten-dollar tip, just for the hell of it. That had left him pond-bottom broke, but today was another payday.

The girl's hair seemed to be darkening so far away across the room, behind the counter. She was wrapping something in paper. The blonde with the white headband was still here, one booth away, staring out at cars and darkness. She looked at him; he looked at her, then down.

The refrigerators were making a steady loud noise. Sausages hung in the air. Finally nothing could be seen outside but the reflections of the cars. The waitress was clicking at something, moving food processor levers. How sweet she was! It would be impossible for any man she'd ever known to emulate his tenderness.

Do you want me to take this away? she said to him.

Maybe I'll just keep looking at it awhile, he said.

It was very black and pretty out the window at eight-o'-clock, just as it had been the previous night when he'd run past his ex-wife's house, running back along the dark street, running back from San Pablo where a man had chased him yelling that he was going to kill him; once he'd crossed Grove Street he slowed down, wondering if he'd see his ex-wife. He didn't *want* to see her, exactly, but he sort of *hoped* he would. He never did. If he had, his heart would've curdled so tight as to snap the scar tissues. Standing outside the house, he remembered the day that his best friend had told him that her friend Colleen had just moved in. He had never met Colleen. His best friend said that she was very pretty. He wondered what his ex-wife had told Colleen about him, and whether he could creep into Colleen's room and kiss her, to be unfaithful to his ex-wife . . . But in fact he had slept with no one since his ex-wife.

Nine-o'-clock.

You want *lots* of lettuce? the thin girl was saying to a woman in blue. You got it.

He got up slowly. — Will you go out with me? he said to her. Please?

He was already looking at the floor so that he wouldn't have to see the disgusted pity rushing at him from the girl's face.

No, I don't think I could do that.

Please? he said, longing to kill himself.

I'm sorry.

He went out.

New York, New York, U.S.A. (1990)

He always sat in one of those chairs whose cushion was the color of canned tomato soup, in one of those chairs whose arms curved round to embrace your kidneys, at the table in the corner where the brick partition began. From this location (his loneliness reflected in the spoon) he could see one TV on a sports channel bright and silent, and the two fans spinning circles of shadows across the pennants that hung from the ceiling like sleeping bats. Above the brick partition reigned the paintings: the ocean scene, the phony horse, the discreetly blurred nude, the happy child—and beyond them lay a wall of lace locked in place by brass posts. Through this he could occasionally find flickers of action from the bar, but he preferred to gaze down the length of the brick partition, past cash register and coffee pot, where he could sometimes see the waitress who interested him. He did not love her; he did not know her name. But he was sorry whenever he didn't find her there. He had not yet learned when her shifts were because he did not come every day. Often enough she was there, blonde and Irish, rubbing her nose as she said something on the phone.

When she got the bone out of her throat and her ear out of her shoe, by then they'd hung up the telephone! a drunk was shouting.

On the television a man was in the driver's seat, closing the door of his car, and his arm was immense, bigger than his shoulder.

The door to the kitchen swung and glittered. He thought he saw his waitress's face through the diamond window.

She passed the small white table with two settings: two forks on the left, and a knife and spoon on the right, then salt, pepper and flowers, always wilting flowers. He had never sat there. It would have been too sad to sit alone.

Someday he would take this waitress out to dinner and they would eat at that table. She would get up and serve them both, or else no one would serve them and the food would come by itself, sliding like the black plastic tray on which she brought his change, Lincoln's wry face uppermost, his edges curling upward toward the distant fans.

Berlin, Germany (1992)

S o. You want to come with me? the blonde from Mannheim said in that calm slow voice.

Well, I don't know. Maybe. Can I kiss you?

She flinched. — Depends on where.

How long will I have with you?

Well, you know, we won't have all night, but I won't hurry you.

How much?

One hundred fifty deutsche marks.★

I don't have that much.

No? No credit card?

No. I'm sorry; I wish I could. I didn't know it was that much. I talked with a girl last night who told me a hundred . . .

Nothing?

No.

It includes the price of the room.

I can't.

She stepped back.

I wish I could, he said again.

You know, the blonde from Mannheim explained, the more you pay the more you get.

I'm not surprised.

You want to try?

OK.

Ja?

Sure, I'll try it.

The blonde from Mannheim unlocked the door, and they went up wide stairs. Just past the landing, where it could no longer be seen from the street, a red carpet began. These last stairs pulsated like blood vessels. Inside the salon where the loitering crowds of ladies in lingerie were pinkened by crimson lights, the red carpet thickened into something resembling endometrial lining, and he felt as if the blonde from

★ In 1992, 150 DM was about U.S. $94.

Mannheim had led him into the womb of a ruby grapefruit. It was very dim and spacious and he walked beside her into this soundlessly cinematic dream of a brothel, a dream he'd had many times before.

She took him into the first room on the right. It had a red carpet, and the double bed had a red bedspread. The casement was open. She closed it and began to undress, which didn't take long. He laid the money down on the table.

I must go pay the rent, she said. Please undress.

He took his clothes off and lay down on the bedspread, which was warm, damp and smelly. After awhile he lifted it up and got beneath it. There was nothing there but a bare mattress covered with crumbs of something like old scabs.

The blonde from Mannheim returned and said: For what you gave me I can do nothing except with my hand.

Can I kiss you?

Never.

He looked at her. Then he got dressed.

The money is gone, you know, said the blonde. You can't get it back.

Why isn't that news? he said, tying his shoes.

You're not angry?

No, never mind, he said.

She followed him to the top of the stairs.

Well, then, goodnight, she said.

Goodnight, he said emptily.

He came back down onto Kurfürstendammstrasse where it was a late September night and a double-decker bus passed among streetlamped trees like a ghost. Greasy squares of sidewalk throbbed with the U-bahn's moling. Two men played a duet on electronic keyboard and xylophone. A crewcut boy in a denim vest sat with a knifeblade between his teeth. A clean straighthaired woman stood inspecting haloes in a jewelry shop; the haloes were watches. A little past eleven, a guard came and drew shutters over that window. Now the haloes were transubstantiated into denizens of the kingdom of squares.

For the purposes of free enterprise there were illuminated glass cubes displaying towels or else white lingerie on black dummies with roses. A blonde leaned against the nearest one, chewing gum alertly.

— You want to go back up with me? she said. I can make you very happy.

Can I kiss you?

No.

Some whores stood intense and still. Others in big boots waved to him with cheery wolf-whistles. He went to three of them and said: I'm sorry I don't have any money left but can I just kiss one of you?

OK, darling, laughed a redhead. I'll kiss you. — She sucked at her gum for awhile, strode up to him, pulled his head toward her and spat in his face.

Antananarivo, Madagascar (1992)

I speakee you good! I speakee you no problem! I sleep under you hotel?

But afterward she drew her hand across her forehead, wiping the sweat of amazed disgust.

Once she had put her clothes on, she raised again her lovingness, like a man lifting an immense load of green bananas onto his head, and whispered: No problem. I likee you! No problem! I likee you! I speakee Mama come back here six-o'-clock morning.

She got dressed in the dark, whispering again and again to him in pidgin her lies of reassurance. Then she asked for money for the taxi. He gave her thirty thousand,★ which was the rate for a full night of that work, and she kissed him on the lips and went out. He had already forgotten her face, but there stayed with him the delicious feel of her hair, which she had braided with fibers from some plant so that it felt like hempen rope intermixed with velvet, and he remembered the sugary taste of her nipple and the salty taste of her vulva, the *energy* of her blood when she first approached him; in an instant she'd been writhing and begging on his lap in the disco while

★ In 1992, 30,000 Malagasy francs was about U.S. $16.

she pierced his mouth with her long wet tongue, and he remembered
how as soon as he'd entered her all that had paled to patience, but
most of all he remembered the rich smell of her, a smell of roast
coffee, chocolate, shit, soap and fresh sweat, a smell which had re-
pulsed him slightly at first but which he grew to love faithfully in the
course of that hour because of its strength: he trusted her fleshly
richness.

But she never came back.

He'd known that she wouldn't, but waited just the same, unable
to sleep in the sweltering room of rainforest planks whose knotholes
let the mosquitoes in, and outside he heard music and dancing and
laughing because it was New Year's Eve, so he could not sleep, and
finally he went out to see if he could join them but they'd gone into
closed houses; and as he stood taking this in, a chalky dog loomed
out of the dirt's darkness and he went back upstairs to his room where
he sat smelling the stink of his sweat and waiting for the night to be
eaten like so many others and listening to the mosquitoes around his
head.

Her smell stayed on him—at first a mere pale greenish stalk, but
then when for loneliness he pressed his face in the pillow where her
head had lain it expanded like a mango tree's cracked and crumbled
bark; it became an orchard of palms whose trunks were thickly sprout-
ing everywhere with ferns.

Weeks later he spied her by daylight, a barefoot woman striding
rapidly down the road with an immense basket on her head, her arms
easy at her sides. He watched, and she didn't see him. And he said
to himself: Her cunt is one of those roadside huts in which any can
take shade—any of these muddy barefoot men in patched pants! So
why won't she shade me? Why won't she shade me?

Then it was night in another town. Night it was, while the two
women he'd rented sat over their coffee, and he over fresh white
lychee-fruit juice, and his women were swishing flies off their brown
arms and laughing, tranquilly scratching insect bites, while motorcycles and pousse-pousses went by and the one who'd made him so
lonely went into market across the street, the market which offered
pineapples and melons. He could not get away from her, it seemed.
He wanted only her. His women chatted. Charlotte *sans culottes* was
always grinning, laughing hoarsely at him and the other woman, slap-

ping her thighs. She'd be a good loser. Tonight, although he'd paid her off, she'd attached herself to him and the other woman like a leech, coming all the way to the Bras d'Or to get him to buy her coffee, but so lazy she wouldn't walk like they did; she had to pay the pousse-pousse both ways. It had been an expensive coffee for her.

He said to Charlotte: Are you lonely?

She laughed until she cried. Then she said: Always.

She laughed again quickly, so that he wouldn't believe her. Then he knew that she was telling the truth.

And you? he said to the other one.

Not with you, my love. — She for her part tried so hard to be sincere that he knew she must be lying.

So they were both lonely! Imagine that—and him, too! All lost and falling!

The whore who'd left him came out of the melon store, licking fruit pulp from around her lips. He stood and blocked her way.

For a long time she didn't recognize him. Then she said: OK no problem! I sleep under you one more time, you me two ladies? OK I speakee you good! I likee you very good . . .

He said: Why didn't you come back?

She gazed at him without answering. Then suddenly she'd wriggled past him, was running down the street so that the other two whores gaped; almost gone in the darkness, she screeched over her shoulder: *I no likee you! I no likee you!*

Nairobi, Kenya (1993)

Every evening was a parade of crowd sounds, honking horns, calls, chantings and whistlings, and yet he never saw any parade. Maybe he needed to look again, persevering like the toilets in Nairobi, which often work best on the second flush; or maybe he was the parade, and everybody else a spectator: the whores on posts with their feet stretched out before them (big smiling whores in blue-jeans and sandals, smiling because they had all the time in the world), the men sitting on switchboxes, the birds rushing like the crowded buses, like the cigarette smoke whirling up from beneath men's top-hats and baseball caps. He obtruded himself upon the Kenyans' attention in just the same way that the diesel-smoke crept along the pavement in swirling melting ridges like blowing snow, flickering across people's shoes and steel shutters and gratings and across the uniformed guards outside the shops. He paraded on. Taxi drivers grinned wide and white, elbows out the window. He went past the yellow honeycomb of Nyakio House whose windows were melted in, and he came to the striped posts around the perimeter of the concrete island by Moonlit Limited where the whores always began to sit in the late afternoon. There was a dark girl at a post, chewing gum, her cheeks bulging out and shining white in the streetlights. He hurried past her and saw another one in a doorway and her eyes made his eyes explode into flames. He went on. The twilight smelled like cigarettes, curry and armpits. Through that continuous grimy roar men rode in open vans, packed like soldiers. Dark men in pale suits and hats sat on a low wall that curled around a dirt parking lot for taxis. — My friend, can you give something to eat? Something small? — They were unlike the beggars in Madagascar, who upon receiving money immediately asked for more. The children, however, were the same—sly, insistent and treacherous. When a grimy waif—boy or girl?—pushed up against him like a calf as he walked, grabbling in his pockets, he felt helpless. — No, he said. — The child snuffled. It worked its snotty fingers deep into his pockets, digging and scratching while it clung, its head against his crotch; he wearily said no and no. Everyone was watching him. They pointed at him in the way that people point in Nairobi, reaching up at the sky. He did not want to hurt the child, and he did not want to be hurt for hurting the child, and he did not want the child to take his money. Finally a man shouted and pushed the creature away.

Outside the National Archives, a crowd began to shout because the police were beating a thief. They shouted: *Justice, justice!* They were shouting and running. He walked on. A man came with a razor and tried to cut his wristband and he kicked the man hard in the stomach so that the man sat down in the street with a very surprised look on his face, and he went on; that time he ran on. He saw the rainbow Cobra bus with the big snake painted on the side, and on the other side of it the whores were waiting. One of them reminded him of a woman he thought he had seen in the heat of the afternoon: a woman in a loose black dress of ankle length, with a black shawl over her midnight hair, only her eyes white as she moved across the parched dirty sidewalk like living shade; now she was wearing a pink miniskirt and no bra.

At the entrance to the movie theater, a cat emerged and ran under a car. In a doorhole of a moving twilight-colored bus, a dark man's smile screamed white as he banged on the side of the bus. People often walked with their heads flung back. Two security guards came slowly out of the theater, one thoughtfully tapping his truncheon against his palm. The birds were flying faster and faster, and the lights of the bus blinked balefully. A man sat smoking. He appeared to be sucking his thumb. A woman in a blue blouse and a yellow skirt sat with her legs up, cheek on wrist, and when she saw him she opened her legs wider, put her middle finger between them, and gave him a smile. But he would not do that anymore.

A man was roasting khaki-colored corn at the corner. Another man leaned on upraised knee at a post, smoking. Foliage wept from the yellow eyes of streetlights.

A woman in pink curved her flirty neck from behind a mound of garbage. A fat girl in pink, the same one he'd seen the day before, came up and took him by the hand. She said softly: I like 'ee. Less go.

I'm married, he replied as gently as he could.

Please, we do busy here, she whispered, pointing between his legs. I like 'ee! I like!

Again he refused her, and this time saw her smile's hurt. As she walked slowly backwards to the car against which she had leaned with two slenderer sisters (their hair twirled into delicious snaky ropes), she never took her eyes from him.

He began to walk away, past the staring man who pushed up froggy glasses, and the striding brown-ankled people who watched the potholes and muck-mounds on the sidewalk, and he smiled and waved to her and she waved back, and he knew that she could not possibly be hurt but he knew that she was hurt, and as he turned his face away from her for good the loneliness struck him in the chest so hard he almost groaned.

LUNCH

New York, New York, U.S.A. (1994)

New York, New York, U.S.A. (1994)

Faces at lunch, oh, yes, smirking, lordly, bored or weary—here and there a flash of passion, of dreams or loving seriousness; these signs I saw, notwithstanding the sweep of a fork like a Stuka dive-bomber, stabbing down into the cringing salads, carrying them up to the death of unseen teeth between dancing wrinkled cheeks; a breadstick rose in hand, approached the purple lips in a man's dull gray face; an oval darkness opened and shut and the breadstick was half gone! A lady in a red blazer, her face alert, patient and professionally kind like a psychoanalyst's, stuck her fork lovingly into a tomato, smiling across the table at another woman's face; everything she did was gentle, and it was but habit for her to hurt the tomato as little as possible; nonetheless she did not see it. Nodding and shaking her head, she ate and ate, gazing sweetly into the other woman's face. Finally I saw one woman in sunglasses who studied her arugula as she bit it. It disappeared by jagged inches, while across the table, in her husband's lap, the baby watched in dark-eyed astonishment. Her husband crammed an immense collage of sandwich components into his hairy cheeks. He snatched up pommes-frites and they vanished in toto. When the dessert cart came, the starched white shoulders of businessmen continued to flex and shine; the faces gazed at one another over emptiness, maybe happier now that they had eaten, unthinking of what they had wrought.

BRANDI'S JACKET

San Francisco, California, U.S.A. (1993)

San Francisco, California, U.S.A. (1993)

San Francisco, California, U.S.A. (1993)

I hadn't seen her for years, and every time I happened to be in town and got a chance to go to Haight Street, I wondered if she was still alive.

One day I saw her and called out her street name. She didn't come flying to me as she used to do; she was older and a little more tired. But she came; she came. She remembered me right off. — Sure, you're the one I used to con all the time and you'd never get mad!

I remembered a little boy who used to panhandle with her, and whomever's hand I'd put the quarter into, the other's hand would fight to snatch it. — How's your son? I said.

Her face lit up. — Only twelve, she said proudly, and he's already doin' time for armed robbery! He's so bad!

She dug a scrap of greasy paper out of the trash can and wrote her phone number on it. The next time I was in town I called her and said if she wanted to come over she could make some money.

She came running upstairs throwing herself into my arms and kissing me with delicious greasy lips. Her hair was well oiled. Even in that first embrace I felt her trying to pick my pocket.

We went upstairs and she said: I wanna have your baby. Please will you gimme your baby? I wanna little girl. I had one but she died in a crib death. How about it? You wanna make a little love? Just gimme

55

some money so I can go and get some rock. I'll be right back—I promise!

So she was a crackhead now. Before it had just been freebase and some other things.

I knew she wouldn't come back, but I wanted to see what she'd do. I gave her twenty and told her to leave her jacket behind as a hostage.

Lemme borrow yours then! she said.

You just go out without any jacket, I said.

OK, OK, OK. An' I'll even leave my pipe—you *know* I won't be goin' *nowhere* without my pipe!

She put it ostentatiously into her coat. I pretended not to notice when she palmed it back.

After an hour had gone by, I had to go away myself, but I thought that since the jacket really belonged to me now I might as well see what was in the pockets, whose domain had been considerably expanded by holes, so that the whole lining of the jacket was hers to store things and hide things—how precious!

There was no crack pipe, of course, but I found three lighters, a tube of Vaseline, lots of dirty tissues, a hamburger wrapper wet and yellow with oil, a broken cigarette, some matches, and finally, like some sweet secret, a little Tootsie Roll. Something about the Tootsie Roll touched me, I don't know why. It was like her, the dearness of her hidden inside all the greed and the lies, the goodness of her that the badness drew on and exhibited and used for its own selfish work.

I left the coat in the hallway where she could get it if she ever came back. I wanted to keep the Tootsie Roll but that would have been like robbing her of her soul. In the end, just so I wouldn't feel like a complete chump, I stole one of her cigarette lighters. The bus took me down Haight Street. Suddenly I saw her, soundlessly arguing and pleading and whining with a man. I waved to her but she didn't see me. Later I took the lighter out in order to strike an idle flame, but then I saw that it had no flint. I wondered what would have been wrong with the Tootsie Roll.

BUTTERFLY STORIES (I)

Phnom Penh, Cambodia (1991)

is razor was a Happiness Double Blade, made in China. It lived in a phony gold box whose phony silver lid was spring-loaded like his other wife whom no one dared to say a wrong word to. New and quiet, the razor waited for him. He pushed the stud and the top flew open. The tray where the double blade went had been engraved with a repeating pattern of leaves which dazzled him almost as much as if he were standing at a waterfall's edge peering down into some deep gorge tapestried with the heads of palm trees. The tray could be raised, too, clicking against the lid's underside with a flimsy metal-on-metal sound. The bottom of the tray was a mirror just large enough to reflect either his chin or his upper lip; which should he choose? The secret space beneath, which reminded him of a hiding place in a false-bottomed coffin, held a half-cylindrical recess for the handle, which was grooved with diamonds formed by the intersection of slanting lines; and next to the handle-niche a sunken rectangle waited to reclaim the double blade's shield.

In his underwear, with a towel around him, the journalist looked at his moustache in the mirror for a moment and then closed the empty box. He'd clicked and screwed and twisted the razor's three parts together. The naked blade he'd handled with nervous loathing. It was by no means a safety razor. He remembered a winter day long ago in school when the other children had debated which death would be the worst. One small girl whispered that she was afraid of fire. A boy had seen his sister drown, and thought that was the worst. But the boy who was going to be a journalist had known at once that the most horrible thing would be to have his throat cut, to feel the razor sawing and slicing through the skin and muscle and soft cartilage of his neck. For years it made him go weak just to see barbed wire.

He put the box down on the night stand and rested the razor beside it. Solid and silvery, it caught the sunlight in its many whirling grooves.

Through an interpreter, his wife (whom he'd met a week before) had told him that he looked old with his moustache. He'd told the interpreter that she could shave it off, and she smiled with timid pleasure.

So you're gonna let her shave you, huh? said the photographer, lying bored and sick on the other bed. The shades were down, but through the slits where the fit wasn't perfect the sun still swarmed, turning everything to sweat and corruption. The photographer's whore lay on top of him, giggling and moaning and squirming even as the photographer cursed her, rubbing his stubble with the back of his hand.

You could use a shave yourself, the journalist said. I bought you one of those razors, too.

How much?

Oh, about two bucks. Maybe it was one buck. I don't remember.

The photographer flushed with fever. — Get me the bucket. I'm not sure if I'm gonna puke.

The journalist's wife tapped softly on the door. He leaped up and let her in. He knew that it was embarrassing for her downstairs because everyone looked at her knowing what she was.

Hello, Vanna, he cried happily.

She almost smiled. Then she came with him to the bed. The other whore laughed, and his wife paid no mind. She lay wordlessly down in her black spangly dress with the green ribbons, and he lay beside her. He put his head in her lap. Very softly she began to sing him a sad song which he could not understand. He fell asleep with her hand so light in his hair that the harsh sun-time seemed not to touch him, and he could feel himself grow younger as he slept, more handsome and strong and perfect for his new wife. When he awoke, the light from outside was a screaming orange, but much of the heat had gone out of it. He felt pleasantly damp with sweat. The photographer and the other girl were asleep. His wife (who was amazed by freezers and dental floss) lay against him in her black dress, not sweating, breathing steadily with eyes closed. He raised his hand to caress her and she opened her eyes.

Remembering, he sat up and handed her the new razor. He pointed to his moustache. Her face lit up. Her redwaxed lips curved up lovingly, the lower one widening and shining like her once-scared eyes beneath the dark-peaked brows. A circle of light kissed her nose.

Between her narrow brown fingers (the nails painted the same apple-red as her lips), the handle undid itself, turning until it separated into a hollow silver bone. She lifted the inner plate of the guard off its three screws and set it soundlessly down. Then by the side-edges she took the pure blade whose exposed double meetings of steel and nothingness could so easily have sliced his eyes out or slashed his wrists down lengthwise to burst open the blue arteries of his life. Her smile widened, and he began to sweat.

The photographer had sat up. — Don't tell me you're gonna let her shave you dry with that blade! That's a good way to get cut, man!

I guess I'll make her happy, the journalist replied.

Again he laid down his head in his pretty wife's lap. He made up his mind not to wince away whatever she did. But as he gazed upward at the approaching blade, he decided that it was better to close his eyes.

The first pass of the blade caught the hairs of his moustache painfully, matting them up against the steel edge as they twisted and ripped from the skin. He could almost hear the hairs roaring out. He had not changed his expression; in that respect he lived up to his resolution; but perhaps she saw that she'd hurt him because after that she shaved him in smaller, more nibbling caresses. He could not tell whether she'd cut him yet or not. He was no longer afraid. He lay quite naturally on her lap as she bent over him, uttering her little hisses of concentration and pride. At last she was finished. He opened his eyes. She held the mirror before him triumphantly. He saw his upper lip immaculate and pale, younger than the rest of him (it had not been exposed for years). He got up and looked into his compass mirror so that he could see his whole face. A pretty young boy looked back at him—the true husband of his wife.

Bangkok, Thailand (1993)

The girl from See Sar Ket sat behind the bar with her hands in her lap. There was a long silver cross between her breasts. He bought her a drink, so she came and sat on the stool beside him and pinched his thigh.

I go Kambuja to find my wife, he said. Me no butterfly.*

Oh OK, she said. Broken heart.

Thailand to Cambodia (1993)

The woman beside him on the plane was going to Battambang, because after twenty years of paying detectives she'd finally found her sister. Her father had been killed. One of her two children was dead, and the other would be twenty-two now; he was still missing. The woman had pearl earrings and bright red fingernails. She said she prayed every day.

My sister have three children now, she said. She is old. I want to get her out. I can work hard for money to pay her visa. But I have to wait.

He supposed that she if anyone would understand him. On a page of his notebook he wrote: *I am searching for the lady in this photograph. Her name is Vanna. Can you help me, please?* He asked her to translate this into Khmer for him, so that he could show it to people in Phnom Penh. But she turned away, saying: I prefer not. Because my Cambodian writing is now me embarrass. — For the remainder of the

---

* Philanderer.

flight she tried to talk with her other seatmate, a German who rudely ignored her.

Phnom Penh, Cambodia (1993)

Phnom Penh was so utterly different that he began to clown around with riels and dollars and taxis so desperately that the Cambodians shook their sides while he almost cried. The bicycles were almost gone. It was all cabs and everything was new and they wanted you to pay in dollars.

In the hotel where his wife had shaved him they had mirrors now and refrigerators and toilets, televisions and bedside phones with music on hold and automatic redial. He couldn't believe it. The price had tripled, but they charged him only half again as much as before, for old times' sake. He asked for the maid he remembered, and she came to him with a cry of joy. He said to her: I came here to find Vanna. Can you come to the disco, please, and help me?

She shook her head so miserably. — I am very sorry, she whispered. I cannot go there. No good. I want to be married, so I cannot. I am so so very sorry.

Never mind, he said. I love you like a sister.

Her salary was thirty dollars a month. He slipped her a twenty. At first she wouldn't take it. She kept saying: Why you pay me?

He said: Because you are my sister.

She rolled the twenty tight in her hand and thanked him in a whisper.

He went into the nearest restaurant, where a girl sat playing some electronic game, and two men were drinking Tiger beer, so he ordered a Tiger beer, trying not to cry, and he arm-wrestled one of them and won, felt dizzy with beer after no breakfast and no lunch, and pulled out Vanna's photograph.

Her name not Vanna, said the old proprietress, whose skin was bleached gold like lemongrass. I know her. Her name Pauline. Wait.

She took the photo from his hand and walked away. He wondered if he'd ever see it again.

After an hour went by without her coming back, he stared at his empty beer and his dead heart exploded with hope because maybe she might actually be doing or finding out something.

The floor pattern was a series of three-dimensional squares which bulged and trapped his drunken eyes.

The proprietress's middle-aged daughter sat nibbling at her finger-tips, and the granddaughter read a newspaper with her bare feet up.

The proprietress came in and said: She change house.

No good, eh?

She shook her head.

To restore the past, which cannot be restored, it is most expedient to perform rituals. Belief, while useful, is not indispensable. With his Happiness razor she had once made him young for her. He would youthen himself against all censure, so that by sympathetic magic he could become hers again, hers only. No matter that being hers was as impossible as being young. As he passed a beauty parlor, the women called to him, and he let one lead him into that white bright mirrored place of music; he couldn't get over the newness. The woman who'd hooked him was very beautiful and kept asking if he was married. He allowed that he was. — You no like me? the beautician said, putting his hand on her breast. — I like you very much, but I'm married already, he said. My wife lives here. She's Cambodian. — She didn't understand a word. — He signed to her to cut all his hair off, which would render him monkish, so she washed his hair twice, smeared a beauty mask all over his face, struck his forehead with her clasped wrists in such a way that the bones made a strangely musical clacking sound, shaved his face and neck hair by hair with a straight razor, and then brought a huge dentist's lamp with which to besiege his ear so that she might clean it with no less than twelve instruments: ferruled feathers of various sizes, loops of fine wire to dislodge his lifetime of earwax, and even a fine razor to cut the hairs inside his ears so as to strangely pleasure and tickle him and sometimes spice him with keen short-lived pain. She warmed every implement upon the lamp's lemondrop face. The hot feathers anointed him with sleep. Every time he turned his head to look at her or see what time it was she slapped his cheek lightly, saying, *Sa-leep! Sa-leep!* She spent half an hour on each ear. Then she did his fingernails. After peeling off the facial and purifying his now angelic countenance with a chemical-scented towel she combed his hair and then presented him with the bill: seven thousand riels or three dollars, as he preferred. He paid her ten thousand, and she clasped her hands *Ah khun.*★ In the next chair an UNTAC† soldier from Germany was getting the works, too. *Das Leben ist hier so gut!* he laughed to the soldier, and the soldier, unsmiling, gave him the victory sign. He turned to the mirror. No matter that she'd never cut his hair. Once again he looked so young and handsome—ready in case he might meet his wife.

Phnom Penh, Cambodia (1993)

The streets were now grayish-brown canals as in Thailand, through which the shiny white UNTAC police cars and the motorcycles and the cyclo drivers ferrying their passengers under sheet plastic all swam, honked and hulked. Sandalled people waded, holding umbrellas.

In the café where he passed that rainy hour (it being too early for the discos to open), old men with puppet-string necks leaned forward so that he could see their ribs change angles under the skin. Dinnertime. The proprietress brought the chicken in a great tub. Her husband, who was an ambulating skeleton, mopped the dead flies from the glass case with a paper towel. He hung the cauliflowers, lemongrass and eggplants in the upper storey and stuck the chicken pieces on hooks, while the son brought blocks of ice. A man in a dripping black raincoat rushed in, bearing an immense prism of ice that was hollow like a glass brick. Slowly the glass case lost its transparent

★ Thank you.
† United Nations Transitional Authority in Cambodia.

freedom, becoming instead a cabinet of morbid curiosities silhouetted against the rain. At last it was closed, and the skeleton-man stood beside the man in the black raincoat, looking out at the rain.

As for Vanna's husband, he sat looking across the street-river at the striped awnings of the New Market, knowing that the disco was almost in sight; and his heart suddenly rose.

But he kept believing that this was a spurious double of the city, that the true Phnom Penh, where the disco was in which Vanna had always worked and always would, must be farther east. This was another way of saying that he knew he wouldn't find her.

A cigarette stand girl told him that her business had cost two hundred and fifty dollars to establish. That was how much she made in a month. He had brought five hundred for Vanna; now he was happy; now that sounded like enough.

It began to rain harder. In his camouflage raincoat, he saluted and greeted all as he had done two years before on that armored personnel carrier in Battambang; they smiled as before, but as far as his heart was concerned he might as well have been inside one of those blocks of ice. He was not exactly sad or lonely. He was simply a marionette pulled by strings of resignation.

As he splashed in his sandals through the calf-deep streets into which squatting children pissed, he saw that there were new lights, sometimes even neon, trembling jellies of light that lay on the black night he sank his legs into, that night between steely grayish walls and shut windows, that liquid night of dark crowds walking slowly, some bearing lighted cigarettes like torches, that night of glowing trucks splashing; and he came to a man. He and the man had never seen each other before. He said to the man: *Je cherche ma femme.*

The man looked at Vanna's photograph. Then he said: *Je demanderai si ma femme la connaît.*

Non, he said a moment later, with the young wife peeping out through the open door. *Pourquoi vous cherchez cette femme?*

Parce qu'elle est ma femme.

Je comprends. Mais pourquoi vous la cherchez?

Merci, said Vanna's husband, suddenly exhausted.

He went another block and came to where the disco was, and it was not there.

Maybe I made a mistake, he thought. He went up and down the next two streets on either side, soaked to the knees.

No, he said to himself, it's not there.

Three blocks from where it had been he found an absurd new whorehouse shaped like a wicker beehive. The motorcycle drivers at the entrance stood silently aside. He opened the door and went in.

The ceiling was an immense wheel whose infinitely packed bamboo spokes recalled for him the density theorem of numbers. The circular bar had a circular island with bottles on it and ashtrays crammed with cigarette butts. That was where he sat. UNTAC soldier-boys were playing pool beneath the tigerskin-hung walls. The jukebox sang "You Ain't Nothin' But A Hound Dog." There were tall girls in bathing suits moving about. They did not look Cambodian at all. He said hello in Khmer to the barmaid and she did not understand.

Where are you from? he said.

I am Filipina. Me, her, all from Philippines. Manila.

How long have you been here?

Two weeks. All girls very news. This bar very new.

He pulled out the photograph, which now had a water-spot on the corner. — I'm looking for my wife, he said. Have you seen this person?

She called the other girls, and the soldiers looked at him with the neutrality that comes just before anger, because he had stolen their girls, and the women all inspected the photo and said: No. Never seen that one.

He bought a beer to make the barmaid more helpful. She made him pay in dollars; Cambodian money was no good there. He asked her where he should go next and she told him the Martini. — Many Kampuchean girls there, she said.

If I paid you, would you take me there? he said.

We are not allowed to go out, the girl said carefully. Not ever.

Oh, that's a great job you have, then, he said wearily. He wanted to crush the world under his heel.

Have a good night, Ernie, a soldier said, and he saw another soldier walking beside a girl, going into the back. No, the girl was right. Only the soldiers went in and out. There were no Cambodians in this place at all. He was the only one who wasn't either a soldier or a whore; he was both.

Three dollars for the beer. He left a twenty on the bar and went out. He heard a seashell's silence behind him.

Girl good? Girl number one? laughed the motorcycle drivers in the rain.

He took out Vanna's picture. — This is my wife, he said. Which of you will take me to my wife?

A raindrop fell on Vanna's mouth.

Phnom Penh, Cambodia (1993)

The motorcycle stalled in deep water. He and the driver knee-waded between bamboo fences which leaned in darkness, push-ing the motorcycle down a prison-like corridor of bamboo in which giant rats swam. The driver cleared the engine. — Quickly, quickly! he cried. — They yawed back into the night. Occasionally motorcycles of other dreams passed like lonely motorboats. This street was a dark lake whose window-shores very rarely shone.

They came to the Lido now, and at first when he saw the sign he thought: Yes, must be the place because it was about here that that hot low dark disco used to be. But as soon as the motorcycle driver began to slow down he saw a doorway with crimson-carpeted stairs and he knew that it was not the place. He took out the photograph, now somewhat more spotted with rain, and held it out to the woman who stood there, but she brushed it aside impatiently. The next woman took it for a moment and shook her head. — No use, said the driver, who was actually a very good person, but Vanna's husband waited until some more girls came out; they shook their heads and sent him away. It was a mark of their business sense that they did not try to entice him into spending money on a drink or on them, *locum tenens;* seeing the photograph, they seemed to calculate that he would not be worth their effort to persuade, and they were right. So they sent him on his way. At the Pussy Doll, the Savoy and the Tilden it was the same.

Hee, hee, hee! laughed the cyclo men in raincoats when they heard that he wanted to marry Vanna. One bouncer analyzed his face and pronounced him Japanese. Their opinions of her showed a like sense of the exogamous. They concurred that she was Vietnamese, hence hated, enemy. When he told them that she was Cambodian, they said: Ah, very good! but he could tell they didn't believe him.

Old! Ugly! Vietnamese! the whores laughed over that sad and skinny image of his wife in the straightbacked chair in the hotel that didn't have straightbacked chairs anymore. *Whaiiiieeeeeee?*

Because I love her, he said.

Does you loves her? For all night? Hee, hee, hee!

Phnom Penh, Cambodia (1993)

Seeing the photograph they usually yelled for him to go away. They looked him up and down, peering over each other's shoulders, and laughed, not always derisively. In only one bar did the girls crowd around him, looking into his face with something like hope that if he could fall in love and marry a whore, then maybe somebody might marry them someday, too.

Phnom Penh, Cambodia (1993)

From among the sneering girls came a girl whose name was also Vanna. Snatching up the true Vanna's photograph, she stared at it and then shrieked in disgust.

Phnom Penh, Cambodia (1993)

At the Regent he entered through the gate and then crossed a grand courtyard to the steps which led to this temple of flesh where women stood, and as he ascended in his rolled-up sodden trousers they jeered. The motorcycle driver nudged him; he passed Vanna around . . .

Yes, the motorcycle driver said. They have ever seen her.

Ever? They have or they haven't?

They have all seen her before.

When? When?

I don't know. They have never seen her.

At the Martini they all said that they knew her, and two girls in a bar by the Russian market in dresses of netting and sugarcaned starch insisted that she worked at the Lido.

Phnom Penh, Cambodia (1993)

S o they went back to the Lido. A woman sat outside looking old.
At first he thought her the madam. She was merely another dancer who'd accomplished too many dances. His wife probably
looked like that now.

She know her! cried the driver, so happy for him. By the river, in
floating restaurant!

You believe her?

She say she know her, said the driver. She have house by the river,
but she change her house. Now she work at floating restaurant. Yes.
No. She have ever seen her.

Phnom Penh, Cambodia (1993)

I t seemed almost a platoon that set out for the nightclub where his
wife, who might or might not be dead, might or might not be
working. There was the husband, of course, first, last and foremost.
He had his driver to speed him there through the rainy streets. At his
side rode the dancer with her motorcycle driver. Two other motorcycle drivers followed for a time just to keep company with their own
amazement. A dozen barefoot kids in torn gray rags ran behind them
laughing; they were, however, soon forsaken. The two supernumerary
motorcycle drivers duly recollected their responsibilities to Cambodian commerce; they peeled off. (And speaking of Cambodian commerce, they passed the false Vanna, who was riding on a motorcycle
behind a suited man; Vanna's husband nudged his driver and pointed
to her but the driver only laughed: You cannot be Kampuchea. Your

nose too big!) So there were four who arrived at the market in front of the floating restaurant, and the motorcycle drivers stayed to watch their vehicles while he followed the Lido girl up the gangplank over the water where two women patted the Lido girl down and he offered them his thighs and buttocks to pat down, too, but they only laughed, proving him not consubstantial with the Lido girl, who led him onto the deck around the floating restaurant, led him under weird still lights on the black water, and girls girls girls lined up on the porch as they came in. In that season they seemed to like black skirts with silver belts. They strolled with heads tossed back and pouting lips. They had rounder fleshier faces than the Thai girls. Some had a Chinese look. Every now and then one would go to the railing and smoke a cigarette, staring out into the water and the still Cambodian darkness.

There was a disco ball like a die in the darkness, waiters in white passing on creaky boards over the water. One waiter seated him, so he ordered Tiger beers and a plate of nuts for the Lido girl. The Lido girl said something and nodded at him. To the waiter he showed Vanna's photo, his logotype.

Just wait and they will inform you, said the waiter.

He sat outside with devitrifying eyes, unmoved by the dancing or the dark-clothed figures at white-covered tables. He and the Lido girl had nothing to say to each other. He watched as an UNTAC guy from Holland with a nice ID got pulled inside by his Khmer girlfriend.

You must come back tomorrow, the waiter said. (They all spoke some English now, it seemed.) She did not come because of the rain. Tomorrow, ninety-nine percent, one hundred percent, she will come. Come to this table at seven or eight-o'-clock.

The woman from the Lido took his hand, pointed to herself, and said: Dancing?

He patted her shoulder. — Me-you brother-sister. I dance only with Vanna.

She nodded sadly.

What is this one's name? he asked the Cambodian at the next table. The Cambodian had been an interpreter until his identity card expired.

Dounia, he said.

Oh, that's her name with the foreigners. What's her Khmer name?

She shook her head and refused to answer.

Well, then I won't give her my real name, either. Tell her my name is Sihanouk.

At this everyone choked with laughter.

I'll see you tomorrow, he said to the former interpreter.

To the former interpreter this was an even funnier joke than the last. — You see, he chortled, tomorrow I will be—*absent!*

You must go for Dounia at the Lido tomorrow at seven-o'-clock, the waiter interposed. She will bring you here.

She'll bring me to my wife?

Your wife—ha, ha, ha, ha! Yes, yes—to your wife!

Phnom Penh, Cambodia (1993)

That night he slept less than well, poundinghearted as he was by the probable insaturation of his wife (no matter that she was dead). Actually he had terrible dreams. In the morning he was exhausted. He could not add up his stacks of riels when he paid for anything. He forgot his hat in a restaurant and the waiter had to run after him for a block calling out. He thought about the coming and final night and hoped without believing.

In the hotel lobby, men in immaculate white shirts and black loafers rested Rolexed arms on the knees of their creased trousers. The billboards showed telephones and overflowing steins of beer.

There were still the narrow alleys paved with black mud where men repaired motorcycles, ladies carried pots of steaming soup, and barefoot kids rode plastic cars, but now the alleys pulsed with generators and the formerly empty shopcaves were selling pigeons and refrigerators. At the hairdresser's where two years before the woman had laughingly cut his hair and made gestures of marriage, this same woman now looked at him and said: No.

The hotel maid was very busy. He gave her a hundred dollars. The lobby swarmed with UNTAC men from Malaysia. They were taking more than forty rooms, the maid said. He went outside and watched small fishes drying on a wooden trencher on the sidewalk.

A block or two from the hotel a Japanese girl in a kimono was weeping before a stern man in a golden robe; this occurred on a color television in a black-on-white room of shut gratings and dirty chessboard tiles in which people barefoot and in sandals sat in rows of lawn chairs, some couples close together, a girl in a striped shirt in the back row with her chin in her hand, smiling in amazement. He sat in the row of skinny men who smoked cigarettes and drank Cokes. Every time someone opened a can it sounded like a pistol-shot.

The maid's family had invited him to lunch. They wanted to see the photograph. He showed them, and they burst out laughing, and the brother-in-law said: But she is old!

Phnom Penh, Cambodia (1993)

As he came into his room the other maid said: Sir, I am very poor. Buy me gold rings, buy me gold bracelets!

Oh, he said. Boys do that for their girlfriends. Are you telling me you want to be my girlfriend?

Yes, she said.

Well, come in then, he said, crooking a finger. All he would have done was give her five hundred riels and shake her hand, because he was married to Vanna. But she didn't know that; she shook her head and ran away.

On his bed was his laundry, which still another maid had left with this note:

Dear frined
&ee you a soon.
Love and all good wises of you.
your frined,
Love

Well, he thought, someone loves me anyway. — This en-
couraged him, so he went out and showed four motorcycle drivers
Vanna's photo, but they said: No good! Maybe more than thirty
years old!

Phnom Penh, Cambodia (1993)

e went to another hairdresser's shop, and even though a man
did most of the work, even though the people weren't friendly
and the water they used to shampoo his hair smelled like stale
meat, still the woman scratched and scraped the lather into his head
with her fingernails most pleasantly; for a few moments he felt as he
had when Vanna shaved him.

He passed one of those tapering glass cabinets of cigarette vendeuses
with red stacks of riels in the topmost shelf, and reminded himself:
Two hundred and fifty dollars. I can easily do that for her.

It began to rain, so he returned to the room and slept for an hour.
At six-o'-clock he went down without hope or enthusiasm. He flip-
flopped his rubber-sandalled way through the hot ankle-deep street-
ponds, looking for a place to eat. He wasn't hungry and hadn't been
for days. He saw a sign that said CAFE and went inside but it was
only a bar with a brand-new bank of slot machines. Crossing the
street, he encountered a restaurant whose long tables were covered
by stained white cloths. New money proudly illuminated glass cabinets of beer and soda. Outside the double glass doors, motorcycles
rolled in magical silence across the silvery black wetness, and neon

string wriggled. For a moment those activities seemed almost mean-ingful and he remembered some place of lights and hot exciting rain where he had been alive; at the same moment he experienced a pas-sionate flush of hope and belief, and then that died.

Two young waitresses stood behind him, watching. At last he pulled out Vanna's photograph. There she was in the hotel that didn't exist anymore, sitting in that teakwood chair in her starchy gauzy disco dress of rainbow colors. He loved her sadly but without shame.

Madame? said one.

He nodded.

Madame you? said the other incredulously.

Sure. Why not?

They looked at the picture, then at him, then burst out giggling.

The restaurant was replete with music and empty chairs. The songs were sung by a Cambodian woman with a shrill yet very beautiful voice whose turned vowels reminded him of a harpsichord's metallic loneliness. The chairs were all pulled back a little as if skinny ghosts were sitting in them. He felt a longing for death which passed as quickly as the earlier gush of joy. Outside, a white UNTAC pickup went by, possibly to a nightclub. A very dark truck passed in the opposite direction, heaped with hideous earth like the cargo of an-other mass grave.

The lady behind the bar wore a night-blue dress and a long golden necklace. She was older than Vanna, but no one laughed at her. She opened a plastic bag of cashews and poured it out onto two saucers for the waiter to take away. When he had gone, she slipped a single nut happily between her teeth.

The singer sang: Ah, la, la, la.

It would be seven soon. He felt very nervous.

Phnom Penh, Cambodia (1993)

The Lido was completely empty and dark. He went upstairs. Dounia was not there. The second floor was half as huge as a city block. Its windows looked out on the street. Mirrors, neon-strings, glowing beer signs, mirror-pillars, loud music and the whirling disco ball—these things just made him more alone, because no one was there. He swam the expanse of dark tables, avoiding the light which whirled meaninglessly on the dark and empty dance floor. It was almost terrifying. So empty and huge! After awhile he saw a man sitting alone in a corner. The man looked at him, got up, and left.

Nobody, nobody. Nothing but heat and darkness with a dead voice singing. He rose and redescended those red-carpeted stairs to wade again in the streetpools that little boys pissed in, and he stood in the rain waiting for Dounia among the motorcycle drivers and their neutral headlights. She did not come. It was half-past seven, and he was desperately afraid that his wife might come to the table of rendezvous at the floating restaurant, find him not there, and go with another man. He would not wait anymore.

A cyclo driver took him down that quietly puddled street, past the silhouette of a woman walking and the pale form of two strolling men. They made a left down a wide boulevard of fences, walls and monolithic buildings with black windows. He thought that maybe the Ministry of Foreign Affairs used to be here. Trees overhung a ragged black river in each gutter; over a driveway one incandescent bulb blinked crazily. Mosquitoes bit his feet. They passed a glowing sign that said NO PROBLEM; ahead, a faded banner in Khmer overhung the street. Trees squiggled down like multivulvaed mushroom caps. The night was cool.

The cyclo driver had lost his way. He pedaled him into new darkness lit in lightning-flashes by the occasional barfront. They paralleled a long wall with high dim ornaments, and he remembered that this was the Palace. At each corner a sentry stood in the dark with a rifle over his shoulder. They passed a park of many frogs and then joined a lighted road with two-storey villas glowing and billboards and al-

most shut gratings and people leaning from balconies as he remembered. Now in the night many changes had come undone, so he
began to hope again that he'd find his wife and that she'd be as she'd
been. The light and music did not bother him anymore. Behind a
hill of garbage a beggar-woman was squatting. Darkness hissed and
sparkled from between her thighs. Reddish cans of motor oil gleamed
almost comfortingly in a window. Then they made the last turn, and
he saw the long low spiral of lights at the river's edge. Dounia waited
there.

Phnom Penh, Cambodia (1993)

She sat beside him among the other jades and sylphids, saying:
friend; not smiling in her spiral-frosted dress and gleaming gold
necklace and watch. The narrow eyebrows he remembered from
Cambodia, these dense inverted U's. High heels clicked on the
squeaking boards. White teeth cracked nuts. Earrings and hair darknesses and tight bras lived around him; wide belts shone with silver.
Girls wearing butterfly barrettes sat at the white-clothed tables,
waiting.

Then a woman came whom he was sure he'd never seen before.
Young, beautiful, full-figured, she hopped on his lap with a cry of
joy. Later he'd think that now he knew how the prince in a fairytale
felt when his enchanted wife became someone else. He simply could
not believe that it was she. She was talking to him with hisses and
ahs and ais, laughing with sparkling eyes to find him come back to
her, and he could not believe in her. She was getting humiliated now;
she thought he didn't love her. She went and sat quietly on the other
seat, not looking at him anymore. He gazed out at the bonnets and
polka-dotted butterfly-shaped ribbons and the girls in quilty dresses
walking with their hands on their hips.

Vanna? he said to her.

She nodded.

The other woman took the photograph out of his hands, pointed to it, to her, nodded.

OK, he said, defeated. You can be her.

He got two motorcycles and took Dounia and this new, false Vanna to the hotel. He hired one of the clerks to come upstairs and interpret for him. He asked her some questions that only Vanna could know the answers to, and she knew all the answers. The clerk said: She want to tell you, sir, before, when you with her, she very sick, very skinny! Now in health again!

He believed.

He thanked the clerk and Dounia and paid them both off. Then he sat alone with his wife and he put his arm around her, but she sat unmoving and he wondered how much his unbelief had hurt her.

Phnom Penh, Cambodia (1993)

Vanna's nipples were long and thin as he remembered; they were the beautiful rusty bloody color that he remembered (Cambodian rubies tend to the brownish). Her urine was a robust color because she was menstruating. He could smell it on her breath and in her sweat. Her skin was neither warm nor cold. She lay so still, barely breathing, the sheet rising and falling over her breasts, her dark hair on the pillow. She had the same slender fingers he remembered.

She kept tweaking his nose, gently pinching him as he made love to her.

He gazed into that oval deeply beautiful face with the arched eyebrows and red red lips, and he knew it at last. He believed, he believed!

She was very anxious and restless all night. Later he found out from the hotel maid that she'd been expecting him to take her away with him on the airplane in the morning. He would have if he could; but she'd never written to him; she'd told the maid she'd lost his address . . . So he had no ticket. Maybe she didn't love him. How could he have known he'd find her?

In the morning she was standing in front of the mirror, slowly combing her hair by the light of the open door because there was no electricity. Her forehead was hot. She'd put his hand on it and made signs of fever.

He said again: I love you.

She gazed at him but did not reply. Probably she'd forgotten what that meant.

Phnom Penh, Cambodia (1993)

You are very lucky, the hotel maid said to him.

The hotel maid had watched the Khmer Rouge kill everyone in her family. Now she was poor and unmarried.

Phnom Penh, Cambodia (1993)

He told her not to come to the airport with him this time because the soldiers might cause trouble for her, and he said goodbye to her in the lobby where the maid had been interpreting; once more he told her that he loved her very much, nose-kissing her hand with that intake of hissing breath her countrymen favored. Everyone in the lobby cheered. She came outside with him. He said goodbye to her again, more quickly and casually because all the cyclo drivers, taxi drivers, doormen and motorcycle drivers were grinning and one man yelled: You go sleep her now hotel? so he did not want to bring any more shame to her who was too pure to be shamed as she had shown at the restaurant which before had been decrepit but which now was tiled and air conditioned; as before the waiter set a menu only in front of him, and he passed it to her. Then he remembered that this wife of his could not read. He said to the waiter: Ask her what she wants. — She take rice soup, said the waiter. — Now he remembered that she had always ordered rice soup before, too. Probably she was too shy to ask what they had, and so she chose the one dish that she could be sure of. — The rice soup had fish in it. Every now and then, with perfect naturalness, she tossed her beautiful head and spat fish bones onto the marble floor. The business suited ones regarded her sneeringly, and she was not shamed. So now most likely she would not be shamed if he'd taken her in his arms again, and it was even possible that by not taking her in his arms he was shaming her; and yet he remembered how in the wedding studio she'd posed beside him with such inwardness, maybe aloofness or reluctance even, never reaching for his hand; that was why he thought he was being good in merely waving, not looking back. He did not want to look back anyway; he was afraid of his own grief. Now a dozen beggar-children came running. He gave each of them five hundred riels; he'd already given her five hundred dollars. Their dirty hands closed enraptured, and other dirty hands came whirling around him like September's leaves in his own country of four seasons; and by the time he'd finished filling them, his vision had been choked by hands—not hers, not her incredibly brown slender fingers . . . so he got into the taxi and then as he raised his palm-edge to his forehead to salute them he saw her standing among them, and he waved and she waved and the taxi began to pull away and he saw her trying to smile and she stood there among the beggars, wringing her hands.

Phnom Penh, Cambodia (1994)

O ne dry season he came back. Cambodia was a kingdom again that year; the slogan was *NATION—RELIGION—ROI.*
Do you know the floating restaurant? he asked the taxi driver.

But now no, the driver explained. Government everybody go away. But now everybody stop the work, because government no have.

So where do those girls go now?

I don't know.

Phnom Penh, Cambodia (1994)

W hen he got back to the Hotel Papillon, the desk ladies said: All your friends have been dreaming about you! and they gave him a ten percent discount. He went upstairs and took a bath in yellow water that smelled like sewage. The walls were starting to get dirty again.

The cyclo drivers said they remembered him, which might or might not have been true. Kien, the short one, the dirty one with the slight stubble, the wide eyes, and the hat with horizontal stripes, said he remembered Vanna and could find her. The husband told him to please do it.

He went out to talk with the cigarette vendors and he ran into the friend of the English teacher who couldn't speak English. The friend didn't remember him. — You want to sleep with Vietnamese girl? said the friend.

He didn't. He'd had enough girls. — And you? he said.

The friend giggled. — No, he laughed. I don't like.

In the restaurant they brought him a menu with a living cockroach on it.

Phnom Penh, Cambodia (1994)

The next morning the phone rang three times. Every time he lifted the receiver and said hello he was cut off. When he went downstairs they said to him: Your wife was here.

He felt a sickening dread in his heart.

Your wife, she come here every two weeks. Just waiting and waiting for you. Why you don't bring her home your country?

He looked at them and could not answer.

Phnom Penh, Cambodia (1994)

At eight-o'-clock the next morning the phone rang in his room and when he picked it up there was nothing but the noise of somebody dialing, and he hung up. He went downstairs, and the reception ladies said: Your wife was here . . . and his heart turned over in terror—not the tiniest gladness, only fear and lonely dread. The ladies said: She come back in ten minute. — He sat down to wait. After two hours she hadn't come, and all the fear had become grief that she'd somehow found him out and had run away from his wicked emptiness; he felt so ashamed and hated himself so much and he longed for her. An hour later she came; and this time the joy flowered and exploded like fireworks in his soul and she drew away from him in shyness but then reached out her hand and then her arms were around his neck and she was giggling with tenderness. He knew that she was the one. He believed in her and knew that she was for him.

The last time he'd seen her she'd been at the peak of her beauty; now she was a woman, not a girl.

They went to a restaurant and she spoon-fed him and he was embarrassed. He tried to spoon-feed her too, but she said she wasn't hungry. She said that she was very sick. She had been sick for months. She touched her forehead and made signs for fever. He supposed that she had AIDS.

The taxi driver took them to a place that said **BLOOD TRANS-FUSIONS** and led them in, beaming. She sat in a dirty room that smelled sweet like old mouthwash. A weary lady with a headlamp that took up half her face inspected her and said that she had rhinid allergy *aigue*. Vanna leaned toward her so attentively from the rusty steel chair with her feet canted beneath in a ladylike way. The lady with the headlamp had a kind frown; she was oldish and patient. She put on her glasses, which were very thick and dark on top like eyebrows, sniffed, and leaned down to write something very slowly which he could not see from behind the wooden stand with its four dropper bottles like relishes. Everything happened so slowly, as if in time with the shuffling footsteps outside.

He'd given Vanna fifty dollars, and she pulled the money out from between her breasts and gave it all to the lady with the headlamp as a tip. Then they went out to the pharmacy to fill her prescription. She swallowed a little of the first medicine, made a face, and never touched it again.

Phnom Penh, Cambodia (1994)

She said she want to cut out her eye, sir, because last time you leave, she take some medicine to kill herself, and it make that blind place in her eye.

He looked at her. Her face was merciless.

She say she have heavy headache for six months now. She want to kill herself if illness is incurable. Maybe she is joking. She say she don't want to be cured. She just want you to buy her a motorbike before she dies, because she is maybe joking again.

Phnom Penh, Cambodia (1994)

That night she took him by motorcycle to the Ambassador Hotel, where he'd never been before (nor had he wanted to go); maybe it was where she worked now; and the lobby was massive, empty, gleaming and dark like the crypt of some inhuman giant not yet dead; and in the corner lay a subcrypt on either side of whose stairs a security guard stood, one man and one woman, and the woman patted his wife's body down coldly and degradingly and the man gazed upon him in silence; then he and Vanna went downstairs to that basement disco of almost total darkness where the music was loud and a woman was singing a song of terrifying shrillness. They sat down and Vanna ordered some food. The vast walls sucked up all light to such an extent that he could not even see what he was eating. After awhile the disco ball came on. Vanna gestured impatiently. She wanted him to go up and dance with her. He went. They were the only couple on the dance floor. Gazing around him into the blood-vessels of darkness corpuscled by people, he occasionally made out the flash of spectacles or a watch or a gold necklace, but mainly he knew the presence of others by their cruel and scornful laughter. The lights were dazzling and the song went on and on. He felt extremely naked and ashamed. At last the song ended, and at once a double line of dancing girls came to join them. The girls faced one another, trudging toward each other and away in a weary factory step to conserve themselves for the long night ahead, while Vanna danced on, never looking at him, and the girls giggled sneering over their shoulders and already he was getting tired. The song was a love-song with English words. It had already gone on for ten minutes (he looked over every time that Vanna checked her watch) and he was bursting out with sweat because he kept trying to ape the steps his wife made so that he wouldn't disgrace her any further; and finally the song was over and they went to sit down. A man in a necktie and a sickeningly pale shirt approached their table and said: I want to dance with her. — He looked at the man, looked back at his wife who sat appraisingly, and he said nothing. — The man shook him by the shoulder. — I want to take her my house and bed her now, you Mister understand? — He looked again at Vanna, then said to the man as calmly as he could: She's with me. If she wants to go with you, that's up to her. Vanna, do you want to go with him?

He made a gesture of her going with the man, and she nodded, started to get up, put her hand on the man's arm, and he looked away from them, choking with shame and bitterness and sadness; and then his wife had evidently taken pity upon him because the man was going away (and later he wondered: Had she begun to go with him because she'd wanted to or because she'd believed he was commanding her to?); but his wife was now dragging him nervously back to the dance floor; and suddenly he understood the rule, which was as brutal as life: As long as he could keep dancing with her (and paying to dance), she'd still be his. As soon as he became too tired to go on, she'd be compelled to dance with someone else. — This next dance, by the way, was a very strange and crowded one of men and women in nested circles moving very slowly around the floor, groping their arms and fingers like swimmers in a nightmare of cobwebbed jelly; and he was able to regain his strength. — The following dance was a fast one. He had to keep wiping his forehead as he danced. No other man was dancing all the dances; only Vanna and her troupe, those girls who continued to move so dreamily; Vanna, it seemed, was enjoying herself, because unlike the other women she danced with superb energy, practically leaping while they shuffled (but on the other hand she never looked anywhere but at her watch). An hour later he was gasping for breath, but he said to himself: If those girls can do this then so can I; and he watched carefully through his fog of sweat to learn how they shuffled and glided in such wise as to expend as little energy as possible; he began to copy them; but his wife continued as fresh as ever.

He hung on. At the end of the third hour it was over. He paid and paid and then they went back to the hotel. Even through an interpreter she refused to speak to him, and he never found out what he had done wrong.

Phnom Penh, Cambodia (1994)

In the morning she had to go to work. She and her friend were selling wine. She said that she would be back at two in the afternoon (so the ladies at the desk interpreted). Of course she was sometimes late. She hadn't come back after two days.

Phnom Penh, Cambodia (1994)

He was very hungry and thirsty because he had waited to eat with her. He walked and walked all day, half crazed. Every now and then some policeman with a Kalashnikov would stop him and practice English upon him and then he'd have to buy the policeman a beer. Or a man would say: Excuse me, sir, what is your nationality? and then: Where are you from? and then: Where are you going? and then: When you arrive our country? (they all seemed to have studied from the same phrasebook) and then: How long you stay? He always answered patiently; he had no right not to. He passed the site of the floating restaurant (nothing there now), and he turned up a dirt road where girls were unloading huge sacks of rice. The Tonlé Sap was aswarm that afternoon with drifting boats like up-curved dark leaves or maybe seedpods because the seeds were souls, three or four of them, well spaced, in each craft; some of them were standing and lethargically poling; and there were also people bathing and washing in that greenish-gray water where the concrete sloped steeply down from the pavilion in whose shade some beer- and toilet-paper-vendeuses squatted or sat upon their sandals listening to xylo-phone music there just opposite the weird red and yellow roof-scarps of Sihanouk's palace which rose so impossibly steep and tapered like a lock of his wife's hair after she'd shampooed it and he'd pulled it up from her head in a fairytale horn.

He went to the market which so long ago he had passed through but never been a part of; she'd brought him to that district when he'd bought her the first gold bracelet; and the swarming crowds no longer affected him. Maybe nothing did. He said to himself: These people are here to enrich or glorify themselves, or maybe to pass the time. Any of those choices wearied him so much now. He felt very tired. He realized that he was getting sick.

After a long time he neared the hotel, which he was beginning to loathe. He passed by that restaurant where he'd eaten just before beginning his search for her the previous year. The chickens and vegetables still hung upside down inside the glass case, but the streets were dry and the skeleton-man had grown fat. Then suddenly he saw the place where he'd gotten his hair dressed that last time.

A different girl got him. His girl saw him halfway through and cried: Hello, hello! — The entire time that the new girl was doing him, even when she struck the back of his neck with skillful wooden-sounding clackings of her knuckles and wrist, he remembered that first time now years ago when Vanna had shaved him; and at her brother's flat she'd giggled at him and said something in Khmer; when he asked the brother what she'd said, the man hung his head and replied: She say, who shaved for you? Not so good! — Not surprisingly, her brother was an ambiguous soul. At first he hadn't known that he was her brother; he'd assumed that he was the doctor because he'd made an appointment with an English-speaking specialist about her fevers and headaches and they'd set out on a motorcycle to go there, but, perhaps because she'd never had any headaches or perhaps for some other reason, she'd led him around an almost bright sky-blue cyclo with yellow struts whose skinny-legged old driver had been in an accident and held half a lemon around his bleeding finger, and into a hot doorway and up these four flights of dark and urine-smelling stairs to what he'd supposed was the doctor's house; and sat for awhile with the old lady who he did not yet know was her mother.

The man came in quietly. — Hello, sir, he said.

Very pleased to meet you, Doctor, he said.

No problem, replied the man after awhile. I am her brother.

He wasn't her brother, of course. Pol Pot had killed all her brothers and sisters, along with her parents. But he was himself an orphan and he had also been raised by this weary old woman.

At any rate, what she'd said about his shaving made him smile. Later he realized that maybe this was her way of offering to shave him once more. He no longer possessed the Happiness double-bladed razor because one day when he was travelling his suitcase had burst open and the metal box flew out, opened, and scattered parts far under the conveyor belt of his life's airport. Certainly she spoonfed him with rice with her own hands at her stepmother's house that day. It was all so confusing. So why hadn't she come?

He went into the hotel finally and the maid who now was always busy said: I'm sorry I forgot to tell you your wife came yesterday afternoon and waited for you a very long time, maybe more than one hour.

Phnom Penh, Cambodia (1994)

What did she say?
    She was afraid maybe you were angry with her.
    No, I'm not angry. What did she say?
She said maybe at night very very busy in restaurant.
You think she meant the good busy or the bad busy? he said.
I don't know. I'm very sorry, she replied, her face filled with pity.
He said nothing.
Have you been to the restaurant? she said.
No, he said. I don't want to see.

Phnom Penh, Cambodia (1994)

The next morning the phone had not rung, and so he went out
    to get fried rice and two orange juices for his breakfast. The
    swarm of cyclo and motorcycle drivers that always rushed to
meet him shouted: Does you forget her?
    Never, he said.
    Among them was one who closely observed him and his affairs;
this man slept in his cyclo facing the hotel, opening his eyes whenever
anyone passed in or out. On that third morning without Vanna the
cyclo driver smiled evilly and said: And last night you sleep your wife?
    The other thrill-chasers drew in breath and listened.
    It gave him particular pleasure to look the man in the face and
reply: Of course. My wife is with me every night. She always has
been and always will be. She's my wife.

Phnom Penh, Cambodia (1994)

ater she came back to him, that day or another day; he didn't remember anymore, and why should it matter? When he came into the lobby and saw her sitting tensely with another girl awaiting him he knew that none of it had been her fault, that the misunderstandings would never stop, that he would never ever stay with her, that he loved her violently (he was very ill now with the same headaches and fevers that she had), and he took her so gently upstairs and kissed her. There was another night when he had to bring the desk clerk up to interpret again and the man said:

Please, sir, she say to you: She afraid for old age have no house. She say please buy for her a nice house. She afraid now go your country, better she stay here.

How much would that be?

Forty pieces of gold.

And how much is forty pieces of gold in dollars these days?

Seventeen dollar, sir. No. Forty-two. No. One thousand fifteen dollar. No. One eight seven hundred.

Oh. I knew that all along.

He was extremely sick now and could barely stand. The only other thing that he later remembered was that the next time his wife disappeared he'd gone to a house of Vietnamese prostitutes to get shaved, wanting to imagine that she was shaving him like that first time, so of course he did not even get a woman but instead was presented to a very stern man who wielded an immense straight razor and suddenly he knew that the man was going to cut him. The man was almost finished now. The razor had rasped over his lip and across his naked sweating throat. The man was shaving his cheek now and he gazed into the man's face and the man smiled unpleasantly and by reflex he began to smile back and at once the razor sank deeply into his cheek.

HOUSES

Roberts Camp, Wyman Creek, Deep Springs Valley, California, U.S.A. (1986, 1979)

On a melancholy night in the hills, my companion's stove sputtered and extruded wiggling yellow flames from behind the weeds. The moon was the only happy thing; and it was out of reach, above a slanting black ridge. Another ridge slanted the opposite way to meet the first in a V. This second ridge had been tinted greenish-gray by the moon in demarcation of its separateness. Whereas the first ridge could not be construed as anything but a silhouetted phantasm, the second ridge was as evil as doom. My companion did not see or know this, nor did I tell him, even when the ridge began to unlock itself: what would have been the use? Along its shoulder and down its front, black tree-balls waited out the night. I am generally fond of trees on account of their gentle unconsciousness, but these I feared. They squatted there with a purpose, as if they might be demons lurking with their heads on their knees, perhaps

91

planning to inch down the hill come moonset, and get me. Either they would not harm my companion or else his fate was immutable, because he could not see them, so there continued to be no reason to speak out. Evil black cabins, gutted and stinking, hid like turds among the tall wet grass by the creek, or proclaimed their wickedness on the rock piles. Inside them, everything had been ripped from the walls. They were dark, and they stank. They were horrible. The walls had been cut with hatchets and blown out with shotguns. The windows were smashed, the stovepipes ripped out, and the thresholds piled with plaster. Every fixture had been gutted. The floorboards were stained with deer blood where lazy hunters had drained their kills. Flies had come and gone, but there was still a stale sweetish smell.

Years since, some other boys and I had come here by horseback. I remember how the creek looped through a rockwalled meadow; my buckskin dipped his head to drink, and suddenly we all saw the cabins standing tall and lonely. The canyon appeared to end behind them, although it didn't; only life and meaning ended here. Several structures were ruinous even then, whole walls' worth of planks having been prised off for fenceposts or firewood; but I'd choose to call them melancholy, not evil—strange stages for a theater of lizards, snakes and jackrabbits. Lupines and mariposas grew at the edges of those wooden caves, thriving in the shade of overhanging roofs; and the sun projected straight-arrow rays and trapezoids across the darknesses of back walls. Had I been a young child I might have liked to gather quartz crystals from the hills and lay them out in rows upon those floors strewn with lumber and scraps of tarpaper; I might have tried to make them intercept those long spears of light. But the resultant streams of prismatic color mean little to me now. I see in black and white. — These cabins, once used by cowboys and linemen, were older than the century. A half-crazed recluse built the first shack back in the days before White Mountain City went from one tent to half a hundred tents to a ghost town. In those days you borrowed freely, and then repaid with interest. Even in my time the cabins were a little like that. I'd slept in them half a dozen times; the windows had no glass, and the bedsteads had no mattresses, being now mere high flat platforms of solid wood, more comfortable than the mosquito-ridden grass by the stream. I remember how the bare floors were shiny and golden with desert sunlight; and at night sleep always came quickly so that the cold dewy dawn surprised me like a glimpse of my horse's head through the window. I'd borrowed an old silver spoon from one cabin for a summer, and when my horse took me back there, I left it on the old lace doily and added a cheap pocket-knife because that seemed like the thing to do. The next time I rode that way, the knife and spoon were still there, and somebody had left a fork, too; missing one tine, but still a fork; someone had thought and cared. What next? As the mathematician C. H. Hinton wrote: *. . . we are accustomed to find in nature infinite series, and do not feel obliged to pass on to a belief in the ultimate limits to which they seem to point.* I guess he was right. Now the fork and knife and spoon were gone, and the bedsteads were smashed as if by idiots at war. Now they were dead houses. Therefore they were evil houses.

My companion soon fell asleep and snored loudly. I sat watching the evil houses and the evil trees.

The next morning we continued into the high country, where everything had a grayish tinge—grayish-green bushes, grayish-red rocks—and everything was hot and prickly: thorns, prickly pears, nettles, and thistles. Sitting up among the pyrites, you could listen to the creek talking to itself, the faint hiss of the grass-pennants in the wind, the hums of flies and the discussions of birds where the shale spires and saddles were fractured into vertical planes seamed with quartz granite. Some of the rocks were embedded with minerals that glittered like stars. Others had been traced with concentric rings, as if they were trees. They were all hot to the touch an hour after sunup. Outside of houses, we're easily influenced, it seems. I have often seen patches of lichen on Arctic stones, forming a schematic of planetary orbits around the sun. Here, even the lichen—bright orange, bright yellow—hid from the sun in rocky fissures. I wanted to hide, too, but not from the sun. Of course it would be useless. Those houses would see me as soon as I'd clambered down to the creek to drink. Their windows saw a long way.

My companion said: I hope my house is all right. I didn't lock the back door.

All at once I, who had no home, understood why the cabins at Roberts Camp had not assaulted his brain. His own house was evil and had already eaten him . . .

Herculaneum, near Napoli, Campania, Italia (1993)

The Angel of Forgetting wanted to be the kindest angel. She went down to the roofless open places, the lacunae walled with diamond-angled brick. She came into the old house and began to unbuild it. The little boy said: I lived here in the old centuries. I lived in this house.

Around the edges of that squarish pit of ruins, graying apartments whose balconies fluttered with trapped white laundry rose from beards of ivy, and the sounds of auto horns floated down. A living child cried, and his anguish sifted down.

Did you hear that? said the Angel of Forgetting. — Ah, that pretty little bird!

Letting down her hair with a windrushing sound, the Angel of Forgetting overflew continents of surviving plaster. She strode the pillared yard of palms, click-heeled corridors roofed only with marbled sky. The little boy walked behind her, whimpering. Grass and weeds grew atop the jagged wall-ends.

In the room of gravel and moss, the Angel of Forgetting knocked down walls to let wind and birds in. She was being kind.

The little boy said: Don't you know me?

The Angel of Forgetting smelled a memory somewhere, like a pattern of a few dozen tiles. Sniffing, she raised her arms, swam the sea of graffiti-waved grayness, marched down narrow streets sunken like dry cobblestoned canals. Some rooms were hollowed out to store water or oil or grain, each opening being an upturned bowl with a ring around its hole, so that the darkness inside widened like a woman's breast. The little boy didn't follow. He stayed in his house.

Ah, ah, she said. Here it is. Here's the heart that needs to bleed!

She'd found the House of the Deer, in whose ultramarine violet sky of tiles golden-brown greyhounds leaped up at fleeing deer. Wreaths of leaves writhed like banners across heaven, and twin peacocks lived above.

She swept her hair across the tiles, and they faded. Slamming her heel down, she made thunder and the walls fell down.

Then she returned to the little boy's house.

The little boy sat looking at her in the pale-tiled rib-roofed chamber of echoes, sitting on his dolphin-tiled floor.

The little boy said: Don't you know me?

The Angel of Forgetting said: I'm not your mother.

The little boy said: I'm the Angel of Death. I lived in this house.

She shrieked, flew up, and ran along the many low ridges of various curvatures which hunched gray and yellow against time. Her wings fell off. She ran under the wall's narrowing archy darkness, that smell of sand in her face; she was sand in the little boy's hourglass.

The little boy, whose cheeks were burned purple by the Angel of Forgetting's death, kept twisting around to look at the woman who was getting off the train. He said: Don't you know me?

She replied: I lived in your house.

He said: I'm the Angel of Death. I lived in all the houses.

She said: You can't kill me, because I know you. Besides, I don't believe in angels.

The little boy started crying, but she said: You always do that. That's why I left. I got tired of your crying. Why don't you go kill someone?

Why don't you know me? he sobbed.

I do know you, she said. I died in all the houses. You never killed anybody but me. I'm your mother, and you were born dead.

The little boy stopped crying. He grasped the woman's sleeve. He said: Who built the houses, Mommy?

Your father did. He wants you to come upstairs. He has a new house for you now.

Then she shoved the little boy down, knelt upon his chest and strangled him. He squirmed and choked for a long time before he died.

Did you hear that? said the Angel of Forgetting from upstairs. — Ah, that pretty little bird!

San Diego, California, U.S.A. (1988, 1992)

Down in the golden grass near San Diego where houses and new houses terrified me, families lived the California life, saying to one another: If you can't feel it, never mind it. — A black lizard crawled and stopped. He heard what they said, and wanted everything to be true. Like ants on rocks, bees among thorns, flies and then rocks, grass-shadowed rocks, the houses went on forever.

If only I could blow up the aqueduct, I said. Maybe that would stop them.

The lizard crawled and stopped. He heard me before I heard myself.

In the desert I hear the clink of climbing gear or the clink of rock before I hear the sloosh of water in my canteen. I never hear my own voice.

The lizard heard and didn't hear. He heard desert birds talking to each other in long bright monosyllables.

Tomorrow I must die a little for your joy, the lizard said. He didn't hear his own voice.

Every time's a little drier than I remembered, I said. I didn't hear my own voice.

We both heard the slow double-beat of eagle wings.

The eagle saw cacti dead one day, green and blossoming the next. The eagle followed clouds like the branch-widening shadows of trees on narrowing rocks.

The gray dirt is covered with golden flowers, said the eagle. He didn't hear his own voice.

My voice was a bitter salad of Joshua tree flowers. The lizard's voice was a man's legs warmed by the sun through dark trousers. The eagle's voice was a long day.

Others were building new cities in the east, where life is blue space, where so many beaches and low dry mountains are overhovered by vultures. I heard the cities growing loudly. They grew like the voices on their radios, and cars made noise between them. Forests of houses mingled with palms in the canyons, orange-roofed condos and hotels, everything owned, but green ran through it like revenge. Ivory-nippled mission phalli became erect on palm-starred hillsides, the palms bushy, grainy like phosphor from shooting stars. Houses built themselves with hammering rackets. Garage doors hummed shut. Lawn mowers ate my scream. The lizard crawled under a house and said: You can study something for years and have no conclusions, but that's not to say you've gotten nowhere. — He didn't hear his own voice.

The eagle said: This desert might look green if I fly high enough. — He didn't hear his own voice.

I saw a girl naked outside a house and said: You're too glowing to find meaning in, but I can find meaning around you. — I heard my own voice.

She said: I can't hear you until you kill the lizard under my house.

I caught the lizard and said: I'm going to kill you. — He was screaming but I couldn't hear him. I killed him, and the girl and I poisoned his body together. We threw him on the road and watched. The eagle came to eat him and I said: You're going to die. — The eagle couldn't hear me, and I knew that and laughed. The eagle rose with the lizard in his beak. Then he screamed and the whole world heard. He fell out of the sky.

The feeling that I had to become something left me then, in that house where she and I always lived naked together. I knew that I was something, and did not feel trapped. Yes, I became something more evil and more good. Now that it is over, I can say that I was happy.

Once we went outside to look for lizards, but found none. We comforted each other, saying: Here we'll always hear flies. We'll always hear wind blowing until our ears ache.

Omaha, Nebraska, U.S.A. (1990, 1991)

Snow geese ascended from pond and field like leaves returning to the trees. I could hear them crying like Indians. I could see their flickering shadows by the hundreds on the ground. That was in Iowa. The difference between Iowa and Nebraska was more arcane than the shading between silver and rust on a corncrib, but crossing back into Nebraska I saw ever fewer snow geese. Omaha was not the chalice. Outside the city, among the grasses, tawny, red and brown, fields of barley watched the bluffs on the Iowa side, those steep bluffs which commemorated themselves with trees. Pale light, chilly and dusty over the plains, weakened as it crossed the river. Maybe that was why there were no snow geese anymore. Naturally I discovered birdbaths in the backyards (starlings by the dozen), houses window-eyed and door-mouthed like Chalcolithic ossuaries. One house even owned a picture of a snow goose on the wall. That house would have denied that it was jealous or that it worshipped icons. I never saw anyone stop to gaze at the picture, which does not mean that it was without influence. While its situation was not lethal, however, that same pale light declined even further en route to the living room, where there were power tool ads on the TV and blonde cheerleaders yelled prettily.

Like a chicken on a june bug, said the TV. Six-thirty to go in the third. Looks like a *pass!* Got that little laceration over the eye. Don't wanna put a Band-Aid on it. Facing third. This Ace speed drill looks right to me. Not a cloud in the sky here in Oklahoma.

A cheerleader shot her arm up and did a miniskirted somersault, momentarily displaying something like the underside of a mushroom. She was from Nebraska.

That pass went right through Nebraska, said the TV. Nebraska's gettin' blown away thirty-five to ten. They've beaten the stuffing out of Nebraska. And the fullback today—a hundred seventy-seven yards. Let those guys go back to Lincoln. Let's not rub it in.

In Omaha there were little houses in rows, spreading trees all the way to the malls, the place dusty tan with the blue-green blotches of trees. But in the empty old town, the railroad depot still offered its chessboard floor and waiting benches as finely finished as pianos. You could take a train to New York, although that wasn't as easy as it used to be. At the Bohemian Café, where they sold ceramic bottles of Jim Beam shaped and painted like Czech girls, and the waitresses in traditional dress were themselves shaped like bottles, bearing magnificent quantities of platters on their brawny arms, food travelled to and fro according to the same laws, in a union of love and shame, leaving the restaurant inside people's bellies, rolling past the neon beer-lights of bars in the Czech section, entering the little houses in rows, becoming flesh, then dirt at last, dusty tan dirt under the blue-green blotches of trees. It changed into plants and animals. The blonde cheerleader who'd shot her arm up on TV was made out of Nebraska, but when she came home from the game she'd have atoms of Oklahoma inside her. This I have learned by following the contours of universal law. Those atoms would not receive their due, either from her or from anyone she'd ever meet, but for all of that, they wouldn't go away since doing so would have left them even more emptied of their Oklahoma selfhood than remaining a part of somebody who had once at least paid lip service to the sovereignty of Oklahoma. And so the blonde cheerleader would marry, move to Iowa and die, becoming dirt, then barley, but at that point the suppressed principle of Oklahoma would bust out in an angry taint; she'd be barley that the snow geese wouldn't eat. The end would be autumn, as they say, but the middle was midsummer lying heavy on Omaha on the day that the blonde cheerleader came home to tall light-globes, signs on poles, lines of concrete splitting the grass. Summer besieged Omaha's chilly warehouse-wide supermarkets whose white aisles (mopped and polished continually) could fit six shopping carts abreast; there was a whole lane of nothing but potato chips. Outside, the summer said: *I am Omaha. Without my formative activities, humidity could not quarrel with the absolute. You sweating people know it, and that's why you hide from me. That's why you go inside your cold supermarkets to buy red-white-and-blue cheeses with tinsel stars on them for the Fourth of July.* Behind the supermarket was the house where the cheerleader lived. I never met her, but I believe that she too had a picture of a snow goose on the wall. From this house the cheerleader's father drove her past all the other houses to the bus station. She was going to Iowa to visit the boy whom she'd marry. Her father thought that she was going to stay with a girl from school. The ticket window was just opening. She stood her guitar on end like a longnecked pear as she finished her root beer. Then she lifted it and made it keep her company to the trash can. She came back to her place in line and played an inaudible melody. Something flickered against the window, and she heard a bird crying like an Indian. It was only a starling. For a minute she wanted to go home; she didn't know why. If she didn't say a word her boyfriend would hardly notice. What he wanted was to see her in her underwear. Maybe this time she'd let him. He and his friends had watched her on TV for the Oklahoma game. They'd said: looky here, and they'd said: a nice batch. She thought she heard the bird crying again. She didn't want to live in Iowa even though she knew that she would. Tonight for him she'd take off her under-wear. Tonight she'd take his penis in her mouth. She didn't know that he had a bet about that riding with his friends. His friends said: Just pull her head down. Worst she'll do is slap you. — When she saw him she was scared for a second; she didn't know why. She didn't like his house. He grinned. The pale light was very intense as it came in through his windows. He was cleaning his shotgun. He promised that come Christmastime he'd bag her a goose.

La Loma, near Mexico City, Distrito Federal, Mexico (1992)

The cardboard house smelled of urine. The door was part of a packing crate curtained with flower-print cloth. Inside, an old sofa and a chair squatted on the rubble. The dresser was the shell of a dead television. The rear wall was the long brick-edge of the factory that all the other cardboard houses embraced. There was sunlight on the bricks.

Next to this house was a mile of others.

Every month or two, the army came to burn these homes. The people watched. Then they came back, because they did not know where else to live. One old man asked the army what they should do, but the army did not know.

Whenever it rained hard enough that the train policemen could not see, the people leaped onto the factory trains to steal cardboard bales. Some of it they used to make houses, and the rest they sold.

(The toilets were also cardboard boxes. When they became filled, the people built others.)

In a sense the people had a desperate kind of freedom. Nothing was theirs, and so they could never lose it. Their houses could not eat them. Roofed with corrugated metal, those improvised dwellings an arm's length from the hot and sunny tracks swelled full of puppies, chickens and bright laundry. The railroad was like a street walled with cardboard and planks, curving as the tracks curved.

A dirty little boy in galoshes that came up to his knees was laughing. A man approached slowly, carrying baskets of water for his family. Children peered from the rusty stalls between houses. They played on the tracks. Little girls walked brown-legged in skirts. Their clothes were very clean. A beautiful woman with a blouse that shone like metal came running down the tracks. She ran past a house whose walls were made of tires. She ran past the wall of rusty iron where someone had scratched a round and happy face with big breasts. Laundry blew in the wind. The black slits of darkness between trousers and dresses expanded and contracted with the wind. The woman ran from tie to tie with easy grace, not needing to look down anymore. She was coming home. She ran to a house of cardboard where her mother sat in the doorway, smiling to see her come.

A week later the army arrived. When they had finished, the boy in galoshes wept. I want to go home.

Our home is everywhere, the woman comforted him. Don't cry. Come help me and my mother. I'll teach you how to build a house.

UNDER THE GRASS

Hanover, New Hampshire, U.S.A. (1968)
Mahebourg, Mauritius (1993)
Bangkok, Thailand (1993)
Roma, Italia (1993)

Hanover, New Hampshire, U.S.A. (1968)

Your little skull's a light-globe to help my shadow lead me as you did when I was your brother, older than you but small like you, afraid of the toilet's cool skull-gape at night. You always held my hand. Now please take me down the slippery dark path, down between the crowds of palms to the lava-walled, frond-curtained river of broad and rapid waterfalls. Until now I've scrubbed at the stain of your face on my brain's floor, your sky, your headstone—I never wanted you to come back! But whenever you did (your ghost some ignored dog to raise itself hopefully at every word), I convinced myself that you loved me most, because when I thought of you I thought of you alone. Can't you understand that I'm afraid of you? (You're only *caput mortuum*.) Now take me to you.

(Thus my briefless brevet, blotted, illegally disquisitive, which must be sealed with a crimson spider.)

Under your moldy stone, you radicate where the lava's tapestried with mossy crotches, ferns, leaves (dark and pale) so subdivided into heart-leaflets as to baffle my eyes. Within all this fineness, almost as fine as the humid air, I find something finer still, a spiderweb on whose lattices hang a huge yellowbodied spider, vertical, legs wide and strong, waiting. Closing my screams with phosphorite consolations of words that hiss out like hollow jets of flame, I uncrumble your chamber's riddled copper to reach you lying in the black dirt's guts. I sweep back your hair, breach your skullhelm in the muggish air. From behind your hinges and bismite-yellow pivots the crimson spider scuttles out. He rushes on his sister with a bravery as bitter as camphor, determined to gnaw her as I once effaced you with my exclusionary conceit. But the golden one snaps him up. His legs fibrillate. A single crimson droplet tumbles from strand to strand, is drunk by my warrant now validated:

They told me to take care because you were littler, but I forgot. Brawny ropes of water captured you. The fishes asked to drink your gurgling breaths. The mud asked to kiss your eyes. The sand asked to fill your mouth. The weeds asked to sprout inside your ears. Outside the night skull, a tunnel of blue light led you to India. Inside the night skull, your blood became cold brown water.

They said: Where's your sister?

They said: Where's your sister?

When the sea draws away from lava-islands, a thousand rills of white run down, like Grandfather's hair-roots. When the water dribbled out of you as the desperate divers breathed into your mouth, each drop was whitish-blue with the lymph of your death.

That night I had not yet drunk the ginger of sunlight that made my soul walk widdershins: My little sister was dead! No one had liked me, but now everyone would be nice to me because you were dead. I had not yet drunk the perfervid ginger of sunlight because our mother and father came to my bed with the minister to say to my night skull: *Julie is dead.* Choking, I turned to the wall until they left. Fat white tears rolled like pure light behind bamboo. In the morning my tears became a waterfall partially and temporarily catching itself on ledges. — I heard your sister died, they said. — I nodded with tinsel rectitude. I had the passkey to peachworms. Your death was a great gift you gave me.

Your coffin, that closed vacuole, went bitch-hunting for the blackest dog of all, the black and rotting bitch called earth, whose nipples feed leeches, rats, worms and moles, her ill-assorted blind sucking whelps. — Suck the blackest opium-tinctured drop, said the minister as they lowered you down the ropes.

Immensely long skinny leaves of fear (spider lily, *crinum asiaticum*) grew around my throat every night like thick sad trees over a lava hole where the sea comes sadly in. You rushed as a yellow skeleton into every dream. If I screamed myself awake, you waited until the long skinny leaves of sleep choked me back to you again. You came clacking and scuttling like a yellow spider until I screamed crimson tears. A package arrived from the post office of dreams and you skittered out to punish me. Something smelled bad in my closet and everyone knew that you were rotting there. I walked a hotly endless course of graves that suddenly whirled like marble trap doors beneath my feet to pitch me down to black liquescent corpses whose stench screamed through my dreams.

Our parents gave me a toy of yours to totemize you by and told me to keep it forever because you were never coming back. When they were gone, I buried it in the garbage so that it couldn't hurt me with its horrifying screams.

Outside the night skull, you looked for me to hold your hand, but I only screamed.

Sometimes we used to visit your headstone, under which your bones lunged muffled in black dirt. Our mother would cry but I tried not to cry because then you would hear me and get me.

I made your birthday gutter out like wax-light and scumbled the slime-slaked anniversary of your death. I forgot every word you ever said and the sound of your voice and how we played like salamanders, but Mother mothballed your dresses in a cedarwood chest where every year they went smaller and yellower (although I never looked) as your face grew along with mine. Now you're my white witch.

Suppose I'd never done what they never said I did, my execution-eering I mean, would I still have been brazed to ferocity year by year by the memory of your blue face? My blood-writing has quarried you, but I wish that you were still my sister, dancing above the grass.

Mahebourg, Mauritius (1993)

If the waiting room of a train station is a windblown world, an airport's waiting room subdivides itself more neatly into nations. Gate One was the Hong Kong flight, and in the seats of that country sat ever so many Chinese, some with broad coarse-pored faces like old woks, others delicate and meager, the ladies in flower dresses, smoking cigarettes. At the next gate was the Paris flight, and there sat the white people speaking French. The loudspeaker called them, and they were gone forever like a convoy to Auschwitz.

There was a Chinese with gold tie-clasp, bearing loaves of brown-wrapped boxes, and I asked him how to get to the important place.

We stay here for transit only, he replied.

Boarding closing now at Gate Number Three, the loudspeaker said. Boarding closing now at Gate Number Three.

At once the passengers went rushing down the long air-conditioned hallway with airplanes and jungle mountains painted into every window, and the people were carrying guitars, luminescent duffel bags, and long cardboard tubes, and began moving faster and faster, like ants being pulled into a vacuum cleaner. Evening was coming. The purple-gray clouds raced.

I wanted to reach my sister, I said. She's dead.

For this kind of thing you need to contact the Authority, said the Chinese, the Highest Ministry of the Authority. The Authority, they can try to do something. But you may not be welcome, as you may be aware.

I think she was called to the wrong gate, sir. I think she went to the gate too early.

Ah, this will pose some problems for the Authority.

A Chinese with a shaved head and skinny glasses aimed his cigarette at the man's head. A black-eyed old lady hunched her shoulders. I realized that they were fellow petitioners.

I don't mean to trouble you, I said. It shouldn't cost you much time, because I know where her skeleton is.

The man lifted the cheeks of his yellow face so that his glasses became very vulnerable.

It's never easy, he said benevolently. It's sometimes difficult. You must do something of your own choice. There is a center for this. There is an organization.

I've been to so many organizations, I told him. I've sung at all the graves. But they never answer.

So, vanity is one of those characters of eastern people, Oriental people. But you must make mistakes.

And she never answers me. Except that sometimes when the wind blows I hear something that almost sounds like words—

The man had sat down by now. He ducked his face backward until his eyeglasses became wells of disaster. He began jigging his knees and snapping his fingers. He said: They are speaking some quite old ancient language which is quite strange to the younger generation of Chinese. To be exact, it is half a language, half a dialect. If you are not well trained you cannot catch a word. So it is like half and half.

And you, sir, aren't you yourself connected with the Highest Authority?

Thank *you* very much, cried the man in alarm. Thank *you* very much.

Then do I have any chance?

I think the situation will remain more or less the same. By more or less, I mean *more* or *less* the same.

And if I behave better or become better in my heart?

That is a range of uncertain territory. It is not easy to be realistic. That is not compatible with the status of your life.

There was a little Chinese girl in a white dress and white shoes who was beckoned by a grinning Indian into the place where they awaited the flight to Bombay. I wondered if she had died, too, or if she really somehow belonged in India.

Maybe I could petition them differently—

It is not a complicated process. It is simply a longterm process.

And what if I just went and dragged her back?

In the first place, if there is a conflict, both sides will keep their small islands. That will not affect the Hong Kong area. But we reserve the right of military use.

After that he would not talk to me any further, perhaps regretting that he had divulged so much, so I went through the Hong Kong gate when the loudspeaker called me. Hong Kong was the next world. As soon as I got into the taxi, the driver said: I think you look for girl. You want girl?

Yes, yes! I cried in excitement. Has she come here?

He showed me a binder comprising color glossies of Chinese prostitutes, each woman smiling beside a shiny red car, each glossy professionally mounted onto ivory cardboard. I looked at every page, but my sister was not there.

No, I said.

I big uncle but you only big boy! You want girl? Look girl! Police a colosatopoli! What! What! Police a close a door! What! Please close a door! You wear low face, I no talk you! I hate you, 'cause Negroes make big problem in your country! You want girl? Look! Photo girl! Many, many! She standing by taxi! Good smile! Look, look, big little boy!

Bangkok, Thailand (1993)

On the night that the photographer and I returned from Burma, we went to Soi Cowboy to pick up whores. Long swaying arms, black breastcups, lights slowly pulsing across the mirrored tiles—these things both excited and refreshed me, but only at first. Something bad might happen. I felt this like a cancer's tenderness in my throat, not yet knowing that I felt it. I thought that I was happy. Breasts rose and fell, thrusting in and out. Ladies slowly raised and lowered their legs, smoothing their briefs down out of buttock-cracks. The girls who were not dancing slipped on their terrycloth robes and served drinks. The photographer ordered a beer and I had a soda-water. The two of us were, as I have said, quite satisfied with ourselves. Last week we'd rescued a child-prostitute from a nightmarish brothel in the south (no matter that she didn't like us); and in Rangoon just now we'd made a contact who could take one or two Burmese girls back home if we could break them loose on the Thai side. We figured that since we were heroes we deserved what heroes get.

As always, I picked the first woman who approached me in the bar. I had not even seen her ascend to that platform ringed by cold black railings around which white men grinned, the altar of bikini'd bottoms, bobbing heads, pale oval faces that blossomed with long cigarettes, long legs, and wriggling black triangles between soft brown thighs, and I did not care. I was simply lonely. I wanted a human being that I could touch.

She said she was twenty-six, but looked ten years older. She was plump and brown, with steel earrings and large black eyes. — Sure, I said. I'll buy you out if you want me to. — That made her very happy. Possibly she could see that I was the type who overpaid. I was being a hero again.

When we got to the hotel room I said: If you want to stay, OK. If you want to go, no problem. You stay, you go, I pay you the same, OK?

I want you make love me, she said. Me no man, nobody, very lonely please.

Afterward I had a dream in which my mother said: You mean you really don't remember the box? and I said no, already terrified, at which my father began to tell me. He said that you had not drowned at all. You had disappeared. After several days they finally thought to look in a large wooden box that I had left in the yard—a coffin, of course, in which you lay rotting. I woke up either screaming or thinking I was screaming.

That was when I realized that everything I had done was for nothing, that no matter how many young girls I saved I could never undo or appease, that my meeting with your ghost could never be friendly because you waited to send my panic dreams whenever you could; and when I died at last, then the true punishment would begin.

The Soi Cowboy woman's eyes were open. She looked at me.

I had a bad dream, I said. My sister is dead. You understand?

She nodded and touched my head. — You hurt here?

I nodded.

All through the next morning the Thai woman shied away, coughing tired garlicky breath and watching me unsmilingly with big eyes. Every few minutes she'd ask: You no good here? gingerly touching my forehead.

No problem, I said to her. My sister is dead, you understand? She nodded.

So I have bad dreams about her. No problem. Never mind.

But she would not trust me anymore, and so once again, sister, you'd had your revenge as easily and purely as an antler of sunlight slitting a woman's throat on a passing bus.

Roma, Italia (1993)

So I let my shadow lead me down to the stain, even though you wouldn't hold my hand (I was only your symbiont). They say that the Cross with the anchor means salvation, that the olive branch is a symbol of hope. I found those symbols scraped into white shards of marble in the dark tufa walls of Saint Callisto's. I found them in the graves shelved with cool earth. Man-worms bored these caves into the world, some rounded, all so low that my head met the shadow of my head. Looking up into a skylight now very far above, I saw moss around that hole from which I'd been born from within my marble pillar of secretness. I'd dreamed nine months in the crypt of the Popes, their names carved in Greek, all tombs rectangled with darkness; they'd been opened to remove the remains from the danger of the barbarians. But now I'd been born; I'd squirmed down the long narrow hall that was textured with stone like a palate.

Catacomb, honeycomb of the slow bees of souls, the slow crowd in the halls, where do you keep my little sister?

Not in Saint Cecilia's tomb, where the marble corpse lies on her side, offering three fingers in remembrance of the Trinity. You won't find her there.

Tell me, catacomb, and I'll leave fresh flowers in the webbed niche around your daylight.

No, I'll never say.

Then I'll raid your fossae, dark shelves and side-chapels; I'll sweep the dust from your shallow ledges where babies turned to bone.

But I got no answer save the smell of earth and breath. Although I lit oil lamps shaped like fishes, the round eyes of Pope Urban's fresco would not speak to me; the pale cell of Saint Sebastian's burial was empty. I lit an oil lamp with a whale carved on it (Jonah in the whale, Christ in the tomb, both three days, I think it meant). I said: I've been in this tomb for three decades; now tell me, where's my sister?

No sound, nor glimmer from any of these dull crumbling gray rooms of darkness where they still celebrate Mass! — Very good then, said I, I quit; I'll now be coming up from the darkness into the day!

But upstairs there rushed no sun, only long weird dark corners, dark under low arches; above that a marble-floor Roman mausoleum with flower-inscribed circles on the ceiling, faded fresco-strokes like the petals of dried flowers; steps twisting back down, white like Roman tombs; upstairs still, a church on top of that Roman tomb— the ceiling seventh-century, they said, and grave marble personages blooming from the walls.

No shard of brick stamped with the Roman seal knew your whereabouts; below me were too many receding halls of darkness (some areas still to be excavated, they said, still secret places underneath).

Nonetheless, my fond young skull, I must praise myself as only a king can crown himself: I sniffed you out behind the smell of stone, nosing down stone's barred wells and chambers! For you I frightened my eyes with blisters of torchlight on the restoration seal, crying: I'll wrap you in linen, then close you away with stones!

So then I heard a bone-clack; then when your leathery mummy-heart began to pump reddish and yellowish stains across dying frescoes, I thought I knew you, and ran down tiered, narrow, high-arched halls, your heart-drum thudding louder through those volcanic walls which crumbled under my fingernail-scratch; and the sweat of your rotting body bathed my forehead—no matter whether the ceiling was flat or arched, no matter that its plaster sparkled as if with mica— what tragedy and waste and uselessness! But I found your stone.

Among gray moss was the empty spiderweb, beyond it your copper casket's fragments shaking and rattling upon the membranes of your panting heart!

Remembering that the Pope was killed in Callisto CXX, I wondered whether you'd done it, wondered when you'd eat me, who'd seal me behind this rough wall, this dusty hedge of darkness whose leaves were bones.

So I swept back your hair, but you said: I'm not here.

Where are you then?

Clack-clack clack, you laughed—then: Ask the girls from Firenze who drink the sun. Ask the girls who sing a-la-la-*la!* and "Ciao, Maria."

JUST LIKE ANIMALS

Burma and Thailand (1994)

Burma and Thailand (1994)

When D. and I went to Burma we went by horse. I was not so very sick then.

The guide did not have a horse. He was, however, his own horse—his legs being long, bony and brown; his sandalled feet small yet heavy like hooves, his wide eyes set abnormally far apart, almost in his temples. From my mount I gazed down at his wide shoulders cutting through the beginnings of dusk. Often I have been around shy people, and I know that timidity takes many different guises, among them a stolidness or sullenness which some people are deceived into categorizing as a bad disposition. This was my first characterization of the man. He could not understand my speech at all, nor I his; as for D., she hailed from the south, which for him must have been as mysterious as another country. There were many rivers in which he waded knee-deep, then mucky places full of flies and pale yellow butterflies. Wet ferns kept slapping me in the face. The guide, soaked and stained, walked almost at a run, leading D.'s horse whenever there was a difficult place. I could not believe how strong he was. I had just been to Burma a few days before with some Karenni insurgents, and then I had been the strong one because I was tall and well-fed with long legs and so many years of vitamins and meat inside me. This man never quickened his breathing. He was lean and all-enduring and he scarcely said a word.

Bill, I so sad for him, whispered D. when her horse was beside mine. He is just like animal, only working, working all his life, no thinking. I so sorry. I want to give him something.

I understood now that the man was not shy at all, simply unconscious. He rushed along with extraordinary confidence, superbly fitted for what he was doing. I longed to gaze into his face to search for signs of happiness because his strange narrow excellence was so perfect that I wanted it to give him pleasure. But he never looked back at me.

Sometimes the horses lowered their heads to drink from the streams they splashed in, and he stopped patiently. He never drank, although his neck and shoulders had long since darkened with sweat. In her pack D. had a can of soda which she had been keeping for herself. She called the man's name. He did not seem to hear. Cupping her hands to her mouth, she shouted as loudly as she could. Then the man halted and turned back toward her, his eyes incurious, not bewildered or annoyed; he seemed to be looking at her only by accident. She gave him the soda, and he drank it down in one breath, threw the can into the jungle, turned wordlessly and strode on.

I so sad! D. wept.

At the thickening time of dusk the path was frighteningly high and steep. Actually it was not much of a path at all—or maybe too much of a path: —so many refugees, guerrillas, smugglers, and their pack animals had trodden it for so many years that the earth was worn shiny like polished wood. It undulated with ridges of harder dirt and craters made by the hooves of horses, where our own horses now stumbled. Imagine a hand's spread fingers, enlarged and endless, thousands of fingers, going on for many kilometers, and they are made of dirt. The gullies beneath them are knee-deep and sometimes waist-deep. These were the depressions made by the hooves of many horses over the years. My horse was tired now. He refused to go on. He was a wiry little horse, almost like a pony, and when I took my feet out of the numbing rope loops that served as stirrups I could practically touch the ground. I slid off him and led him up the hill, clinging to roots with my free hand, tripping and sliding into those eroded traps. The guide had never stopped. He was long gone with D. and her horse, high above me in the darkness.

When my horse recovered his wind, I got back into the saddle.

The night was very black and cold. I had to trust my horse because I could not see. The way was almost terrifyingly steep and narrow. I felt the presence of invisible precipices on either side of me. The poor animal panted and snorted and shivered, the sweat on his shoulders now as cold as dew. After a long time I saw the silhouettes of D. and the guide on a high ridge illuminated by starlight. D. called to me lovingly. Before I could answer, the guide continued on, leading her horse away. My horse saw or smelled D.'s mare and cantered to join her, which afforded me some comfort; it seemed to me that I had been travelling alone in the darkness for a very long time, although probably it had been less than an hour. The guide strode so briskly that the horses had to trot, never slowing even when he went up and down cliffsides in that pitch-darkness. D. kept calling his name in terror; but it was as she had said, he was just like an animal. He rushed on without drawing a rapid breath, drawing us along the naked backbones of those unpleasant mountains by habit and instinct. He was one of the strongest men I ever met, and among the least moved by other human beings.

Every time the fever came back, hot sweat oozed from the insides of my ears like drops of boiling oil in a wok. When that happened I became very dizzy, but I knew it would do no good to call out. As for D., she was pregnant, and continually nauseous, so that the jolting of her horse agonized her, and she whispered that she had a great fear that she would fall. Sometimes the guide would be swiftly striding straight down some wall of scree so steep that the blood rushed to my head as my horse picked his way and sometimes stumbled. Ahead of me, I heard D. sobbing in pain and terror. If she screamed his name long enough and loud enough, he'd shake his head as if in surprise, then come running back to her solicitously. He was not callous at all. She'd tell him to please go more slowly for her baby's sake, and he'd nod. A moment later he would be striding just as rapidly into the mountain coldness, smoking a cigarette, with one hand in his pocket. He was not hostile or even intractable. It was only that there was something immovable about him. He was pure and good and wanted to please, but nothing could prick him through his animal dullness. —We are fashioned, so it's said, of dust and clay. And perhaps in abodes of poverty, where health, learning, shelter and security are not birthrights, the soul is not a birthright, either. Could it be that these men I've met who are just like animals own no self, contain nothing in their skulls but brutishness, possess no feelings for other human beings save fear and lust and greed; or, even if they feel love, experience it only as a dog or a horse does, without understanding? In these insensible ones do only dust and clay have life? — It was all that D. and I could do to stay on our mounts. Twice my weary horse grew ill-tempered and threw me. The first time I fell only about seven or eight feet and struck rock, tearing my left arm open. I could hear the guide striding rapidly on, while D. screamed his name. By the time she'd managed to stop him I was back on my horse. The second time, a couple of hours later, I fell about twenty feet and as I was falling I thought that I was going to be seriously hurt but I was caught by a treetop which gave way and dropped me into a thornbush. The thorns broke off inside my raw arm and began to burn right away with some quick-acting nettlish venom. Far down the mountain ahead, I could hear D. weeping and calling the guide's name. He returned at last with that surprised look and helped me back on my horse. D. asked how I was and I said I was OK and she screamed: Why why *why* you say that? You *no* OK! Oh, you make me very angry! You talk strong, talk stupid! — But by then her words had faded into a distant wail because she was already far down the mountain again, pulled behind the guide like a balloon on a string. My horse picked his way, carrying me down into the dark. I kept one hand tightly on the wickerwork pommel; the rope that served as reins was wrapped around that hand; my other arm, the one that was swelling now and filling me with warmth, I kept a few inches out from my face, to catch the branches and briers that sometimes leaped for my eyes.

Finally it was very cold and I saw stars far below me on my left and on my right, and then we reached the minefield warning and were inside Burma.

I closed my eyes, but the drops of sweat that oozed out of my skull were so painfully hot that they glowed right through my eyelids, hued like the brownish-orange license plates of Egyptian taxis.

The guide brought us to a dark cold safehouse where a man with a lacerated face sat smoking cigarettes, and then he turned to leave. He had not even asked us for his money. Clutching her belly, D. stood up and uttered his name, in a feeble voice which matched her pallor; and he turned toward her. That was when I knew that he was not deaf. D. told him that we'd return across the mountains with him in one or two days; would he kindly await us here? We'd pay him when we were back in Thailand. He nodded and left us wordlessly.

Our business in Burma, which was animated by propaganda, machine-guns, and other categories beyond the animal, was not completed as quickly as we had hoped. On the third day we returned to the safehouse and learned that our guide had left with the horses. We never saw him again.

D. remained ill from the ride, and was bleeding from her womb. She would likely have a miscarriage. As a special favor, the insurgents arranged to bring her back by truck, for which I was very grateful because I think walking would have killed her. It did not seem wise for me to accompany her since my white skin would attract notice at the checkpoints; and in fact the people who took her back were all arrested. — Since there were no horses, I set out on foot, with two brothers to guide me. I was quite a bit sicker then.

I cut a bamboo cane to help me, and wobbled along, hot and cold. White streamers of rain sped suddenly down from a cloud. At the Weekend Market in Bangkok I'd once seen a man rattling two sticks together as he wriggled a toy snake of many papier-mâché joints across the sidewalks. My fever was now like one of those snakes. It wormed burningly and freezingly up my spine and gnawed my brain. Long creepers reached into my sickness, bewildering me with immense skinny trunks like bars across the cliffs of greenness. Sometimes I succumbed, and slid down my pole to sit on the ground and let my teeth chatter until my mind began to unthink itself. Then I'd arise and continue up the hills of hot and mysterious forest. Past the mine-field warning sign there was a steep cool meadow grazed down almost to sand, and then the true mountains started.

The elder brother ran far ahead. He circled widely like a dog, I think because he'd never gone this way before. I think I could have found the path alone but it was very nice to have company in case we were stopped. He gazed at me with reptilian indifference. Then he disappeared again. The young brother stayed with me. He was a different kind of animal, I don't know what—perhaps some kind of rodent, maybe one of those giant slum-rats which fear nothing and march out from beneath houses in a cold and lordly way. He glanced over the jungle as we went; possibly he was watching for mines. Neither of the brothers was as strong as the previous guide, but they suffered and endured in silence like animals, never speaking to one another, scarcely even looking at each other as they strode on bloody-footed in their wretched sandals. I thought of the driver of a bus which D. and I had taken from Mae Hong Song to Bangkok. Like so many of his colleagues, the man had begun the nineteen-hour journey by drinking a bottle of liquid speed. Then he drove the mountain road as rapidly as he could. He did not actually get to Bangkok any more quickly because the hairpin curves required him to decelerate almost to a stop whenever he tacked; what he did suc-ceed in accomplishing was making poor D. and about half the other passengers vomit. The ticket-taker, a thin boy of perhaps ten years, smiled apologetically, bowing and clasping his hands as he passed out plastic bags for people to throw up in. Nobody said anything to the driver, who continued to nod happily as he gunned the bus into another high-speed lurch. Nobody moaned or changed expression. They vomited in silence (even the restaurant proprietress, even the bar girl, even that longlegged soldier whom I'd seen carry two suit-cases through the hot brightness of the night), filling the humid air with stench. I don't think the bus driver was a cruel or malicious person. I believe that his soul had simply been compressed to the same meagerness as the horse-guide's. He was doing all that he knew how to do. He could have been an executioner, and doubtless would have dispatched his quota of shrieking or pleading victims with a calmness which had never known empathy; and if he could have been an executioner then somebody else could have been a judge, pro-nouncing death sentences without feeling any agitating impressions; and if we can judge we can do anything.

Descending a mountain of trees whose fat leaves swarmed as thickly as beetles, I felt myself again lost and alone; I staggered feverish among broad-topped trees and narrow grasping claws. I wondered to what extent I too was but an animal. Once on a night plane voyage from Mauritius I'd been stricken with loneliness and let my fingers touch the thigh of the pregnant woman beside me. Her flesh was soft and burning hot through her silken dress of white flowers upon blackness. Her face was young, dark, full. She opened her eyes and silently shook her head. I withdrew my hand, ashamed, tortured by my own nature.

It was, of course, only my self-consciousness which had created the torture. Had I been a true animal, I would simply have ravished her, doing what I had been made to do, like the young brother beside me, who twitched his nose, sniffed and bared his teeth. His dirty fingernails were like long claws. — To him and his elder brother, of course, I must certainly have been a pale white dull-eyed beast, stumbling and sweating, unspeaking, the draft-horse of my destiny among these grand trees with many trunks that grabbled downwards into root-galleries. We were animals together, wading across the streams. In our adjacent prisons of aloneness we bore the touch of wet pale leaf-hands with points, gracious fingers the color of Ceylon tea, fingernails growing downward, piled hand on hand as if for some game; we were patient and unresisting like animals when our raw feet bled.

Now we'd passed both places where my horse had thrown me. We were coming down through fog and pale green trees, wading streams, approaching the smell of woodsmoke amidst high and cool plantains. I was sick—oh, very sick; and my legs threatened not to carry me. Icy droplets of sweat sizzled on the griddle of my forehead, and my feet ached. If you have ever been footsore, I mean really footsore, as if all the cushioning had been squeezed out of your shoes, and when you sit to rest, your feet burn where they touch the ground, as if the world had become a hell of flaming spikes; if you lift them, they swell to aching with weary blood, then you will know how I felt by the ninth hour, clambering up an embankment of spear-shaped plants. The elder brother was not in sight; we'd failed to glimpse him for three hours. He'd taken all the food and water. I looked at the younger brother's muddy blistered feet and asked him: Are you OK?

Never mind, he said.

He possessed the nobility of the animals. He suffered without remark. I myself suffered quietly because I could barely speak.

We came to a plant with a twenty-foot stalk from which gargantuan leaves hung down. The younger brother drew his lips down against his teeth. Sniffing and twitching his nose, he licked the plant's green skin. Then he straightened and continued on his way, never glancing at me. It seemed very natural to me then. He did it because he was an animal and he had the knowledge. I was but a golem with a fever that melted my flesh away and exhausted me to the roots of my eyeballs. Once I dropped my stick. It was a wonder to me how after I'd so painfully dragged it close, the younger brother, seeing my weakness, instantaneously whisked it upright and stood it next to my body for me to take. Yes, he was a superior animal.

When we arrived at the safehouse in Thailand at last, the elder brother was waiting. In my fever the banana trees around me seemed to get bigger and bigger. I was desperately thirsty, and thought that the two brothers must want something to drink, too. There was a refrigerator case full of beer and filtered water and other things. I gestured to them to choose what they wanted. They each picked a bottle of liquid speed and drank it straight down.

I got a taxi-bus to Mae Hong Song and they rode with me. I had told them that they were welcome to stay in the hotel room with D. and me if they wished it. But twenty minutes into the ride they tapped on the window and the bus stopped. We were at a crossroads. One road led south to Mae Hong Song, and the other road led back across the border to Burma. They jumped out, and the last I saw of them they were running at full speed toward the horizon.

EXALTED BY THE WIND

The Slidre River, Ellesmere Island, Northwest Territories, Canada (1988)
The Slidre River, Ellesmere Island, Northwest Territories, Canada (1988)
The Slidre River, Ellesmere Island, Northwest Territories, Canada (1988)
The Slidre River, Ellesmere Island, Northwest Territories, Canada (1988)

The Slidre River, Ellesmere Island, Northwest Territories, Canada (1988)

Up the snow-choked gorges went tracks of musk-oxen as of foot-dragging skiers. I felt trapped and gloomy. The wind had not come yet.

At eleven in the morning the world was blue and white and perfect with hard-snowed clarity—the reification of some extreme ideal. The whole island, vast and by temperate standards almost lifeless, was in effect its own planet, low, blue, white, and brown, the horizon often no more than knee-high, so that heaven was all around. A realm of the Platonic Forms might be thus. I seemed to see nothing but solidified space without a predicate. It was a blank page of all possibilities, not excluding loveliness and terror. Absolute potentiality was a very wearisome thing to any imperfect being (such as myself) which crawled across the gravel flats. By now my companion and I had come a considerable distance from the coast. The Arctic Ocean having vanished from sight, we were left with only a cold and ugly river to follow. Muddy canyons grooved the land with dreariness. But a new force, no less inhuman, was entering the realm. I could feel it and did not know whether to fear it. My companion said nothing.

By eleven-thirty mist had covered the sky, except for a blue-gray line at the horizon. Lenticular clouds rushed at right angles to the ridges.

There was a white plateau (although it was not really a plateau; it was a river-edged valley, but because there was snow on it I could not see any difference between floor and wall anymore), and above the plateau was a thin blue smudge of sky, and above the sky was a white plateau of cloud with its own humps and mounds and appendages; there was nothing else.

A breeze began to deaden my fingers inside the mitts.

How are your gloves holding up? I asked my friend.

Not bad, really. — He was stretching out socks over the gas stove. — There's a couple of dry spots here, he said.

The wind increased.

My friend got into his sleeping bag, unzipped the vestibule door and lit a cigarette. — Kind of a much different day from when we got up, he said. Looks like it must be melting out there. Or it may just be the way the light changed.

An hour later, when the wind began in earnest, the shriekings of it precluded sleep. The tent-poles bent, quivered and lashed, and the tent bulged concave and convex, while snow blew up from the ground and worked itself into shifting patterns of continents between tent and fly, constantly changing and scattering like the harvest of a kaleidoscope. Ice from condensation rattled down on our sleeping bags. Somewhere in the storm could be heard the loud and regular cries of a seagull.

Suddenly I knew that there was something for me in the wind but I did not have the courage to take it. Thus the wind was but the increase of my despair. My heart stumbled into the deep wide ditches of tundra polygons treacherously covered by snow.

The Slidre River, Ellesmere Island, Northwest Territories, Canada (1988)

n the end I did sleep, and I dreamed. When I awoke, my companion was still sleeping uneasily. Everything was quiet. I unzipped the tent flap. Outside, the country was magically white and clean. The land had been scoured down to brownness in great long tracks across the valley; elsewhere the snow was neatly raked into drifts, mound after mound of them, and the river stones were black and white. A fierce white light hung above the ridges.

The Slidre River, Ellesmere Island, Northwest Territories, Canada (1988)

'd dreamed that I walked up a round ridge-mound into a cloud, and the wind got stronger and stronger and threw sleet in my face so that I grinned and ducked my head and climbed so happily; then the wind threw sharp ice-crystals into my face and pushed me; and I staggered but outspread my arms like flapping wings, joking with the wind. Gaining the summit, a wide upturned bowl of snowdrifts and tan pebbles, I turned myself around so that I was looking back the way I had come, with the wind at my back; the wind became mine. I felt the steady eager thrumming of it between my shoulderblades, pressing at my back and legs with unerring force.

Below me, corkscrew trails of snow whirled across the plain and fogged the ridges. They blew across the land like parallel wave-crests. The fjord also flowed in that direction; the wind was pushing it, wind-ripples greenish-grayish-gold.

I raised my arms to my shoulders, and opened them wide. I laughed as the wind lifted me under the armpits and bore me up into the blue sky, where the clouds floated like drifts of ice. I flew far.

I came to a place where the ice was gray but gold-bordered. It seemed to glow from beneath. On the white snow-beach I saw the black silhouette of a woman, with white fur-ruff around her face.

The Slidre River, Ellesmere Island, Northwest Territories, Canada (1988)

The snow was raked into parallel ridges half a foot high. Ridges ran also between the black rocks that protruded from the snow-covered river, so that they seemed to be lined up in rows. The scene expressed above all an unearthly *precision*. Once again golden plant-stalks rose above the snow; the faraway ridges were blue, and all was calm.

The wind began to keen, and I closed my eyes again. In my sleep the wind caught me and carried me to the woman with the fur-bordered face. She kissed me. Then I heard my friend unzip his sleeping bag and open the outer door; I heard the match strike and smelled the sulphur of it; I smelled the cigarette smoke. Opening his eyes, I saw the smoke mingling with the steam of my own breath. It was another cold and dreary day. Yet somehow it did not seem dreary anymore.

In the afternoon the sun came out, but the snow and wind kept on for a long time. Finally the snow stopped and I lay in the tent watching the fly flap away from the tentwall in the gusts so that the wall became sublimely white and perfect for a moment before the fly's writhing shadow lashed it; all day I watched the sun-play and felt that I needed no more.

Later my companion and I came to a mound of frozen sand and

stones like the one in my dream, and as we started to climb it the wind swooped to chill our faces numb and white. And yet we both were laughing, too. By the time we reached the summit of that up-turned bowl the wind was almost strong enough to carry us away. I wanted to be carried away. I said to the wind: Please carry me away. — Then my companion rushed past me. Before he disappeared in a lenticular cloud, I saw that his eyes were closed and he was smiling tenderly and his arms were outstretched as if he were about to em-brace someone.

THAT'S NICE

Split, Dalmatia, Republika Hrvatska [Croatia] (1994)

Now I want to know who will pay for the car, said the rental agency man. I have been to the bridge to get the car and it was very dangerous with all those bombs.

That's nice, I said.

In America you could not leave the country before you paid for this type of damage, he said.

I don't like to be threatened, I said. If you threaten me I won't help.

He sat there in my hotel room and stared at me while I sat on my bed looking back at him on that Sunday morning.

Why did you go there? he said. You must tell me why you drove that dangerous bridge.

Why don't you ask Mr. A., I said politely. He was driving.

He's dead, the man said. (I could see that he had no sense of humor.)

Well, then, why don't you ask Mr. B.

But he is also dead.

I guess you're out of luck then, I said.

We stared at each other some more, hating each other more every minute, and the church bells tolled outside, and then he got out an album of color photographs which portrayed the car from every angle.

As you see, it is completely damaged, he said. Destroyed.

Which photo is your favorite? I said. Why don't you give me your favorite one and I'll take it to my agency.

At first he wouldn't do it. He hated to part with any of the glossies in that collection so pure and complete, but at last he selected a good one that showed how the driver's side had been smashed and twisted and riddled.

That's nice, I said. That's very artistic. Here. I'll show you a couple of nice pictures, too.

I got up and went to the other bed and took the envelope of contact prints.

This is Mr. B. after I pulled him out of the car, I said. Isn't that nice? He was my friend for nineteen years. And this one here is Mr. A. Here they both are in the front just before I pulled them out.

Mr. A. was driving? the rental man asked.

That's right. See how the first burst got him right in the head? I'll be happy to make a copy for your collection.

He looked away. — So you will stay here in Split?

No, tomorrow I'll go back to Mostar, I said. It's so nice there.

Why? Why do you go back to that dangerous place? — That was what I expected him to say because that was what everybody else said, but he did not say it. He was not so interested in future whys because he was first and foremost a rental man.

When do you come back? he said. I'll be waiting for you.

Tuesday night. That's when Mr. B.'s family is arriving for the funeral—

So they will be in this hotel? he said, eyes lighting up for the first time. What room number?

I want you to understand something, I began.

I already understand everything, he said. But who will pay for the car? Ten thousand six seven hundred dollars! Who will pay for that? I ask you, who will pay?

No, you don't understand everything, I told him. What you don't understand is that if you bother Mr. B.'s family with this matter in any way I will not help you anymore. His mother is old and has a bad heart.

Then who will pay?

I did not sign the rental agreement, I said. Legally I have no responsibility. Morally I do, so I will try to—

You are also responsible, he interrupted. You also chose to go there. I have rented to journalists before. I know how you are (this last he said with stunning contempt).

I promise you, if you disturb Mr. B.'s family in any way you will receive no help from me, I said. I will not be happy. Right now I am very happy because I enjoy talking to you so much. If you bother anyone but me I will be quite unhappy. Then maybe I will not be very nice.

You were very lucky, he said. So you must pay.

We understand each other there, I said. What you say is very true and relevant to all walks of life. Thank you for imparting your philosophy to me.

His cellular phone rang just then, so he had to go off to Sunday dinner with his family. He was eager to go now because the food would soon be getting cold. Before, his business with me had been quite urgent. I offered to buy him a drink and show him still more photographs of my friends' mutilated bodies, but he would not stay. So I sat alone on the bed, looking at the damage estimate, which was typed in a language I could not read, and I was unable either to laugh or to cry.

FATHERS AND CROWS

Joshua Tree National Monument, California, U.S.A. (1988)
Charlevoix, Québec, Canada (1990)
Algonquin Provincial Park, Ontario, Canada (1990)
Algonquin Provincial Park, Ontario, Canada (1990)
Mission-Sainte-Marie, Midland, Ontario, Canada (1648)

Joshua Tree National Monument, California, U.S.A. (1988)

Peter returned to the mount called Olivet whenever he could, at first because he sought yet for signs of Him Whom he worshipped, but once he'd taken upon himself the first black mantle of priesthood, once he had founded his church, his craving for JESUS lost its ache and became instead a wholesome nostalgia: — This place, he said to himself, is where I became what I am. — And he meant this not out of any sinful pride, for he fully expected to die for the LORD as JESUS had done (and we know that in this he was to be gratified). So Peter walked the path of hardpacked quartz pebbles; his robe caught and tore on the gray bushes; he ascended the way his FRIEND had gone and looked up at Heaven until his face was sunburned; he sat on the spot where the two Angels had appeared, and there he rested all day, smiling with his head in his hands. In the evenings that cut like blue and ancient knives, birds pelted the sky in droves, sounding their different notes, and the Joshua trees seemed to stretch upward as their shadows lengthened; *His* shadow must have become impossibly, mournfully elongated as He had risen (but the silhouette of His face would have remained as it was, a face of ordinary proportions, bowed upon a great pillar of cooling shadow)—and the Joshua trees whose arms invoked all directions like the crooked legs of spiders began to tremble in the wind, and the ridges to the west turned purple with black tree-dots, while the ridges to the east, receiving the last of the sun's low-slanting rays, glowed hot and pink above the darkness.

For the sake of this same sentimental archeology, Peter occasionally returned to Golgotha, ignoring the cries of the more lately crucified because they were *not* the ONE; so paying them witness could only erode his recollections of that Crucifixion which he was bound to consider final. — *Water, water!* moaned a man on a cross. — Oh, what a cursed place this was! — But Peter's occupation must now be to overcome such impressions. Kneeling with clasped hands, he lowered his head and began to search for beauty in the ridges below him, whose tan boulders were ridden with cracks so that they seemed to be stacks of half-melted bricks from some old time, and channels and canyons of the same rough rock ran between them, all edges sandblasted smooth, but their stone-flesh was grainy with sharp quartz crystals that could scrape hands to bleeding. Yucca plants grew in fractures or little beds of sand; their shadows were very sharp. Sometimes a sandbed led between two slanting boulders that gave like a gateway onto some plain or plateau bounded by ridges of again the same rock; those places were gray with brush. Immense squawbushes shone iron-gray like tumbleweeds forged in some smithy; they bore no red berries to refresh the Savages; they bore nothing but grayness; the only green things were piñon pines or the straight shaggy trunkposts of Joshua trees, in whose green brushes crows sat. In sunny places the heat was burning; in the shade it was cold. — Peter could see nothing beautiful there. — Sighing, he proceeded up the Road of Tears, which wound monotonously upward, not steeply but steadily, and the wind gusted colder and the shrubs grew grayer and the Joshua trees smaller, while the way went from bowl to bowl in the rocks. In each bowl the horizon was very close, being bordered on every side by a ridge of the same tan stone, and in each bowl a cross was erected, on which a man hung dying while his guards played dice;

and Peter averted his eyes and strode on to the summit, from which he could see many dead black hills below, fretted with shrubs and the silvery trails of flood-washes, and then the far flat plain of bluish enigma, stained by cloud-shadows, upon which the great whore *Jerusalem* walled herself in to her pleasures, and the plain stretched past Emmaus all the way to the Dead Sea, which was then the color of the sky; and a great dark range of dark blue mountains made the final horizon. But where Peter sat was only reddish dirt with the ant-hollowed flute of a man's thigh-bone sticking out, and flakes of quartz or feldspar, and feeble patches of grass huddled in shrub-shadows; — so all he saw was a great anthill of decay swelling above a world of iniquity, but I am sure it was only because he was not quite high enough; had the guards considerately raised him up to the fork of a Joshua tree and nailed him thereon, he might have seen what CHRIST saw: the lovely cacti, over which the delirious CHRIST murmured and waved His hand as He blessed them (but of course His hand was nailed fast to that cross of gray splintered ironwood, so that to those watching below it seemed only that He struggled feebly for a moment, tearing His wounds a little more so that another trickle of weary black blood ran down between the hard-baked clots already on him), and He smiled at the gardens of cholla cactus which only He saw, loving them for their spines, which were as intricately whorled as rose coral; he smiled upon their greenish-orange fruits, which were like hard raspberries; He sent His affection to them on account of the beautiful green they glowed beneath the gray bushes where woodrats lived; in His greater self, which was never maimed or fettered, He kissed the hale gray buckhorn chollas; He embraced the strawberry stems of calico cacti; He smiled in such delight to the rustling leaf-music of the creosote bushes, whose waxy leaves, though olive-green and soothing like stream-plants, were nonetheless almost as sharp-edged as those cholla spines which shimmered silvery and lavender like delicate down upon their lobes and joints, which twined caress-ingly about each other in that dry sand and they seemed softer than hare-fur until you got closer to them and saw that each joint was like a sea-urchin and their shimmering was a shimmering of barbed spines (but cactus wrens could nest in the chollas, and the Cahuilla Indians could gather and eat the cholla-fruit); so CHRIST married the fuzzy-soft chollas, and he took to himself the detached chollas lying in the sand like fallen gray stars; and He married the pencil-chollas, whose pale green cylindrical leaves were rolled tight like promises; they too were spine-studded, but every spine was precious, and so emerged from a diamond on the leaf; He resurrected the dead gray-white cholla skeletons that decay had reduced to hollow wind-tubes; nor did He neglect the others, the jojoba and the desert senna, the ocotillo, which rose, woody, split, and spined like fish backbones, to a height of fifteen feet or more, like the upright of His cross, and its gray wood was cracked and helically green-veined; but it glowed with orange cactus-flowers . . .

Peter loved none of these weeds. But he loved to look down the mountain Golgotha at a certain ridge-fold where a single green tree rose; that was where he and the guards went to drink at a certain hour because there was a tiny oasis there; in the oasis it was cool and a wide shallow stream trickled through a muddy tunnel between the great cottonwood palms, whose bleached fronds stirred about their trunk-waists like the grass skirts of dancers, and the sky fluttered blue as turquoise between their green fan-fingers, and they spread ever so many happy green hands all around themselves in thankfulness, and cattails made a wall against the heat, and the water glittered in the darkness and the palm-trees rustled and between them it was so dim and cool; it was almost like being in a forest, but not quite, because there were not enough trees and their scales were sharp plates like reptile-scales; but at least the fronds were soft; they did not cut your hands. — Peter felt contented when he thought upon that grove. And he said to himself: My CHRIST is in the grove, not the grave. — And the guards made a covenant with Peter that neither party would molest the other, for each was but rendering service and allegiance as he was called upon to do.

Charlevoix, Québec, Canada (1990)

C he hills were like green breasts. In the vast mounds of forest blue and green rose skinny white birches so needy for someone to embrace them. Sky-blue massifs rose ahead and behind.

The Baie Saint-Paul was wide and blue, pale blue like a sea. The far shore was but an uncertain congealment of haze.

The priests were Peter's sons. When they saw the immensity before them they whispered: We shall make no covenant with you.

Algonquin Provincial Park, Ontario, Canada (1990)

P ère Jean de Brébeuf made no covenants. But he followed the Spiritual Exercises of Saint Ignatius, and being thus directed (according to the limits of his strength) up the great river of prayer called Time, he came at last to the Seventy-Second Rapid— *viz.;* the Thirteenth Apparition of CHRIST, Who manifested Himself to Saint Paul, and also to the Holy Fathers in Limbo, from which state He freed them. Around this Rapid rose the blockily fractured cliff-faces covered by trees standing one below the other, the crowns of those spruces and aspens shadowing the bases of those above them; they went down and down, until began the rock that dropped sheer to the brown river below. At first he saw the river flowing far down below him, between trees on which autumn and evening already shone with a pale yellow light; he seemed to stand with JESUS CHRIST, Savior of the World, atop the faded cliffs gray and cool that rose to crickets, resin, ferns, red maples, forest shade, crowned by sky still luminous as in afternoon; but this position Brébeuf considered highly presumptuous considering his unworthiness, and so his soul leaped into the river, allowing itself to be borne back down the Three Falls of Humility, where he was much bruised and scratched by the river-rocks, a mortification which afforded him some consolation for his many faults. Now he permitted himself to clamber back up the Sault of Election, to ascend to the Current of Patience which again washed him back to the commencement of the Third Week, to rise from the Sixteenth Rapid to the Third Isle of Prayer, to swim from the Twenty-Third Rapid back up to the Seventy-Second, which he pulled himself up by great might and main, wedging his feet between boulders to brace his climb as the cataract spewed down upon his body and the walls shimmered high and narrow above him like rocky-hued rainbows.

In fact the weather was rather grise—*viz.;* dull and gray. It chilled him but he would make no covenant with his loathsome body, no matter how much it shivered.

Algonquin Provincial Park, Ontario, Canada (1990)

A sick woman saw in dreams a man dressed in black like Père Brébeuf, whom they called *Echon*. In the dream it was Echon who touched her with fire, at which her fever became much worse. When Tehorenhaennion was called, everyone in that longhouse greeted him most respectfully.

The dogs must not howl, he said. I make my cures only in silence.

A girl took the dogs out, and also a bear-cub in its cage, which had begun grunting.

It is my rule to require the sick one to be carried into the woods, to see the SKY, said Tehorenhaennion after a pause. But today there are clouds. This cure will be difficult.

He bent over her and began to blow upon her and suck at her body where she was most swollen. Very soon he had found five hairball charms which Echon or some other witch had sent into her.

The case was most serious, and he had little hope that she would live. However, he turned to her relatives who were there and showed them the witch-charms before he burned them in the fire, concealing his doubts, for sometimes belief alone would assist a patient to recover. Now he gave her a potion to drink which would open the way to her navel—the seat of her disease—and said to her: *Have courage!* and she smiled most gratefully and replied: Even now I feel eased . . . and her lodgemates began to be very happy, although for fear of him they did not show it, but then the potion mounted to her ears, which began to swell, and so she died.

You tricked us, a man said to him. Why did you fail?

Tehorenhaennion regarded him calmly. — You did not give me all the presents which I asked you for, he said. Where is my pipe of red stone? Where is my tobacco pouch?

The truth was that Echon had used magic which he did not know. Echon was the most Powerful and malignant witch whom he had ever fought. He would make no covenant with him.

Mission-Sainte-Marie, Midland, Ontario, Canada (1648)

Corn hung yellow and bright. The pigs wanted it. They were grunting pigs with huge pink ears and dirty faces and there were flies on them. The flies wanted pigsweat and blood. Not far away, udders hung. The brown calves wanted them. And the mooing black cows with swollen brown udders, they wanted to be milked or sucked. They had great glistening eyes; they lowed loudly in the hay.

The furnace eye was uneasy. The flames curled back.

Priests stared from the open casements, knowing the furnace eye, wondering when their covenant would be burned. They watched the aqueduct drain down to the South Compound. The water continued through the narrow canal, just a canoe's width; it exited the lock all gray, narrow, a little waterfall through the square arch; and then it left the tables, candles and beds to become again the river it had been, deep and black, streaming with white reflections of palisade-poles like bones. Across the river the Iroquois crouched in hiding. They wanted everything they saw. They wanted to make everything scream and burn.

The flies came and came; they got everything. Then some corn dropped down to the pigs at last, and the pigs got it. Milk jetted from udders into pink mouths, the mouths of calves. Now practically all that's left of those days is Québec's Chapelle des Ursulines with its rose window and rose-windowed arch; but if one looks into space as one reads or rather recites from one's Bible (the eldest daughter looking up at one, the other children eyeing each other silently), it's possible to see how the furnace eye blinked and widened. But the priests never succumbed, never made any covenant, even when they canoed fleeing from their burning Mission. Yes, the fire came, and the Iroquois also gained their own desire, singing: *Hé é é é é* . . .

DOING HER HAIR

Madagascar (1993)

While the roaring gray rain cooled down Madagascar for a minute, she greased her hands, then combed her hair back again, combing the grease in until it shone, leaning forward naked on the bed to watch her progress in the cracked plastic mirror (one of the few items of baggage she'd brought from home). She made a greasy twist down the back of her head, the center one. Then she began to form the others. Leaving the comb in her hair for safe-keeping, she inserted the rollers, holding each in with a forefinger until it was securely pinned. So steadily she assembled a long spine of those cylinders along the center ridge of her head like a sort of mohawk as the rain slackened and thunder sounded close but not loud, and she commenced combing and twisting around her temples. She was making art as surely as the barefoot craftsman who hammers wood with a wooden mallet, squatting on fresh sawdust. Her fresh head slid forward and back as she peeked in the mirror. She sang. A loud clap of thunder made her laugh. Her gold ring shone dully in the dim light of the hotel room as she pinned the last comb in the back, the whites of her eyes large with concentration in her chocolate face. Now she could embellish herself with the new earrings he'd bought her, she nodding, talking fast, rows of twisted locks curving back around the side of her head. Now she was ready to dance with him at the Discotheque Kali where white shirts and blouses glowed blue in the fluorescent lights just as the tonic water did; and a man stood behind a pillar, his face the color of blood, his necktie like the blue tongue of a black snake, and he was watching, grinning with hard eyes. Perhaps the man liked her hair. (She was always doing her hair. Sitting on a bed in the Hotel Roger with a towel around her middle, she put her hair up with the same sweet concentration as when she squatted to piss on the sidewalk.) In the Hotel Anjary she did her hair, but did she do it for him who loved her or for the man whose face was the color of blood? She loved to dance but she feared the discos because the robbers owned them; why was it that she must do her hair for robbers? Maybe if she did not make herself more beautiful the blood-faced watcher would not watch her. But he never said anything about the blood-faced watcher to her because she feared the robbers already and he did not want to make her more afraid. In the corner, behind another row of black pillars, beer bottles shone full and empty; behind them, a line of white shirts spanned the wall like skulls. The faces above the shirts were entirely gone in shadow. These were the gangsters who ran the Kali, and the darkness they hid in was the same essence which they manufactured outside, extruding it past their bouncer at the door, past the beggar-boys in carnival masks who waited just outside, past the men who sold brochettes in the street (cautiously wise, she visited only the brochette stand owned by the *patron*), past the taxis waiting to take her one block for two thousand francs because it was cheaper to pay two thousand* than to go beyond the taxis, where it became dark and lifeless and men stood playing cards on the hood of a parked car, and after them it became truly dark, even darker than in bed when the blackly humid night pressed its hands down on his lungs, because this other darkness was moist with the breathings of robbers.

It was moist; it was raining again. She needed to do her hair.

Dawn found the two of them a green and rolling rainscape, green gestures of vegetation in fog, the dark fingers, beseeching hands and benediction-laden palms of it, looming through the mist in a rattle of insects, trees drinking moisture like green cotton balls, ferns bowing politely, then building green walls inset with stars of darkness. She did her hair. Because she had a toothache, she could eat only soft things,

---

* In 1993, two thousand Malagasy francs was a little more than U.S. $1.

so she gobbled ice cream and cream-filled pastries as the raindrops rushed innumerable as ants in the hole of a dead snake.

She bound her hair around black threads of yarn until she was more impressive than the barefoot girls who walked with entire forests of leafy twigs on their heads; she strung her hair with the rain-strings that stretched down the sides of rocks into moss-lips and corn-hairs and tree-capillaries, drumming and splattering down; her hands became fernclaws bristling with rain. Seeing her, a brown man cinched his awning tighter against the rain. She took a shower and wrapped her wet hair into tight black licorice twists which she made sure of in her cracked mirror. She made it shine more brightly than the whites of her black eyes. She put her lover's hand on it; his fingers followed and loved her hair's soft raw studded coarseness. Now she was almost finished. Running into the rain for her hair's sake, he picked a red kana flower, a blue fasis berry, a red round coffee bean, a yellow blossom with a black center; and she took these things smiling and hunched over her mirror like a woman washing clothes in the river. Now once again she was ready to go dancing with him at the Discotheque Kali.

The taxi crawled across the pitted beige surface of the night which rattled teeth and windows; they went down dark meat- and diesel-smelling streets, and the light from bottles in a bar could not outdo her hair, and they passed the *épicerie* whose doors were open wide like a whore's legs, and dirty white walls and dirty white dresses glowed in the headlights. The strings of sausages silhouetted like amber beads compared not at all with the boldly twisted segments of her hair which ran suddenly like the rain down the dirty walls of his life behind which occasional lights burned weakly like failures. Men walked into the darkness of her hair like skinny spiders. She would not dance with them; she danced only with him. Her hair kissed him so that his eyes could not be doomed anymore by the row of shirts like skulls where the big watchers sat. The blood-faced watcher stood behind the pillar. The fluorescent blue swirl of a white miniskirt as a girl danced among girls lured the blood-faced watcher for a time; his mouth was like the lighted aperture in the wall where they sold cigarettes. But then all the watchers at once saw the lover with his very dark girl who nodded her heavy head to the music, drinking beer. They had seen him and her already that night at the robber-infested restaurant whose greasy concrete floor and grease-streaked concrete walls enriched the flies on the tables while beneath bright bare bulbs the gangsters grinned and punched each other's wrists and fat whores laughed and went in and out of the bathroom; the whores sat at the corner table, smiling bright-toothed, their hair braided into darkness; but the hair of the one he danced with was as flowery ricefields under hot purple clouds. A man leaned against the wall by the bathroom, a cap low over his eyes, nodding, smiling to music. A fat whore in denim shouted *ah yah yah,* slapping her thighs. The belt around her was as big as a railroad track. The music got louder, and she clapped her hands, which were as big as hams, with a deafening booming sound, and then the gangsters came over and asked to be bought drinks. He was wise with her wisdom; he bought them drinks. A whore asked him to buy her dinner and he did, so as a favor she whispered to his braided-haired darling that the robbers planned to stab them that night. That was how it had been in the restaurant. In the Indra the darkness was better for the watchers. The blood-faced watcher came and asked the lover to give him money. As for her with the lovely hair, the others waited for that with their knives. Once they cut it off the rain would stop forever. In the village where everyone was sitting in trees, one last time a tiny waterfall would fill a brown pool that fed bright green ricefields, and then the waterfall would stop.

SPARE PARTS

Mexico (1992)
Highway 88, California, U.S.A. (1993)
Mogadishu, Somalia (1993)
Roma, Italia (1993)
Mogadishu, Somalia (1993)

Mexico (1992)

The train passed slowly away from flat white-sand-floored towns whose trees spread lushly pubic shadows, and then it whistled and began to accelerate, leaving a squat palm askew, slicing the pale blue sky a thousand times with the glittery slats of its blinds. The horizon was slate-blue like a thunderhead painted with dust. From those sandy towns men in tank tops and shorts stared out, sunglasses covering half their faces, and they absorbed the passing train darkly from behind baseball caps. At Caborca the men who stared wore cowboy hats. They leaned in the narrow strip of shade adjoining the wall (the wall was yellow on top, brown on the bottom). Just past the station, men in cowboy hats lay wearily in the space between offices. The train kept pace with another track, grown stale with wiry grass that writhed and whipped in that hot wind that came from the dry hills. The train passed a wall made of old tires. Then it went away.

There was laundry under a tree in a sunken place. On the far side of the road, which had accompanied the train across dry riverbeds,

140

began a pale-green-grassed desert befogged by trees. Blue and red bush-pocked conehills lay ahead. Once those were reached, the road would end at last, like a wailing lover who'd run alongside as long as she could, until she collapsed breathless in the desperate sands. But for now the road went on, in panting little zigzags which never grazed the train's progress.

The train crossed a slanted plain which ended in gross knobs and knuckles. These were the hands of other dying roads, which went down into the earth; they went nowhere, but their hands refused to be buried; they clutched at distances they could never catch. The train left them all behind.

Inside, the music streamed on as reliably as propaganda. In the evening, when the shadows of the blinds curved around his arm like vertebrae, the songs seemed friendlier, perhaps as a result of simple contrast to the loneliness which existed between him and this woman who slumped in the seat with one leg up, eyes closed. Later, to his intense surprise, she leaned her silent head against his arm. He watched the veins on her tanned hands. Then it was night, and morning.

Years later he'd drive the freeway past the place where she used to live and the sadness of it screamed at him; he wanted to chop down her exit sign. Years later he'd look out his window into the rain (the maple tree was taller than before), and he'd watch the cars go planing by in their troughs of wet grayness, and he knew that no matter how long he looked out the window she'd never again come past the ivy tree to turn in at the streetlamp, slowly crossing his line of sight in her new red car (it must not be new anymore; she probably had another) as he leaped up and ran down the stairs so that he could open the door like thought as her finger approached the bell. He remembered the first day he'd met her when they went walking in wide horse-meadows and he climbed the fence first and then turned to her and she leaped into his arms, so shy and skinny and lovely but not shy after that.

She was still sleeping. Her head had been on his shoulder all night, but now she made a face in her sleep and turned to press her forehead to the window.

Continuing south to loud waltz music in the front and mariachi music in the back, they crossed a yellow-brown plain cut with deep sandy washes where cattle lurked like lost souls and the cement vaults of cemeteries were painted blue and orange. Gradually it became greener. That was probably his fault. Everything else was. There were still chollas and ocotillos, but there were also dark green mushroom-shaped trees.

Past rusty-pale railroad cars, they saw a half-naked brown boy on a bicycle, whitish houses plated with curvy orange tiles. Between the blinds of his window the list of monotonously strange entities went on, retreating down forsaken roads. The time was coming when he'd want to tell her so much because he wasn't with her anymore, but at the moment they continued together, so he had nothing to say. It was not a question of boredom; it was just that they were caught up on all each other's secrets so that the next moment would also die easily, leading to death the moment beyond it like that girl who was taking her little daughter for a walk along the railroad tracks. There was a wattle fence, with great trees inside; then laundry drying under an aqueduct, a family bathing in a curvy river, prickly pears, long, whiplike fingers of cactus . . . The gray-blue sea kept breaking white and clean against a coast of scrub and thorn and cactus, the cacti like mutilated hands planted at the wrist. They were so far away now. They'd gone almost to the end. Two vultures passed overhead. Long shady combers broke shallowly on the beach, the water getting lighter as the sun got higher.

Across the aisle, a man in a T-shirt slept on his wife's shoulder, his breasts and belly jiggling like his massive brown arms, and the water giggled and slapped in the jug at his feet.

There came another stop, where people fanned themselves at flowerclothed tables and tried to sell the passengers Tropicana, corn and bread. And she was still with him, so he didn't need anything; he had bought a bottle of mescal which he shared with the other men and so they all told him that she was the most beautiful woman on the train. At the time he took it as a matter of course; later, after they'd passed the end, he tried to remember what the other women had looked like but he couldn't. In the train of his memory there were men and there was mescal and the men taught him how to sing sentimental songs like "I am the king but there is no queen" and that must have been true because there were never any women but her. The train had not gone away yet. He gazed down those wide dirt streets defined by low white houses with curvy orange-tiled roofs, fenced and treed, and he was so lonely. The fact that she was with him made no difference even though she loved him, even though they still had time; they'd not yet come to the end of the end. He held her hand tight.

Once the air conditioner was fixed, the train went into the blue mountain-walled highlands welling with cumuli whose white fringes caught the light almost like jewelwork.

The rain came down hard enough to hurt, and then the air was fresh and good with clouds still over the mountains and the smell of licorice.

In the place between cars he pulled her shirt up and held it out the window to soak it in cool fresh rain while she laughed. He loved her so much. Her inverted nipples were raspberries.

The train was rolling faster now to crosscut the breeze, past rusty rails and toilet paper, heading southeast toward the cool mountains; swaying up the canted greenish-brown plain that dim gray train crept, almost empty, through the high mountain tunnels. Ahead, the next car's row of ceiling lights could be seen slowly swaying, and a silhouetted passenger dwindled beneath them. They emerged from the tunnel. It had been raining again, and the sky was still gray, with pale orange streaks of evening. The greenshagged wilds were muted in that light, like distant mountains. Granite and then foliage ghosted by, close enough to touch. The train accomplished a perilous trestle and then a man with a medal was smiling, leaning out the window where the open air came in between cars. They descended the steep green ridge-churned villi'd slopes, rode down to the town past blue mountains, and it was dark. Through the blinds he saw the swing of a flashlight far away along the axis of a fence, flaring warmly between trees in the mountain village where they'd stopped. She said to him that it was still only the middle of the end. In the west the sky remained pale like a piece of manila paper. The train began to move again, passing a wall that was boulder-scaled like an immense crocodile, and a few houses flashed dully like skulls behind the trees and then they were out of the village. There was nothing left but dark mountains.

In Guadalajara they changed to a sleeping car. He thought that he would never forget the station's plain of tiles whose particular brown matched that of a smoked cheese; all the families sitting in the long

darkstained pews subdivided into prisons by metal handrails; because
he said to himself: the next time I am here she won't be with me.
— Then they got on the sleeping car.

The warm orange light of the lefthand lamp, the only one on, was
reflected on the khaki-painted walls with the globular texture of
sweat, its original rectangular shape degraded almost into an oval as
he lay sweating against this silent one who lay reading the guidebook
with her knees up, her shadow-head growing hideously when she
raised her real head to see the map better, and the train increased
velocity so that lights like stars flowed by in stripes between the blinds
which they'd closed when they were making love. Her bush sweated
between her thighs, a wide brown-black wave at the edge of her flat
white belly whose navel held a single drop of sweat, and the rectangular lamp outlined the ridge of her nose in gold, and a sickle-shaped
goldness adorned her cheek just below her gilded eyelashes. They lay
side by side in the narrow and threadbare bed in this narrow room
as sturdy as a submarine, built in the U.S.A., with the original English-
language instruction plaques still on the fixtures: **CEILING,
EMERGENCY.** In this he took a curious pride. These trains had
long since been abandoned by his countrymen in favor of newer and
inferior things. For how many years now had the trains continued
across Mexico? No doubt they broke down sometimes, but they got
well and struggled on through the fleeing decades.

Someone was knocking. He got up and dressed to show the ticket
to the conductor. When he was finished she'd turned her head in the
other position so that her feet were beside him. She'd turned the
righthand light on so that now the khaki paint was much whiter and
brighter and there were two reflections in it, one on each side of her
magnificent shoulders. She lay on her belly, reading. The hairs between her buttocks made pleasant shadows. They continued eastward,
past darkness.

In the morning, the bed back up inside the wall, the two wide red
armchairs basked, warming their faded felt in the murky light that
also pleased prickly pears, plantations and white horses along the high
river. Then they went into a tunnel; and the armchairs and the world
were gone. Far away, a cloud-brain brooded atop a broad blue pyramid. That was the end of the end.

He said: I'll never forget.

But she only smiled bitterly and said: If you remember everything, what color was the thirteenth house we saw after Mexicali? White, he said defiantly. It was white like your underpants . . . Then their lives together were over, and they got off the train.

Highway 88, California, U.S.A. (1993)

Sunset on the snowy rock-wrinkles haired with pines and spruces trapped him; sunset was as dreary as the evergreens crowded to shade last year's dirty snow. Last year he'd gone this road with her in the morning. They'd left the motel room in Tahoe on a snowy icy dawn whose light spread before them like the rest of their lives; and a man whose wife had left him gave them a ride to the junction. The man could hardly keep his eyes open. He had been driving all night. He was going to drive over the mountains to San Francisco. The lovers were worried about him. They warned him that he might have an accident if he didn't sleep before he went his winding icy road, but they were happy and he was sad so that he could not hear them. When he let them out, they were very glad to be free of him. His sadness had choked them like old snow. (Now the sadness of the one who remembered made him squeeze his fingernails into his palms. Did she ever remember now?) They stood in new snow, kissing. She said that the cold made her legs prickle, so he kissed her legs and then she laughed and said that she was warm. Half an hour later, two ladies who were going on a ski race picked them up and let them ride in the back of the carpeted van among bright clean skis. They let them out at breakfast time where the road made a T, east into California, west into Nevada. The lovers were going to Nevada. They waited for three hours, getting discouraged, and then a boxer came and took them down into the place where the desert day opened up before them like an endless noon.

It was the same time of year as then, but the rivers had not been so swollen that year. He would never see them with her again. This year they were pale and rushing, brown and white-flecked, drowning bushes.

The sun struck peaks with clanging strokes as it sank, dyeing them a lurid orange which made his heart pound with fear and despair.

The mountains of sadness were left behind. He said to someone, he didn't know who: Please don't ever let me see them again.

Then he went down into the green-gray evening desert.

Mogadishu, Somalia (1993)

P haraoh asked Moses news of the former generations, said the teacher, and Moses said: Their names are with my Lord, in a Book. My Lord never errs or forgets.
That book was the atlas. The atlas contained the rain upon her breasts in Mexico. It had cloud maps, kept track of all the water in the world. The atlas contained the browneyed dog in the van, brown-eyed, brownhaired, red, blacklipped, standing with its forelegs on her knees, trying to lick her; and she was laughing and he was laughing and the man who'd picked them up was shaking his head with a smile as they came into the high desert flats just past June Lake with the purple-brown mountains smeared with snow and purple ridges behind where he had kissed her and kissed her, sleet pelting on his camouflage raincoat which he did not wear anymore because it reminded him of her. — The teacher took a stick, dipped it in a pot of thick black ink, and wrote that verse on the long narrow piece of wood which was knobbed at the top like a weird tombstone or a cross-section of a bowling pin. The teacher had the whole Qur'an in his head. For each lesson the little boys would write one day, wash it off the next.

Outside the school's walls, brown kids with their long dirty shirt-tails hanging out played games of throwing rocks and running in the shade of roofless buildings past which soldiers' trucks rolled. (Very ancient buildings, a man said. Two hundred years.) Birds flew over the missing roofs. A kid cleaned a dusty piece of canvas with his hands, and a long gray iron-breasted truck with soldiers in it came speeding around the road. Where the road turned away from the sea there was a wall with two bites taken out of it, and then the road dwindled into trees and soldiers slowly trudging across a street-horizon in the direction of the Green Line, the dangerous place. A brown man in white walked steadily down the white sand road, whirling a stick. On a ledge in a white wall, people sat, and water ran slowly from a silver bowl which a boy poured over his hands.

He did not want her back because he could not have her and also the rest of his life which contained matters which had caused her anguish, but of course he wanted her back; he wanted to wake up beside her; he was so lonely for her. In the atlas it said DRAINAGE BASINS and UNPRODUCTIVE AREAS and LOST LOVES and FOREVER LOST LOVES. *The principal meteorological factors which impose severe natural limitations on human activity are temperature and aridity.* — The boy poured water from the silver bowl.

The boy poured water from the bowl. Beside him lay a long narrow piece of wood which was knobbed at the top like a tombstone. A verse was written upon it in black ink. He looked up at the boy with the wooden slate, and wanted to ask which verse it was, but the boy did not understand. He wanted to ask where the gazetteer was, so that he could locate the rains which had fallen upon her in Mexico, but the boy did not understand. The boy spoke to him, and he did not understand.

Roma, Italia (1993)

No, no, it wasn't that she'd died; no, she hadn't gone down into the rotten arches of darkness that crumbled like cheese. And it wasn't that he couldn't be hers again, contingent upon certain modifications which he could (but would not) readily make in his character. He knew where she was; if he was determined enough he could find her. But he refused to rewrite the inscription on his secret obelisk. She'd told him that in that case he'd chosen to give her up. And it was true. — But, as Husserl says, how fares it with *animal realities?* He still wanted her. That being so, his deductions then proceeded thus: (i) When your wife dies and you die, you'll meet in Heaven. (ii) When your wife dies, and you marry again, and then you die, you'll meet both your wives in Heaven. The wife and the other wife will both be with you, loving you and each other forever. (iii) Since Heaven and forever are both beyond time, whoever is meant to be in Heaven must already be in Heaven now. (iv) Therefore, everyone you love, living or dead, is already in Heaven waiting for you.

So he descended beneath the Sunday noon of empty streets stretched tight like drumheads (a woman sounded them with her gold-flowered black high heels); so he went into the catacombs. She hadn't died. She wasn't in Mexico. That night he ascended the Spanish Stairs' white smoothness etched black in the texture of a full moon. He bought a pocket atlas in Italian; opening it, he addressed her and said: Since you are also in Heaven there must be two of you. Therefore one of you can be with me. That's reasonable, isn't it? I'm not asking for you. I'm only asking for a spare you.

He confided this into the atlas, which he then closed and tied with black ribbons. Then he left it in a church. He hoped that maybe it would call to her like a signal beacon.

Mogadishu, Somalia (1993)

At the Petroleum Market, where they'd steal the eyeglasses right off your face if they could, a lady robed in blue flowers sat on a dais at one of many covered stands whose tables were separated by thick wire mesh. Tins and jugs and bottles of molasses-colored oil stood on the tables beneath the roofs of corrugated metal.

Some of the tables were fronted with rusty steel. White dust and buses blew past. A child, grinning with effort, rolled a rusty oil drum in the sand. A lady in yellow and black glided through the dust. These stands ran a long way down Population Street. They sold gasoline and diesel, direct from Mombasa and the United Arab Emirates; they sold Comet and Caltex and Pelo 400 and Ocklube. Oil cost fifty thousand shillings for ten liters.★ The air reeked of oil. The lady in the blue garbashar was laughing, swatting flies on a post.

A big red truck with many brown feet and knees high on top drove down Population Street past a rusted Soviet tank. It was bound for Bardera. The passengers had paid thirty thousand shillings each. Suddenly the truck ran out of gas. It stopped, and the driver ran to the lady in blue and bought a bucketful of gasoline from her.

Another man stopped for fruit. There were both mangoes and oil on Population Street. Next door to the lady in blue, bananas had been strung like washing along a wire in a mango stand roofed by corrugated metal.

There was a man who came walking down the street holding onto his eyeglasses, and he peered into every stand of rusty metal with mangoes and limes and glasses on top, but then he'd walk on, shaking his head. Finally he came to the place that said **SPER PARTS**.

On the whitewashed facade of the spare parts store was painted a camel, a glass of milk, a yellow fan belt, a blue carburetor, a red and yellow battery, and a blue and black tire, all bursting with speed like cartoon rockets. The spare parts came by ship from Japan to the dusty white beach where the sea swirled green and stinking against a sharp lava-like rock (it smelled as cheap postage stamps do when they're licked) and people with brown skinny legs sat barefoot on blue steps outside a blue door with one panel blown out; the spare parts sailed between the American battleships on the blue horizon; they passed the rusted red and yellow Soviet ship; and they arrived at last at the seaport where a handcuffed boy rushed by in the back of a jeep and crowds waited and hoped for the job of carrying sacks of rice. The spare parts kept company with a white wall veiled in white dust; then they passed through the curtain of camelbone beads in the cement

★ U.S. $15.

doorway (a cassette playing loud and scratchy), the doorway over which was written **SPER PARTS**.

The man went in. — She left me in Mexico, he said. I need spare parts.

Allah, Allah! cried the proprieter. My business pays just enough to eat! I don't dabble in those things . . .

(Across the street, two men squatted in a pile of automobile components, sitting side by side, sorting them as slowly and deliberately as if they were moving chess pieces.)

So you can't help me get a spare wife?

Can't help you? I won't help you! You must not ask such things.

The man smiled. — How many wives do you yourself have, Farhan?

I have three, but for me it's no problem; I'm Muslim! And for me there was no pimp such as you wish me to be—why won't you leave me alone, you odious fellow?

And how did you choose them?

Why should I tell you?

I ask you respectfully.

The first wife—ah, she's my real wife. The second is my girlfriend, and the third . . . well, she was a beautiful girl I saw in the market. And, you know, I made a mistake. To marry more than one Somali girl is very difficult, because you must love them more than twice a day; it's impossible sometimes! You think you have problems. And they like to corkscrew their buttocks wildly; they're different from all other girls. I get so tired. So, my friend, I choose only one per night, and you cannot believe the jealousy . . .

Ah, so that's how it is. Well, for me there are two women. They are really the same woman, but one, she has a double in Heaven. I don't want to disturb the one on earth, so—

So you want to kill yourself? That is a great sin, although for guns I do have some spare parts.

No, Farhan, I don't want to do that. Do you have a spare atlas?

You mean an address book. I don't dabble in those things. What you ask is very shameful. If you persist, someone will kill you.

He had a notion that she might know where her double was. He suspected that she might be somewhere within this equatorial duct, bridge or trough. He breathed the hot white wind of dust. — I want an atlas, Farhan.

Oh, well. Not every want can be remedied . . .

A donkey's-load of wood, a month's worth, cost about fifty thousand shillings in those days. He took out a hundred thousand and told the man to find him an atlas—a spare one would do. Then he stood waiting, his mind partaking of the same wide empty flatness as Military Street (which used to be Lenin Street).

It was definitely somebody's spare atlas, even grimier than the one he'd bought in Italy (his then ladylove had wrenched her hand out of his and begun screaming: I think you're crazy buying that goddamn shitty thing! You'll regret it, I tell you! and after that she'd refused to speak to him beneath that milk-white sky; they departed from congealing pillars, walls and fountains lit falsely by lingerie windows, furcoat windows, bookstore windows, house-beasts and ships of state blind-windowed; and he tried to take her hand but she pulled away with disgust or anger or simple loathing, sitting beside him in the cab, reading her own map). An obsolete Africa, white as a salt island, floated in a turquoise sea; bearing appellations from the Second World War: French West Africa, French Sudan, Anglo-Egyptian Sudan, French Equatorial Africa, Military Territory of Chad, Belgian Congo, Tanganyika Territory, Southern Rhodesia, Northern Rhodesia, Italian East Africa, Italian Somaliland (which was why the Somalis didn't like Italians), British Somaliland . . .

Mogadishu was in Italian Somaliland. He positioned his electronic magnifying loupe upon that spare country and gazed down. The fibers of the paper were very white and bright (in the atlas he'd read that Somalia received more than nine hours' worth of mean annual bright sunlight—second only to the northern area encompassing Libya and Algeria; no wonder the page was bleached!) Slowly and carefully he let his eyeball drone like a spy satellite over the flats of Shabellaha Hoose, proceeding eastward to the humid sandy beach, which he tracked northeast to Golweyn, Shalaamboot, Marka, Jilib, Dhanaane, Jasira, Banaadir, and now, experiencing that accustomed white and yellow Adriatic feeling despite the rubble and tanks (he wondered whether Dubrovnik looked like that these days), he approached Muqdisho, which was spare for Mogadishu; he zoomed in upon roads

(Stadium Street, Military Street; here was Population Street and he found the place that said **SPER PARTS**), ruins, military sites (there was the stadium, still sandbagged by Marines, a machine gun mounted up high, pointing out, barbed wire at the gate). Down, down, down. In that country of sand, the most brightly colored things were the women's clothes. Loftily he gazed down upon the tops of those poison-trees called *booc*. He watched their pale green broad-lobed leaves blow in the hot wind. For a moment he gazed down at the Green Line which divided the city into factions. It was a yellow wall pocked and pimpled and made of lifeless white and yellow rubble on which crowds of chocolate-colored people sat barefoot. Looking up at his giant blinking eye, little girls in red or yellow garbashars stood and tried to sell him packs of cigarettes. Turbaned men nodded at him, smiling. Then someone shot a gun at him. He watched the golden bullet enlarge itself in the longitude-latitude crosshairs of his loupe, rising toward him like a torpedo; he did not think it could reach him, but as a precaution he zoomed back to lower magnification so that he rose high above the entire continent of Africa with its neatly lettered countries; he could almost see the page number; and now he zoomed back in again because surely the bullet had fallen to earth. He saw people sitting in chairs under a great toothbrush tree for shade; he dialed the infrared setting and watched the steam rising from the tops of their heads; then he switched back to NORMSPECTRUM and watched a lady bent almost double, carrying a can of water. He saw a woman in black and yellow slowly trudging through the sand. He saw a half-naked man squatting in a high barred window (a thief who grimaced at his immense searching eye which hovered overhead like God; the thief said: I am afraid for airplane).

Panning past smoking garbage in the sand at the base of a wall, he spotted her (or the spare her) at the wheel of her red car. She was just now passing the U.S. Embassy, whose sign read: JIB: WARNING AT-4 ANTI-TANK POSITION. THIS WEAPON HAS A 60 METER, 90° BACKBLAST. WHEN IN IMMEDIATE AREA, SEEK COVER DURING ALL CONFRONTATIONS AT FRONT GATE!

In exultation, he rang a wooden camel bell with a wooden clapper.

Farhan rushed to look. — This a woman drive car! he laughed. Very fantastic! You say she is your spare woman, spare wife?

Yes.

The proprieter wanted to look again. — Oooh, I see her naked arms! he giggled. You know, my friend, before the war one could see girls on the beach dressed in European fashion, which is to say in bra and knickers, but these have fled, and now there are only rural girls here.

She's not a rural girl. She's from New York.

Is she jealous?

I really couldn't say, Farhan.

You know, my good friend, they tell a certain story that one Somali man had four wives, who were all jealous. So he said to them: *Turn around, close your eyes and I will tell the one I love the best.* — Then he tapped each one on her buttocks in turn and sent them all away happy. But me, I don't know if it's true. Maybe it's true. I don't dare try it, because my wives might only pretend to close their eyes. I think your woman is jealous, yes? Because she has a jealous face.

You must have better eyes than I do. Even at maximum magnification I can't see whether she's jealous or not.

But she left you?

Yes.

Why?

I had someone else I wouldn't give up. That's why she left me.

Listen, my friend. Somali girls don't attach conditions. If they see you with another girl, they either say nothing or they ask for a divorce, but they never say: *If you want to stay with me you must have only me.*

He bent down and looked into the loupe again. Now he could see. She was driving toward the Green Line.

The internal combustion engine was one of the West's many presents to Somalia, and I would have to call it an *a-a-mmah,* which is to say a bequest for evil purpose (the example given in a treatise on inheritance law being money left by a Muslim to build a Christian church); but nonetheless her little red car looked sporty.

That was when he saw the other red car.

On the enemy side of the Green Line, just past the former police station, rose another camp on the dung-hued sands of the former technical institute, one of whose walls bore the scrawl: CAMP OFFISH. Refugees, their faces wide and brown, were standing at the base of the barbed-wire-topped wall, among weird mounds topped with green plastic; those were their houses. The women wore deriis and garbashars. They carried babies in sacks against their stomachs. They smoothed their garments down while the first grade of the SOS Children's Village counted one to a hundred in a deafening scream and the schoolteacher conducted with a twig. There was a little child not much more than a brown skull on skinny legs, his toy a plastic bag on the end of a string; he stood touching the shiny red car, the spare car in wonder. Now through the loupe the watcher's eyeball saw many little girls with dark brown faces. One in a white dress who had big black eyes ran inside a cave roofed with green plastic; a moment later she came out, holding a white woman's hand. The white woman was the spare of the double. He looked down from the sky and wanted to lick her bare shoulder and arm.

Sliding the loupe back along the page to his side of the Green Line, he saw the first double pass two cars with UN flags. Farhan was saying something but he didn't listen.

He thought about the way that Somali men who are friends walk so happily with their arms around one another's waists. He wondered if the doubles would do that. And he wondered if there would be room for him.

On Population Street it was getting dark, the evening sky like a crude oil painting, with solid white and gray cotton-blotches of cloud unrolling in its pale blueness; and so people were getting afraid of bandits and the petroleum market was closed; but Farhan's lantern flickered brightly down upon the atlas so that the two red cars approached each other bathed in afternoonness.

Farhan was still going on. He said that in olden times a Somali girl's dowry was one hundred camels, one horse and one rifle. Then it became five camels, and now it was only one camel, which could cost anywhere from one to five million, depending on the kind of camel.

Farhan gasped. Coming down Population Street were dozens of red cars, and a boy whose legs he could almost have circled between thumb and forefinger came running out and threw a stone through the windshield of one spare car, and the spare woman inside pulled over and jumped out cursing with that thin shrill anger he suddenly remembered very well, and then somebody shot her from the shadows. The other red cars continued on past. They appeared to be heading for the Green Line. Looking desperately through his loupe, he now saw the army of red cars approaching from the other side. He saw that all the doubles looked very angry, and they all carried guns. They were getting close enough to each other now that he could see where exactly along the Green Line they would meet. He could not bear to watch anymore. Moving the loupe away from the Green Line, he saw white soldiers patting black boys down for qat. He saw a spare Farhan going with his brother to pray in the mosque. He saw a lady in a yellow garbashar. The lady knocked on a green metal door. Inside was a sandy courtyard with one donkey and many smoldering fires. A skinny child came and let the lady in. When the metal door had closed behind her, and nobody in the street could see, she threw off her veil and looked upward at him with the deadly dark glide and glitter of a tiger snake. She was one of the doubles. This time he was mesmerized by the approaching bullet.

AT THE BRIDGE

Coral Harbour, Southampton Island, Northwest Territories, Canada (1993)
Coral Harbour, Southampton Island, Northwest Territories, Canada (1993)
Coral Harbour, Southampton Island, Northwest Territories, Canada (1993)
Coral Harbour, Southampton Island, Northwest Territories, Canada (1993)

Coral Harbour, Southampton Island, Northwest Territories, Canada (1993)

I came to the bridge and there was no one there. It was ten-o'-clock on a sunny night that echoed with seal-hunters' rifle-claps, and I needed water. That was why I'd turned my back on my tent beside the lake of howling dogs and set out for the noise of water. The river was very close. Children swam in it every day, although they allowed that it was not as warm as Fossil Creek where I had camped on the night that the wind blew my tent almost to pieces. The town had a swimming pool, but that year it was closed for repairs and so they swam by the bridge.

As I went I kept to the socket of high ground around the water (the rest would have engulfed me above the rubber of my tundra boots). That night the mosquitoes were so thick that I could literally snatch them out of the air, and the sun left double orange-egged reflections in two ponds. I scrambled onto the raised gravel dike they called a road, passed a pond of rich green grass as delicate as vermicelli, for all the world like a Cambodian ricefield, then turned off the road at the river, which sucked itself down from a glowing violet lake of eerie shallowness before it slithered toward an orange-painted bridge that said I LOVE YOU and NAKOOLAK and other things. The water shimmered orange with an indistinct reflection, a slightly pale water-color of the sun-trail, and then went under the bridge, around low rocks, and out to its mouth of ice.

And no one was there.

The children had finished swimming for the moment—no reason; they sometimes swam at midnight. But even had they been there it would still have proved too late for me, because I could not be a child anymore, although I passed well enough for children to like me; and even if I'd become one I would not have been able to kill birds in flight with a single stone; and so it was too late. As for the fullgrown ones, I was not of their kind, either. That afternoon I'd seen two beauties swimming. One had a boyfriend and one didn't. The one who was alone had smiled at me, and that was too late, too. Another true or false love would only make my soul more sadly vicious. Then there were the young men, to whom women and everything came easy. — You wanna catch a polar bear? they'd say. No problem. All you gotta do is get your gun and shoot. — So their company was also salveless to me, my jealousy being a ptarmigan always half-seen, half-buried in my mossy hopes. In short, it must have been only because I was a selfish spoiler that I stood lonely on the gravel below that empty bridge, watching the mosquitoes attack my knees, listening to the river flow out into Hudson Bay, where it was almost too late for ice.

I felt that I had to make something of my condition. Like the glowing gold outlines of grassheads, I was bordered by a trick of light—oh, a real border too, but nothing with the power to detain me in such brilliant monotony.

The people in the four-wheelers on the road above, their parkas open to the breeze they made, sometimes smiled and waved at me. But I was alone.

That was my difficulty. My circumstances were no different from anyone else's. A boy had come to my tent and I'd asked him what he would do that night. — Go to the bridge and watch people swimming, he said. He was happy, more or less.

They came back, two boys and two girls, and called my name. I was more lonely than before. I stood at the bridge and watched them playing. They were walking from shadow to sun, and they reached the rocks and then the water. They were wading, the girls carrying their shoes, the boys not. They'd gone to the mossy island. They were in the violet water, bending their knees and calling out in Inuktitut as they picked their way between sharp stones.

Two more boys came running up the road.

Hi, called the girls. You gonna swim? You gonna swim?

I was watching them to see what it was that I had lost. They seemed to make no motion without a purpose, and to do nothing that they did not want to. They did nothing to fill time because they swam time and breathed it. They flapped their arms against sodden shirts, stood still, put bathing suits on, all with the quick confidence that doing these things was right and that afterward there would be other good things to do.

A truck went by and drenched me in white dust.

I knelt down to fill my water bottle from that stream well spiced with stones, that stream which curved around the curvy horizon. I felt the cold touch of a mosquito against my face. When my bottle had surrendered its last bubble of emptiness, I climbed back up to the road again. The bottle was very chilly and heavy in my hand. I stood at the bridge, and two couples I'd seen in church came on their four-wheelers and greeted me. They asked the children if the water was warm. With them it was different. They weighed possibilities, with easy indulgence. They could take or leave anything. But, just like the younger people, they owned their lives.

I was at the bridge and everyone was there. And I was alone.

Coral Harbour, Southampton Island, Northwest Territories, Canada (1993)

A ll this changed on the first day that I went swimming. The coolness, the novelty, the loveliness, all these things engrossed me so that I was like them, learning the blue and green and brown lives of water, speaking with shouts and stone-splashes to the kids wrapped in towels like Arabs. Water ran from our lips. Happily straining reddish-orange faces swam around me and teased me. Little kids were riding me, clinging to me, calling my name in the water. A small girl braced her skinny brown knees against the current and crossed back and forth, dancing from stone to stone. We were always throwing stones at pop cans which we floated down the current, or trying to wing birds, though I made sure never to hit a living thing because I was not a hunter; my friends were quite good at striking a mark. They taught me about the strange current on the south side, right by the bridge where the little birds lived, so strong that you could not cross the creek without angling upstream. I let it catch me, and was caught up in life.

Boys kept diving off the bridge. The girls were dressing and undressing on their side. When they came out they shivered.

At ten or eleven at night, when dusk rose out of the island like fog, the river beneath the bridge darkened until it resembled the purple altar-hanging with its polar bear and stars, its two igloos, and its man and woman entering the yellow-windowed church. I had felt rejected by the Anglican god until the second Sunday, when the white-gowned priest shook my hand, and they sang one hymn in English; I realized that that was for me. On the third Sunday a man loaned me his battered hymnal, and the priest preached part of the sermon in my language. I loved that church. The youngest children were screaming, crying, talking, giggling, going in and out to their hearts' content, leaping into the arms of their parents and kissing them. People smiled at me at the church door. I was happy to be with them. That was how it was swimming, too. Entering the cool rocky water, trying not to stub my toe or be knocked backward when kids jumped onto my shoulders, I agreed to underwater contests with all comers, especially with the nine-year-old boy who chewed snuff and with the fat boy whose glistening black pants upturned as he stood on his head underwater, bringing up a rock, spouting through his mouth.

It was just before nine. The sky was pale blue, with a cold evening wind. The sun was somewhat low in the sky. The boys hunched over, pulling their caps lower against the mosquitoes. They kept asking questions about my Indian girl. They'd seen a nude I'd painted of her. Was she Inuk? Was she mine? What color were her pubic hairs? What color were her nipples? Was her hole thick? Did I lick her hole?

But I could handle them. One of them, the kindest ugliest one, had already confided to me: In this town, we answer a question only by *I don't know* and *probably*. — He was the plump shaggy one in coveralls who'd taught me that in the dialect of this town hello was *kujalu*, which actually meant *let's have sex;* he'd taught me that goodbye was *iti-pau*, which really meant *your ass is full of coal*. I'd said kujalu to a serious man on a four-wheeler; the man stopped, gazed at me, and inquired politely: Are you a prostitute? — The shaggy boy and his friends laughed so hard they fell down onto the tussocks frosted with pale green lichens. After that I saw the shaggy boy every day. He'd drive up in his Fourtrax, pink-brimmed cap pulled low and backward, stand on a rock, and ask all the shivering kids if the water was hot. No matter what they replied, he'd lean over, squinting at the water, blink, and drive off to get his bathing suit and towel. On that very first night when he'd teased me, he taught me about I don't know and probably.

So come on, aye? How deep was her hole?

I don't know, I said, poker-faced like him.

Did you get her pregnant?

Probably.

Yes or no?

I don't know.

Then they slowly grinned. I was one of them.

Maybe I'm gonna get one tonight, too, said a twelve-year-old.

I got fifty girlfriends and they're all pregnant from me! a nine-year-old cried proudly. (I'd met him on a hot day of grey dust and white dust when a wedding cavalcade set out for Fossil Creek. He was the one whose big brother had seen a polar bear that day about six miles out, just swimming.)

You gonna dive? said the shaggy boy.

Half a moment later, creamy white splashes formed around the reddish bodies. I flitted with them through the exquisitely cold water. I watched those kids throwing stones, crawling into shallows, calling: le's go, aye? back and forth between the two grassy gravelly shores under a chilly purple-colored wind.

Coral Harbour, Southampton Island, Northwest Territories, Canada (1993)

It was a gray chilly evening and everyone was at the bridge. The girl who'd stolen my best Polaroid crouched on the railing, shouting: All right, you motherfuckers!

Come on, Lydia, jump! they shouted up from the water. Five, four, three, two, one!

If you talk like that I'll never fuckin' jump!

As I approached, she shouted at me: Get out of my fuckin' way!

She looked like a boy as she stood here on the bridge with her wet hair gray against the skull—very different from when she'd been in my tent, lounging so sexually, swearing and smoking cigarettes. — By now, practically everybody who swam had come to see me. The boys would visit my tent three or four at a time, burping and farting, drinking from my canteen and spitting jawbreakers into it when they talked, then sucking them out, trying on my hat and glasses, shouting with laughter at how stupid each one became in them, joking about fucking dead seals, telling me that if when I shat I wiped my ass with a rock then any seal I shot would sink, making hangman's nooses in the ceiling—good company, in short. The

shaggy boy loaned me his favorite thing, his electronic keyboard, for a night and a day without my dreaming of asking for it, and I listened to it play "Ave Maria" over and over, the dogs pleading and cursing across the water. The ten- and twelve-year-old boys were always giving me snuff. A boy brought me a dried hunk of the caribou his brother had shot two weeks before in Arviat; another brought me a piece of his mother's fresh-baked bannock. He was the boy who collected the offerings in a vessel of sealskin, then held them high above the altar until the congregation had finished singing the hymn.
— When you come back, we'll go out there to the place of birds with sharp tails and get their eggs! he promised me.

Beaks, not tails! said his friend.

No, tails. A beak is a tail. A bird got two tails.

Is that girl your girlfriend? a boy asked me. He was one of the ones I knew from backfloating and glistening, heads and bodies sparkling with windy light.

Probably.

Is she *always* naked?

Probably.

Is she pregnant from you?

No.

Why? he cried in surprise.

Sometimes girls came to visit, too. I lived in a fine spot that summer, in a place between two lakes where my friend was a chalk-yellow flower with the lemon-yellow center, and another friend was the long woolly sausage of a willow bud. Brown birds danced through the moss. When my guests got close I'd hear them exclaim at all the birds. — One girl said: My grandmother saw a big black bird in the morning when she was young. Bigger than this little house. It tried to catch kids. — I'd hear the girls unzipping my back doors since my front door was broken; I'd hear them unlacing their boots as they knelt upon the giving, prickly-brittle mound of lichens. I knew them; I'd seen them on Sundays listening to the the little white-robed trio at the altar; I knew those girls' slender arms and the way their shirts worked up to flash their bikini-breasts in the water. They called each other sluts and talked about the boys whom they wanted to fuck. They shot my pistol. They asked for liquor, which I didn't have.

Sometimes boys and girls would come together. When my tent was crowded, a boy would just pull his coat over his shoulders and his girl's shoulders so that they could kiss in private. That reminded me of the bridge, too, where the women tented inside towels or quilts as they changed. Everything had begun to remind me of the bridge by then. It was as if this island where water pulsed around me between long blue windblown pond-fingers were inside a paperweight. There was nothing but this. Alone in my tent at night, chilly from my day's swim at the bridge, I dreamed of grabby willow-islands and also good flat stones to cross, but grassy mossy bogs on either side. The world went chill and grey as more clouds thrust their elbows across the sky. And in the morning when I heard my friends coming, I knew that we would go together to the bridge. I felt interested in their loves, being but a spinning camera eye which could not and must not love them because I would never come back. — The girl who'd stolen my best Polaroid and the boy who always got into trouble loved each other, I think, but they never visited me at the same time. My best Polaroid was of him, and that was why she stole it.

Do you swear? she'd said.

No.

Why? she said contemptuously. Do you use drugs?

Sometimes.

Why not all the time?

When at last she jumped, unannounced, long after everyone had given up on her, I saw the dance of her white breasts through her wet T-shirt, the fierce downward point of the running shoes she'd swiped from one the younger kids and then she was in the air but still very far away and then with the ripping-cloth noise of a gyrfalcon swooping to protect its nest she plunged into the cold brown water with a roar and a splash, bobbing back up immediately among the other orange faces rising and falling in the dark water which was occasionally stained orange by the bridge's reflection.

The boy she loved, the one in the Polaroid, was the boy who'd slit his wrists because he was caught breaking into the mayor's office, "just to see what was there," and his mother (he was adopted) said that none of her *real* offspring would have done that, so he said: I'm gonna die, Mom.

He sat in my tent, playing with my scare pistol. — I think my uncle saw I slit my wrists, he beamed. I told my cousin if my Dad don't change, I'm gonna go all the way!

Minutes later he was swimming and laughing.

After the girl who loved him jumped, he clambered up the chickenwire-lined gravel wall of the bridge, passing the small girl who clung peering at a baby bird, until he stood beside me in the spot where his admirer had stood, and in lordly summer silence the two of us surveyed the black turtles' backs of rocks under the greenness and brownness, and kids' skinny phosphorescent bodies making waves like obsidian arrowheads.

Dive in, Jobie! cried she who loved him. Splash me good or I'm gonna quit!

He pretended to look away from her upturned face. Then, smiling, he dove. The river exploded with his splash (the lake where the river came from was a swollen gray cloud with orange bloodstains on it).

Oh, my toe hurts! cried a water-spouting girl.

What about my balls? he shouted, and they all laughed.

The girl who loved him stood where the water was only knee-deep, her wrists clasped across her breasts, watching him and shivering. — Let's go to the other side an' dive! she said. Then she crept all the way into the cold water.

The boy in the Polaroid's cousins were clinging to him and he was shouting: Get the hell off! and they were all laughing. He was so strong and perfect; he fought the strange current inch by inch with girls hanging on him and shouting: A world record! and when by dint of great shoulder-flashes and whirling arms, spray shooting from his rich black hair, he succeeded in touching the rock where the bird's nest was, he only smiled modestly and said: Clear water, anyway. — But the girl who loved him stood shyly on the other side where he had not come to dive, and she was alone.

The shaggy boy's little sister, kneeling in a wet blue shirt, was not alone although nobody kept her company down at the river's mouth where she could still see three figures poling very slowly out in an aluminum canoe, the bow tipping down almost to water level with every stroke of the tall figure, and then they vanished behind a sailing ship in the middle of the harbor. The shaggy boy's little sister was wringing out her swimming clothes in the brown water, tossing and turning them quietly as if she were cooking strips of bacon She was the ten-year-old who'd burned her nose smoking a cigarette. Water ran down her pouting lips.

Coral Harbour, Southampton Island, Northwest Territories, Canada (1993)

Coming back from the river with the white crosses of the grave-yard ahead of me, I found the sun more rubicund, fractured with splinters of dark cloud. I took the high road, the only road, already seeing the hemisphere of my tent across that lakey plain which was interrupted by half-sunken rocks, clumps of grass, tussocks shared by mossy lichens and flowers, and the occasional dwarf willow colony creeping across the flatness like sturdy wire unraveling leafily in any direction. Summer was rushing in tune with the yellow rhapsody of wind-dancing buttercups. The darkness was oozing back. I inhaled the reddish sun-jelly, the sweets of evening seemingly comprised of melted berries.

When I stepped on one gray slab it grated down upon another rock with a terrifying snarling laugh.

After half a dozen hours of being tentbound by a windy rain, I heard birds sing again and came out to find one of the strangest and most beautiful skies that I had ever seen: pale beams of light descend-ing like spider-legs from a gray cloud's body, and then other patches and pools of the same light, more and more fantastic in shape, strings of flying pillars like leads in pack ice. Scarcely an exhalation of air. The birds called, the grasses did not flinch, and then a gust came after all.

I walked through town. The boy from Arviat had a brown bird in his hand, a little brown baby. He let it go. He said: Maybe if I keep it the mother is sad. And maybe in just a few minutes it will starve.

One time I was playing with a baby bird and it died so quickly from starving. — I went through that low flat town of small houses and passed the nursing station, the well-fenced reservoir (which still had chunks of ice inside), and came back to the open road, the bay on my right, a long low snowsquiggled purple cape on the horizon, and then clouds and wind.

They said that the girl who'd stolen my best Polaroid liked to talk about suicide. They said that her parents were always drunk. They said that her parents didn't want her. (Sure, I know her Mom and Dad, said a white guy in town who always fed me on beef stew and pie because he pitied my tenty existence. He was a good and great and generous man who hated the notion that someone might see that he was good. He gave away money and time left and right and flew into a rage when people thanked him. He sat in his coveralls of wrinkled water-metal, resting on his laurels, a veteran of forest fires, mining accidents, bar fights and bad acid trips, bored and weary in the overheated hotel, worried about his blood pressure, watching adventure videos, keeping count of the number of N.E.'s. — What are N.E.'s? I said. — Nipple erections, son, he explained. You must be a tenderfoot not to know that. Have some more pie. Yeah, I know her Mum and Dad. I know them, all right. Can't take care of their own children. They both work in my crew, *when* they work. I don't want to lay anybody off, 'cause they need the work. I hope I don't have to lay them off. But I *hate* these two lazy bastards. They should have their tubes tied. I *hate* this place. Soon as my contract's up, I'm out of here. I *hate* those fucking Inuktituks. They think this hellhole's the best place in the world and no one can tell 'em any different. Well, everyone shits on the Newfies, but one thing you gotta say for 'em: they don't got an Indian problem. Took care of that first thing.*) So that was the story of the girl who'd stolen my best Polaroid. Her life was like some cold wide shallow pond rushing straight at her with fan-shaped waves, the wind picking up now, not yet strong enough to throw more than foam in her face.

That was all I learned, and I didn't see every twist her courtship took, because it wasn't my business and after all I had my own swim-

---

* The Indians of Newfoundland were hunted down and exterminated in the last century.

ming to attend to. (One sign of spiritual development, Buddhists and Christians agree, is drinking more water and enjoying it more, so swimming must be good for you, too.) I swam until my hands went numb and red. They were fiery when I got out and started walking home, the sun low over heaps of rock. I had no towel, so the shaggy boy loaned me his. He was one of the many souls who seemed to be looking only into your eyes but who'd suddenly point off toward Hudson Bay and cry: Look, Bill, a weasel, weasel! There, there! — They could all see things which I couldn't. Sometimes they seemed uncanny to me. They lived on their island amidst the ruins of a race of giants. The boy from Arviat rode me on his four-wheeler out to Kirchoffer Falls, where the water was sea-green and seemingly gelid: transparent, swirly, filled with bubbles like bath gel. The mosquitoes did not find us right away. He showed me where to walk up and down the poppied stairs of cliff. I scanned the inukshuks* on the opposite bank, which was also a long cliff comprised of slabs of reddish rock, here and there a paler gravelfall; and then he showed me the Tuniit house, a rock-rimmed pit in the moss.

The Tuniit were strong, said the boy from Arviat. So strong they could lift a big rock or a polar bear with one hand.

What happened to them?

The Inuit killed them, I think, he said. A Tuniit man had sex with an Inuk woman, and an Inuk man got so mad he killed many, and the rest ran away.

When I asked the shaggy boy, he said: Some sailors came, and then they got sick. All their wives died, so they couldn't make new people.

So they're all dead?

All dead, except maybe one or two. They don't know they're Tuniit, 'cause they got adopted.

What would you do if you found out you were one of them?

I don't know. Nobody would touch me then because I'd be too strong.

The next day I saw that the girl who'd stolen my best Polaroid

---

* The inukshuks around Coral Harbour were particularly well constructed. Their job had once been to scare caribou. They had no job now. Each one crouched with its stone arms extended and its stone knees bent, as if crossing a stream. Every time I looked at it, I thought that it had moved.

was holding hands with the boy she loved. I was happy for her. I went to her and said that she was the strongest diver I had ever seen. I said that she was so strong that she must have a drop or two of Tuniit blood, and she laughed proudly.

Do you think Lydia's pretty? the girl beside her said.

Sure. I mean probably.

Really? You really want to fuck Lydia?

Probably.

Do you like *every* girl in this town? said another girl in amazement.

Probably, I said.

Why?

I don't know.

Who do you like best?

You, of course.

If you come live here you'll get a girlfriend, said a girl comfortingly.

Probably, I said.

Now it was midnight. Three boys were silhouetted on the bridge railing against the yellow light. Lydia's cigarette illuminated the breast of her multicolored parka like a Christmas tree light. — Guess this'll freeze me or kill me, aye? said her new boyfriend, diving in. Soon everyone was peeling down, some entirely, and playing in the cool greenish water, boys and girls together and secret. Some came out to sit again on the gravel bank.

Lydia's boyfriend lit a match and said: I like it here, 'cause it's tundra, aye? We got the fattest caribou.

THE BEST WAY
TO SMOKE CRACK

San Francisco, California, U.S.A. (1992)
San Francisco, California, U.S.A. (1992)
San Francisco, California, U.S.A. (1992)

San Francisco, California, U.S.A. (1992)

The crack pipe was a tube of glass half as thick as a finger, jaggedly broken at both ends because the prostitute had dropped it. She kept talking about the man down the hall, whose pipe still wore a bowl. She said that that special pipe was for sale, but the john figured that he'd already spent enough.

The john was of the all-night species, family Blattidae. Having reached that age when a man's virility begins to wilt flabbily, he admitted that his lust for women grew yearly more slobbery and desperate. Every year now he fell a little farther from what he had been. In his youth he had not considered himself to be anything special. Now he recollected with awe how his penis had once leaped eagerly up at the merest thought or touch, how his orgasms had gushed as fluently as Lincoln's speeches; those were the nights when ten minutes between two trash cans or beneath a parked car had sufficed. His joy now required patience and closeness. That was why he'd paid the twenty-nine dollars to share with this woman whose brown body was as skinny as a grasshopper's this stinking room whose carpet was scattered with crumbs of taco shells and rotting cheese; among his possessions he now counted the sheet which someone had used to wipe diarrhea, the science fiction book called *The Metal Smile*, a gold mine of empty matchboxes, and all the wads of used toilet paper that anyone would ever need to start a new life. He'd bought the room for the night, and after that he was going to go back to work and the prostitute would live there. Maybe that was why she worked so hard at cleaning up, hanging the diarrhea-sheet over the window for a curtain, picking up the hunks of spoiled food and throwing them out the window, sweeping with the broom without bristles, sprinkling the carpet with water from the sink (which had doubled as a urinal) so that the filth would stick better to the broom. Maybe that was why she cleaned, or maybe it was because she had once had a home where she'd raised her children as well as she could until jail became her home, and although they took her children and turned them into somebody else's (or more likely nobody's) it was too late for her to shuck the habit of making her surroundings decent; or maybe she worked so hard just because she was fond of the john (who was generous), because she wanted him to be happy and comfortable with her.

If it wasn't for whoever left this mess, there'd be no roaches, she said. I've lived in this hotel all the time and never had no roaches.

He sat on the mattress with his arm around her while they smoked a rock, and a cockroach rushed across his leg.

I'm not afraid of any human being, the prostitute said. I'm a single female out there, so I gotta be ferocious so they be respectin' me. And I'm not afraid of any animal. But insects gimme the jitters. All them roaches in here, it's 'cause whoever was in here before was such a slob. If I ever meet that motherfucker and he pisses me off, I'll say to him: You know what? You remind me of your room. Ooh, look at that big fat roach!

Certainly the big fat roach was blameless for being what it was. And the prostitute was likewise faultless for not wanting that roach to crawl across them later that night, once they turned out the bare bulb which reflected itself in the greasy window. Biting her lip with disgust, she slammed her shoe against the wall over and over until the bug was nothing but a stain among stains.

I really hate them roaches, she sighed, loading her blackened pipe with more whiteness. They just gimme the creeps. You know, in the Projects, you catch 'em with crack. If you cleaned up your place too good and stuff and you can't find 'em, just lay a rock out on the table and they'll be swarmin'! Shit, there's another one!

She snatched up her shoe and pounded the wall.

She was picking bits of rancid cheese out of the chest of drawers with three drawers gone while the john lay watching the roaches. They seemed to be accustomed to the light. They scurried up and down the walls on frantic errands, ran across the carpet, whose water-stains and burns resembled the abscesses of half-Korean Molly down the hall (another whore said she kept picking at herself); and one roach even climbed that foul bedsheet draped over the window.

The prostitute came back to the mattress and they smoked another piece of rock. She'd loaned the pipe to a whore who'd bought bad stuff, so it stank of something strange. Now she kept running water through it, but that didn't do any good.

Nudge that rock down into the end that's burned blacker. The john knew that much. Don't push it in too hard, or you'll break the mesh which is already almost gone. She'd taught him that. Just tamp it lovingly in with the black-burned hairpin. Lovingly, I said, because crack is the only happiness.

The prostitute celebrated whenever she got a big rock by buying a lighter whose color matched her dress. She held a red lighter tonight to keep her red dress company. She was wearing red shoes and a red headband; red was her favorite shade. He'd seen her in the black cocktail dress that she put on when he knocked at her door and she was embarrassed because she thought she looked old; he didn't care how old or young she looked because he loved her, but she closed the door and wouldn't let him in until she was beautiful for him in the black dress which thirty seconds later he was urgently helping her pull off; and he'd seen her in the foxtail outfit that reminded him of women he knew at the horse races, but most often he'd seen her wearing the hue of vibrant blood. She lit the rock and breathed in even though the tube of glass had been broken so short that it burned her lips and tongue when the rock was only half cooked; she breathed in because when she was eighteen her first husband had brought a two-by-four smashing down on the crown of her head, and after that she'd never had very good balance; that was twenty years ago now. And one of her daughters (she'd been very little then) had said: Mama, don't *ever* worry about falling, 'cause I'll always be next to you, and if I see you start to go down, I'll throw myself right down on the sidewalk so you can fall on me! — It made her cry sometimes to remember that. Her daughter didn't walk beside her anymore, and so she smoked crack.

The john was looking worried. — Crack isn't addictive, now, is it? he said.

Oh, no, honey, the prostitute smiled. It's just a psychological thing.

And later, in the night, when she spread her legs for him and he worried about AIDS, she said to him: Oh, don't worry, honey. You can only get AIDS if you're two homosexuals.

There were two roaches on the wall, and she got them both with her shoe in a slamming blow like the one three months ago that had left her permanently blind in her right eye when she was being raped; now she couldn't read a menu anymore.

Inhale it slowly, hold five or six seconds, expel it through the nose. That was her way; that way was more mellow. If you did it too fast you might get tweaked. First the head rush, then the body rush.

Don't inhale so hard, she said. That's the difference between white boys and black boys. White boys always inhale too fast, 'cause they think if they do they'll get more high. You white boys are just greedy sometimes. Black boys know better.

He felt the smokebite in his chest as he held it in, and then the rush struck him behind his eyeballs. Now his heart began to pound more fiercely. His lips and tongue swelled into a numb clean fatness like a pussy's lips. The feeling that he had was the same as long ago at the high school dances when the boys and girls had stood on opposite sides of the floor and the music had started but he was too afraid to cross that open space where all the girls could see him as he came among them to ask one to share her beauty with him for a dance, so his heart pounded faster and faster, until suddenly he was going to the girls anyway to say: Will you dance with me? and the girl giggled and her friends giggled and she looked quickly at her friends and then at him and said yes and he was going into the music with her, holding her hand. It was in exactly that way that his heart was pounding, except that there was no fear in his excitement this time; no matter how rapid his happiness became it remained tranquil.

Well, laughed the prostitute (who always became more talkative the more crack she did), another main difference between white people and black people is white people have reputations to protect when they buy drugs. Black people don't care. — And she laughed.

Ahead waited the long night of her going in and out to do her business which she pretended not to be doing, believing that pretending would keep him from feeling hurt, when actually he wasn't hurt at all; she was trying to be loving by protecting him from what she was doing, while he was trying to be loving by letting her do whatever she needed to do. Meanwhile they both smoked crack. Ahead of that night loomed the night when he took her out for dinner with his friends and she was late because she had to smoke crack and then at dinner she excused herself to go to the ladies' room where she smoked crack and came out weeping as though her heart would break because she was convinced that all his friends looked down on her, so he embraced her outside as she soaked him with tears begging him to return with her to that hotel on Mission Street whose gratings and buzzers were like airlocks, so later that night he did come to her, and when he lay beside her on the dirty mattress and took her into his arms her face was burning hot! Her forehead steamed with sweat that smelled like crack, that delicious bitterclean smell even more healthy and elegant than eucalyptus or Swiss herbal lozenges; she ground her face into his chest and whispered something about the Bible as her sick and glowing face burned its way to his heart. — There was a woman whom he loved who was a scientist. When he told her what had happened, the woman said: That fever, that night sweat, that dementia about your friends, well, it sounds to me like AIDS, particularly the very early stages. — But another friend just rubbed his stubble and said: Her sweat smelled like crack, huh? She must be O.D.ing on crack. Happens all the time! — Ahead of that night crouched the night when the john woke up in his own bed wanting crack. It was the middle of a moonless time. He had no crack. He said to himself: If only the moon was here maybe that would cheer me so that I could sleep again; but ahead of that night laughed the night when he woke up from a dream of crack with the

moon outside his window as big and round as the abscess on the
prostitute's foot which would not heal, and he lay wide awake needing crack.

They smoked crack, and he lay in her arms staring up at the long
lateral groove-lips of the moulding reflected in the mirror of the medicine cabinet, whose shelves had all been wrenched out, and he began
to smile.

Look at that! he cried. Look at all those roaches running crazy
across the ceiling! I guess they must really be enjoying themselves.

The woman cackled. — I s'pose they be gettin' a contact high
from all the smoke up there. But it kinda pisses me off, 'cause they
can't pay me no money!

They both laughed at that, and then they did another piece of rock
in the best way; she approved of how he smoked crack now; the best
way to smoke crack is to suck it from the tube of broken glass as
gently as you'd suck the crack-smoke breath from the lips of the
prostitute who's kissing you.

San Francisco, California, U.S.A. (1992)

The john remembered the nights when he was still married and
lay in the darkness of the guest bedroom watching golden hall-
light, listening to the rush of his wife's high heels as she adjusted
her dress and necklace in the main bedroom, his grief and anxiety
hideous while his heart ticked with the clock. He had decided that if
his wife asked him to come, he would say: Why should I? but then
he thought that that did not sound sincere (and he was actually very
sincere), so he decided that when his wife came in he would just say:
Convince me and I'll go. His wife was almost ready now. It was cold
and dark outside the window. He knew that he was missing his last
hope by lying there while his wife put the penultimate touches of
lipstick on. He was terrified that his wife might not even come and

look for him. If she did not at least ask him, he could not volunteer to go with her. She went into the bathroom, where she must be checking herself in the mirror. Now she came out and turned off the bathroom light. He resolved that if his wife came in he'd say: I'll go if you want me to, honey. Now his wife was making the rounds of the upstairs, turning off lights. She paused. Perhaps she was wondering where he was. He could not move. He would not move. He heard her go downstairs. She was clicking her high heels rapidly through every darkened room, including the living room where the unlit Christmas tree slobbered its sticky shadows of shaggy foulness; she must be looking for him; she was back at the bottom of the stairs now, and he heard her picking up her keys. So she was going to leave without calling for him. He lay breathless with tension. She called his name.

Here I am, he said.

Where are you? It's all dark up there.

Here, he said with effort.

She came up the stairs and turned the hall light back on. He heard her going into each of the other rooms again. At last she entered the half-ajar door of the guest bedroom and stood peering to see if he was there. He could not say anything.

Are you sleeping? she said hesitantly.

No, he said.

She turned on the light and looked at him.

I'm going to go now, she said. I'll be back in an hour. Maybe an hour and a half.

I'll come with you if you want me to, honey, he said. He was surprised at how easily the words came to him. It was as if some grace of husbands, wives and desperate angels had helped him.

Oh, don't bother, said the wife. It would be too much work for you.

It's up to you.

You really wouldn't mind? said his wife. Don't worry about it. I know you don't want to.

She stood there waiting for him to encourage her hopes. He strained his every effort to say the words again that would make her happy, but even as his mouth opened he knew that he was going to fail.

You—you heard what I said, he gasped out.

Her face became resigned again. — Never mind, she said. She turned out the light. Tears had begun to gush out of his eyes just as she reached for the switch, and it is possible that if she had waited another three or four seconds (or if he had somehow been able to make her do so), she would have seen them.

She went down the stairs, opened the door and left him.

San Francisco, California, U.S.A. (1992)

Again he ascended the stairs between the two gratings, and tall black men made way for him on the landing because if he was white he must be an undercover cop.

Who you lookin' for, officer? one of them said.

He said her name.

You a cop?

No.

You a paid informant?

No, officer, he said.

The black man laughed grimly.

He got to the top of the stairs where the second grating was, and the lobby man who had buzzed him was already standing on the other side of the grating with his arms folded.

She's not here, the man said. She just now went outside to do her business, so I reckon she'll be back before long.

They always said she wasn't there, and she was always there, so the john wasn't surprised. — Can I wait on your stairs? he said.

Help yourself.

He descended a stair or two to show his respect for the workings of the hotel, and waited, looking alertly through the grating like a zoo-barred jaguar waiting for meat, watching and waiting until just past midnight he saw her pass across the lobby on one of her constant errands. He was here to tell her how she made him feel. He called her name, and her face lit up and she came running to make the lobby man let him in.

Thank you kindly, he said to the lobby man.

The lobby man gazed expressionlessly away. At least he didn't charge the john five dollars to get in.

I was just thinkin' 'bout you! the prostitute said. I was afraid you'd quit me. Come on!

She ran ahead of him up the back stairs by the toilet, and there was the man who had laid out his or somebody else's possessions on the stairs, including pennies and nickels, and stood patiently waiting for them to make him rich. The prostitute had already run high into the smoky darkness above him as he picked his way past more loungers, and then he had caught up with her and she'd taken his hand. Soon now he could tell her. Men like salt-encrusted pillars of carven ebony walled them on both sides, looking on silently as she kissed his lips and thrust her tongue repeatedly into his mouth. He wondered if he was tasting other men's sperm. She slipped her arm around him and led him to the room where the two lesbian whores lived. The lesbian whores did very well in that hotel by renting out their room to strangers for five dollars for fifteen or twenty minutes. That was why they were so well furnished. They had a TV and even a single bed. The prostitute (who knew that the john would pay her back) gave the white whore some money, and the white whore slipped out. Inside the room, another white boy was sitting on the bed. He was smoking crack and he was very nervous.

Y'all make yourselves comfortable and I'll be *right* back, the prostitute said, as prostitutes so often say, and the john thought to himself: Why not? What do I care if she doesn't show? I have all night, and I haven't even paid.

The white boy offered him a piece of rock, and the john thought again: Why not? because the prostitute was still there and she was serving him so tenderly, holding the crack pipe to his mouth, lighting it, reminding him not to swallow the smoke or he'd get nauseated, and then the feeling hit, the good feeling, and the prostitute grinned and went out.

I don't like this, the other white boy said. I gave eighty dollars. Well, forty was just business, you know. But forty was to get me some more rock.

You'll see her again, the john said. You can trust her.

Usually I take her to my place and she stays the night, said the white boy. I don't like this place. This place is dangerous.

The john could not tell what exactly the prostitute meant to this other person. He wanted to find out. He wanted very much to find out.

How many times have you done her? he said.

Oh, two or three times. Maybe four or five.

Listen, he said to the other white boy. Can you do me a favor? When she comes back, I need to speak with her, just for five minutes. Then you can take her home. I won't get in your way.

I don't wanna do that, the white boy said. He was out of crack, and so his hand was clenched around the crack pipe and his face was sweating.

OK, the john said.

They sat in silence on the bed, and then the black whore and the white whore came in to get toilet paper. — Your friend sure is keeping you waiting, they said. That's rude.

I'm gonna go talk to her, said the white boy. I need some rock. I gave her money. I need rock! Where's her room?

Number sixty-four, said the john. It's a real nice room. Lots of company scuttling up and down the walls.

The white boy went out, and the white whore sat down next to the john on the bed while her lover sat in the corner. The white whore (who had been going out with the black whore for eight years) was wearing a very lowcut dress that showed her rich plump breasts, and she bent toward him a little to make them move and said: You wanna like *do* anything?

Just then somebody knocked on the door. The black whore unlocked it, and the white boy came in. — She said she'll be down in a minute, he said unhappily.

So, the white whore was saying to the john, you think you might like a date?

You're beautiful, he replied, but I've already got a date.

Well, what if she don't come back?

Maybe then. I don't know. Maybe then.

Anybody got any rock? said the white boy.

She sure ain't showin' you no respect, said the black whore.

I don't like this, said the white boy. I'm getting very upset about this.

What makes you attracted to her? the john asked.

Oh, I don't even know her name exactly, the white boy yawned. It's just I run into her on the street sometimes.

Just let me know if I'm in your way.

No problem, dude. We can all hang out. Once she comes back, you and me and these other girls can go to my place and party.

You wanna date? the white whore cut in, her eyes lighting up. I'm sorry my face is kind of a mess. I got into an accident. But if you wanna date me I'll be real good.

You see, the white boy said, I gave her eighty dollars.

Eighty? laughed the black whore in the corner. You gave that bitch *eighty?* Shit.

I'm getting like *tense* now, said the white boy. I'm afraid I might do something.

I'll take care of it, the john said.

He went upstairs to sixty-four, and just as he was about to knock the door across the hall opened and an ancient Asian lady in a night-gown stuck her head out and flapped a moth-colored titty at him and he bowed with his hand on his heart, at which she closed the door. Behind the other door, the prostitute he'd come for was saying: Just gimme a dime bag, just this once. I swear I'll never ask for no more favors.

He knocked.

Who is it? the prostitute shouted in her fiercest voice.

It's me.

I'm comin', I'm comin! she cried impatiently.

I've got to go now, he called, smiling a little. I'll see you another time.

That worked wonders. The prostitute practically flew out the door in her eagerness to keep him, and they went downstairs.

These two girls are coming with us, the white boy said.

Oh *no* they are *not!* the prostitute cried. Ladies, I don't mean to disrespect you, but this is my business. We gonna go to his place and kinda get established, and then if we need you we'll come an' get you *then*.

So I'll meet you at two A.M. at the corner, the white boy was whispering to the white whore.

Come on! the prostitute said.

The two johns got up and followed her into the lobby where the manager studied them from within his glass cubicle, and the prostitute (who could tell by taste whether crack was good or not) opened the grating and they went downstairs past the black men and through the second grating and onto the street.

I wouldn't be doin' this for just anybody, the prostitute said to the white boy. But you're such a dynamite guy. You're my baby. I love white boys.

That was the first time that night that the john's heart ached. The prostitute always told him he was a dynamite guy, too.

The prostitute ran across the street and bought the white boy some of the crack she owed him. Then she called laughing: I love white boys!

The john put his arm around her while the white boy stood watching. — I love two kinds of crack, he told her, the kind I smoke and the kind between your legs. — She laughed and laughed.

Thanks for letting me come along to your house, he said to the white boy. I sure do appreciate it.

No problem, dude. We'll chill out and party, you know, just a couple of mellow crackheads.

Everything OK, baby? the prostitute said to him. Soon we'll all be doin' some really good rock. Danny here don't mind. He's quality, he really is.

They got to the white boy's house, and the prostitute and the white boy were kissing. The john looked away.

While the prostitute was in the bathroom the white boy said: Come into the bedroom for a minute. Why don't you sit down on the bed with me for a minute?

You sure I'm not in your way? the john said. You paid for her. I didn't. I can take off anytime.

Let's you and me do her together, the white boy whispered.

Sure, the john said. You go first. That's only fair. Besides, it's your place.

No no no, you don't get it. Let's do her *together.*

Oh, I'm not exactly into that, said the john, watching to see if the white boy might suddenly scream in rage and pull out a knife or gun. — I only do girls.

I'm not queer or anything, the white boy pleaded. There's nothing to it. We just turn out the lights, get under the covers, and you won't even know whose mouth it is.

Well, I'll have to think that one over, the john said, wondering if he would be able to knock the white boy down and run if the white boy turned out to be coeval with the white boy in the newspaper who kept other boys' heads in his refrigerator. He decided that he could take the white boy easily. The white boy was very pale and puffy and unhealthy. If he had a gun, of course, that would be different.

Please, the white boy said. If you don't do her *with* me, my whole evening will be ruined.

The white boy was weeping. Because he had broken so easily, the john felt fairly sure now that he must not be dangerous. He put his hand on the white boy's shoulder and said: I just don't think I can do what you ask. I'm really sorry. How can I make it up to you?

Never mind, the white boy said in a desolate voice.

The prostitute was still in the bathroom. The white boy went and opened the door.

Can't you see I'm tryin' to shit? said the prostitute.

I just wanted to give you this T-shirt, the white boy said, peering in eagerly. I thought you might like it.

Thank you, the prostitute said. I appreciate that. You're a real dynamite guy.

When she came out, the john said: Well, I have to go.

What's wrong, baby? said the prostitute. Come on. Smoke a little rock with us and relax.

She took some of the white boy's crack and gave him a nice big hit. He felt the feeling again, the happy excited feeling, and for a moment it was so strong that he couldn't talk. He exhaled through his nostrils, and his nose went numb. He could no longer feel the weight of his body's sadness.

Why don't you stay over? the white boy said. It's so late. You don't wanna be out on the street.

Maybe I'll just take a stroll around the block, he said.

He put his coat on, and the prostitute gave him another rock, holding him tightly so that he could not get away. — He's my baby, she said to the white boy, embracing the john desperately. He's the best. He's dynamite.

I guess I'll go now, said the john.

What's the matter, baby? said the prostitute. Listen, come on into the bedroom and tell me what's going on. Excuse us for a second, Danny.

Sure, the white boy said dully.

Now what's goin' on? said the prostitute, sitting beside him on the bed with her hand on his knee, looking into his eyes like a worried mother whom he must not disappoint.

He wants him and me to do you at the same time, he said, in a low voice because the bedroom door was open and he did not want to hurt the white boy's feelings. I just can't. I'm sorry.

He said *that?* cried the prostitute in amazement. *I* don't do that!

It's okay, he said. Anyway I'm going to go.

She sat motionless on the bed.

The white boy walked him to the door. He looked back and she was sitting on the bed crying. — Please come 'ere, she said.

He went back to her, hesitated, and said: I love you. Then he strode out without looking back.

THE BEST WAY TO
CHEW KHAT

Nairobi, Kenya (1993)
Nairobi, Kenya (1993)
Nairobi, Kenya (1993)
Nairobi, Kenya (1993)
Nairobi, Kenya (1993)
Nairobi, Kenya (1993)
Nairobi, Kenya (1993)
Nairobi, Kenya (1993)

Nairobi, Kenya (1993)

She could open soda bottles with her teeth. Her plump and delicious lips, her nipples swollen from nursing babies, her succulent clitoris, these and other dainties enthralled her customers all night, until at last they must snatch greedy gobbets of sleep. She never let anyone fuck her up the ass because that would be trying to fool God.

When he asked her if she loved him, she opened her eyes wide in the bed and said: My God! How can you ask me that? I treat you like my own husband!

One night he was chewing khat with her and her sister, holding each one's hand in the theater's darkness. Her hand was hot and excitingly sweaty. The sister's was cool and getting colder, because the sister chewed khat too much. She said: When I chew khat, I can't stop. Just want to chew more!

He remembered the boy at the Twenty-Four-Hour Green Bar, fallen asleep with his head on the table, pale like riverbottom sand. — From smoking brown sugar, the sister whispered.

The sister caught the smooth red skin of a khat stalk between her teeth and pulled, ripping it away from the bad green flesh inside, like a hyena nuzzling the dirt sideways to snap rotten meat in his jaws.

The sister kept passing him fresh stalks of khat even after he'd had enough. She gave him chewing gum so that his mouth would not go numb and dry. Her hand got colder and colder. She laid her head down against his neck and watched the movie with a silent smile.

The other one, his love, burned his hand with her hand. She chewed khat in silence. He could not stop thinking about the way her thighs glistened with water after she had shaved her pussy. Her pubic hair had been lush like the black lump on a lion's neck, but not long-stranded like an American girl's, not like the bundle of leaves hung from street signs or tobacconist's signs to betoken khat, because the heat of Africa always made her crop it into a darling checkerboard. This time she had gone farther and shaved it all off with his razor. Now it itched. With her free hand she kept scratching herself and then stuffing khat into her mouth.

The two sisters had different mothers. Both mothers had been circumcised (they cut only the sweetest part, his love whispered). When the sisters had become women, they'd refused to let that happen to them. The sister's mother was a fat old lady in a blue and red kerchief who sat very slowly sifting the grit out of red beans in a wicker basket, picking out pebbles with one hand. The courtyard, bright with dripping laundry, smelled like piss.

The heat of his true love's hand drenched him with lust. Her hot wet fingers encircled his in just the same way as the black areolas ringed her nipples, not mere virginal speckles of some untested theory of circumnavigation, but solid disks from breast-feeding, sturdy like steel washers. Her hand was equally strong. Its grip came from work. Twice a week she washed her clothes and the baby's clothes, scrubbing and wringing them in her iron-hard palms. She was always bending over the baby (his bald round face slightly more orange than hers), always putting on his little shoes. She'd taught him to shit nicely on a scrap of paper bag on the bathroom floor. She cleaned him and carried him and spanked him a hundred times a day, striding tall and brown down the street with a ten-pound bag of rice under her other arm. The baby cried and she bounced him gently. (As for the man, he thought to himself: to mate with a widowed lioness, the lion first kills her cubs.) On her slender well-callused feet one toenail had been split by a stone years before. She had scarred knees. Her hair was always stiff and greasy with sweet oil.

The sister's hand was very cold now. Lovingly she popped a stalk of khat in his mouth.

Nairobi, Kenya (1993)

There was a long pale green plain with dark green trees topped by flattish elongations, and then far away a blade of sky-blue mountain, translucent like church-glass. The plain was stained with crawling emerald shadows by the clouds. Its grass was frosted with seedheads. Low green trees shone with white thorns. A leopard was in a tree like a mass of white stars in muscular darkness. — No, I fear to see a wildebeest, his love said. I fear the strange high shape. — His love said: I don't like Masai, because they don't fear animals. They live just like animals. They drink blood. — Near the leopard was a buffalo like a lump of burned wood, black-eyed, humped atop his skull like a coolie's hat. Almost in sight of the buffalo, a cheetah lay under a tree like a puddle of speckled milk. Then came dirt roads and shanties and the muddy place behind the wall where his love sat by the open door, cleaning rice. The low bubble of the camp stove was a loving voice. She had once been a girl with skinny chocolate knees who uncapped soda bottles with her teeth.

She was dicing a fresh steak, bending and laughing with her friend who'd just come in and was sitting on the bed. She chopped up onions and carrots and added giant spoonfuls of cooking fat.

When Kikuyu lady get married, they buy for her a cow, she said. When I get a cow, I sell it, buy a business.

There were happy Kikuyu songs on cassette outside and she sang, her mouth a circle. She was serious and stately, calm and happy, tall and brown; she said she was fat because she used to chew too much khat.

And me, I'm fat because you take such good care of me, he said.

When we get married, I must feed you in front of all, she said to him. I will give you big cake, very big cake, so that all know I take good care of you!

But her best friend said: I'd never stay with a white man without money.

Nairobi, Kenya (1993)

The baby was upon him like a leopard leaping with meat in his mouth, his spots shimmering with his breath. The sister was in his eyes like the three dark stripes on an impala's backside. Only his love lived aloof; she was busy working; she was the only one who worked.

Water ran down the diagonal channel in the concrete, gray with oatmeal, flecks of wasted food in the bottom, while the yellow soles of her housegirl's feet flexed very slightly as she stood on the concrete riser, leaning against the long communal basin like a man standing at a bar, scrubbing pots slowly, expressionlessly and thoroughly, while his love, her skirt tucked above her knees, worked ten feet down the same channel, her bracelet shining, her wrists white with suds, her ankles flecked as if the baby had spat on them again, and she scrubbed the clothes one by one in the soaping basin and then scrubbed them again in the rinsing basin there in that courtyard with the bathroom smell; and then she wrung them out and pinned them on the wire. (The sister was asleep. Every day she slept until almost sundown. Then she put her earrings on and went out to chew khat and get drunk. She never paid rent. She was much happier than his love, whom he rarely heard laughing outside her home; he could remember only one time when the baby was on her lap and she was throwing litter out the window of a taxi.) The baby took the pushbroom and played with the water in the channel while inside one of the still-shut blue doors someone else's baby cried determinedly, and the lady beside his love bent over a plastic basin, twisting and scrubbing, and she and his love laughed gently together. The baby stood and peed into the gutter again, picking fretfully at his sneakers. Then he threw a passionfruit rind in and stepped on it. By now it was nine-o'-clock and she had been at it for two hours. She darkened the courtyard with her cool dripping clothes hanging from the wire, baffling the unpleasant sun. She cleaned out the gutter and scrubbed the floor with a brush. None of the other ladies ever did that; she'd taken it upon herself.

In the third hour she did the jeans and jackets, scrubbing them with a hard brush on the concrete floor she'd washed; she rubbed in soap powder with her hands; then she went about her folding and straining and rinsing; while in the darkened room the housegirl peeled garlic, considering deeply over each clove, making each as perfect as a white tooth.

In the smoldering forenoon the pot, bubbled continually, the women smoking cigarettes and gossiping with the bird-nodding of gazelles' heads. Whenever the baby was bad they grabbed him and made to cut his penis off with a big knife or burn it off with a lighted match, and when he screamed they laughed.

Now at last it was safely late, the house not too hot anymore but cool and blue inside; and after dinner the baby sat on the floor eating rice with a spoon. The soles of his feet were already thickly callused. He'd grow up to be what he had to be, just like her first husband, who'd beaten her. (She said: Every time a woman gives birth, the pain is so great that she wants to punch her husband!) She bathed the baby in the plastic washtub and let him splash and play. Then she rubbed his body with Vaseline. When he became fretful and bad, she gave him a capful of cough medicine and he fell asleep on the bed. Then she went out to do more washing, while the girl with the furrow-woven hair sat hunched over the pot, slowly chopping chard.

Later, happily lying beside her white lover in the cubicle of the rich couple, who even had hot chocolate powder, she listened to her little radio. She said: If I get rich, I'll buy a nice house, buy my mother a car, buy my children everything. — Her hands and buttocks were more lovely than the dapplings on a giraffe leaning down to browse on a bush, the giraffe's flesh brownish-yellow with dark brown spots like a fresh buttermilk pancake. Her soft brown thigh was delicious with sweat.

Nairobi, Kenya (1993)

The room was now cozy, lighter, cool because it was night. The neighbors told each other good night from one cubicle to the next. (Her sister was out whoring and chewing khat, never riding the zebras of sleep.) The music was low; bulbs glowed beautifully above the dirty white walls. Her delicious musk-mound floated him away from himself just as khat took him out of Kenya, past Moronie's low tree-balls bunched together under the broad cloud-cauldron of volcanoes; past the dark lady with the golden nosering and golden earrings (her head and shoulders wrapped in a cloth of blue and white stripes, blue and black sunbursts); past Moronie's bulk of hairy greenness, past the spittle between the hot black teeth of bays; and all the way to Madagascar's rivers the color of tomato soup, braiding broadly down between clouds and tree-destroyed places. She rolled on top of him, and he whirled westward to Somalia, where khat was qat and the sellers sat on a carven wooden chest beneath a green plastic awning. Ladies sat on the curb with double handfuls of qat, swishing flies away with the green stalks. A Somali in a station wagon pulled into the special parking lot, waving a plastic bag of qat, and began to chew and spit. He said: I don't need to eat anymore! My food is qat! —

He recited the roster of qat: gangete (the best kind), gese, lare, harere from Ethiopia . . . Everyone was chewing qat. His head began to pull the rest of his body a little into the air; he discoursed with the others on all subjects of this world, his analysis complete and certain; she pulled him on top of her and was kissing his lips until she'd sucked him back into Kenya where qat was only khat and there were not four kinds; her sister lay drowsing half-naked against him all day making chewing sounds, dreaming of khat. It was night again, and his love was in his arms.

Nairobi, Kenya (1993)

She explained to him that President Moi was a devil-worshipper because on the twenty-shilling note was a picture of him with a snake around his neck. — To be a devil-worshipper you must kill someone in your own family, the one you love the most, she whispered. You must do it in front of the other devil-worshippers. If you get rich from devil-worship and then leave that church, your riches will leave you. — President Moi's bodyguard had seen the snake and thought that it was hurting the President, so he killed it. President Moi got very angry and had him murdered.

She said that Moi had killed so many people. She knew that he was a devil-worshipper because her rent had doubled in one year to eight hundred shillings a month.*

She was sleepy now. She yawned and scratched her cunt. After he went away he found that she was still with him, because in the hair below his belly tiny black scabs appeared, itching more every day, and finally when he caught one between his fingers he saw that it was not a scab at all, that it had writhing legs. Then he knew why

* In 1993, this was about U.S. $40.

she had really shaved her pussy; and he remembered how she used to scratch between her legs without saying anything.

She was in his arms.

Nairobi, Kenya (1993)

ow it was dark, and crowds stood in the streets. Someone had tied a bundle of leaves to the sign for Taveta Road. The night was cobalt violet with pale gray swirls of cloud. A woman smiled and said: jambo,* and he knew that he would never be lonely again. The buildings pulsed with shouts. The whores stood in the darkness, their sun a single strip of orange windows above.

Past the alley where men stood pissing against a dark wall, his love's sister disappeared, sinking without sight or sound. The police had caught her.

They waited an hour to be sure. Sitting at one of the restaurant's scuffed and mismatched tables, they ordered the cheapest dish, which was mutton stew and passionfruit juice. Heavy chairs grated squeaking on the echoing floor. Parade music momentarily drowned the bus horns outside as a guard came in between the tables, swinging his truncheon.

I give him one hundred shillings, his love said. He find out for me.

She went over to the man and they spoke for awhile. When she came back, her face was almost the same. Only someone who knew her very well could have told that she was almost in tears.

He say, you a cripple and you fuck me up the anus. Sometimes I want to cry, I tell you. I tell him, maybe he know that because you fuck *him* up the anus!

While the police laughed over a newspaper behind the tall booking desk, a sergeant came in with a beggar whose face was a black

* Hello.

drowned lady-mask in a ruffled collar of dead grass, and she carried a skinny child of indeterminate morbidity which did not brush away the flies from its mouth and the mother was wailing in grief and terror so extreme that it was a wonder they did not begin crying instead of laughing at the booking desk; of course at the booking desk they never noticed. The sergeant kept his hand on the beggar's shoulders so professionally that it almost seemed he was comforting her. Really, of course, he incarnated the foul-smelling sandy sprawl of a lion snarling over the meat between his paws.

They catch her without a home, his love said in a whisper. That's why she is crying. Now they put her in the cell for three months or six months.

The sergeant took the beggar through a door, and almost immediately they heard the rhythmic screams. He could not keep himself from looking at the booking desk where they smiled back at him behind all their riches of contemptuous knowledge. He could see that they knew him. They knew him just as well as the beggar-boys who if they weren't given money started shouting: White man, why you take our African lady? — They knew his love, too. She didn't want to visit her sister in prison because if she did they'd stare her down in exactly the same way, saying nothing, and then if they ever caught her they'd shout: It's your turn now! Where's your husband now?

Nairobi, Kenya (1993)

But every day she took the bus into town, searched the prisons, paid out bribes, until at last they let her sister go.

Nairobi, Kenya (1993)

She put on a faded yellow dress, picked up the clothes her sister had thrown about in drunkenness, took off her shoes and scrubbed the concrete floor. The room smelled like the sister's unwashed body. There was a single bed where the two of them slept with the baby, a roof of corrugated metal held in place by two crossed two-by-fours from which a bare bulb hung. Every wall was in touching distance of the bed. The view outside was a concrete wall. She opened the door, and knelt outside on the sunny concrete, leaning in to scrub the floor. So strong she was, so able in this world of pain. The police had shot her father; her two mothers could not help her; she rented her body to live, and she lived. She nourished her baby and her sister. Nothing could crush her until death. She was pure and her name was Rose.

There she was, tall and brown, sweeping.

ALL HE HAD
WAS HEART

Sacramento, California, U.S.A. (1992)

Sacramento, California, U.S.A. (1992)

There were two boxers on that square platform covered with red, white and blue, and one of them was going to lose. The hometown boy got all the cheers. The other boy was from Mexico. They'd brought him in to lose. The crowd booed when he was announced.

The hometown boy's manager had a fresh towel on his shoulder. He took it and rubbed down the hometown boy. He patted his back and shook his hand. To look at him, the hometown boy could have been the Mexican boy's brother. He gazed at the Mexican as brothers gaze at each other, the look of people who've known each other a long time.

The Mexican boy's manager was already gone.

They pranced like horses waiting, each boy in his corner staring at the other.

As soon as the first round started, they began to look even more like each other. They were both skinny and quick. Their puffy pouting lips and wooden faces stylized them like the eyebrows they raised to stare at each other through their sweat.

Carlos, Carlos! Knock 'im out! called the hometown boy's manager. Kill! Do it! Use your right!

Use your jab! shouted the Mexican's manager.

They danced lightly like art mannequins.

The first punch landed on the Mexican's face with a sharp and puffy slapping sound.

I could already see in the Mexican's face that he was beaten. I don't know if he knew it yet, but I did. He was not trying to win anymore. He was only trying to survive. It was heartrending to see him backing away, never landing a punch, retreating behind his own sweat, no longer seeing the hometown boy's gloves coming. Later on the hometown boy, soaked and panting, would say to the press: Yeah, I feel good. I was hitting him where I wanted. I just kept going 'till he didn't want to throw no more. — The way he said it, anyone could see that it was nothing personal. He just had to win, that was all.

The hometown boy's manager felt the same way. — A right, Carlos! he shouted. In the face! Hit 'im in the face! Yes!

At the end of the first round, each of the two boxers sat limp on his stool. Their managers poured cool water on them, took their mouthguards out, poured bottles down their throats, put their mouthguards back in.

The bell sounded. The fighters came together, embracing in a tender stranglehold.

The Mexican's manager was in agony. — Don't wait, baby, don't wait! he called out. Go for it! Come on, Ernesto, move it!

They flailed, and drops of sweat exploded upward from them with each punch.

The hometown boy punched and punched the Mexican in the face while the Mexican sagged against the ropes. The ref didn't stop it quickly enough. Finally the Mexican fell. Everyone leaped and cheered and beamed. They leaned back, nodded tightly, smiling and pointing, making thumbs up.

He got back to his feet before the count. He was better off than the boxer in the previous match who'd taken a kidney punch and lay paralyzed with pain, a bubble forming between his lips while everyone clapped for the winner. He was better off than the boxer in the next match whose blood would run into his eye while the ref shook his head and the opponent paced and the crowd shouted: He's all right!

Let 'im fight! — The Mexican was better off because he fought on. He and the hometown boy were both hinged skeletons, sweaty and veined, their shorts darkening with sweat. He was trying to punch now. His punches met the hometown boy's like hands applauding.

Hunching, dodging, dancing, they hissed their breaths like snakes as their faces gorged purple. Amidst the crowd's raw shouts, their open mouths proclaimed a mystic silence. A fat girl put her hand to her mouth yelling: Whoo-hee! and the Mexican's manager was calling: You gotta win this round, Ernesto! You gotta fight! Get down, come on! You gotta fight! and the hometown boy's manager shouted: Hit 'im upstairs! and the ref crabwalked carefully round, wearing his quizzical look, and the smell of musk came and the Mexican flailed bewilderedly as the hometown boy punched him and the hometown boy's manager shouted: That's it, Carlos! Jab 'im! and the Mexican would not quit. Any second now I expected to see him go down with his lips shaping a mindless square. The hometown boy's blows slapped into him with a sound like a bullwhip striking a cantaloupe, and somehow he took it. He and the hometown boy were each doing what they had to do. There was no malice, only sweat and pain. The hometown boy was tired, too. He needed to win, and the Mexican would not give up.

At the end of the second round, the ref bent over the Mexican as he sat panting on his stool, and he said something very quietly. The Mexican nodded quickly. They pulled his hands out of the gloves, powdered them, slid the gloves back on. In the other corner, a man was powdering the hometown boy's sweaty face and chest. Then the bell rang, and they were both up again, dancing. Their low brown masks of faces flickered between their upraised double fists.

Look how he steps right in to close with that Mexican, a reporter said. He's got no respect for him.

There was a crisp slapping sound, and then the Mexican fell. The crowd thrilled: Ohhhh! — The ref leaped in and counted. The Mexican got back up. His sweaty face was elongated in wild gasps between the flashes of blue-gloved fists. His neck-tendons strained.

Get on him, Ernesto! cried the manager despairingly. Ernesto, keep your head down!

Hit 'im right through his body! somebody called out.

A hit to the head! The Mexican fell down on his back and lay limp with his mouth open while the crowd screamed with joy. The referee knelt over him. The Mexican nodded brightly and got back up. The hometown boy rushed at him exultantly.

Hit 'im, hit 'im! a man shouted.

Another punch! The Mexican was whirled around by the force of it. He sank down against the ropes. His head dropped and his mouth-guard rolled out.

There was an old man sitting beside the press section. The old man said: This guy's a butcher. They should never have brought that Mexican in. That Mexican didn't have nothing. All that Mexican had was heart.

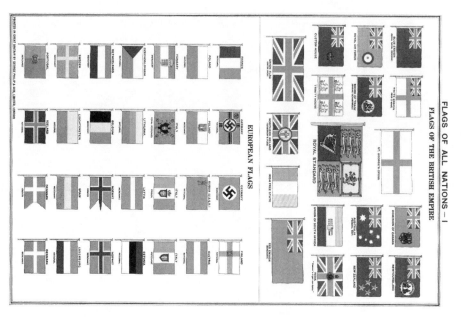

FLAGS OF ALL NATIONS – I
FLAGS OF THE BRITISH EMPIRE

EUROPEAN FLAGS

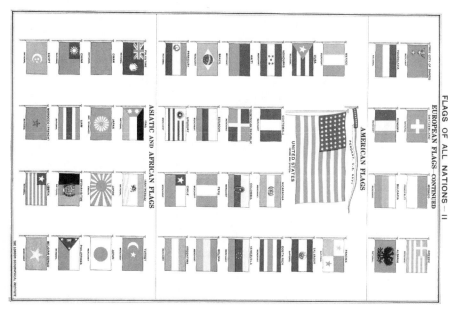

FLAGS OF ALL NATIONS – II
EUROPEAN FLAGS CONTINUED

AMERICAN FLAGS

ASIATIC AND AFRICAN FLAGS

197

THE ATLAS

Montréal, Québec, Canada (1993)
Cornwall, Ontario, Canada (1993)
Port Hope, Ontario, Canada (1993)
Pickering, Ontario, Canada (1993)
Guildwood, Ontario, Canada (1993)
Napoli, Campania, Italia (1993)
Orillia, Ontario, Canada (1993)
Washago, Ontario, Canada (1993)
Bangkok, Phrah Nakhon-Thonburi Province, Thailand (1993)
Cairo, Egypt (1993)
New South Wales, Australia (1994)
Mae Hong Song, Mae Hong Song Province, Thailand (1994)
Bangkok, Phrah Nakhon-Thonburi Province, Thailand (1993)
Boston, Massachusetts, U.S.A. (1993)
Bangkok, Phrah Nakhon-Thonburi Province, Thailand (1993)
Boston, Massachusetts, U.S.A. (1993)
Bangkok, Phrah Nakhon-Thonburi Province, Thailand (1993)
Mogadishu, Somalia (1993)
Bangkok, Phrah Nakhon-Thonburi Province, Thailand (1993)
Yangon, Myanmar (1993)
Orillia, Ontario, Canada (1993)
Washago, Ontario, Canada (1993)
State of Vatican City (1993)
Mount Aetna, Sicily, Italia (1993)
Lutton, Oklahoma, U.S.A. (1968)
Herculaneum, Near Napoli, Campania, Italia (1993)
Sydney, New South Wales, Australia (1994)
Phnom Penh, Cambodia (1991)
Tamatave, Madagascar (1994)
Sudbury, Ontario, Canada (1993)

Mexico (1993)

Allan Water, Ontario, Canada (1993)

Savant Lake, Ontario, Canada (1993)

Taxco, Guerrero, Mexico (1993)

Sioux Lookout, Ontario, Canada (1993)

Reddit, Ontario, Canada (1993)

Ottermere, Ontario, Canada (1993)

Malachi, Ontario, Canada (1993)

Diesel Bend, Utah, U.S.A. (1992)

Thailand (1991)

Chiang Mai, Chiang Mai Province, Thailand (1993)

Bangkok, Phrah Nakhon-Thonburi Province, Thailand (1993)

Winnitoba, Manitoba, Canada (1993)

Rice Lake, Manitoba, Canada (1993)

Yangon, Myanmar (1993)

Battle Rock, Oregon, U.S.A. (1994)

Los Angeles, California, U.S.A. (1994)

Budapest, Hungary (1994)

Zagreb, Croatia (1992)

Sarajevo, Bosnia-Herzegovina (1992)

Key West, Florida, U.S.A. (1994)

Samuel H. Boardman State Park, Oregon, U.S.A. (1994)

Key West, Florida, U.S.A. (1994)

Sydney, New South Wales, Australia (1994)

Mendocino, California, U.S.A. (1994)

Sarajevo, Bosnia-Herzegovina (1992)

Karenni State, Burma (1994)

Sydney, New South Wales, Australia (1994)

Karenni State, Burma (1994)

The Great Western Desert, Northern Territory, Australia (1994)

Key West, Florida, U.S.A. (1994)

Elma, Manitoba, Canada (1993)

Paris, Département Paris, Région Parisienne, France (1995)

Winnipeg, Manitoba, Canada (1993)

Roma, Italia (1993)

Cairo, Egypt (1993)

Berlin, Germany (1992)

Philadelphia, Pennsylvania, U.S.A. (1994)

New York, New York, U.S.A. (1994)
The Nile River, Egypt (1993)
Ho Mong, Shan State, Burma [Myanmar] (1994)
Marakooper Cave, Tasmania, Australia (1994)
Jerusalem, Israel/Jordan (1993)
Antananarivo, Madagascar (1993)
Bangkok, Phrah Nakhon-Thonburi Province, Thailand (1994)
Antananarivo, Madagascar (1993)
Vatican City and State (1993)
Afghanistan (1982)
The Pas, Manitoba, Canada (1994)
Churchill, Manitoba, Canada (1994)
Pond Inlet, Baffin Island, Northwest Territories, Canada (1990)
Tokyo to Osaka, Japan (1995)
Avignon, Département Vaucluse, Provence, France (1995)
San Francisco, California, U.S.A. (1995)
Churchill, Manitoba, Canada (1994)
Churchill, Manitoba, Canada (1993)
Churchill, Manitoba, Canada (1993)
Churchill, Manitoba, Canada (1994)
Home (1994)
Delhi, India (1991)
Churchill, Manitoba, Canada (1993)
New York, New York, U.S.A. (1991)
Home (1995)
Coral Harbour, Southampton Island, Northwest Territories, Canada (1993)
Churchill, Manitoba, Canada (1993)
Toronto, Ontario, Canada (1990)
Poland (Dreamed)
Eureka, Ellesmere Island, Northwest Territories, Canada (1988)
Churchill, Manitoba, Canada (1994)
Nevada, U.S.A. (1993)
The Slidre River, Ellesmere Island, Northwest Territories, Canada (1988)

$\mathfrak{H}$ e had used up every place now. Everywhere he went, he'd say to himself: There's nothing for me here anymore. No more nowhere nobody.

He had finished.

Once life had been as mysterious as a Sierra lake at dawn. That was when he believed that things would happen to him. Now he understood that nothing would ever happen.

It was time to go back to Canada.

Travelling, especially early in the morning, is equivalent to dying, swimming through a night of sleep-choked houses, carrying one's baggage the last few steps to the place where it must be surrendered, entering the irrevocable security zone, then waiting in monotonous chambers to be taken away. This was how he now voyaged through his days. Of course he knew that living, too, is a likeness of dying. Living means leaving, going on trying not to hear the screams.

Almost silently the train departed its tinsel of darkness, metal, concrete and glistening glass. It left another train behind. Then it struck the sky, which had been bright, cloudless and noisy with seagulls since five hours past midnight. The atlas opened as he entered that morning of birds. For a moment he vaguely remembered those summers that adolescents have, when they think they are about to irrevocably change. Montréal continued under its plague of sleep. Apartments, hotels and warehouses were but monuments.

He sat beside a French-named family of Indians: the plumply phlegmatic young mother, disinclined toward rippling her own peace, her four- or five-year-old daughter, who was the most "native"-looking of them with her cedar complexion and long black hair, then the old grandmother complete in spectacles and purple. The grandmother was reading a book about how to live in Paradise forever, her crumpleskinned arm flat across the type, her glasses crouched on the tip of her nose, her lower lip puffed out. He decided that he wanted to live in Paradise, too. He tried to have faith that the train was taking him there. Maybe it was. No more nowhere nobody.

They crossed the river of small green islands.

In an hour they were already in Cornwall, riding the green ocean whose spray was leaves and needles foaming gently against the sky. Another train passed so rapidly that it became a sky of reddish flickers in the lefthand windows.

The Atlas   203

When the train broke down and another train had to push, the Canadian ladies merely said: Ooh, this is exciting, eh? — Only one person complained, a man who was going to be late in London.

They crossed a shining river, greeted the shiny roofs of metal sheds, and then said to each other: You meet the most interesting people on trains.

I was raised on the prairie, a woman said; which was enough to make him long for the prairie miles ahead. Canada was already making him well. It was an infallible country. What heart-wound or soul-wound could remain unhealed by Canada balsam? How could death ever gnaw away Canada's birches in full-leaf? Why, those leaves had the power to compose an entire yellow-green sky! The grandmother's book was true. He had come back to Paradise.

Passing along the deep brown railroad ties they reached the forest's end. Wet fields of pale green with trees between the rows, a silver silo, long streams of blond hay on the emerald fields—these things now refreshed and greeted him.

Then, like the forest, the world ended in a darker coagulation of blue sky that went on forever: Lake Ontario. Trestles, canals, white-washed box-houses; they'd reached Port Hope. They continued without stopping. The center was not at the center but at his left hand, which addressed nothing. On the left, nothing but water (lightest closer to shore, with occasional white diagonals across its middle surface, almost all the way to its thick dark horizon-line of blue).

Not a lot to see, though, once you get west, eh? a man said.

No, not a lot, a lady said. We were there once. We got on the flat prairie.

Now and again trees rose tall and summer-leaved around the tracks, and another reddish train-body hurtled by, but then the water would be there again, nearer or farther away.

Pickering's the most special place, the lady said. Wait till you see Pickering.

More semicylindrical hay bales, then a hot, wooded suburb, a vast golf course, a river half-shored with concrete, two men fishing at a sandy spit choked with seagulls—these manifestations he'd finished with. Maybe that was why they didn't stop at Pickering. As for Guild-wood, that town came into being as a hot wasteland of pipes, bull-dozers, weeds and apartment towers, but Canada itself could not hurt his Canada. He remained unburied even yet, and they changed at Toronto. In the waiting room he remembered all the waiting rooms of his life. He remembered a crazy old man in Napoli with bandages around his ankles who'd come stamping rhythmically across the floor, raising an army of echoes. The young men put their hands in their pockets and leaned forward grinning. They shouted: *March, march!* Now suddenly it seemed that all his deeds and hopes and memories were no more than the old man's echoes. But he said: Never mind. I'm in Canada.

Nobody knows what this government's gonna do, a man said. I'm taking a ten percent pay cut in September.

Well, it has booms *and* busts, though, Alberta does. That's the thing. Those oil stocks keep gaining.

Trees as woolly as German participles, pale green, and all the two-storey white houses; yellow flowers, maybe dandelion or mustard (he couldn't tell because the train was going so fast now), like wet stars in the grass; a brown creek; a ferny forest not yet overthrown; a scudding lake with sailboats on it and roller-skaters around it; smooth green pebbles under the water; these were the letters constituting CANADA. Now the land was greener; Orillia was hot and green and shrubby. His joy bloomed bright green like swamp algae, and there were white and purple blooms in the grass. The train honked by the boy on the rusty watchtower in Washago, his bike on the weed-fringed road beneath. The boy called something soundlessly. The lady in the facing seat looked out the window and opened her mouth to reply. He saw her teeth and behind them the inward glistenings of her throat. Her tongue pulsed. Then suddenly he was assaulted by all the useless scraps of language he'd learned: A ring seal was a *nutsiq*. A harp seal was a *qairulik*. A bearded seal was an *ugjuk*. No more nowhere everywhere.

Now the crowds of nations and memories overthrew his joy; wasn't there a place where they ran sugarcanes between two motorized cylinders to squeeze the pale green juice? The two cylinders were weariness and despair; and they extracted the freshest liquid from his thoughts, leaving him the husks while the abyss drank everything else, catching each green drop on its coal-black twitching tongue. He had a fever headache, and drops of sweat exploded on his forehead like grains from a shotgun, dense, heavy and painful. The black tongue drank those, too. — So many souls and countries weighting down his atlas—eternally everywhere everybody! — He remembered all the women he'd loved and waited for, all the friends and hopes like fruits in the compartments of an upslanted tray, brown ocher terraces, mottled walls covered with Arabic writing, remembered the happiness, blessings that had come and passed away; and he remembered ants in an anthill. He remembered a late night plane to Australia when he sat in dull amazement observing a woman's struggle down the aisle, a massive gilded vase in her arms; then a man dragged a bulging garment bag which swiped at everyone's faces—useless things people serve and pray to in their useless lives! He remembered ants crawling by the hundreds across his hands in the Blue Mountains of New South Wales. He remembered ants in Mae Hong Song. He remembered Bangkok. Behind the grand oval windows of the massage parlor, ladies with numbers, ladies as numerous as ants sat on stairs of pink carpet, each woman a memory for many men whom she mostly did not remember (although the men remembered her, discussed her with one another and made claims, just as each anthropologist argues for the superiority of his own natives); and the women's hands were clasped upon crossed knees, and no doubt they were sitting there still, even as the "Hudson Bay" clacked farther up the track; the ants were waiting to become memories like the Somali women in flower-robes and stripe-robes and check-robes who sold mangoes inside the corrugated metal boxes under pale yellow-leaved toothbrush trees of Mogadishu. That was it. You waited to sell or you waited to buy, but in any event you waited, your consciousness essentially contingent as Hegel had said somewhere; so the Somali women waited and three Thai girls in tight blue ankle-length dresses ran giggling to the elevator. They were through for the day. — But a girl in street clothes entered like wintertide, passing through the hot velvet darkness where viewers and buyers fed upon each other (one girl lay on the sofa there, and another in a bathing suit trod her back quite lovingly). The new girl folded back the drape that hid a long hall of mildew which stretched to the dressing room where girls sat tweezing themselves before the mirror, and she went in and the drape closed and so she vanished. Behind the oval windows, her colleagues sat very still beside their purses, occasionally running a hand through their long hair. A tall German came in, and they froze into winning statues.

Just a massage, or a real Thai massage? said the German. Fifty dollars with sex?

Yes, said the obliging necktied boy, who'd just smashed a journalist's camera.

For the girl in, uh, red? said the German.

OK, sir.

Soon the girl in red was bending her knee in a kind of curtsey and gesturing the German into the elevator.

Next three Thais came in and drummed ballpoint pens on the glass very thoughtfully while the barman swivelled his stool and tapped a pen on another stool. The three Thais lowered their heads and tucked in their shirts.

Body massage? said the necktied one.

A girl in a bathing suit strode rapidly across the pink world. More girls inhabited its steps now, and they fixed their perfect unmoving heads in the direction of those three men who leaned and drummed and worried about prices. Whenever the girls sat down, they arranged their hair, tucked their skirts up to show a little knee, worshipped compacts, licked lips, then became mannequins. In Thailand were people acquainted with the adamantine heads and shoulders which we call tombstones? *Beneath this Stone are Deposited the Remains of Cap. John Mackay.* Stared a skull with fish-scale angel-wings. Mackay's headstone was canted and darkened. How much farther would it sink this year? H. P. Lovecraft had written that certain gravestones were keys which could be turned to unlock the infernal regions of space. Did all those American flags hinder that? It was Memorial Day in Boston. He sat down upon the mellow green grass fed by so many rotting carcasses of people who had once worried about prices or showed a little knee; and the graves went on like all those houses on stilts just outside Bangkok, each house a patchwork box of rags, an island in canal water green with algae; those were the tombs of poverty, perhaps worse than the tombs of death, perhaps not; and stones weighed down that old burying ground. A panhandler, a paunchy bully, came rattling the money in his paper cup, moaning: I'm doin' real bad! Do you have anybody buried here? and when he shook his head, the panhandler said: There's always room for you. I'll be waitin' for you at the gate because *there's no way out!* and his face split with terrifying glee.

When the women came down from the elevators alone they always looked happy. They gave little slips of paper to the barman to write on and file, and then they went back down the hall of mildew. The boy in the necktie stood in front of the oval windows and added up profits aloud, smiling. (His favorite thing was to go dancing. But whenever other boys asked him how often he went, he'd hang his head as if caught in some lie.)

And he, the traveller and erstwhile weary watcher, thought: This is not the train station or airport, where travellers pass and go, but a hot round world of women going round and round. Only the men disappear.

But then another woman was finished for the day; she smiled and departed, under over somewhere nowhere.

He exulted, and said to himself: Yes, we'll all disappear at last. We have that to hope for. — He'd become a Buddhist like them.

And so he was permitted one more memory which had to do with waiting, a good one this time, because in the belly of a golden tower, Buddha's plump white red-lipped face hid itself, floating above gold robes and white hands and folded knees on shelves of fishy silver, waiting, not watching, willing to let itself be seen but not displaying itself; and in a niche beside it a woman offered fresh leaves and stood praying while another girl sat with her feet tucked behind her and leftward. After many long moments of gazing downward and ahead she pivoted on one of those two crossed feet, pushed with her toes to lean forward, bowed, and bowed again. Then she vanished.

Now he too would disappear. He was going to travel to the world's edge (which lies in Canada), and he was happy.

They came to a wide, still, blue-gray lake, a river with tree-islands perfectly oval like lily-pads. His joy was strong and wide like the ferns around the trunks of birches. Those ferns resembled immense pale green lichens. Every place seemed a luscious place to spend a summer or a life, remote and serene like those sticks almost sunken in weedy water. There was no flaw in this landscape, because it was full of nature and loneliness.

'Tis purty in here, he heard a boy say. All the trees an' stuff.

His joy deepened like black bogs and black pools in the grass.

Clouds of pale leaves and dark needles swirled by. Sumacs, butter-cups, ferns, dandelions gone to seed, grand beech trees, two chrysanthemums in a pot on the topmost strand of a barbed wire fence, forget-me-nots, daisies, reddish boulders gaping out of the softness in the little towns where washing hung between spruce trees like sails too bright and perfect for the whitish plain of water—it was all home even though he'd never seen it before.

The people that are in the sleepers are really nice, but the people that work there are snooty, a little girl said.

The train curved like a silver river.

They were playing cards in the observation car, making fans of their red-backed cards, passing and bidding and drinking Molson in cans as they rode high over so many rock-lipped black pools in the moss, all those ancient folks doing crossword puzzles and showing off pocket knives and laughing and saying: We all gonna get old some-time, but not yet! and everyone happy. — What's trumps? Hearts is trumps.

He remembered Mount Aetna's broad white fang floating in blueness.

Dead trees among the live ones, long blonde grass on the knolls between pools, every now and then a bird winging off the marsh; these things scraped away the last of his unhappiness, which fell into a birch gorge at sunset, into the brown water-mirror of nowhere nothing far below. Thinking he saw some creature in the water, he remembered his friend Joe, who'd said: And the dream was, I was swimming in the Connecticut River with my first love. This girl was a virgin. We were both virgins when we got it on. And her name was Janny and she had long red hair in a ponytail. We were swimming underwater. I remember the sunlight and the trees. We were swim-ming underwater, and things were green and then the water was so clear. Swimming underwater, and all the sudden I hear a voice—a voice! I say, how can I hear a voice? I'm underwater, I'm underwater! And the voice kept saying: *Joe, Joe, Joe!* And I realized that I was gonna drown! I didn't wanna hear that voice; someone's shakin' me: *Joe, Joe, Joe! It's chow time!* And just then they show up with the cornmeal and the beans, and I'm back with bars in front of me! And I say, Oh, no! I'm gonna go back to that place! 'Cause beans and cornmeal, it's the same meal every day. You know, it wasn't anything to wake up to. On my birthday, somebody else gave me their beans. Back in jail again. Nothin' to do but race the cockroaches. Oh, you

catch 'em, you shake 'em hard, and you put 'em on the edge of the
bed. You race 'em for cigarettes. The stupid cockroaches wouldn't
have a sense of direction. You'd have a finish line, but *they* wouldn't
know where the finish line was! They'd just take off anywhere. But
you'd just take their legs off, an' *influence* their direction! I mean, that
was if you wanted to win the cigarettes! You'd have a limited quantity
of cigarettes; you had top cigarettes, and you'd roll 'em real good;
that's one thing I learned in jail, it's to roll 'em, roll a damned neat
cigarette. We had plenty of time to do it, so we'd roll 'em real good,
tight, tuck 'em all in. It wasn't like nowadays, when they give everybody like ten cigarettes a day. We had ten cigarettes a *week,* so you'd
save that cigarette, an' you'd use it for barter, and you'd use it for
favors. Trade it for some cornbread. So the cockroaches . . . I had
one cockroach; it didn't last too long after I pulled its legs off. Most
of 'em got away, though. At nighttime you'd catch 'em. They'd run
across your chest. It was real hot at night. You'd sleep like this, with
your arms folded. And they'd come out of the bed. They'd run across
your chest at night. You'd catch 'em, wrap 'em up, save 'em till
morning. The toilet paper was a stiff type toilet paper, a manuscript
type toilet paper. I mean it wasn't very good for wiping your ass, but
you could write on it. It was the brown paper people used to wipe
their hands on. So we wrapped 'em in clothes, stuck 'em in the
pockets of your clothes. I had this one G.I. jacket with buttons on it,
it was really worn out. I was the Omega Man. I had a button with
the omega sign for resistance; I was resisting the draft . . . Yeah, I
was drafted. I gave 'em a lot of shit. I was 4-F. I'd joined the Marines
when I was seventeen, wanted to go and kill some Commies. Even
lied about my age. But I got in trouble sitting on the bench when
the big black sergeant called my name and I couldn't hear. He'd been
sayin' it for a few minutes. I said oh shit. I was the only one left. Get
over there! So the lieutenant talks to me, he says: I'm sorry, son,
you're just too deaf. He says: You can't pass the hearing test; you
flunked all the hearing tests. Well, I was real sad and everything. I
went out and said to myself: Well, what are you going to do, kid? I
told all my friends: Well, I'm not going. They all shouted: You lucky
bastard! — Well, after that I went to college, and in college I got it
straight. I had history professors, radical history professors. I realized
the whole thing was a scam and I got pretty pissed off. Then we were

real wild. We went wild and made a lot of shit, made a lot of noise because we wanted to hit 'em where it hurt, in the pocketbook. So I got a couple of banks, would trash the street just to make a scene, you know, because my buddies and civilians were dying in Vietnam; everything was all *injustice,* like in Nazi Germany. You had to do *something!* Can't just go to school and get your degree, you know what I mean? — I didn't burn down any buildings, just threw a trash can through a bank window. Trash can was on fire, too! The police came and charged us. We backed up, threw some bricks and bottles and stuff. The police charged again. Then they caught a guy I was with and they beat the shit out of him and backed off and I went to pick him up and all the sudden I felt the darned *presence* and I look up, and they all got their pig masks on and they said something to me: *budufdudufuu!* so I says: *Fuck you, pig!* so they smashed my glasses, split my head open, and I started running down the street and one cop came up behind and hit me on the back with his baton: *whop!* I got away, and some Harvard students pulled me into the dorm and they stitched me up. One guy starts to stitch me up, and he says: No, no, let me do it, I'm a third-year man! They were arguin' over who was gonna stitch me up. I went to school the next day. Both my eyes were black and I had a split-open head and the newspapers were saying: **15,000 RIOT IN HARVARD SQUARE,** so all the teachers knew what I was at. I was one of the movement heavies. Twice in two weeks I got a chokehold from the authorities. So I did that for awhile, and then I started hitchhiking. Had to eat, so I'd sell my blood—oh, many times. You get into town, you sleep in the park, you'd be the first one to get up in the morning, six-o'-clock, go to Peak Load or Manpower. If they didn't call you out that day you had to do something to get money. It wasn't like those spoiled brats they got nowadays or the homeless people. You had to find money. The only way to do it was through work or sell your blood or jerk off, sell your sperm. Oh, you find out. I saw it in Oakland. In fact, I did it in Greece twice in one week. I did it in Utah, I did it in Atlanta; it's just something to do for five or ten bucks. There's nothing to it. Two times in one month, that's too much. You almost pass out from selling your blood twice in a row. Selling your blood isn't much. It's just you get five, ten bucks, you know. But that's a lot of money if you're on the road. Five dollars is really a liberator. Well, now it would be more like twenty dollars. But let me tell you about five dollars. You got five dollars, you can take fifty cents of that, walk around town, find a day-old bakery. You get a loaf of bread for twenty-five cents. And then you're all set. Tie that to your belt, stick the rest of the money in your shoe, keep your change in your pocket, put the three dollars in your shoe, put it between your big toe and your little toe; you're all set, you can sleep anywhere; no one bothers you, as long as you take your shoes off at night, put 'em under your head, use 'em as a pillow, wrap your shirt around 'em. It's a typical thing to do. That's if you're sleeping in a boxcar with other bums around. I wasn't that desperate then, either. Look, if you're hitchhiking around, come into a town, get there early enough, it's a freak town like Denver or Salt Lake City or something, you sleep in the park in a dugout or some baseball park or something, at the first light you get up, and the night before you've looked in the phone book to find out where the Peak Loads and the Manpowers are. Labor pool. So you're first on line in the morning, even though the regulars they're gonna get the jobs. 'Cause you gotta get the job, gotta get that ten bucks, twelve bucks, whatever. Hell, day-old bread only costs a nickel. You just wrap it up, tie it to your belt and hitchhike, hop a freight train or something, and you have a day-old bread on your belt and you're all set for days. Bread and water, that's fine. Cigarettes would be good, too. And then go to sleep, dream good dreams. Everywhere I went, though, I remembered swimming underwater with my first love, and waking up in that lousy jail to find it was just a dream.

As he rode away from Joe he recollected how in Herculaneum steel bars had been installed by the Museum staff in so many of the streetfronted rooms to prevent anyone from damaging the frescoes; thus these curatorial efforts formed an empty afternoon of ruined jails, like Joe's barred rooms reminiscent of prostitutes' cages in Thailand or India. And he wondered which of his own memories were like that, in sight but out of reach like place-names on an atlas page which the eye grazes over. A squirrel descended a tree headfirst. I want to remember my first love, too, he said to himself, but his love was in out up down everywhere everybody. (At the train station in Sydney the man by the turnstile said: Out you go. Off you go. Off we go. Now, where did you want to go?) He'd been too promiscuous. In Cambodia, where everyone talked slowly and dreamily, where even the beggars walked slowly, he could look through the gratings of the restaurant windows and see the cyclists' heads go slowly by. At that time he hadn't finished. He had never wanted to reach through the grating and touch one of those shiny blue Russian-made bikes as it slid by. But the next time he went there the cyclists had begun de-composing into memories; motorbikes had injected themselves onto the scene, in accordance with the smog dialectic. He said: I guess I should start remembering these bicycles. He said: I want to remember my first love, every time everywhere forever. In the French restaurant across from the Hotel Papillon, boys in clean shirts slowly, almost silently tried to sell him things. They squinted and wrote out the prices in thousands of riels, and began to pray the count of bills when-ever he bought something. The hundred-riel notes were jungle-green, with a socialist face, stern and green, hair cropped back like some Viet Cong general's. He could almost remember his first love's face. The city seemed empty that first time. Had so many been killed? Of course Bangkok had been very crowded; most other cities would seem empty after Bangkok. The boys in clean shirts went out, and he could see them through the restaurant grating and then they were gone.

They passed an abandoned beaver dam in a winding river that reflected everything in the hue of a sepia-tinted photograph. The river was widening, the trees lowering. Admiring the turf of the winding banks so overhung with bushes and rich grasses, he said to himself: This is Joe's river. If Joe were here with me he'd dive beyond those grimacing branches of dead spruces to be with that virgin he loved; he'd find her here. What kind of jail would that be?

Rocks furred with blueberry bushes sank their snouts into blue lakes. An osprey flapped low with open talons. Knowing that very soon now he'd vanish forever from the atlas, he felt a happy excite-ment. His eyes drank from ponds whose rich mud tinted them the color of wine.

Then sunlight crazed the river strangely, turning it the exact hue of a sheet of yellow paper on which his first love had written: *Last night I dreamed we were both in a double bed with the covers pulled up over our heads. We were wearing karate type pants. You had longish hair. It looked really dark against mine. Our legs were stretched out in front of us and there was a cat purring between mine. She was black and white and her head was resting against my knee. It was all very warm. The cat got up and walked over my stomach to my chest. She started licking my breasts and neck. It tickled and you were laughing and I pushed her away. Then I woke up. At first I felt really happy. My body was excited but I was so tired and warm, I curled up. I began to think about you and suddenly I panicked. I had this irrational fear that you were just pretending to care for me to "get even." You were going to make me care for you, let me love you, and then, for educational purposes, to justify your own pain, you were going to cut yourself off completely from me. I got out of bed and reread all your letters from this summer. At that hour they struck me as dignified, careful, cold, impersonal. Then I cried myself to sleep. This morning I put the letters away and thought: sad, silly girl.* And on the back of the sheet, almost at the bottom, she'd written: *I don't really want to ask you this and I won't ask it again but I'm rather insecure today. Do you love me?*

Did I? Do I? So many years ago now she'd married somebody else. Now she had cancer. On the envelopes to her letters there were thirteen-cent butterfly stamps. In the upper lefthand corner was the address of where she'd been when she was a girl. If he ever went searching for her, he wouldn't go to the house where she lived with her husband and three children. He'd go back to that town of streets now empty of people he knew, long and empty and wide like the boulevards of Tamatave. He did not really remember the town of her girlhood at all. Memory is declivous, sinking of its own weight into the mucky ponds. That new virus he'd read about that converts a person into black slime in three days, perhaps it was but the counterpart of what forgetting does more slowly to the soul. For he could remember the excitement he'd felt when her letters alighted in his mailbox one by one, but the flagrant fragrant emotion that had rushed into his lungs when he'd opened each envelope so long ago could only be faked now, not recapitulated. The letters were now near as old as he and she had been when she'd written them. Once he started to reread them, but some were typed and some were written in her intense and crabby longhand; he'd read only the typed parts because he was tired and his eyes hurt. *This is getting too long,* she'd written, and he thought: I guess that's true of my life. *I meant to be civil but not chatty. I am selfish and nasty now, hardly nice. I like my life the way it is now because it's mostly private and very much my own.* Then she'd crossed two or three lines out and continued: *I'm being rude. I just want to go away and think again.* He thought that he remembered (he wasn't certain) spending an hour or more trying to make out the rude part, and now if he really wanted to do it, all he'd have to do would be to call the CIA. It wasn't that he didn't care; his mind and soul had gone so many times abroad, each time ensaring him in new experiences from which, struggling to get free or to dig himself deeper, he'd dusted and buried his past. That muffledness made him wonder whether the fact that he still loved her (or at least her memory) might be grotesque. Everything made him tired. Thinking of her afforded him pleasure even now; but those stale letters were like draghooks to pull him down. Closing his eyes, he watched her signature form itself like sky-writing on the insides of his eyelids. The words she scripted could never change. Time had split her farther and farther from what she had been. At least they were *her* letters. *His* letters would have been worse. The reflections of grass-tufts in dark water all around made it seem that the land was just as green underneath and that it floated on darkness. He'd go under to find the women who'd loved him. He'd live and leap on the islands of red rock in the forest. A bird winged like his heartbeats.

A mother read to her child: *In the forest, the Iroquois were waiting for something.*

The sky was a ceiling of blue crystal held up with white pillars of birch carpeted so richly with evening ferns. It was that time when the light goes out of lakes.

Near Sudbury it got sandy with hard white dunes and it was grassier and rockier but there were many fish-ripples in the streams. The reflections of birchtop and sprucetop serrations were almost black, and blue cloud-reflections swam in the brown sky. Birch groves fingered evening's green wall with their skeleton hands. That long train the sheen of evening grass followed the sky.

Now the trees began to rise up taller into the night, and the fish-rippled ponds were tarnished blackish-brown. He saw a sudden gash of blue and white light on a lake whose tree-reflections were wide enough apart to let in a little last sky-color, and then he put his head down in his seat and slept.

The next morning was skygray and evergreen. Tall narrow firs were packed together as tightly as poles in a palisade. (He remembered Mexico's railing-teeth on grinning balconies.) Behind and between the tops of them, other trees flashed, helmeted guards of each other's greenness. Then suddenly from the pale bushes rose tall and grizzled stalks like arrow-shafts. There had been a fire here, perhaps three or four years ago. Now the birches returned to flash their skinny white throats, their striped white necks, keeping the firs and spruces small; now the spruces choked everything else out.

Really pretty muskeg, a mother was saying to her children.

Mommy, can we live here?

Well, do you see all the standing water? That means there's lots and lots of mosquitoes and blackflies.

But he thought to himself: They feel it, too. They want to live here, too.

In a field of gray ponds and grass-haired water, he saw three little black ducks.

Past a lake which they crossed by trestle bridge there were an Anglican church, a red building, a log house and upended aluminum canoes. Indians stood in the high buttercupped grass, watching the train. The boys and girls pretended to hit each other, laughing. The older ones just stood there. They loaded some boxes and coolers onto the train, and a few of the teenagers got on. That was in Allan Water, Ontario. Then the train went west.

Half an hour later they reached Savant Lake. There were more Indians, in flannel shirts, old sneakers, windbreakers, tall rubber boots, baseball hats in that town of long ago whitewashed houses among the flowery grass, tall white crosses, some trailers, a propane truck, then more birch trees.

He had begun to believe that this might be one of those perfect days which are sometimes given to you so gently and lovingly that they are half over before you comprehend their perfection. Amidst blackened backbones of dead firs sprung crazily with lichens he re-membered the steep streets of Taxco, Mexico, narrower than your outstretched hands, whose stones had been worn dangerously smooth; sometimes there was grass, sometimes a smell of urine, always cool darkness from behind the window-grilles of the overhanging houses; he'd walked there with a woman he'd loved, held back from her heart by arch-windowed, bar-windowed white houses—a world of white houses with cryptic windows to make them into dominoes under the awnings where the juice-bottles stood; and now he didn't know where that woman was anymore.

And the Bible said: *Do not desire her beauty in your heart, and do not let her capture you with her eyelashes; for a harlot may be hired for a loaf of bread, but an adulteress stalks a man's very life. Can a man carry fire in his bosom and his clothes not be burned? Or can one walk upon hot coals and his feet not be scorched? So is he who goes in to his neighbor's wife; none who touches her will go unpunished.* They transected a lovely gray water-plain with brown highlights. The sun shone on spiderstrands as fine and blonde and precious as the hairs he found on his pillow after kissing the first girl he ever loved. And the Qur'-An said: *It was said to her: Enter the pavilion. But when she saw it, she supposed it was a spreading water, and she bared her legs. He said: It is a pavilion smoothed of crystal. She said: My Lord, indeed I have wronged myself, and I surrender with Solomon to God, the Lord of all Being.* A pale blue lake was sublated.

An old Polish lady got on at Sioux Lookout. She'd lived there for forty years. She had three children, eleven grandchildren and one great-grandchild. She said she picked lupines as high as her shoulder —red, blue, yellow, purple, so beautiful! She ate beaver meat all the time: not just the tail, but the whole beaver, boiled an hour, then roasted. She loved to eat black bear meat, too, but beaver was the best, served on a plate of wild rice. She said she'd had a good life and was still having one. — When you get old, you know what you have to look forward to, she said. So why not go on enjoying yourself as long as you can?

She thought he was crazy to be going into the wilderness alone.

Now it was blue and white in Heaven instead of gray, so the land was the color of blueberry bushes in summer and the lakes were the color of blueberries.

Can I try beaver meat in Winnipeg? he said.

I don't know. I have no one there, so I never go there. Find an Indian.

She saw some teenagers drinking from a water bottle. — They brought their own water, she said. That is very good.

Fringy frothy green growth, moist, cloudy and sprucified, guarded an island like a swimming stegosaurus. They passed a still lake's black-streaked white cliff; and a memory of happiness flashed in him like some crescent-shaped brown pond, rock-shelved and hid in birchy wilderness. Everything was good; goodness was water trickling down sunburned rock.

At Reddit he spied an island whose small steep-roofed house was half hidden by trees; at the lake's edge was a dock and a canoe. He wanted to go wherever the canoe went but already it was gone and they passed a station that said BLUE HERON and MOCCASINS and SOUVENIRS; they passed Ottermere with its birch-clumped mowed lawns; then Malachi, the last book in the Old Testament, hence the last town in Ontario; beside a low-wooded lake he read the sublinear gloss: two moose and a black bear . . .

Between Malachi and Winnitoba, which is the first town in Manitoba, he recollected for accidental reasons Diesel Bend, Utah, where he'd gone north through the green fields walled in by trees, the little farms and white houses all embraced by those chalky cliffs in which fossil fishes are sometimes found; these, too, were tree-greened . . . and farther ahead lay the blue blue mountains that made you know you were going north. Families were sitting on the porch in the evening or hoeing their gardens, and beautiful white horses swished their tails, and everything smelled like clover. Diesel Bend was not so different from Winnitoba. But, like a platter of Mexican marzipans made to resemble miniature fruits (papayas studded with chocolate seeds, strawberries, pale green pears), while in color and sweetness they might approximate each other, there was no sameness anywhere (his clawing at identities but a failure even when he looked out into sunlight, his self but a grimacing face in chill sea-foam). No two things are not disparable, although life's proprieties pretend otherwise. His first love's letters lay sweetly in their envelopes, whose righthand edges had each been snipped just so because he'd loved her so much that he didn't want to mar anything with her writing on it; each envelope was from her to him, with a thirteen-cent stamp on it—but how disparable! The one that had been addressed in crayon contained a page which said: *Of course Tina thought I was fantastic or unique.* He had no idea who Tina had been. He was fairly sure that he'd never met her. His first love had passionately snatched up so many people, bringing them to her heart; and then when they hurt her or she tired of them she'd throw them away again. He'd be surprised if she still knew Tina. He'd be astonished if she still thought about whether or not she was unique. That was what adolescents did. He had done it. *But it wasn't because I was; it was because of the life I led, living in a suite with six young men, drinking bourbon straight in my footy-pajamas in front of the fireplace, knowing the owner of the local Irish pub, seeing a cardiologist, an internist, having physical problems unique to my age, making love, roaming Philly, spending afternoons at the zoo like a child, balloon in hand. When the dope came in I sometimes had to weigh it and check it. But I am the same as I always was, mostly. I am not so unique now because the novelty isn't there.* She had tried so hard to be bad, to be glamorous, to have adventures. And she'd had them. Then what? In Thailand all the rigid figures relax into motion again at the end of the national song. (The train passed narrow-needled cones of green.) A mutual friend, now dead, had once told him that she was not and never had been unique. But everybody is disparable, and everybody dies. *In answer to your picture: there are no squares, right? Only in three dimensions and I didn't know that counted. Are we getting to know one another quite well? I don't know you too well. But I suppose I'm willing to learn as you let me and to let me know you as you wish.* The sweet earnestness of this young girl aroused his tenderness. Now he could be good to her. He could give her money and let her be and do whatever she pleased. That was goodness, wasn't it? *I think this is an awful state—being in love. I wonder why people do it. I was happier not loving. That's a lie, you know. You are all I have in my life now that can make me happy. Of course you are also capable of making me miserable. After all, I am still feeling like a part of me is missing.* He read that in amazement. Did I really have the power to make another person happy or unhappy? Was I ever that much alive? *Jesus, I want to die of leukemia, too. Perhaps we are too much alike in thought.* And now she had cancer and he didn't. The weirdness of her having wished that so many years ago chilled him. He had wished it, too, solely because she did: a true puppy lover, he'd yearned to be counted among the hues of her iridescence. Neither of them could have known what leukemia was. He supposed that she knew now. *I'll do what you asked about the drinking. I suppose if it were for myself I would continue to drink and smoke. I want to die young, you know, and in disgrace.* But then sodden mossy trees bloomed in his brain with white mushroom cups around which regiments of ants hurried on their voracious errands. It was cool and humid in the bamboo tunnels between dripping ivied boulders as high as two tall men. Water leaped down like liquid dirt, spewing and dipping in clumps as of an old dog's hair, seething into brown pools whose mist was drunk by pale yellow butterflies beneath those living fishing rods that grew down,

steadying themselves with spade-shaped leaves, reaching wooden feel-
ers into the water. That was the place of reddish-brown waterfalls
near Chiang Mai; that was the place of cool sweat and slippery jungle
paths. He'd ridden a train from there back down into the lowlands,
the ricefields whose muddy rivers relaxed from time to time by forming cloudy puddles in which the travelling sun was reflected. An occasional tree rose out of the rice, with water around its roots. The
bitter smell of diesel-smoke was exhaled by the train. The cloud-map
rushed across square lakes of green-stubbled water. His wife put her
arm around him as they passed an old ruined wat with dogs loping
its edges (white birds on the ricefields), then another small wat rising
gold-curlicued and red-roofed in the fields and his wife, his dear and
darling wife, was whispering: *I love you same same crocodile . . .* He was
beside her in Bangkok walking to the seafood restaurant, every street
calf-deep in brown water, so the two of them splashed barefoot—so
pleasant to feel the warm dirty water against one's feet—and at last
they arrived at the restaurant with its decorative tree dried leaves and
all, studded with lights, ice and crabs in the windows. You could
order *Steammed Crab in Shredded Jelly, Fried Frog with Garlic, Peppered
Paisa Serpent-Head Fish,* or *Steammed Crab with Anything.* Ladies whose
arms glowed with gold bracelets nibbled happily at breaded crab. The
windows steamed themselves up against the hot rainy night. The waiters in their immaculate black vests and bow ties always smiled. It was
a very happy restaurant, and he was happy; he said *I LOVE YOU* to
his wife. (She cried later, of course, because he had to go away.)

    We're going to stop here and pick up some guy we threw off the
other day, said the conductor. I hear he's got more money now, or
at least some blueberries.

    Rice Lake, next stop! shouted the conductor, and there was a lake
with grasslike tufts and clutches of wild rice, some sky-spaced
pines . . .

    He saw nothing but a one-row station and grass—maybe a town,
maybe not.

    I want to make love with you before I grow old and ugly, one of his first
love's letters said. *I want someone to enjoy what I have, now, while it is
sweet and strong. I want to be hard, with many facets and moods. I don't
want to be stable. I want to be stable and secure. I want to be loved. I want
to spin, pushing myself around and around, living a fast, crazy, creative*

destructive existence. I want to give myself away and throw myself out a twentieth-storey window. And I want to live with you, away from everything. I want to lie in a bed, garden, laugh and weep. I want to have a baby.

How many twentieth-story windows can you throw yourself out of? he wanted to ask her. That has sometimes been my life. But unfortunately when I aim for concrete the ground always turns out to be Jell-O and goose-down and rubber. That's why you got the cancer and I didn't. Nobody can kill me. Not even I can kill me. You had already been married for years the time the bullet jammed.

Suddenly he wondered what would have happened if he had left college that last year and hitchhiked those two thousand five hundred star-edged miles in order to make her truly know and believe that he wanted to be with her forever. At the time he used to sleep with her letters under his pillow. He was still a virgin.

Probably she was already seeing someone else.

And now, which everybodies, somebodies and nobodies didn't he see?

But he had to know. The telephone slept like a tiny white shark. He seized it by the flanks, lifted it from the plastic it dreamed in, and dialled.

Mrs. Teitelbaum is sleeping, said the nurse. Is it important? Should I disturb her?

No, it's not important, he said. I'm an old friend. I just wanted to know how she was doing.

I want to know that, too, said the nurse warmly. Let me go upstairs and check to see if she's taken her medication.

He waited and then he heard the receiver being lifted on the other end and he knew that it was his love and even five years before his heart would have soared but now his hair had begun to turn gray and his heart never soared except when he smoked crack, and anyhow it was only the nurse who said: She says she'll call you, maybe next week.

Where do you come in? she'd written. Have I lied to you again? Have I made promises I can't keep? Have I hurt you yet again? Shit. I warned you, I told you, I deny responsibility, but in the end, if it hurts, it'll be my fault. I DON'T KNOW. HOW CAN I KNOW? WHAT IS HAP-PENING? Oh, I don't know if I love you. I don't know if I don't. Sex is a weapon. It will be used. It doesn't hurt me as much as it hurts the men. We're friends, we're lovers? No, we're not lovers. I am not and never have been lovers with anyone. I will write you before I leave. God, I'm not sure about all this.

Now he did feel something. With all his soul he wanted to say to the girl who no longer existed that it was all right. (Outside the train window rushed the gunmetal dapplings of dark ponds. He saw a squirrel's raised tail in the leaves.) He wouldn't embrace her because she wouldn't like it. He wouldn't demonstrate through any gesture of puerile romanticism how she who once had been the center not only of his selfish desires but also of much of the goodness and generosity which slept within him now remained and would always be his—no matter that he'd long ago lost of her all but the memory; as someone in his past she'd yearly become (in a secret all too well kept from himself) more and more a part of him, her trace so permeating him that he was hardly conscious of it. The proof was the physical weight of the grief he felt (as if he were carrying a backpack of leaden sadness) once he understood that she might die within months. You see, he loved her so much. — He'd confine himself to stating that nothing was or had been her fault, and even that communication could be reburied under his breastbone if its presentation would interrupt her (on the rare occasions when he did telephone her and got beyond the nurse, she'd say: Who's this?); he'd explain that he had no desire to ask anything of her because he had other wives now and would never be lonely. He only wanted her to be happy if she could. If she had any notion of how he could help her, he would do whatever she asked. He'd lay everything out for her with the utmost service and ceremony, just like the waiter at the Hotel Thanada in Rangoon who put on his glasses whenever you ordered, then carefully polished each utensil that he brought you, making one trip for the fork, one for the knife, one for the spoon, cleaning each of these in a once-white rag before setting it noiselessly in front of you on the greasy tablecloth. That was service from the heart. If she didn't want that, he would think kindly of her and return to his various rushing trains. But that scared girl was not there anymore. He could not find her, no matter where in the world he went. She was gone. She was not dead yet, only gone. She did not need his love and care anymore. She never had, because what he'd possessed she never wanted. Now she needed chemotherapy, and then pills to stop vomiting, and a wig to hide her baldness, and more pills for weeping and for pain.

He began to dream, going someplace that he could not remember which made him feel serene. In the gloom of his dreams, brown mosquitoes hung like dust-motes. He sank inside Battle Rock, outside him seedheads of grasses shuddering and hissing in the violent wind of a cloudless afternoon, the sea slightly greener than turquoise, black-berries ripe and past ripe. What a tangled quilt of reeds, ferns, thistles and poison oak there was on this high rock of tall grasses blinking in the wind like eyelashes; and he was underneath it. The globe turned outside of him; outside of him life sped like the winds that pressed any lighthouse cape in Oregon where golden grass-stalks locked the sun in a million-barred prison that continually writhed and gnashed its lips, with the wild sea all around. He might have slept. Then blackberry spiders crawled over him, brilliant silver spider swarms that soothed him with mosquito shade and warmed him with maple leaf sunshine. Time was infusing itself into him; he was healing or perhaps just changing. The train traversed the sky. Green boulders, brown water, everywhere no one forever. At twilight a dark stream sped down its own cusp and became white, the crowded drops playing arpeggios on rock and then separating, falling separately together to the brown pool below that was ringed with fernclaws. Old man's beard hung from dusty shrub-walls. The undersides of maple leaves were translucent green windows to the twilight. He left them behind, ascending a steep gray path toward the dreariness of night rock. — Close your eyes, said the girl in the treehouse, lowering the shirt and pants from the string as if she were bringing a hanged corpse back to earth. — Still close 'em! — The other girl closed her eyes obe-diently, dancing around on the lawn. — He fell crashing down from his dreams. But when he awoke the train was still bringing him safely away from everything; and the man across from him who was getting old offered him a sausage and then fell asleep quickly and unknow-ingly; in rest the man looked so happy and refreshed; that was what he'd needed; his head lay on the back of his chair as trees trotted by, the ground with them rolling back up like the receptacle cylinder of a scroll. And he who watched felt that the dreams had left a strange and special residue inside his skull, one of those mineral salts that makes a candle burn in spooky colors. It was like a Sunday in Budapest when pigeons, families and middle-aged women paused before the windows of closed shops. What was in the darkness behind those displays of sparseness? That is what we ask our minds when we're afraid. The greenish river curved creamily round the pilings of the greenpainted bridge, every rivet of which was green. Across the river the tree-crowned cliffs had been cut away and cragged with towers and domes of its own substance. That was Gellert Rampart, and crossing the bridge he'd found it choked with garbage, the aged domes now tarnished, cracked and reeking of the piss of drunks. But it rained birds sideways along those streets of flats textured like waffles, and he liked that. The plum trees were flowering white and pink in Budapest, and a fat raven hunched his shoulders on a branch, picking at wet wood. On the side of a dumpster it said HEJ HITLER. Hitler, it would seem, was still a place-name in many atlases. A stout old man paced slowly down the path, both hands behind his back and locked around a chisel. It was one of those Sunday afternoons in the middle of spring when the wet grass (already transcendently covered by dandelions) became all the more enriched by the sky's gray, while the clouds, so deliciously bruised by the pressure of their own rain, became greener like wet moss on a slate tombstone—all this going on around a coast of steep red roofs which had long since frozen their gestures into spires. Then the thunder began, a little before the rain which now commenced to break out of that sky of polychromatic grays. The birds continued to sing. It came down so hard that he could see it dancing like dust or smoke off the roofs of cars, and whenever it struck the sidewalk it seemed to form stalagmites of water stretching explosively back upward. The streets were so wet now that they crackled like bacon under the taxicabs, and the blush of headlights across a streaming auto's rear window was every bit as subtle as the cloud-shades had been. So that was Sunday, and the next morning he bought his ancient landlady some chocolates in the Lebensmittel store just around the corner from Red Love Massage; and at the train station he changed forints for dollars and deutsche marks with the Algerians who stood near the pillars in the waiting room. His Algerian preferred to speak French. The Algerian agreed that deutsche marks were probably best. He said that he had been in Beograd before the war but not now; he had no advice on what to trade there. Men in fat coats passed, smoking cigarettes; old women in shawls carried bags; old men took only their hats; a tall bald man whose face resembled a sardonic Roman emperor's passed unanswerably, and the Algerians huddled around their pillar and whispered. His future stretched on like the long groove of double railroad ties that went past that bane of the Algerians, the official moneychanging office; and the tracks continued past the travel agencies, the news stands, whose foremost publication showed a woman licking a curvy penis; went on past the stand of canted fruits and escaped at last from under the arches of glass and black lines like cables or wires, some of which formed a face with a gaping mouth; and then they went on under the white sky all the way to Beograd, where he knew that he would be the enemy. Perhaps that was why he went there; he'd always been attracted to lamias as well as chimeras. It is perhaps too easy to say that self-destructiveness is an attribute of certain members of the propertied class. Poor people destroy themselves in their own way. By Lenin's standards he lived a meaningless life which required infantile romanticism to stimulate a spuriously healthy blush in the tissues of pale lassitude. By his own standards he was simply looking for something. He wanted to see the world, that was all. He wanted to know and love the entire atlas. As far as Beograd went, fear was a secretary typing up a long list of scary reasons. He had once been a secretary himself and knew that lists are always revised. Two years previous, in Muhammed's bar in Zagreb the list of reasons not to proceed to Sarajevo had been voluminous, so it became irresistibly prudent to figure out what to do upon arrival at that city's sandbagged airport, now surrounded by snipers. As the brochure from the 1984 Winter Games had put it so magically, *The noble Olympic spirit experienced full satisfaction in Sarajevo, and for that reason it will certainly in the future attract travellers from all over the world who are desirous not only of new natural but also of new spiritual horizons.* — Fine. Here I come. — So he was buying thick sweet dark Tomaslav beers for sundry members of the secret order of Bosnian Dragons (whom the Serbs in Beograd would later assure him existed only in enemy legends) and in return the Dragons were explaining to him exactly how easy it would be. — From the airport go by car to the UNPROFOR encampment, a big man said, gesturing like a falcon stabbing its beak into the meat of another dead bird. At UNPROFOR you can telephone our commander. They have a nice yellow building, about a hundred and fifty meters away. But you must be very careful because anything could happen to you. — And then what? he said. — Tell them to hang in there. Victory is ours. — I want to run through this one more time, he said. Can I walk to this yellow building from UNPROFOR? — Yes! the man said. — No! said another Muslim. You must request five soldiers to escort you. — You must go by car, insisted a third fighter. And never go alone. — Best to go alone, opined a fourth. That way you'll be less conspicuous to the enemy. — I get it, he said wearily. And will UNPROFOR ask me any questions? — Oh, those Serb-loving bastards! the Bosnian Dragons all shouted. Tell 'em to fuck their mothers! — That was when he had realized that he could not expect and would never have any good advice when he went to wars because wars were by definition processes which strove to make advice obsolete. That was why children, old ladies, mapmakers, commandos and wise men all got holes in their heads. Perfect. There was webbing over the windows of the Hercules, and evil yellow lights glared out of the steel ceiling. He remembered all the hours and days spent on airplanes when they wouldn't let anybody look out the window even when overflying beautiful Greenland because that might pale their movie which crawled so nauseatingly and inanely upon its soulless screen. At least there would be no movie today. A man in green fatigues leaped in and mounted to the cockpit. Another soldier came, slammed the entry hatch behind him, shone his flashlight through that steely room, and also went forward. Just before that one disappeared, he turned back to the traveller and shouted over the engine (for the engine was howling like a spoiled child): After you talk about places you'd rather be, there's not a hell of a lot to say! — It was not going to be a nice day. — A moment later the comedian stuck his face back through the opening. He was smoking a cigarette. He shouted: No rules in war! In Beirut some dumb broad told me smoking's bad for your health. I says to her, I says, that's the least of my worries! — A tight-lashed stack of cargo boxes quivered as the plane began to move. His own bulletproof vest embraced him comfortingly, heavy and firm like a wall against his back and his first love in his lap. The groin protector came down almost to his knees. He tightened the four straps still further so that the weight and rigidity they empowered could more firmly encourage his hollow, fuming stomach (the rest of him was cold, numb and ever so slightly drizzled with sweat), and he felt calm and satisfied that he had prepared himself as well as he could, having not yet learned that a certain grasshopper-green Warsaw Pact vest obtainable only through illegal trade covered the armpits and that special cylinder of flesh beneath the chin, the black market vest's shelter for which consisting of a doughnutlike collar that might be useful as a neckrest for snoozing on long bus rides: You forgot about your carotid artery! sneered one of the many well-wishers one meets in this life. One nick from a bit of shrapnel and you'll bleed to death! But not *me*, buddy, *I* went Warsaw; *I'm* protected! — Trembling, roaring and buzzing, the Hercules departed. The atlas slammed open. And then it was very hot and loud and nothing happened for a long time, and through the window-webbing he saw pale brown hills, bare and riven earth, a vast lake of blue, slightly tinted white. So this was the vortex. The plane was circling again. They were going down. The cargo hatch was already opening as the plane hit the runway, and hot white light poured in. Somebody was shouting. As he ran across the tarmac he saw two plumes of black smoke far away, and he heard a thud. A crash. A thud. A thud. A thud. Among the red-roofed houses across the runway one car moved in the next hour. One house appeared to be raggedly half-finished, as if the workmen didn't know the meaning of a straight line. Black smoke was coming out of it. A thud. He entered the airport sprinting, and they told him to sit on the floor behind a wall of sandbags. A departing journalist in a flak jacket of slender stopping power was pacing, unable to stop whistling. The man lit one cigarette after another with shaking fingers. A crash. A terrifying boom. The UNPROFOR security man behind the desk, which was actually a slab of laminated plywood and fiberboard resting on a radiator and a stack of sandbags, glanced out the window, mildly interested. The nearest minaret had just been brought up to date with a new hole. The security man thought for awhile. Then he got out his camera and took a snapshot, like a dutiful tourist who'd paid admission to a castle or museum of small merit. — Five observers got hit by a mortar round the other day and had to be evacuated, a soldier was saying, and another soldier was explaining on the telephone: Well, we watch to see what they're firing and when they're firing, and write down the serial numbers, so when they say we have only five weapons we can say, look, there are nine hundred and seventy-three fucking weapons and here are the fucking serial numbers. — A French freelancer came in limping. He'd been at the cemetery, filming the latest funeral, and was awarded two shell fragments in his leg. — The traveller, the new boy, sat against his sandbags taking all this in, and finally, recalling the directions of the Bosnian Dragons, said to the security man: So, how do I get to the UNPROFOR encampment? — The security man laughed in his face. — That's your problem, buddy. You can talk to MOVCON if you want, but the answer's gonna be no. — There were good UN guys, too, who shook his hand whenever they went off shift and said: See you later. Keep your head down. — He never did reach the commander in the yellow building to give him the message that victory was ours; a week later, in fact, he was informed that the Serbs had captured him and most of his men; the Bosnian Dragons who gave him this pleasant news, before dismissing him with a well-bred rendering of the Bosnian Dragon anthem on a battery-powered cassette machine, remarked that in any event the detachment in the yellow building had existed with no legal basis prior to its liquidation. — After a day of sitting on his sandbags, hoping doggishly for someone to give him a ride, sipping at his bottle of Zagreb tap water, forbidden, like other personnel not connected to the UN, to use the lavatory, some American journalists took disgusted pity upon his lowliness. At a run he helped carry their video camera cases to the car, which received a solitary bullet during the zoom to town; the hole was a few inches from his ankle. There were three journalists in the car. One was very friendly and kind, one was neutral, and the third, a redhead who never forgot her own admirableness, asked what he was doing here. He said that he was writing a feature. — Oh, my God, the redhead said. He's in *features*. — They said little to him after that. But they had rescued him; if it hadn't been for them, MOVCON would have made him go back to Zagreb on the last flight. They dropped him at the TV station, which was thick-walled; later somebody else gave him a lift to the Holiday Inn, the journalist hotel; and that night he listened to machine-gunners playing their instruments like musicians in that dark night, one flashlight illuminating the room while the battery powered radio spoke of bananas, and the man whose room it was moved the flashlight a little further from the window to decrease the likelihood that the musicians would shoot into it; came a shell, and then an AK-47 burst in a nasty hard rhythm accompanied by its lethal sparkles, and the radio kept talking about bananas. No more nowhere never. So he went inside the pale green foliage of Canada (too early yet to find those yellow leaves drilled with insect holes of beautiful regularity), not into the clouds or lake; each leaf was a thought with a voice, and because they all whispered at once, none could be heard save by dreamers who heard them all, and having heard so much, the dreamers could not remember the words. They passed Elma with its cut logs and white cross, and right there the fields commenced so that his dreams had to be hotter and sleepier now, wandering under the short-cropped sod. Then the trees rushed back. *Tonight I am thin and tall: blue jeans and T-shirt, sexy but vulnerable. I feel disoriented tonight. Sis and I talked for about forty-five minutes. I was shaky and a little too intense for her. You are much more suitable as a midnight confessee (confessor?). It did us both good, Sis and I, to talk. Sitting in her room, I felt I was talked into a patch of black velvet. She wasn't visible, and my eyes made funny lights out of the darkness. Maybe I am seeing the aurora that is her "essence." The only thing clearly visible was the top half of her clock and the folds of her bed ruffle. Intimate conversations with a bed ruffle. I want to reach you but you're not there. The waste of my love goes on tonight.* Are first loves always unhappy? This question, which echoed precious, rhetorical, absurd even as he posed it (how desperately serious she'd been! Was her young love better or purer then, that the absence of its object could waste it?) was one he did not know how to answer. Her love had not been unhappy in the end; her husband and three small children had led her to a perfection of a sort (or at least it seemed so to her now, because she might be taken away from them swiftly). — Nor had his own career of the affections been ill-starred. He remembered, for example, one woman gentle and sunny, remembered those long warm beautiful sunny days in her house of joy, the fans turning at different speeds, her hips like music, other white houses seen through the blinds. That had been in Key West. At a quarter till midnight he was sitting in her house with a flamenco album playing; and in a denim shirt she sat with her small dark clipboard upon her jackknifed knees as she smoked a long cigarette, her face a little older than when he'd last seen it three or four years ago but also even dearer, her slender body as taut and lovely as ever. The light from her praying mantis of a

lamp outlined the right side of her long oval face and her right leg
and knee. She was writing very seriously. She lowered her knees,
took a sheet of paper off the clipboard, then brought her knees up
again, and he looked at her and remembered how they'd made love
all afternoon, six or seven hours! and she'd had her knees around his
neck, and she'd had her knees across his chest, and she'd had her
knees bent around his waist; and he'd been kissing her cigarette-
flavored mouth so many times and then he'd taken her pretty little
nipples between his lips. She sat across from him with her knees drawn
up like a sweet little frog and the midnight breeze stirred outside and
the fan made her fern twitch like his straining face between her thighs,
and she sat thinking, with all the oils and graphite sketches on the
walls around her. There was a young girl painted six times into the
same beach scene: once groping and grabbling in the sand, twice
wading in the swirly turquoise sea, once sitting demurely in a wickerwork beach chair, once gangling her skinny legs as she gazed down
at her own wet shadow upon the changing sands; and once squatting
with her knees out, showing teeth and tongue in a hilariously rude
face. Across the room were the drawings that began her "Venus"
series: the constructivist figures which were so elfin and strangely
lifelike, black and white and black and white with powerful skeletons
showing themselves inside the naked girls. (He'd seen how when she
painted the German girl naked she used glowing yellow watercolors
with a few blues and oranges to form the translucent bones inside.
She gave her long slender arms and legs which were bent but still
reaching out for the balance of those beautiful geometries which almost always skulk away from us. The German girl dreamed. When
she painted the German girl she flexed her legs and danced around
the canvas; she said that she had to paint with her entire body.) She
wrote on, not quite smiling. And the next afternoon mangoes were
falling outside and a lizard scurried past one of her half-awake cats as
she came to him on the sofa wiggling the soft tanned toes that he'd
kissed; she was resting now, breathing, her lovely face inside her
folded arms, all of her still except for her waist gently contracting in
a slow rhythm; then she turned onto her back and her homemade
dress rode up above her knees so that he could see again the reddish
goldish pubic hair he'd played with all morning; he'd made love to
her mainly with his hands, her body so deliciously sentient that a long

soft stroking of her back and buttocks could bring her to orgasm as she lay on top of him, riding his thigh (it's all done with hipbones, a lesbian once explained); or a gentle clockwise twirling of his fingers in her vulva could also make her happy. The more hours they spent making love, the wilder he became about her. Whenever he'd given her great pleasure she'd fall down limply on top of him, her breasts and back so rich with sweat that he could draw his hands through it and then lick the droplets off his fingers. During intercourse he felt not only the pleasure and power of giving her joy, and the joy of giving to one who took so happily and well, but also an almost mystical feeling that her body was speaking to his fingers and mouth, saying exactly what was needed and wanted for its happiness, and that because through some miracle his fingers and mouth understood and answered and gave, her body spoke to his with more and more freedom and joy, giving him back all the sweetness he was giving and wanted to give, so that when he slid his hands up and down her back, for instance, his fingers experienced like special molasses seasoned with hibiscus flowers a sensation, as thickly material as that liquid which dripped from her clitoris, and her musky moans perfumed him with joy. He learned her silent signs and ways. When he'd first reach between her buttocks and work his hand farther to the mound of hair, the double lips inside already parted to receive his caress, he'd know by the heaviness of her eyelids and the workings of her throat that he'd found the right way to touch her, and a quarter-hour later, when her pelvis began its first slow inchwormings of joyous measurements, this confirmation that he had understood filled him with thankfulness. — Nonetheless, with her he was impotent. On the very first night with his first condom he'd been able to do the deed, but after that, even though his penis might be rigid with feeling or even need as he played with her during all those hours, it collapsed as soon as he put the rubber on. This was not frustrating for him physically. With her he did not need to ejaculate. He drank his delight through his hands. But he was afraid that no matter how many orgasms he gave her, even when he worked two fingers in deep, thrusting and corkscrewing in ways he could never have done with his penis, no matter how many times she collapsed sweatily against him pounding-hearted, whispering that she was happy, still she might want the other. He was not impotent with anyone else. The reason was simple. She was afraid that without a condom he might give her a fatal disease. Knowing this, every time he put his erection into her he immediately imagined the condom breaking, and then her fear and misery and his guilt, and so his penis would shrink. He explained it to her; she was touched, and kissed him; she understood; but still he worried that she was disappointed in him even though he knew that she wasn't. So that was why he made love to her with his hands. At night, exhausted, he'd fall asleep with his head against her breasts and dream of hands, seeing again Oregon's low barnacled rocks carpeted with kelp's many hands, dark green bulbous fingers open, hands upon hands, the squishy bulbs of fingertips reaching down into crabridden channels where dark snails slowly made their way. Those were the places where the ocean came in, searching out every hidden way. The tide was rising. Green anemones pulsed. Mussels clung to boulders. He slept late beside her, and then they made love all morning and all afternoon. Sometimes they couldn't stop long enough to eat. They made love until twilight. Shy khaki-colored palmetto lizards came out of hiding as it got dark. The two cats chased them or gazed at insects and rotten mangoes, the foliage bending under the weight of its own ranks of fingers, its greenish wrists flexed into downcurves of magnificent idleness which now magnified their authority as the darkness dripped down from the treetops like hot tar and the first cricket began to make its announcements in a voice much less kingly than any voice the leaves would have had if they could speak as they grew down out of darkness. Darkness came like music. Just as in an orchestra the drummer hunches forward, having selected from his convenient palate two sticks with the requisite heads, and begins to thrum one of his giant kettles so lightly, so the first thickening of night rippled quietly down from her thick humid trees as she smiled and kissed her hand to him; he remembered how at the Sydney Opera House the tenor and the soprano had stood before the conductor like a bride and groom before the minister. He saw the flash of trombones as the trio in the orchestra raised them like rifles, taking aim at the musical notes which had called them forth (and again for a moment Sarajevo entered his mind in much the same way as in California a muddy-gray wave can come in, sweeping sideways, having been diverted by a knife-sharp shapelessness of lava, then wheels back home, leaving a semi-circular deposit of sand; amidst the raveling of Florida darkness he recalled the construction of a Sarajevo morning; how at six-thirty it would be sunny, empty, quiet; and then suddenly came the *ka-chonk-chonk-chonk-chonk* of an anti-aircraft gun; a car sped desperately by, and he heard individual shots echoing between buildings; then another car fled squealing, almost tipping over. He heard breaking glass. It was silent and sunny for a moment. A machine-gun burst made the windowpane rattle, and he saw that there was a new hole in the ledge outside. That was how it would be all day. The old mother, smiling and tired, brought in a piece of grenade. — On our balcony. From last night. — The Bosnian Dragons had said: If you are killed we will light seven candles. — That meant that they would kill seven Serbs. — In Karenni State, on the other hand, what he'd thought to be gunshots had been but the explosions of burning trees where refugees cleared the jungle.) The opera interrupted his thoughts. As he peered down the concentric golden rings of an immense tuba's barrel, he wondered if he saw what the doomed fly sees in approaching a pitcher plant. As Lautréamont says, *to struggle against evil is to pay it too great a compliment.* — Should the fly struggle then? Should anybody struggle against his ominous golden destiny? In the secret jungle village the candleshine had been like liquid in the grooves of the long bamboo table when the Karenni soldier in his tunic with the red emblem poured smilingly from a glowing cloudy bottle of Karenni rice whiskey which tasted both sulphury and sweet, while water ran in the bamboo darkness beneath. To fly into the pitcher plant must be like drinking that whiskey, like drinking light without knowing what might happen. How could one struggle effectively against the unknown? And the choir came out, some of them bald and ugly, some frumpy, some overdressed in diamonds, some shrivelled by the light of their own spectacles. The cymbal-player did not have a gleeful face as he himself would in his position but he was compensated for by the happy gesticulations of the conductor. That was how the oncoming darkness felt. Somebody was making it, sifting down clouds of sweet and spicy trickery like the greenish flash of a Li So woman's skirt. It was a very good darkness. The woman whom he made love to with his hands was still writing, so he went out to the atlas and fell into it, the outline of his identity staining place-names below him in just the same fashion that a plane descending into the Great Western Desert of Australia casts its shadow on a land like an immense dead leaf with many veins both black and white; and then, sinking deeper into the lichenous red of that continent darkened by blue haze, it loses itself in uplooming, lands lonely in that vermillion country of purple shrubs and broad low W-shaped gullies, becomes a small silver glint in dirt as red as Mars, its belly almost lapped by yellow grass. It is nothing nowhere nobody. For darkness is so vast and wide. That was the shape of his experience when he went out from the house of joy and descended into the Florida night, meeting at the end of the street a large cemetery hunched behind its diamond-meshed fence, the vaults sometimes three high in an immense U-shaped block like apartments, flowers and flags on the ledges by the nameplates, a fingernail moon overhead, the sound of running water from a dormer-windowed palmridden house across the street. Here and there he saw a low white vault, with palm silhouettes behind. So he spoke to all the dead, asking where they were from, and their silence said that they were from nowhere everywhere, and he wanted to explain that he himself travelled everywhere and perhaps he did explain it after the best conceivable fashion; namely, he said nothing; thus he spoke the language of the dead. — He went back and took his woman by the hand, and they made love until dawn.

But there have been other houses of joy in the world; every neighborhood has one; the gazetteer is riddled with their toponyms, although perhaps not all deserve the name. The center is where we are; thus in travelling we but change our peripheries. One traveller may rule (or be slave to) many, many worlds. And other travellers of course leave the flotsam of their extinguished secret planets and planetoids —a faded photograph, a doll, a lock of hair, a symphony, a mineral brought from who knows where, a baby, a gravestone, a pair of dirty underpants. When he met the surviving wooden panels of Gauguin's House of Joy from that dreamworld we call Oceania—les îles Marquises, to be precise (1901)—he remembered how priests had burned the rest as soon as the artist died, leaving orphaned his bas-relief girls with negroid shell-faces, idol-faces, who dwelled within the world he'd once called "Soyez mystérieuses." A little yellowish-green pigment remained on their faces; their hair was painted red or bluish-green; one tawny-buttocked nymph grappled at a greenish darkness, gazing at another woman's face which shone in isolation like the moon; as it seemed, the nymph supplicated and the moon gazed back at her and the traveller, tight-lipped. On the far left another woman sadly drowsed, faded like so many of Gauguin's dreams—sentimental, pornographic dreams, yet not without merit; the man wanted to be loved, let's say; he was a traveller; he wanted to possess the alien; his flaw was that he was unwilling to be possessed by it. — The other traveller would have loved to see the viewers made up of Gauguin's elect, which is to say, laughing amorous couples, but by the time people got to Gauguin upstairs in Division Forty-Four their feet hurt and they had already seen ever so many images of nakedness. A whitish-grey rainy light came in. A man rushed down the scuffed tiles, following the camera implanted at the end of his arm. A business-woman trod dully along, half-gazing at Gauguin's panels. Her fat husband pointed to the one that said SOYEZ AMOUREUSES— VOUS SEREZ HEREUSES* (a seductive snake basking round that message), and she touched her shoulder affectionately. That was good; he was being good; but she but half looked. Nor was she to be blamed; her legs ached, held so unnaturally angled in the high heels. So she passed on to Division Forty-Five without glancing to see whether he would follow, which assuredly meant that she took his following for granted, and that was not so good. But maybe he had failed to consider the high heels. The man gazed at the moon-woman for awhile, listening to the lines of her face, and then went on. For a long time, almost a full minute, the Maison du Jouir was empty, except for the traveller. Those squat naked women waved tirelessly—joylessly, he hated to say; almost grimly; had Gauguin dis-believed his own message? If so, what an unhappy man! . . . Across the hall, a glass case sheltered his head of Tehura, carved of *pua* wood and painted. Tehura was the first of his thirteen-year-old wives. Gau-guin wrote home that her skin was "an orgy of chromes." Her shiny face was tilted back forever, her dark eyes almost pupilless holes the shape of seedpods. Light crawled upon her cheekbones and forehead. He wanted to kiss her calm, rich wooden lips. — In Division Forty-Five, smiling ladies were showing their little girls Aristide Maillol's *La femme à l'ombrelle* (1895). When they came to Gauguin, they peered at Tehura and the *Maison du Jouir* in silence. Perhaps they were hostile. Perhaps they understood what those women had been to Gauguin

* "Be loving; you will be happy."

and they did not want their daughters to have anything to do with his joy. Perhaps they thought: Old lecher! — In Division Forty-Three, which displayed the works of the École Pont-Aven, they lingered somewhat longer, pointing out to their young females his safely unimpresive still-lives and the harsh Brittany women of his pre-Oceanic period. No danger that anyone would emulate *them*—and, if they did, no harm done! A landlady's calling is rarely despised. — Supposedly Tahitians, a Canadian woman explained. — His feet hurt, too. He returned to the glass case where Tehura's head lived. Behind it hung *Et l'or de leur corps* (1901), whose skin-hues rendered the title a misnomer, being brown rather than gold; Gauguin had achieved beautiful expressions for the two girls, whose heads were cocked in patient curiosity, seeking the traveller's eyes which they would never find. But Tehura was the one. In this new crowd there appeared to be a wave of wood-carving enthusiasts, since on his current circuit round the glass case he had leisure only to notice the shiny dark chisel-marks of her hair before eye-pressure and breath-pressure impelled him. Another orbit. That melancholy masklike thing never looked back at him. Even when he brought his head down against the glass and looked straight into her eyesockets, nothing looked back. It was not that she was nothing, only that she would not look. He was on the periphery of the world. Another orbit. This time he aimed his gaze according to a lesser anger of imperialistic intimacy, and was rewarded by her looking *almost* at him, her lovely, sullen lips not quite parted. Halfway through the next orbit, he glanced across the hall and saw how a crowd was grimacing at the panels of Gauguin's house. A man leaned forward and gazed at *Soyez mystérieuses* with respect. Another aped him, then walked away humming. What hateful and artificial places museums are! But in Division Forty-Three, a man leaned against a pillar and smiled so lovingly upon a Rousseau. That was good. — It was not (be it said) that the traveller wanted to smash the glass case and run off with Tehura's head, although that might well have been the most honest and committed thing to do. Possession is a myth. One enjoys something or someone for awhile, then ceases to enjoy, either because the loved thing is taken away or because life itself is taken away, or simply because enjoyment is taken away, at which time the fabulous head simply becomes a lump of ennui rendered in wood.

There was a yellow field of rapeseed, and then he had to change in Winnipeg.

They pulled out of Winnipeg at ten, the sky still blue but losing color, the lights on in the houses and buildings across the river. Contingent memories followed him like twin blotches of sunlight keeping a train company along the adjacent rails. Hegel writes about shapes of consciousness which have not yet attained to the perfect abstraction so dear to him; that was one way to characterize them; another was as simple crumbs and scraps one held onto, remnants of life's ceaseless giving, like the wasted golden light on the corners and in the veins of the ranked black concrete squares which floored the platform at the train station at Rome, goldness exploding upwards in tiny occasional spangles when a raindrop hit, while the black railings, though they shone as if varnished, remained still. Now the train began to move; the atlas opened, chancy shapes of light rushed down into the seams perpendicular to the direction of travel to make lines of light; then the bright entrance crept by, and then he was speeding on gravelly tracks between fences and trees, observing the widening slices of Italy between train-tracks . . . There was Arabic neon under a hand-painted mouth, the yellow letters crawling like dotted inchworms, policemen in black with white belts and flat black caps and white-striped sleeves, black boots, black moustached faces (Venetian red with a touch of yellow ocher). That was Cairo. *I am very disconnected,* another woman he'd loved had written, *and within ten minutes of your departure wondered why I hadn't called your bluff about running off to Spain. I hope that you are not too sad about everything, and will forgive me for needing things you can't give—and for wanting to—as Ivan would say— "respectfully return my ticket" alone. Being alone is very important to me. I will look into finding you some daguerreotyping equipment next week.* Everybody was disconnected. Everybody retained some meaningless recollection or other, like that part of Karl-Marx-Allee with darkish apartment buildings, the Stalin Wall; when Stalin died, they took down his sign quietly in the night.

The woman who'd respectfully returned her ticket wanted to get rid of ill-made furniture, too. How could he blame her for doing that? First of all, he didn't love her more than the others. She needed to be loved exclusively, because she was sad in a different way than he was. While his incompleteness and emptiness made him so lonely that he sometimes couldn't sleep outside of a woman's arms, her own disease was self-hatred. Once he sent her a photograph in which, so he'd thought, her beauty had been definitively proved, and she thought it ugly, although at least she didn't throw it away. Some gray and cloudy species of dreariness, some foreign chemical or trace, had invaded her and inflamed her with listless sorrow long before they'd ever met, clinging to her like a poisonous mucus, and although he wanted to brush it away he couldn't; he didn't know how. His own need-driven selfishness, which she'd later name his culpability, only added to her hurt. Because she could not see her own excellence, his compliments rang sarcastic in her ears; sometimes he felt so guilty for hurting her that he wanted to kneel down and give her a revolver and respectfully request that she shoot him. How could he make her see how rare she was, how specially strange? Sometimes for a moment she'd smile at him through her guardedness and pain. But he could not be loyal only to her, and when he was with her he couldn't leave her alone. He'd take her hand on the subway, for instance, until she became angry, interpreting this as a kind of exhibitionistic possessiveness or territorialism, like a dog marking ownership by means of pungent liquid irrelevancies, when in fact his was a different kind of selfishness, that same desperate loneliness which compelled him to take her hand again and again until she practically shook him off. He was not really bad, just greedy and unmeritorious. (She wasn't perfect, either.) Behind his screen of consideration, sincere though it was, he operated almost ruthlessly, so that his filthy love-claws hurt her again and again.

Clasping her pale arms behind her back as she gazed into a glass case filled with golden figures in some museum, she might have felt distracted from her struggle against the gray cloud if he were with her, because she truly liked someone to identify things to, thereby confirming her empire of names (when he asked what her favorite thing was, she said: Probably the funerary couch), but he just felt sulky and sorry for himself, remembering the walnut-paneled hotel room in Philadelphia, with snow outside and the hazy peace inside from her cigarette smoke, the old room with its pale beige moldings, its browns and off-golds behind the netting curtains which hid the white sky and brick towers and roofs. The next morning all the snow had melted. The lobby's black and white floor-diamonds swarmed around her when she went out. In the window-ledges, the holes in the heater-grilles were as big as fingertips. The dark wood around them was cracked by the hot air which had fought so many winters. He stood watching her dwindle through the picture window; she was in a hurry to make her train. A rotund man in a black trench-coat stood with his hands in his pockets, his face pale, his eyes glittering like wet blackberries past their season; and the man was leaning beside the brass-bordered mirror. With a strange start of jealous anger, he understood that the man was watching her also. She never looked back. Possibly she didn't know he could see her. His own train, leaving, followed the parallel wildernesses of track, sooty arches and old snow. The blue sky clouded over with ugly birds. He passed buildings, bare trees old and dirty and dreary, crossed the wide straight river. Useless. He gazed at black tree-fingers in the reddish-brown dirt of spring. Broken-windowed houses looked back at him from over the railroad tracks; that was that. She'd said: You don't love me, and he said again that he did, and she said: I believe you *think* that you love me. I believe you love me as much as you can. — He sat there, sad and heavy and guilty. That was in the summer-time when it was very hot. She made love with him only twice that time, once on the first night and once on the last. The first time he'd seduced her and afterward she'd said: It's not fair for you to make me want you. — The other time she'd done it as a surprise, probably out of pity. As soon as it was over she'd gotten out of bed, put on her clothes and sat staring at him from the other side of the room. The rest of the time they were at museums and she said: Come look at this calligraphy. — Memory-pictures crowded past like the high alert buttocks of cyclists speeding so silently down the river drive. Everything which he now recollected on that train was as clear as another glass of horseradish vodka with the meniscus trembling so alertly on the table whose red roses were less ruby-dark than the wine in the other goblets; the pianist sent out happiness in firm rhythms, turning his bald head in swivels of pleasure; the woman in the dress which was a meadow of black roses moved forward to kiss him, leaned back forking her mushrooms vol-au-vent, smiling, her shoulders shining; and the disk below the stem of his water glass burst into a dozen rainbows; and the beauty in the black dress was happy and frowned and ordered more wine, clasping her breastbone. That night the light had been a crooked bamboo pole in the red cushions of booths, and the woman in the black dress had brought his hand to her lips like autumn's river slow and strange. The crazy piano-notes sank into the coriander vodka; and after more coriander vodka he looked up and the woman in the black dress was gone, only the crumpled white napkin which had touched her mouth remaining to mark her. He sat still for awhile. Then he picked up the napkin and put his face to its lipstick stain. After he'd paid their bill he went outside and stood there for awhile gazing down the long street-canals which sparkled with cabs like square yellow beads . . .

He was on that train all night and all day and all night and half the next day, so he came to know the Chinese cook, who'd pretend to charge him two hundred dollars instead of two for a couple of sodas; he'd tell the cook that the check was in the mail and then they'd both laugh; he got a crush on the black waitress, who always smiled and spoke softly and gently when she served his eggs and bacon (she put in extra toast); and his memories spilled ahead like the reflections of sedge-bundles in the ponds.

The river itself was calm, salt-blue in the twilight except for the rich brown shadows that hugged the far side under the trees. He remembered how the Nile, less modest than wide, became greenish-brown where deep, greenish-blue where shallow. Wide wet sandbars were hued like burned corn. The ship passed a yellow sand-hill crowned with tombs like anthills; and a long-necked ibis lurked among the oleanders on Lord Kitchener's island, which was an un-dulating green tree-strip. The tomb is the future. Perhaps that is why some people are not happy at the turning of the year. By chance he'd attended one Chinese New Year in Opium City. Across the border he'd seen the richly colored Hell Banknotes which the Chinese burned for their ancestors, so he expected fire, which there was, but where lay the joy of the future's dreams? Above that monotonous guitar song in a minor key, a strong raspy soldier-voice was singing to wordless people who danced strangely around a smoky sparky bon-fire. — Mainly soldiers from the front, an old veteran said. This festival to make them happy. — Their dark uniforms were thick with sadness as they danced round and round in the cold and foggy dark-ness. Occasionally they did sing; he even heard all voices raised. Clouds of breath rose like smoke above the arc lights in the black

sky. The voices chanted and then were silent. — Strange to admit
that this occasion had no more sap than a dead branch, whereas a
cave he'd once entered in Tasmania had been almost vivacious with
inhuman strangeness from its very mouth where ferny darkness shattered the light into a billion bedraggled strings of limestone like carrots, fat leaves, spearheads; deeper in, bleached cave-spiders surveyed
him from walls textured and webbed; there was a peace to this place
without sadness, a patient transformation of water into rock which
knew little of life and so could not be tortured by it; its history was
written only in candle-white stalactites growing down to a pond. It
had a sky, possessed its still white constellation of glowworms in the
blackness. In that cave there was only eternity to fear. Hell is anything
which continues long enough. He remembered a sunken bubble of a
Jerusalem teahouse whose domed ceiling was whitewashed and
arched, and as he sat in a cushioned niche drinking mulled cider
against the chill a young Jew came to him and drew a picture of a
dove. The Jew wished him *shalom,* which means peace, love, happiness, freedom, and all dreams coming true. He said that the young
dove he had drawn wished only to live. The Jew's sweetness uplifted
him. He was not in hell. But in another niche a man with glowing
eyes, filled with the same pride and tenderness, expressed that spirit
with words that sought to persuade, compel, dominate. His victim, a
young Jewish-American girl, cringed miserably before him. He leaned
toward her and said: Do you really like this country? Do you think
the mentality and spirituality of this country fit you? — I don't know,
replied the girl as bravely as she could. I'm here to find out. — You
see, I know a guy, the man said. He came to open a business here.
But, you know, he was not happy. This kind of thing disturbs me.
That's why I must ask you. — There was no levity in this man, only
a merciless sincerity. The girl struggled to speak, but he silenced her
with a wave of his hand and told her: I think what you have already
seen, that is enough. You must not wait any longer to make up your
mind. — The poor girl was weeping. He would not let her alone.
He said: To be a Jew in Israel, you must have some deep roots; you
must be ready to get married and live the life. Elsewhere, you are
only a Jew. Here it is different. If you're asking me, your place as a
Jew is here. — There was an impressive quality to the man which
only made his speechifying more unpleasant. And yet it was not meant

as bullying at all. Another day he who travelled and watched arrived at the Western Wall, where two checkpoint police in blue knife-proof vests met him in a happy spirit. One of the pair said: Why don't you go in the army? The army's very good . . . —and put his hand on his shoulder. The physical contact felt warm and loving. The policeman was proud of who he was. He wanted to help Israel; he also wanted to give this stranger before him a place in the world. His wish was heartfelt and had to be respected. Beneath palms and white towers he saw a sticker: EVERY YESHIVA SHOULD JOIN ISRAEL'S ARMY. EVERY JEWISH STUDENT SHOULD JOIN A YESHIVA. He ascended the Citadel wall, peered through the slits once used to pour boiling oil down on besiegers; went out and down the narrow street lined with handwoven scarves and tablecloths, rugs, leather purses and belts, fringed bedspreads, mounds of coriander, and, passing a coffee shop which was bright with caged birds he found himself at the edge of the Jewish zone. Green-garbed soldiers with Uzis stood tense and ready. He passed through a doorway and came out into the Arab side where two men in blue windbreakers that said POLICE were forcing couples to disengage hands; and he decided to visit the Aqsa mosque. He took off his shoes. Two Jewish soldiers were sitting on the wide flagstones, guarding rows of soldier-boots. — I'd like to kill all the dirty stinking Arabs, one said. — He entered the mosque, loving the blue tiles inscribed with Qur'anic verses. Some Jewish extremists had planted a bomb underneath but it hadn't gone off. Inside was the same still hollowed-out beauty as in the Tasmanian cave. Calligraphed Arabic letters rose like swords. There were silver flowers and disks on the ceiling, and the pillars were marbled like halvah. He saw some Qur'ans on a shelf at the rear; people were borrowing them like hymnals. He went to look at one, and a man screamed: *Not allowed!* and all the other people in that mosque regarded him with hatred. He went outside and was trying to understand the Dome of the Rock with his eyes when the hour for Muslim prayer arrived and an Arab yelled at him: Okay, the show is over! Get out! — And so he returned to the Jewish side, where two soldiers in green parkas stood beside a metal detector. An Arab passed through the metal detector and it did not go off. The soldiers called him back and frisked him roughly. An Orthodox Jew with long sidelocks set off the metal detector and the soldiers smiled and waved him through. Then it was his turn. The metal detector was silent. They didn't frisk him but they searched his bag. Not looking back, he walked down the arched tunnel, toward the flag with the blue stripes and the blue star . . . YOU ARE PRESENTLY IN THE AREA OF THE WESTERN WALL. YOU ARE KINDLY REQUESTED TO FOLLOW THE INSTRUCTIONS OF THE GUARDS AND TO SAFEGUARD THE SANCTITY OF THE HOLY SITE. THE FOLLOWING ARE PROHIBITED . . . A soldier with a machine-gun strolled slowly across the worn white stones. — The train continued to move slowly as it came into a swollen blood vessel of track, then shadowed a long wall of boxcars overhung by whitish-yellow lights on poles.

Then the train was vibrating across a flatness of dark brownish-greenish grass under a dark slate sky with power towers making tall black skeletons of interlocking triangles and a radio tower flashing like lightning far away under the night's thunderhead. He wandered through sleep that was like the soft wet grass between birch trees.

In the morning he saw that it had rained, and waking quickly he remembered Madagascar right away with the umbrellas unfurling well before six in Antananarivo, rising like mushrooms on cobblestones still wet with rain; the green tree above the sand like an immense lung whose alveoli were spreading green trunks, the women carrying their brooms bristles upward, handles upright like flagstaffs in the hollows of their arms: these brought morning to the dirt street walled with low brick houses. He loved someone there whom he would never marry. She knew that. He had never lied to her. But she waited, and wrote him letters, which he kept in the same drawer as the letters of his first love and all the other loves, and slowly the letters became overaccommodating, desperate, and then bitter, and it was his fault, even though whatever pain his first love had caused him was not her fault; which apparent contradiction demonstrated the failure of classical theories. What physicists call *blackbodies,* namely, hollow heated solids from which radiation passes out through a tiny hole, the rest of the solid being entirely black, prove through their spectra that energy is released in discrete quanta instead of in a continuous stream. He could see himself and the Malagasy woman as facing blackbodies (although her body alone was black), each radiating need and sullen resentment and lust and hope and love and all the other wavelengths in the spectrum, glowing only through their tiny sexual orifices which connected directly with their souls; but the steadiness of hysterical light was only an illusion; they were really and sincerely *pulsing* very quickly as they locked lips and children leaned out and ran while fresh meat began to go rancid in sizzling brick windows; and *he* was the one who had the orgasm of responsibility; he was the one to be blamed. He decided never to go back there and then he felt lonely so he went back there. She stroked his sunwarmed shoulders. She said: *Je constate tous mes erreurs en te disant que tu n'étais pas gentil et tous nos petites disputes, je—je—je t'aimais trop et je t'aime encore plus, voila pourquoi j'ai faite comme cela . . .* — and he said: Please don't talk like that, honey; I myself love you so much. — She said: When I think about you, I cry alone in my house. (A barefoot man in rags came walking past the hot green place where women were washing their clothes in the brown river. He balanced a long narrow cardboard box on his head. He held his hat in his hand. Why was he so familiar, like Madame Bovary's blind beggar? Had it been when the train was pulling out of Bangkok that he'd seen a man sleeping on concrete with his knees up beside a greenish canal in which so many trees reflected themselves as they groped down between blue continents of reflected sky? That man and the one in Antananarivo were brothers who would never meet. But if that were true, were rich men also brothers? And whom was he himself the brother to? Again from the Vatican he remembered snowy double curves of ceiling embellished by golden circles of crowns and angels; from these spheres crossed elaborate wreaths between whose legs lived paintings of rampant lions, monuments, beautiful and terrifying processions, and the ceiling's Saharas of whiteness which separated these entities swarmed with angels. These maps and diagrams were intended to demonstrate to him his relatedness to other beings in this world. Somewhere the two beggars were affixed like stars, still with the same sunken eyes of hunger and sadness, but the Celestial Painter had dressed them in royal purple and their hair glistened and the line between them had been painted in gold. Was there somewhere that those men could truly partake of the existence of angels? He couldn't believe it.) In Madagascar he wanted to explain himself and couldn't. He tried to please her and couldn't. She led him beneath the trees whose heads were as pale and lacy as carrot-tops; and together they journeyed across red and purple earths. — You no same before! she kept saying sorrowfully. Oh, your char-

acter not so good now! — And she turned away from him and played
Malagasy solitaire, sweating in the hot tobacco breeze. She'd gained
a little weight. Her breasts now reminded him of those clusters of
green bananas that hang off the trees like grenades. They were now
mostly silent together, those two, she playing cards, he slapping his
mosquito bites and gazing at the rain that fell upon the street. He
watched the bright white sky, the weird pale green trees spreading in
the square, the dirty kids laughing, showing white teeth. He kept
thinking: What's the use? — He tried to compliment her; one night
he pointed to a calendar girl and said that she herself was that beautiful
and more so. She thanked him spiritlessly. (Before, when he honey-
talked her she'd smile, set down her rum bottle, and give him a big
wet kiss, saying: *Merci, mon amour . . .*) Two days later, unable to
digest the insult after all, she began screaming at him in rage. It turned
out that he'd said the worst thing. The calendar girl was of another
race, hence ugly. — But me no want problem with you, so just smile,
speak thank you! she shouted. Oh, you no good! — It was like the
time in Afghanistan during the war when Suleiman was sick. His
medicine was in his packsack which was locked away; and Suleiman
was too poor to have medicine of his own, of course. Gholam Sayed
kept saying: Suleiman is ill, Suleiman is ill. — But Poor Man had the
key and Poor Man was asleep. Old Elias, the malik of the village, had
warned him never to wake Poor Man. Without Poor Man the Rus-
sians would get them, so his concentration must never be molested.
— Who else has the key, then? he asked Elias, knowing that someone
did but forgetting the name. — No answer, either because Elias didn't
understand or else because by asking he was breaking some com-
mandment unknown to him. Suleiman lay feverish. He asked Suleiman if he wanted him to wake up Poor Man. Suleiman lowered his
head and whispered no. So they all sat there staring at one another
in the hot red dust; and then Gholam Sayed said again, more accusingly: *Suleiman is sick!* — If you care for him get the key, he replied,
angry now. Then I can open my pack and get a pill for him. — The
oratorical effect of this speech was somewhat lost, as he had to consult
his Pushtu-English dictionary for every second word. (He would have
preferred to be as reclusive as a crow dodging under a bridge.)
— Gholam Sayed said nothing. — I don't know how to find the
key without waking Poor Man, he added, or would have, but the

dictionary didn't have the words *find, locate* or *discover.* He couldn't think what other words to look for. He had never been good at crossword puzzles. (The dictionary was really a disappointment.) He managed to say: It's difficult for me. I am a foreigner. It's not difficult for you. You are a mujahid. — Then suddenly Gholam Sayed announced: Suleiman is not sick. — He says he's sick, so he's sick, the traveller insisted. Help him. Or show me how to help him. — It's Ramazan, said Gholam Sayed. Muslim no eat. No drink. — If a man is sick, the traveller replied, then no Ramazan. — At this, Gholam Sayed pointed to Suleiman and said something disparaging. The traveller didn't understand. Then he pointed to the traveller, indicated breasts on him, pointed to Suleiman and said: He want . . . and made his culture's equivalent of a representative gesture which suggested that Gholam Sayed, at least, squatted when he did it. They were all Muslim missionaries so maybe they didn't need the missionary position. Whether or not Suleiman had designs on him, the traveller didn't really care. Walking up the unnerving cliffsides, Suleiman had held his arm. He'd picked fruit for him, held his hand in friendship when they walked. Suleiman had helped him. Suleiman was sick and he was not helping Suleiman. — He said he's sick, so he's sick, he cried. Help Suleiman! — It's Ramazan, returned the implacable Gholam Sayed. Muslim no eat, no drink. — The traveller went to look for the other man with the key but didn't see him, so he came back, and Suleiman was moaning with fever and Gholam Sayed was standing there grinning. — He gave Gholam Sayed a push. (Gholam Sayed had pushed him many times on the journey across the border. Once he'd been weak with dysentery and Gholam Sayed had shoved a machine-gun butt into the small of his back.) — Help Suleiman, he said. — He is no sick, said Gholam Sayed. — You are a liar, he said. — It's Ramazan, Gholam Sayed replied. — You are no Muslim if you will not help your brother, the traveller said, fearing these words even as they came out. Those were the kind of words that made people kill. — I am Muslim, said Gholam Sayed simply, grandly, contemptuously. Suleiman is Muslim. You are no Muslim.

And yet love and friendship were not always skulls with no minds. There had been that wife so gentle and sunny in Key West (no matter that she hesitated to meet him again). There had been the one in Bangkok. As for the others, could there be any whose recollection he'd ever fail to praise? Their tears and reproaches, silences, farewells, laughter and whispered words were marked on the atlas pages like nations. The ones who'd loved him still and the ones who'd sent him away, he loved them all so much that it stopped his breath. Proud of them, grateful he was, to each from the very first who'd flashed her young head, telling him no and not yet and not anymore while she ran her fingers through her long blonde hair, whose absence she now concealed with wigs, to the last one, the quiet one, the one they'd exultantly warned him was mysterious. She was the one who told him that anytime he wanted to die she would help him by strangling or stabbing as he preferred, after which she'd bury him in a hole. She was very practical and had killed before. She had dark hair which she sometimes braided; and he loved to take a braid in his hand, lean down and kiss it. Her pale oval face had a delicious odor. Her big hand would reach for his own and lift it to her lips. Then she'd kiss and lick and suck the back of his hand. He could feel her hot wet tongue on his skin. Sometimes they came together mouth to mouth and her tongue would go inside him and she'd hold him tight and stroke his hair. They held hands for hours. He had fallen in love and told her so. She said she loved him. She said: I'm sorry I'm such a shitty lover. — That was because she wouldn't fuck him anymore. Fuck was the word she used. She'd taught her little son and daughter to say fuck and dick and cunt. On her ancient car, whose transmission was senile, whose first gear was dead, whose front passenger seat consisted of the floor, on which her lesbian friends sometimes coupled— on this car of hers, which she loved, were painted a devil and a woman transacting cunnilingus. An old hippie walked by and muttered: Wow, it's flashback time! — The mysterious woman liked girls, and would sometimes bring him to strip bars, saying: That one's really horrible! or: That girl is so beautiful I want to *eat* her cunt! Look at her pretty cunt! Do you want to fuck her, too? — Sure, he always said. I'd do her. — And he drank his beer. The girl on stage stuck her rear out at them, bent over and studied them upside down from between her legs. He took the hand of the woman he loved, the big warm hand, and said: If you could do just one thing to her, what would it be? — I'd snuggle her and give her a *long, long* orgasm, she replied. — Later it was too sad to view clearly those pictures of the past as he sat in another hot dry hotel room gazing out at a long blue blade of mountain holding up fog and rain. But the first chilly night in their tiny hotel room in Billings when he'd kissed her lips for the first time and taken her big breasts in his hands right through the sweater, he'd known that she had borne him out of everywhere somewhere nowhere, all the way to the capital city of the central continent; the atlas opened. As they made love she gently ran her fingernails over him (your skin marks so easily! she said in wonder); and she fucked him again, whispering that she wanted him to put one of his pistols in her mouth, which he didn't do, and in the morning they took each other again and then she went into the shower and he could not help following her any more than if she had been a taxidermist holding him by a loop of wire through his eye sockets; he was soaping her off when she said: I don't want to fuck anymore. — OK, he said. Are you sore? — No. — He hadn't understood. All day he continued in his joyous ignorance, kissing her mouth, holding both of her hands. She always kissed back, and his penis was firm and ready like his heart. Even though she'd kept her lips closed that last time in bed, he skated along, thinking himself well-shod when all he wore were his assumptions. So together they unlocked the door of the hotel room in Bozeman and she said: Didn't you hear me? I wanted two beds. — He looked at her in amazement. It was a pity that he couldn't later see his own face at that moment, because it must have looked so comically befuddled. — You don't want to screw me anymore? he said finally. — No. — Why? — I just don't feel it. — OK, he said. I'll sleep on the floor. — But she didn't want him to sleep on the floor. She said she'd go talk to the clerk and get two rooms. He asked her not to, please. He would much rather sleep on the floor than face still another humiliation, although he well knew that he ought not to be affected by any opinion of the clerk's; he was weak and shy just then. Then she said he could sleep in the double bed, but he didn't want to. Perhaps he appeared contrary, although he wasn't. Neither is Aadorf (47.30 N, 8.54 E) the same as Aadorp (52.22 N, 6.37 E). She said she couldn't bear to have him sleep on the floor. So he lay just under the bedspread with his face turned away, limbs tensed, alertness stiffly resident in every muscle and tendon as if he were one of those animatrons at Las Vegas (It was taken directly out of the movie and recreated, said the tour guide; it was spectacular to watch them put it up; in one day they'd have an entire

part done!); and his soul correspondingly stiffened into vile green spurious crystal spires of anxiety like tourmaline because there was nothing that his clenched body could do or grasp or fight. He heard her
sleeping peacefully. She lolled naked on the sheet, and the sight of
that body which he had known and thought to know again and could
now not touch inflamed him with rage and grief. After three or four
of those caged hours he double-dosed himself with sleeping pills. She
continued very gentle and open and cheerful. At night when he was
sleepy she'd squeeze his hand and whisper: *You're so pretty!* and although each morning he awoke aching with loneliness and sorrow,
her gentle darling ways always won him over anew because throughout the day she was beside him holding his hand. He felt so happy
with her! He loved her so very much! One autumn's midnight they
were driving from Idaho to Montana in a storm whose white rays of
snow sped towards them in an explosion like silent fireworks; lines
rushed outward from a central perspective point which eluded them
and drew them on as they ascended the pass, snow deeper and deeper
on the road and they had no chains. — This is crazy! she laughed.
It's *so, so* beautiful! Thank you for bringing me with you. — And for
hours of dark snowy rivers she squeezed his hand and he would have
kissed her but it was not about that. He'd cooked elk and venison for
her that night and she had said that it was delicious and he had asked
her if they would be lovers again and she'd said: I'm not sure. — She
said: Sometimes I look at you and I really want you. Other times I
don't. — Her eyes shone when she looked at him, and she smiled
and said that she loved him. He threw his arms around her. She said
that she couldn't decide anything, that she was sorry, that maybe he
should just hit her over the head and take her. He listened and actually
considered it, but for him that game was too fearful to play. What if
he started and couldn't stop? Rape and murder and suicide shone
hypothetically before him, grimly equidistant beacons of love indicated on the atlas page by scarlet pentagrams. He told her he didn't
think he could do that. She said she didn't think he could, either.
Slowly and thoroughly she licked his hand. The snow-trails were like
shooting stars. They reached the summit and began to come down
into Montana where a snowplow whined feebly up the mountain,
with snow thick ahead of it and new snow behind. He felt so close
to her. In pioneer days it must have been that way and more, a man

and a woman travelling on together, helping one another, needing each other, not knowing whether they'd make it. These days there seemed no penalty for not being sure. The atlas opened; easy pages lay ahead. When they came into Missoula an hour later he told her to pick the motel and then said as always: One room or two? and she smiled tenderly and said: Two, and he smiled back and rushed out of the car before she could see him crying. It was absurd. — It'd be a lot cheaper for you if you just got one room with two beds, said the night manager. — I think I'll take two rooms, he said. — He brought her her key as she sat there in the car with the motor on and he said goodnight and ran to his own door several rooms down, but as he set down his pack to pull the key out of his pocket he saw her standing there beside him in the cold darkness smiling and his heart flowered until she said again: Goodnight, and she took his head in her hands and kissed him. — Goodnight, he said. — Then he went inside, flung himself down on his bed, and wept. Did it count that he only wept for five minutes? Anyway, why snivel at all? She did love him. Others loved him. If he wanted sex or just a woman to hold in his arms all night there would be an escort service. There'd been a night when he'd asked her: One room or two? and she'd cried: I don't *know!* so of course he got them one and she undressed and said she felt sleepy and said she just really didn't want to very much now and said: You can jack off or whatever the fuck you want! and added gently: I'm sorry . . . so he'd waited until she made her darling sleeping sounds, hearing which he rolled stealthily toward her until his knee grazed her buttock and that touch alone was able to keep him happy all night. In the morning she rolled into his arms and began sighing and deeply kissing him and they'd made love. That was the last time they slept in the same room. But on the last night of their journey, they went to see a movie about a boy who ran away from home, and the boy was so happily leaving everything behind on that early summer morning of green forests that he who watched was uplifted (throughout that film, which she'd chosen, she held his hand); so he no longer ached or wondered or sorrowed but just kissed her goodnight in the parking lot of their latest motel as she shivered in her leather jacket and he said to her: Darling, I love you so much. — And he strode quickly and happily to his room without looking back.

Later, of course, he cried.

Past The Pas the spruces were as narrow as wolves' tails and there were ripply warm brown rivers. Cormorant Lake was a pale miniature sea. There was swamp, and then muskeg, and white birch flashing and thrumming by. They passed silver lakes in the green-walled dusk.

Came a blue dawn of tiny skinny trees, of lake and lichen. He was approaching the edge of the continent, soft and flat and wet, speckled and boggy. Some lakes were blue with pulsing stripes of paleness in the breeze. Waterdrops struck the train window, making transparent worlds. The ground was now itself a map, the lakes minuscule blue continents in a greenish sea, all unfamiliar, and so many of them, countries he'd never known before. The world was larger than he had thought.

An old Inuk couple sat drinking from economy-sized bottles of ginger ale and staring alertly out the window, looking for animals. The man's dark hands were the color of bloodstains, the web between thumb and forefinger snug over the other wrist. The woman, who was fat, never stopped smiling. Sometimes they spotted small flocks of Canada geese resting on the tundra and watched them in silence. Sometimes the old man divorced his veincorded reddish hands, leaned, coughed, and spat into the wastebag.

The ground was pale with lichened tussocks. The dwarf spruces' branch-ends were like strange green-toed claws. Memories landed on him with a mosquito's six-legged crouch.

They came into Churchill where the land was spongy brown and green, with so many indigo Swiss cheese holes, with flat olive-colored trees along the river's bank, ocher sand-islands, small infrequent patches of snow like crusty flakes of dryness in the soggy boggy ground, and ahead the sharp cracked white ice of the bay forest with patches of bog eaten out of them. The atlas closed. His train riding was finished. No more nobody never. He was in the snow country now.

He had read *Snow Country* long ago one Arctic summer in Pond Inlet when people were hunting narwhals. Pond Inlet lies considerably north of Churchill, and the landscape is different. East of the dump, perhaps a thousand paces from shore, a stream wound through a rich

bed of moss. If you walked up this green S-shaped valley you reached
a triangular arroyo whose walls hid ice and waterfalls. Above, climbing
the black-lichened steps of these white and orange cliffs, you reached
a green ridge that looked down on the sea where a Ski-Doo slid
bravely along one of the last solid spans of ice and the sun was long
and white on Bylot Island. A shot sounded. Water trickled down
beneath banks of dirty snow (which resembled the black-lichened
white rocks). Listening to the splashes of the dying animal, he remembered the book's first sentence, variously translated as: *The train
came out of the long tunnel into the snow country* and *After the long border
tunnel, the snow country appeared.* It reminded him of that Faulkner
sentence *Soon now they would enter the delta.* *Snow Country* is a hundred
and seventy-five pages long, and its palm-of-the-hand reduction a
mere eleven, yet old Kawabata, who they say was shy and wise and
lonely and who gassed himself, not long after receiving his Nobel
Prize, kept this sentence even in the shorter version. It was the back-
bone of the world he must miniaturize. *The train emerged from the long
border tunnel into the snow country.* The snow country was for Kawabata's protagonist the end of this world and the beginning of another,
the country of pure mountains of sunset crystal which all tunnels are
supposed to lead to, the zone of that uncanny whiteness hymned by
Poe and Melville, the pole of transcendence. But on the bullet train
from Tokyo to Osaka, although it was snowing outside and there had
been a tunnel, ladies sat reading glamour magazines or drinking piping
hot canned tea, while businessmen dozed or fuddled over their papers.
No one had been transcended. The snow country was to the north,
but they were going west. Yuki said that the snow country had been
grossly developed since Kawabata's time. (Yuki was the traveller's
wife.) She said that it would be difficult to find sensitively decaying
geishas in the hot springs now. He looked out the window and everything was ugly, dreary and clean. Now they passed Mount Fuji's
broad paleness. Yuki's father had taken her there when she was five.
Her father had put her on a horse when she got tired. It had been
summer season, and so beautiful, she said. The top half of the mountain had refracted a special purple color into her soul. He gazed at
Fuji's dull snow far above so many dull white apartments and could
not see any beauty. *The train was born from the lengthy border tunnel; it
came into the snow country.* Behind Yuki, a man in a silk suit gaped his

lips blackly, the lower side of his mouth sagging from right to left. He looked dead. It was too warm in the car although outside it was very cold. The tiny old conductor, whose cap seemed larger than his head, pigeon-toed his slow and pensive way up the aisle. A girl in a sky-blue miniskirt passed, offering a tray of cartons which could have been anything from yogurt to wine. Now they flashed in and out of so many hollowed-out mountains and it was snowing but they were not and would never be in the snow country. *From the long border tunnel the train came out into the snow country.* There was no border, no special world. Ahead grew more swarms of houses and factories. Fuji was getting closer while she slept. The lower part of Fuji was grayish-green; it could have been the base of a cinder cone in the American west. Smokestacks offered their gruesome twisting homage. Then the train was past. Later they rushed through a snowstorm and it was lovely and white on greenish mountains and raindrops crawled side-ways on the windows. In Pond Inlet the stream glowed mirror-like in the moss, and the mosquitoes swarmed. It was almost windless. The evening was the warmest time. Mosquitoes straddled his chin and knees and fingers; when he slapped one he killed three. Dead mosquitoes smeared his clothes. — In the sun's tail, floes glowed coolly. The Ski-Doo had stopped in a glowing yellow place, and presently the shot sounded. But now the stream was frozen and covered with snow, the mosquitoes were all dead, the narwhals were gone for the year, and the solid ice was back. *From the long tunnel the train pulled out, across the border into the snow country.* He remembered the strange, richly chilly colors which Kawabata's lovers, so distant from them-selves and each other, saw through the frosted windows of the snow country. Life lay outside the windows; it throve only where the sun-set's rays struck snowdrifts, everywhere nowhere everywhere. — He got off the train.

What then? What had he found? What use had he made of his de-vices? (In Churchill's bright windy days, silver-brown light drained curvily in the river's tidal flats, flowers nodding their purple heads, belugas in the river like immense ivory-colored snails, birds overhead. The wheat cars were now open, a few kernels lying on the bottom. He ate them raw, crunching them in his teeth. He saw that the water in the river was the same color as the mud: not gray, not blue, but a sunny silver-blue all shimmery like the belly of a fish.) This book being a palindrome, and this tale being the central and infinitely regressive metonym thereof, one might hope by now to have established the center of our traveller's world, but the Earth itself is scarcely a sphere, only an asymmetric rotational spheroid—that is, a pear—and so the reference point, the map of magma which lies precisely halfway through our atlas, is not quite where intuition might lead us to expect. Then, too, mass displacements occur beneath our feet and no one knows their laws. But, as I've said, cannot we make our own planets wherever we go, with even our own idées fixes or lunar satellites to accompany us in orbits of measurable eccentricity? He'd once breakfasted at a café in Avignon, and the food was good so he returned the next morning, discovering himself to be at the center of a polished world of tables, those square lakes reflecting the chestnut trees' green mottlings and marblings even while shaded by snowy awnings. It was a vantage-point for gazing, as the Frenchmen did, at the sunny greater world of cars and breasty women while imbibing a café au lait so deliciously milky-bitter, the foam yellowish-brown like crème brûlée; beside it a fresh croissant half coiled itself, flanked by two thimble-sized butter dishes, a tiny ribbed cylinder of apricot preserves, and a hot chocolate like a grayish-blue cumulus cloud—everything in immaculate white china, the hot chocolate and its complementary milk in two white pitchers each of which was petite enough to close one's hand around, while the fresh orange juice existed imperially distinct in its silver-clear glass. From his table and the world of tables extended the whole world in a succession of unpredictably angled streets which were sometimes trapezoidal when two old buildings faced strangely; streets walled by ancient stone houses with lion-headed knockers, streets sometimes asphalted and sometimes cobbled, sometimes blistered with stones; some streets were long tunnels of plane or chestnut trees that ran all the way to the city wall which bent around the ends of the world. That was the world for but a day or three, and then he had to leave Avignon. His satellite followed him, revolving everywhere nowhere everywhere. His satellite was the atlas. It flapped its pages like an immense square bird, beguiling and terrifying him with its pursuit. Had he been courageous enough to leap onto the page which spoke most sweetly to his heart, the recession of that moon of his would cease; he'd be troubled no more. But he did not do it; he could not. On the lower terrace of the Cliff House in San Francisco one free spirit of an old fellow ran a strange concession whose hours depended on the weather and his own moods. The business was a giant camera obscura. It cost a dollar to go inside. Within the circular railing lay a world-bowl across which long foamy breakers kept running, tilting and curving and rotating as they ran, the birds overflying them in strange swoops because the world was slowly rolling over! In this world-sea, comber-striped like Jupiter, waves raced upside-down to spill down seal-rocks; and on the beach ceiling out-of-focus people lived feet upwards like flies. Sometimes their world was dismal gray and blurred, sometimes so bright and blue. The lens went round and round. And the people kept walking and breathing, not knowing that they were in the camera obscura's world. A little girl, rightside up now, struggled happily across the sand. Headlight-eyes sparkled like mica on the road above Ocean Beach. Spinning foam-braids brought the world time, and a concave horizon sagged sleepily in upon itself. The girl was lost. The traveller was lost. Lives sped like arrows, and the world turned upside down again with the turning of the great lens. The world was so blue and so excellent, and even though it was just outside this dark room, he could never get there. If he were to climb over the railing and lie down in that pale bowl upon which the lens projected its findings, then he could not get there, either, even though the image of that world might be tattooed upon him. The world was lost, and the more precious for being so. Was that so strange? Was it the secret at the center of the world, that the rest is lost?

The long blue train stretched a good half mile. Everybody had climbed down now into the coolness of Churchill, which is to say Church Chill, the consecrated snow country beyond the frosted windows. He walked around still orange-brown-bottomed pools ringed by rock and flowers and tiny trees. Visited by the striped tapering thorax and ochery-brown head of a mosquito, he let it bite. In the cracks of a lichen-spotted turtle-backed boulder grew moss and then eight-lobed blossoms of a Naples-yellow hue, and hollowed centers, uttering spiders of yellow-orange. He saw fresh bearprints in the sand near the water. He entered the smell of salt, blue mussels, crisp reddish-black seaweed. He did not yet understand the way the plants lived in their variously bordering neighborhoods, sometimes mixing, sometimes bowing in the wind.

For a moment he felt as melancholy as he always did the day before some journey to unknown climes, but then he found himself remembering one of those December nights when he'd come home from a trip, brought the duffel bag upstairs and was asleep within minutes; but he'd awakened early, his innards still flooded with another country's time where high over the cobalt sea there was nothing, then suddenly four low brownish-green islands ringed with brilliant white—Taipei? No, blue space again. Now his half-dreaming eyes found the double wake of a ship; then under a long harvest of cloud some blue and washed-out land where his soul still wandered, unable yet to follow himself to sleep in the far-off winterlands, the insides of his eyelids still imprinted by grayish-blue riverfangs, then an immense harbor with gates and channels; that was the city where his mango-colored wife and children awaited his return, so he prayed for them, lying calmly and at rest in his bed for awhile, making friends with the darkness, and then after an hour or two arose, tiptoed surely down the chilly hall, reached into the back of the closet and pulled on his old Arctic jumpsuit over his nakedness. It was like pulling on a skin of confidence and valorous deeds. He went downstairs and opened the front door and looked out. It was black and cold and raining. The clock said 4:13. He'd slept maybe a couple of hours. He was starving. Because he'd been away, there was no milk in the refrigerator for his cereal. Milk always went bad when he left it. He thought he had chicken soup or vegetable soup, but in the cupboard there was only a can of refried beans. He chopped garlic and browned it in olive oil. Then he stirred the beans in and listened to them sizzle. He found some powdered parmesan cheese and some tomato paste and spooned those on and it began to smell very good. Five minutes and it was done. He sat eating out of the frying pan, warm and happy and alert because he still had the power to move freely within the atlas. Then he opened his mail. More memories of people long unseen and things long undone exploded happily, in the same way that in Delhi the merchants showed him handmade rugs which unrolled like fireworks, red snowflakes, gold diamonds, blue flowers, snow-blue crystals. A woman whom he loved had written him a letter which said: *Often after I spend time with you, I feel almost ashamed afterwards, as if I were just speeding and babbling the whole time. It's like, there's so many things I want to ask you, and so many things I want to tell you, but afterwards I feel like I was talking so fast I found out nothing and communicated nothing. You remind me a lot of my sister, who is also strong and stoic and unafraid, and who won't ever really complain when she is uncomfortable or in pain. Eventually you become so adept at hiding your day-to-day physical or emotional discomfort that everyone thinks you are kind of superhuman and don't feel things as much.* — Maybe I don't feel, he thought. That's my secret, darling. — A woman whom he loved, the one with whom he'd eaten Steammed Crab with Anything, had written him a letter which said: *I receive your letter now how about you. I miss you lot now I'm in Bangkok now I'm always sickness but don't worry about me please good take care of your self you are my distiny. When I'm alone I miss you my dear. Joy she always take good care of me after I feel better. Bangkok it very hot now. I love you much more than I can say I send you my love and kisses. Love you much, your wife,* and before he got to the signature the world went underwater and he sat there sobbing. She was sick, always in sickness. And he had no face. — Opening the next letter, he learned that he would be leaving again soon for still another place where he had never been, worshipping the mystery called motion. *Please good take care of your self you are my distiny.* It was another ten-o'-clock dusk with all the orange melancholy of another summer slipping away, the air chilly and good inside his nostrils, an unseen locomotive thrumming on and on in the dim stillness beyond pale fireweed, the horizon made up of brown Canadian National boxcars now empty of wheat—a hundred or more of them having been unloaded at the grain elevator a mile away where belugas broke out of the river long and black and hollowly breathing and chirping like birds; actually they were whitish like giant snails but the dusk silhouetted them. They were all neck; they were snakes. The energy of an oscillating body varies in proportion with the square of the amplitude of vibration. He tried to sense the combined force at the disposal of those immense creatures and could not. The atlas had closed. Great crates sat waiting to go north on the sealift to Coral Harbour, Rankin Inlet, Baker Lake, Arviat. No place was the end, nowhere never. The end was only in the observer's eyes. After witnessing violent deaths in the semi-elongated progress of his travels, he'd begun to gain the mystic ability to know exactly how the people he loved would die should they too be murdered. He'd be chatting with them on some innocuous subject—cumuli, the Republicans—when suddenly their hideous screams would toll in his heart; he'd see their pâté'd brains oozing greasily out of their foreheads or learn how their carotid arteries would urinate the dark liquid; he'd watch life drain from their faces with astonishing speed, the eyes going fishy and useless, the flesh becoming pale gray clay. It was always his fault. And they'd go on talking, not realizing that they were dead; he'd make himself smile, since it was no good warning them. Soon they'd be broken. That was destiny. And of course he remained well aware that most of these people would not die unpleasantly at all. It was all a figment of horror, some parasite overlaying their healthy countenances, defiantly exposing itself like a cartoon pervert and drinking *his* life; he, not the doomed recipients of his poisoned friendship, was the coward who died the proverbial thousand deaths. But he didn't even fear dying so much; it was more the ritual of watching them end, always in unique ways, the timbre of their screams plausibly calibrated to their well-known voices which he had scarcely if ever heard raised; was this what Biblical prophets witnessed when they gazed with inward-rolling eyes upon their as yet unraped cities? One night what fellow travellers and parlor leftists call "the phenomenon" struck a woman who was on top of him fucking him eagerly, and for a second he thought that his tears were going to explode into her exploding intestines (impish death had blown her stomach open; the insides of his nostrils were spattered with her blood and bile); that was why he wanted to say he was sorry, now while she moaned and convulsed, his penis tearing her open. But she slammed herself upon him faster and faster! Blood trickled out of her mouth. His penis burst out of the crown of her skull (the bone of her snowy like a birch). She screamed. After the Feast of the Dead, souls become turtledoves, as some Indians used to say, but the majority believed that they go together to the Country of the Dead. PIERCE-HEAD puts their brains in His pumpkins, and then the evil dog by the treetrunk-bridge bites their heels, seeking to make them stumble into the rapids where they'll be drowned, and then there is nothing for them but lamentation and complaining endlessly, there in the Country of the Dead. She screamed. He held her more tightly and kissed her; how could he disturb or disappoint her now when she was coming? Afterward he buried his face between her breasts and listened to the heart a mere inch beneath the hot sweatslicked flesh, beating out its song: *I'm alive; I'm alive.* This was the center. He remembered a woman he'd once known for a year or two, a graphic designer, Roman Catholic, a tall brunette (how to characterize a person? what is most relevant?), who'd said to him: I believe that people are here on this planet because they need to learn certain lessons. And I think no one can know what lessons another person can learn. — And now he wanted to shout: What lesson am I to learn from these screams? For a long time that question echoed inside his own mucus-walled chest defiantly, bouncing and flailing against his organs, so of course there was no answer. But one day he asked it sincerely, and then he got a reply. The mysterious woman, the one with the delicious-smelling oval face who had usually slept in her own hotel room in Montana, she was the one who decided to get sterilized. He said: I'll come be with you. I'll hold your hand. — When they stuck the IV in she moaned and said: Oh, it hurts. It hurts, and it feels so cold going in. — Then the anesthesiologist, that representative of superior puissance, took a slender hypodermic, fitted it to the intake port, and slowly pressed the plunger. The anesthesiologist had drawn water from the wells of salvation, and she could not see it because she was locked down upon the table with her thighs spread, and people all around! He held her hand. That transparent liquid which the anesthesiologist had almost lasciviously squeezed into her IV crawled down the tube; he watched it coming closer and then it went inside her hand, scuttled up her armways into her shoulder and up her neck and she whispered: It hurts; it *hurts!* — When it got to her brain she began acting vague, and it went around and around inside her, and each time it came back to her brain she got drunker and wearier and her eyes glazed; then she was gone. He kept holding her hand until the doctor and the nurse and the anesthesiologist made him go outside. An hour later they called him. She was on a gurney outside the blue curtain, and her eyes were closed. (He peeked behind the blue curtain and saw another woman with thighs spread.) He held his darling's hand. When she woke up, the pain was so intense that her teeth chattered and huge tears ran down her cheek. He called them and made them give her morphine. The morphine didn't take for a long time. They had to give her three shots. After an hour or so the morphine began to make her sick, and she vomited. She vomited all night. Sometimes she was too weak to bring it up easily, and then she stuck her finger down her throat, at which the occasionally visiting nurse would make a face. (The nurse also disapproved because his darling hadn't any underwear.) He was beside her with the curvy tray of pink plastic to catch her vomit, and when he emptied the plastic tray for the third time he understood what the lesson was: The screams were so horrible because life was beautiful. He, the dullard, needed to be hunted by screaming throughout his life, so that the fear, agony and grief at *losing* life which they evoked would remind him to cherish it in himself and others. — I also believe in the value of human existence, the Roman Catholic woman had said. I believe there are other human souls coming which want a chance. A lot of stuff I don't understand, but I wonder if accidents ever really happen. I don't think I've ever had one. If I got pregnant, I'd probably take it as a challenge. I'd probably take it as a chance to express some love inside me. I don't believe in judging another person. If it's a young girl, she has to be given a choice. — The next day, sleepy from her omnipotent medicines, the mysterious one said to him: I love you. — How do you feel? he asked. — She smiled slowly. I'm so happy, because I'm *sterile!* — Every day she got stronger. Soon she could get out of bed again. He loved her life's ongoing. He loved his life. He rode the bus and emptied the garbage and picked up dogshit and composed his Traveller's Epitaph: *I can't say I know much, but I've loved, maybe too much; maybe from love I'll get my death. I've seen Madagascar and walked the frozen sea. I have no trade, make nothing but pretty things which fail against the seriousness of rice. I'm not well or wise; I fear death; but I've never failed any woman I loved. I never refused gold bracelets to any wife who asked them of me. When they did me evil I received it gracefully; when they were good to me I gave them thanks. I denied none esteem, never heeded shaming words. I can't say I've done much or been much, but I'm not ashamed of who I've been. I don't ask your forgiveness or remembrance. I'm in the flowers on my grave, unknowing and content.* — But it didn't ring true. He hadn't loved enough (how can one love enough?); and how could he dare to say he hadn't failed anybody? Whom hadn't he failed? He could only say that he loved life. He closed his eyes, and a screaming grey face exploded into crimson gobbets.

That evening the wind was full of vowels, and it said: *ai ee eh uh oh eh ee oh.* He listened and listened again. Then he understood that the wind was saying: *why we never know where we go.* Everywhere nowhere up down around.

He set out for the Barren Lands, always following the coast of Hudson Bay. One of his more reliable and harmless pleasures was to return to his tent after a stroll sufficient to make the cold seem warm, look around one last time at the midnight sun, breathe another breath of that good subarctic air, undo his boots, crawl into the tent, pull the boots off, zip the doorway shut against mosquitoes and rain, and then drink to his heart's content of pure and chilly river water, the bottle having been filled that day by him or one of his Inuk friends from the place where some children swam and others sat with their parkas on. Then he walked to the place where there were no more Inuk friends, nobody nowhere forever, and his walking was completed.

He listened to voices. He loved them. They were always different, although they said the same things; in much the same way that the cries of dogs sometimes resemble those of children, sometimes those of wolves or pulled nails, sometimes those of soccer fans, and sometimes those of dogs.

Then the day came when he realized that he could truly understand some of the words the dogs shouted; and without effort he heard the meaning in the haunting cries of gulls. It was only because he spent so much time alone, eating little; it was nothing special.

He was cold. He shivered and twitched like grass. The skeletons which had been sleeping in the inch-high lichen hills grabbed with rib-claws, vertebral hooks, and tailbone rakes, wanting to pull themselves out of the cold wet place. His lichen-blots were all he owned now, but they were bright enough to keep him counting them in the wind, absorbed like a vampire in wasting all before his dawnless dawn. The grass-columns flashed like skirts.

I know I said I wouldn't write, his first love had written. *I lied. The cancer is back. I'm scared to death. I cannot believe this is happening. I am not vain. I do not care about losing my breast but I do want to live. Do you believe in God?*

Once she'd sent him a photograph of herself at the zoo; and when he found it years later in an envelope with a thirteen-cent butterfly stamp she scarcely seemed familiar. But he had always been bad with faces. A giraffe stretched its neck in the background. Her beauty was what they used to call "classical." It was a face that could easily have been haughty or cold but in the photo she had a sweet little smile and she looked so young, so young. She could have been his little sister; in a few more years she could be his daughter. He was ashamed that he had ever caused her inconvenience or pain. He could never be hers now. He had thought that the picture, at least, would always belong to him; but as he'd wandered through the atlas, the photograph and he had diverged. On the envelope she'd written: *Inside are pictures! Lions and tigers, monkeys cats and giraffes!* and *Hey, did you hear Nixon resigned?* and *If I wrote you in French could you understand it?*

Sure, he said. Try me.

He listened to the plants.

Willow Lady grew slowly out of his thoughts, hour by hour in that summer of perpetual chilly light. The wind was her breath and the wind's voice was her voice. The wind rarely spoke anymore. She had a face like a sly brown mask. She had Inuk eyes. She smiled richly, showing her teeth. Her lean skull was cradled in hair whose stubby woody strands meandered across the moss, holding her safely down; willow leaves sprouted from them in dark green clusters and sometimes there were fuzzy buds. She told him to walk to the waterfall. The wind said: *go.* But he didn't know where the waterfall was. He wanted to find it because he wanted to listen to it and breathe the aerated coolness when he hung his head over the cliffside, watching the white foam softer than moss become brown and then indigo as it rushed away, into the world. He asked Willow Lady how to get there but she wouldn't tell him. There were yellow flecks in the sky, the hue of that stone called tiger's eye.

Skeletons buzzed in the moss.

The tundra became an exploding puzzle. Leaves, flowers, stalks, buds, roots, mosquitoes and bones flew apart, leaving white snow between them.

Long green fibrils crawled across his soul's eye. He saw flowers and leaves glowing happily upon pages of snow.

Low clouds swarmed over the water which glowed with colored threads. The mossy promontories reached toward the Arctic islands.

Now grey clouds came over him, and the water writhed with windy lines like springs, and the droplets sprang apart, leaving whiteness between—an atlas page. He could walk along the beaches and pick up pieces of fossil coal polished over and over by the sea. The sky showed blue-green through the cloud-chinks, while pale blue icebergs bestrode the water in equivalent rarity.

Willow Lady was his wife. He didn't really know her.

He laid his face down in the moss and kissed her cold mouth that drooled fresh water. The wind said: *oh.*

He told her about his wife in Madagascar whom he'd betrayed, about the mysterious woman who "just didn't feel it" when he made love to her, about the sad girl in that hotel room in Philadelphia whom he'd made sadder, about the woman in the House of Joy who made his heart shoot joyously out of the top of his skull, about his wife in Cambodia who needed money for facial surgery and when he sent the money she never got it and so she sent him pathetic color photographs of the operation and after that, although he went to Cambodia to give her more money, he never found her again, about Kawabata's geisha in the snow country, about his friend Joe, who didn't respect him anymore, about the woman in Sarajevo who said that it was too difficult to explain, about his Inuk girl who didn't love him now, who was just a nasty drunk, about the many he'd failed, and the few he'd done well by—he was not even potent enough to fail everyone!—about his first love, one of whose letters said: *I don't need anyone very much. It's a cold feeling, a feeling where I know I should be crying and I can't. During those four days there were many times when I should have cried; I wanted to cry; I hung my head as if I were crying but all that happened was a kind of mockery inside myself showing me that I could out-deceive someone; I could hold my own. I knew during the entire time that I would be all right. In the face of outright physical violence, there's always an escape.* — Sure there is, honey. Just ask any Pole or Gypsy or Jew or Armenian or Cambodian in any mass grave. — He tried to explain that in spite of his weakness he'd remained sincere, that when he thought about the ones he loved, even if he felt guilty or sorrowful at times there lay always beyond those emotions a shining wall of goodness: he loved them more year by year, and their goodness was as an organ-chord of glory in some great cathedral. — Would that be the end? Not yet! One more, one more . . . One more, then, not his first love and not his last, a married woman from Toronto, also no doubt categorized in his FBI file: Jewish, with a husband and a little daughter she loved, smart, a journalist, proud of her breasts, fortyish, with small hands. She liked to go for long walks with him, holding his hand. She had a soft low sensual sexual voice that aroused him even over the telephone. As soon as she said his name he'd be wanting to spread her legs and ride her. He couldn't get enough of her. He was crazy about her. He needed her loving ways. He sensed that she liked handcuffs, although they hadn't tried that together yet. After a long breezy day of walking by the lake it was always so good to go back to her hotel and put his hand up her dress and bring her face down upon his face. Sometimes it would be chilly in the hotel room and he would enjoy feeling cold when he took his clothes off and seeing the goose pimples on her buttocks as they got under the crisp sheets. She brought him life, life! She said that sometimes he struggled in his sleep, but he never remembered that. In those months between "seeing her," as we quaintly say, he sometimes had serial dreams of being a Polish soldier in September 1939, with the Nazis coming on one side and the Soviets on the other, closing in, shooting and killing, divebombing and tankrolling while Hitler in Berlin watched movies of Warsaw burning; he was trapped now in a marsh with a few comrades, all of them wounded, and the sky was red and yellow and stank of gunpowder. The forest was burning and quaking. Nobody could hear anymore. A row of trees smashed down; his comrades were decapitated; he was the last one. Could Hitler see him? Behind, anodized black tanks were crawling out of the ooze like crocodiles. Before him, where the trees had been blasted away, he saw a river clogged with corpses, and then a golden plain of wheat that went all the way to the horizon; the sky was black with Stukas wing to wing, coming toward him, coming down. He dreamed of sitting in an opera box with Hitler and a woman whom he had thought was his, but in the middle of the opera Hitler stood up and began dancing with the woman and nobody else dared to look. He looked though, and Hitler's eyes filled him with pain and confusion. He woke up remembering that dream night after night, struggling to keep his eyelids up so that the dream could not slam down upon him again. But when he slept in the Jewish woman's arms, he felt safe. He felt that she loved him and trusted him. He wanted to be with her always. He wanted to meet her little daughter, which of course he'd never do. Waking up happy and rested, he held her hand, kissed her lips, and she was already rolling on top of him.

She was life. He could fall asleep and know that when he woke up she'd be there. It was permissible to sleep. Even Soviets did it. Her body was still quite firm. She said that she was sorry he couldn't have seen her breasts when she was younger, but he said he was happy with them just as they were. Sometimes they went shopping for toys for her daughter: hologram buttons, ribbons and things; when the fog came in they might stop and he'd buy her a beer; by night they walked hand in hand through Chinatown like obedient tourists, holding hands. He felt that he was good to her and she to him. If she were any other creature she would have been a speckled trout. He would have been a frog. They asked little of each other. She said that she sometimes woke up thinking of him. She said that she sometimes dreamed of him. He never dreamed about her; she simply kept the bad dreams away. He never saw her being murdered. Of course maybe that was because her being married shadowed the relationship with such an obvious ending. That would be something to fear. If they stopped in time, her husband wouldn't find out. Maybe he would never find out. He didn't want to wreck her marriage, to make her little daughter cry. Why didn't he break it off, then? Because they were happy together. The way they were, it couldn't be wrong. Sometimes she was a little ashamed. But he intrigued her, and she was his medicine, his dove like the dove that the boy had drawn for him in Jerusalem. Did she think of herself as Jewish? She said she didn't, but then she'd tell him how one time in a grocery store a mean old lady was picking on a man with Parkinson's disease for being too slow in the checkout line, and when she came to the man's defense the lady turned on her and shouted that she was a filthy Jew. Somehow the old lady could see in her face what she was, she said to him, trembling, and he embraced her and wished that he could send his Polish dreams to the old lady. She told him about her daughter's birthday party. And then she, his dear one, wriggled her hot little body in his arms. She was not the end.

Now only his fingers moved. Willow Lady rustled leaves in his face.

He brought his lips to the ice, which at first was merely a glittering white surface of giant grains and crystals under the blue sky, but as the purple cumuli drew across heaven like the underside of a metal drawer the ice turned bluer and cooler-looking with a yellow line of evil running across its surface, parallel to the horizon—he had a longing to devour the horizons of this world; and here he remembered the white line where a wintry noon ended in Nevada, immense and fluffy, shooting cloud-stuff up into the sky like some defense against falling stars, so vast and triumphant and far away across the plains of tan, rust and beige. His lips did not stick to the ice yet.

Presently the snow began to fall. It fell in big moist flakes that clumped together even as they fell. It did not make a stinging slapping sound like the sleet or the cold dry snow; it pattered very gently down, and kept coming. In four hours there were as many inches. The tussocks on the hills became white fairy mushrooms. On the flats, golden plant-stalks still rose above the snow, not yet choked. Snow kept falling. The ice upon the river hid itself treacherously, and the whitened ridges dimmed gently into the sky. The world was almost featureless. In places it was relieved very occasionally by the black lines and specks of boulder-edges; only where those were swallowed up in white distances could the horizon be approximated. Everything was very warm and still.

This was the soul of it, this rushing and swooping in winged or wheeled tombs, always straining toward some beauty as remote as the sun.

The train entered the tunnel. The atlas closed. Inside, each page became progressively more white and warm.

Willow Lady rolled on top of him and took him in her arms. She rocked him to sleep. No more nowhere nobody. She grew a blanket of leaves over him, and he was even warmer. He lay at the center from which the world rotated round and round and round.

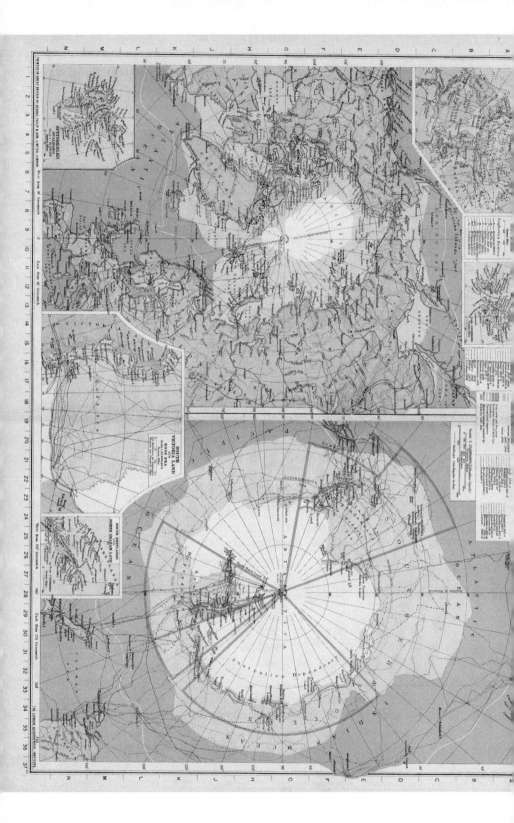

RED AND BLUE

Bangkok, Prah Nakhon-Thonburi Province, Thailand (1993)

Bangkok, Prah Nakhon-Thonburi Province, Thailand (1993)

Past the restaurant lazed a corridor of water-marked concrete, whose righthand wall curved, being the edge of the stadium where I was going to see how proud garlanded warriors beat each other down. A Siamese cat pursued a rat. Another cat sat on the concrete wide-eyed with ears raised, forepaws demurely together. A man was filling a chest with a bucket of ice. A woman emerged laughing from the storeroom from which workmen were wheeling water jugs on trolleys past the stand where soft drink bottles stood as colorful as Christmas trees, and bottlenecks grew from baskets of shaved ice, shining with incredible purity. Soon there'd come a storm of punches and kicks, gloves slapping on the side of the head, because the steel gates were open, and the million-cratered concrete, walled by yellowing whitewashed slats, crouched ready now to let Red and Blue into the ring whose whirly fans now vivisected the overcast sky and made the concrete rings of corrugated metal of which the ceiling was comprised seem to tremble. But it was only four-thirty, and the rotation of the fans was just for practice. They died; the beer and soft drink signs faded; and the sticky air fell back upon my shoulders like a moldy blanket.

Because the concept of two men punching and kicking each other for hire is not unattended by conceptual and ethical difficulties, I'd paid for the privilege of entering the realm called Ringside, founded eons ago by King Money and dedicated to the proposition that others should not be able to get what they haven't shelled out for. Ringside, in short, cost 600 baht,★ but within its circular dominions, practically against the ring, lay a special section for family, trainer and friends, who would soon be leaning their heads back open-mouthed, prancing, shouting *ooooh!*, pushing each other's shoulders; they'd be gloating, applauding, slamming their hips against the stands, bouncing on their feet. I don't know how much, if anything, they paid.

Ringside was surrounded by a thick-meshed fence through which the middle-payers (320 baht) could see, more or less, and behind and above that zone was another mesh fence which demarcated the outer limbo of the 120-baht masses. The early enthusiasts were already there. They gripped the fence like prisoners. The middle zone was still almost empty. Two skinny boys danced there, embraced, kicked high gently at each other's faces while a third boy clung to the mesh netting. They were the ones who a few years later would be working out in the park of sweating flowers. Maybe they already were. Their heads shot up and lurched. They smiled as they struck each other. One boy overpowered another, forcing his head down just as the authorities turned on lights, fans and music, and the boxers entered to be taped up. Cats still wandered about the ring. At ringside the smiling young usherette in red came like an airplane stewardess to take orders for soft drinks and to peddle videos: Thai Boxing: The Hardest Sport on Earth. Perhaps the sport of rape or torture is more difficult, at least for the loser, but kickboxing is certainly hard enough. I could see that on the boxers' faces as they finished getting ready and the men in green came in—men in green vests, that is, with a giant golden jewel on the back of each, and white Thai writing. I never figured out why they were there. The music gradually became louder and more martial. All rose for the anthem. When it was over, all bowed. Then they stood craning and glaring at the ring.

The two boxers entered the ring wearing garlands and yellow-bordered blue robes. They began to sweat almost at once. They

★ In 1993 this was about U.S. $24.

bowed to Buddha. Then they threw off the robes, showing their trunks—Red and Blue. While someone tinged cymbals and someone else blew an instrument as cavernously loud as a Tibetan horn, they knelt and stretched, each in his corner, drinking water held out by his trainer who afterwards hung the garland on the corner pole. The boxers then quickly knelt and touched their heads to the floor.

I thought I might have seen Blue a week before in the park of sweating flowers where men lay knees up on phony-granite benches, breathing steadily, some with wrists infolded across their hearts so that steel watchbands caught the cloudy light, others with their fingers hanging over the edges of the benches; in this park of sweating flowers, a man with what looked like an astral map tattooed across his back (thrashing lines, quartered circles, and captions of Chaldean incomprehensibility) was working out, bending and lifting. He was not Blue. In fact, that night at Lumpini Stadium I did not see a single tattooed boxer. Another man who was not Blue, sporting differently quartered circles on his chest, lay on the press bench by the ginkgo tree, lifting weights. His pectorals were as big as his thighs. He had great muscular tattooed breasts. A third, who now took his turn, carried a great world-circle on his back blessed by many notations. The weights rode up and down. He yelled: *Ho! ho! ho! ho!* A fourth, now lying on the bench, lifted a hundred and fifty pounds, crying: *Euh! uh! uh!* A fifth stood over him, frowning, his neck gold-chained, and they changed places. The frowner's quartered circle glistened as he began. Across the sand, other brown men stood silently swinging fists over each other's heads. Weights rolled silently up and down on pulleys. And then a slender man in a T-shirt walked by. He stopped and watched and smiled slightly. Then he went away. I think he was Blue.

Slender dancing knees, the sharp slap of a foot against a rib—how different this was from the boxing I had seen in the U.S.A., where they only punch—and yet also so similar, because here too are the ones who clap whenever their hero gets in a blow, and here too there has to be a loser, and I hate seeing anyone lose.

At the round's-end bell they sat Blue down in a chair, poured water into a big saucer, laved it over him, encouraging and caressing him. Then he bowed to his garland.

At the end of the second round he shivered as they poured water over his head. They were working at him, supporting his face, massaging his ribs. He was limper now.

At the end of the third round he gazed at his feet on the dirty canvas while they rubbed him down. He barely moved when they poured cold water over his head. He breathed heavily through his open mouth. When they stood him up, he clung with both hands to the greasy ropes.

At the beginning of the fourth round he got in a knee to Red's groin, and then a knee to the hip. Red did not cry out. The boxers never did. They wore the face of someone enduring pain: resolute, it scarcely distorted; it only tightened upon itself.

Red shot a leg up to get Blue in the stomach. Blue did not flinch. Both kept their gloves above their faces. Red got an arm around Blue's neck, punched him behind, hissing *tsss!* and threw Blue down. Arising less than easily, Blue gripped Red in an expressionless embrace which somehow involved the side of a foot against a knee. This was life, was life's bitter sweat in the hourlong moments between intermissions when silver strings of water drip down the boxer's hair, the centurylong moments when knee meets knee and thigh meets stomach, when the heel finally scores the solar plexus. A leg shot up. Blue's wrist went under Red's knee and threw him. The crowd cried: *Eh! Eh! Eh!*—because that was rare; from few of these moments could anything be squeezed but continued clinging and struggling. Blue and Red were embracing at the neck, working their knees around each other's legs and buttocks. A glove in the side, but it was always an embrace. They locked knees around each other. More than anything else I'd ever seen, it was like some new and terrible way of making love.

At the end of that round Blue's arms drooped down around the ropes like wilting stems. He gazed wide-eyed as they washed him, flicked him with a wet towel, lifted his legs. He bowed to the garland. The grayclad judges sat with folded arms, almost unblinking.

In the fifth round Red got in a knee to Blue's kidney. They were head to head, dancing in their pain, holding on while mosquitoes bit silently. Blue thrust out his chin and raised his shoulder, flailing, and the young lady in red brought soft drinks to the spectators at ringside and a white cat came out from between everyone's legs. Red whirled him against the ropes and the referee separated them. Then they danced, but not so lightly. Ankles flashed high like swords. A foot struck a shoulder.

The boxer in the red corner wins the prize, said the announcer.

They took the garlands away. The winner shot both hands above his head, then bowed. The loser walked away.

The stadium was full now of people whose light-colored garments hung in the darkness like moths. A cop stood ready in helmet and jackboots. A fresh Red and Blue entered the ring, threw off their robes, bowed to their garlands; and I saw that the bodies and souls had never mattered; it was only Red against Blue forever, no matter who won; and one kicked but the other caught a knee in his armpit and pulled him down. When they'd come into the ring they were wearing circlets around their heads with stiff rods in back like the handles of frying pans; there was a long tassel that made each look feminine, especially with all the flowers of their garlands; and when they stretched and swayed and flexed, they were like dancing girls. But perfect dancing lasts only for the first round. Soon enough, arms upraised, mouth gaping, Blue leaned weakly on his helpers' shoulders. A dripping towel on his head while they pulled his arms and legs and chafed them, a caress, a shake—nothing could reach him. They boxed at him, trying to show him something, but, panting, he stared straight ahead. After each round, he spat out his mouthguard. They opened his pants and pulled something out. Now they were trying to massage energy back into his muscles. Lifting him, they sucked water from his ears.

Sometimes Blue was on the ropes. I didn't want to see much more. The trainer lifted Blue's slender legs above his head. He'd bowed to the garland at the beginning of each round, but that hadn't saved him from a knee to the balls four times. The man's face scarcely seemed to change, but he burst into sweat and swayed back almost proudly. At the end of the round his trainer looked in his pants, rubbed him down, slapping his hand to make him listen; his head flopped toward the trainer and he nodded. When they raised his legs above his head, he grimaced with pain.

They fell together; the crowd went *ooooh!* open-mouthed. They flailed at one another with spread fingers and the crowd cheered uh-*oh!* uh-*oh!* The fighters' wrists were above their heads as if they desperately strove to be birds.

From behind the middle zone's fence a man yelled advice, trying to teach Blue, his hero, how to punch. But Red threw Blue back down again and kneed him in the groin.

With each incarnation the air was hotter with crowd-sweat, more eye-watering with cigarette smoke. People were betting, fingers raised; people were crying out with deep ritualized shouts. Red won, then Blue, kicking Red in the pit of the stomach although Red kept swinging; Red won, and I sat illuminated by their flashes of pain, shock, rage and triumph—and, so often, just the dull gaze of endurance. They sometimes prayed while waiting for the verdict. Sometimes they ducked back from a blow. So often I saw the sudden mask of disappointment that falls across the loser's face (the winner raises a fist, bows); this mask was stroboscopic,★ flashing each twist in this chain of violent beauty, the puncher's face merely determined, the victim's bobbing under his punches; each seemed about to cry but that was only the effect of grimacing; anyhow these faces were but workings in the molten flesh that worked itself like clay, each skull an anvil for the fisthammer or heelhammer to forge into that ultimate mask of loss as the crowd cried: *Yao! Yao! Eeeeh!* — Sometimes Red and Blue were a pair whom no one cared about or betted on; then the crowds leaned against the fences and grinned at one another, or watched expressionlessly, only chanting and chattering a little when a flurry of punches landed. Then a new Red and Blue would offer themselves. Now the shouts swarmed and rang like a flock of angels, celestial and horrible; but I could see no difference; it was still Red and Blue. Before they began I saw one contender talking with his trainer, the other stretching, balancing on one leg, lifting and flexing the other with all his toes apart, as if in illustration of the futility of stratagems; after him would come the next Red or Blue, nothing ever to be decided. What did Napoleon accomplish, or Genghis Khan? True, the world would be different without them, but the fortunes of the prizes for which they fought continue their shift and ebb.

A judge passed a slip to the referee. Red had won. Then it was time for time for a new head to be bouncing back against the ropes.

★ Or perhaps it was just the strobelike effect of the fans cutting across the light-tubes in the smoky humidity.

They hadn't even gotten to the champion fight yet, but I'd seen enough.

When I came outside it was night and I saw a canal full of rising gray water caked with raindrops. I saw girls in yellow uniforms scurrying to work in massage parlors, and a drenched old man between stopped cars (eight abreast in the rain, and motorcycles darting in between) stood selling newspapers in plastic bags. And I thought: no matter who you are or what you do, life is war.

THE BEST WAY
TO SHOOT H

San Francisco, California, U.S.A. (1993)
San Francisco, California, U.S.A. (1993)
San Francisco, California, U.S.A. (1993)
San Francisco, California, U.S.A. (1993)
San Francisco, California, U.S.A. (1993)
San Francisco, California, U.S.A. (1993)
San Francisco, California, U.S.A. (1993)
San Francisco, California, U.S.A. (1993)

San Francisco, California, U.S.A. (1993)

O n a hot and sinister night when the whores on Mission Street were yelling: What are you parking next to me for? I'm gonna smash your head in, motherfucker! and their pimps only said: You want any shiva? You want any doses?—on that night he turned down Seventeenth and it was dark and empty. Someone whistled urgently behind him in a two-toned signal. Whores and pimps called each other that way when something was up; maybe other characters did, too. It made him nervous. When he got to Capp Street there was only one whore, a demented pimpled mumbler far away down at Sixteenth, and the dark vacuum between thickened with smoky rainy zeroes and enigmas as his anxiety contemplated it. Another whistle. He began to walk toward the demented whore. At once he heard a louder whistle; and looking up he saw a man leaning out a window, regarding him, and the man put his fingers to his mouth and whistled. Instantly another whistle replied from behind him, much closer than before. He looked over his shoulder but could see nothing. A half-suppressed cough came only a few steps behind. He walked quickly to Sixteenth where it was light, and the demented whore pulled up her skirt to let him enumerate the stale jellies of her flesh, but then he heard the whistle again from the darkness of a doorway just behind him; and he was getting angry now, so he strode boldly to the doorway (standing some distance away to delay and hopefully prevent the launching of any blade into his stomach) and he said: Were you calling me?

You want any doses, man? said the darkness shyly. I got me some mighty fine powder . . .

He replied: Now I see. I thought it was you, but it's nobody. Isn't it amazing, to realize that? There's *nobody!*

San Francisco, California, U.S.A. (1993)

In those nights he was living on Mission Street because so many people swarmed there that he could hope someone might actually smash through his soul-eye's smooth flat window to kill him or make him free, but instead the people just flowed down his pane like gray rain. That afternoon there'd been a carnival with fat ladies moving their bottoms in the streets, black-eyed Asian schoolgirls cooling their teeth in the hissing streams of each other's breath, brown girls in black and silver skirts working their lips into kisses; and he'd never forget that coffeeskinned girl on the parade float, swinging her gold-spangled crotch in sharp bursting arcs; now that that was ended and the police had stacked the barricades back into rented vans there remained only the same threateners and bottle-smashers, and above them the same smell of doughnuts in the hallways because the hotel was right over a bakery—preferable to the adjoining hotel, which had married a Chinese fish market for so many do-us-parts that the slime of rotting seafood had leached its way through the wall and summoned the same slow fat evil flies that Lucifer kept under his tongue; no, give me doughnuts, please. Well, he had his doughnuts—the sweet soggy smell of them, anyway, a smell as weary as being alone at ten-o'-clock on a rainy Sunday night in a sleazy hotel.

A voice was saying: He said he was gonna gimme twenty bucks but I need thirty.

He unlocked the door. The old lady was kneeling on the floor, looking up at him in terror while her very dark blood crept slowly down her arm, the hypodermic needle which was stuck in it wine-colored with blood. Her grayish-blonde hair was drawn back tight against her head to make her younger. Her arm had doubled up as if to thrust the elbow forward in defense of her life. She held a bloody paper towel in her hand.

San Francisco, California, U.S.A. (1993)

She wasn't such an old lady, actually. She was just a whore who only got her periods when she went to jail, because she couldn't shoot her speedballs in there. She disliked getting periods, but what she positively hated was being forced to sleep at night. (Everyone knows that whores are nocturnal while johns and prison guards [with some exceptions] are diurnal, which proves at least one difference between the species.) And because he lived with her, because he tried to sleep at night, he dreaded the night, dreaded the smell of old cigarettes and old age, the sound of moaning and coughing in the bed beside him.

He sat down on the bed, and she came and sat next to him. She turned up her half-dead lips to be kissed. — Oh, that feels *wonderful,* she said.

There was a knock.

Who is it? she cried ferociously.

It's me, said a sad shy voice.

Grunting, the old lady popped her hernia back in and opened the door. It was the whore who'd been raped with a vacuum cleaner. (Two days afterward, her stomach had suddenly swelled up, and she fainted from the pain.)

You get it? said the old lady.

Got it right here, the girl whispered.

They heated the bottlecap with the old lady's lighter, untwisted the paper, added water from the brandy bottle (the white stuff in the cap was already fizzing), stirred it lovingly with the needle end.

Just draw it up, the old lady snarled.

I'm tryin' to.

The girl peered down at the mosquito-striped needle. — I left seventy-five, she said. Twenty-five for me, fifty for you.

Let's make it eighty.

OK, said the girl guiltily.

They were almost ready now to bare their arms to the needle, like children who didn't have a ticket to a carnival, stretching their hands out from so far behind the fence.

Well, that came out right, said the old lady with satisfaction.

I'll come back. Where's the restroom? I gotta stick myself in a personal place.

The old lady shot her a glare. — You'd better come back, or I'll hunt you down and kill you.

The girl cringed in terror. — I'm sorry, I'm sorry, she said almost inaudibly. I'll do it here.

Go to the restroom if you want. You heard what I said.

I'll do it here.

Well, stop whining and do it here, then. You need me to hit you? Which personal place is it today?

My pussy.

That's where the happy veins are, the old lady laughed, the needle already in her wrist, the smelly pantyhose knotted around her upper arm . . .

At midnight, after the girl had gone out to make more money (her pussy was already abscessed, but one time when he was with her she'd spread herself with pride and told him: You can always tell if a woman's got a disease by smelling her vagina. If it's not healthy she's got a bad odor. See, I don't smell, do I?), he killed the light. He awoke an hour later to see the old lady kneeling on the carpet, trying to stick herself, walking on her knees to the sink so that she wouldn't wake him when she washed the blood from arm and sleeve.

San Francisco, California, U.S.A. (1993)

There was a black woman sitting naked on his bed, with the old lady wearing nothing but underpants beside her. He knew the black woman well. She was the whore who put makeup on her needle tracks (which she called fleabites). She was the whore who always made the john pay first and then said: OK, baby, you just lemme go out and get my medicine and then I'll be more relaxed. — Whenever she could get away with it, she didn't come back. — The old lady was hitting her with the needle and the black woman's face was turned away and the old lady slyly knuckled her vulva but the black woman said: I been in the pen but I ain't never been no lesbian. I don't have no use for girls, 'cause they don't have three legs! Course, I don't need boys, either, when I got dope. (I dunno about that vein there, baby. Maybe you can't stick that vein.) Dope's *my* sex. Dope comes first, food comes second, and boys come last. Sorry, honey, but your finger just ain't on my list. An' them boys, they should be thankful they're on the list at all. 'Cause if they don't like it I can just go to the store and buy me a rubber husband. Plug it in and turn it on an' I don't need any other kind.

The old lady wasn't listening. She slid her middle finger deep inside the black woman's vagina. Then she eased the plunger down, and the black woman's eyeballs rolled up in gladness.

Sitting on the bed, he glanced at the old lady's sorry arms. He remembered the dark shoeshine place on Sixteenth with the airplane glue smell where he'd come with a broken watch because the proprietor had a round gentle face and his spectacles were alive and his fingers were repairman's fingers, downgrowing piney tendrils studded with sensitivity, so he gave his watch to the proprietor, who took it into another world where a bird flapped on television, purifying all the spools and bins of shoes and boots and purses and jackets, and the proprietor said something to himself in Chinese and took the watch to a pincer-machine, a clamp-machine and then a sewing machine; and smiling quite happily, the proprietor returned from behind the partition on which rubber soles and crescents of a mysterious silver metal waited to come alive, and the proprietor set the watch down on the counter, on which a piece of paper was laid, and the paper said: The Blood of Jesus covers all of my sin.

Sixty-thirty, the proprietor explained. Any time is sixty-thirty. Trusty me.

How much do I owe you?

Three dollar OK?

Sure.

The watch was fixed, and he was happy. Then the proprieter showed his own watch, whose plastic strap he couldn't fix.

The old lady's arm and soul were both like that. She fixed others, for a fee, but how could she repair herself?

San Francisco, California, U.S.A. (1993)

Well, sorry I was gone for so long, whispered the whore who'd been raped with a vacuum cleaner. I got another date, and I just couldn't let that twenty dollars pass.

I don't give a shit about that, the old lady said. Do you have it or not is all I give a shit about.

I'm sorry, the girl said quickly, pulling out the bag of powder.

It only took the old lady only a quarter of an hour to find a vein. The girl watched big-eyed, licking her lips. Afterward the old lady started happily complaining about the black woman, mainly because she wasn't there. — That raunchy stuff is what bugs me, she said. She wears a skirt that barely covers the crack of her ass, no underpants, and she opens up her legs when the cars go by. I went by in a car with one of my regulars and she started flappin' her titties. It was so *disrespectful!*

I dunno, the girl said, embarrassed because she was not listening. I gotta go stick myself in a personal place.

But the old lady would not let her go. She made her listen to the story about the last time she'd gone to jail, when she lost her thirty-dollar coat. When you go into jail and anyone in your hotel sees you get picked up, your belongings are gone on the first night. The black woman said: I don't know what happened to your coat. — But when the old lady got out, the black woman was wearing it when she went down the street. The old lady said: Isn't that my coat? The black woman said: Uh-uh. Anyhow, it's too tight for you. It looks better on me. — In the end the old lady had to trade her for it.

Please, I gotta go, the girl said in agony. I'll come right back. I done my duty.

She ran to the sink, bent her head down, and retched.

I'm sorry, honey, said the old lady. I didn't know you needed to fix so bad.

It's okay, the girl said, smiling nervously in case someone might strike her.

San Francisco, California, U.S.A. (1993)

He heard somebody moan when he began to turn the key in the lock. When he opened the door, the old lady was there, wearily searching for a vein.

He went to sleep and was awakened by a sick smoky smell. She was burning a piece of Brillo pad until the flame stopped being green, because that was the way to remove the plastic coating, which would hurt you if you inhaled its fumes, and when the Brillo was ready she packed it into the segment of car antenna she'd found on the sidewalk and snapped off a piece of and shoved paper towels through with the spoke of an old umbrella to get rid of the lube until it was a good crack pipe, long and skinny and elegant. She didn't care about smoking crack one way or the other. But so many johns did nowadays that she had to be ready. The last time, she'd used a drapery hook to pry loose the glass tube in the bottom of a Finlandia vodka bottle. But she'd gone to jail after that, and since then she hadn't seen any Finlandia bottles in the trash can.

He went to sleep again and began to dream of something whose shape he could not yet see, but from the other world came what the old lady called magic rocks, which were the ceramic bases to spark plugs; one of these could smash plexiglas if you needed to break into a car window, and one of these now shattered the glass of his dream; it was her coughing. She was kneeling in the darkness that smelled like stale doughnuts and rotten fish, holding the needle in her teeth, cutting the plastic baggie of powder, pouring the powder into the bottle cap to sizzle. He heard her whisper to herself: Pay a dollar seventy-seven for a little styrofoam chest and seventy-seven cents for a little ice . . . — Then she twisted the elastic ligature around her upper arm until it sank in and the flesh wrinkled around it. She rolled the bulging vein between her fingers and twirled the needle in, her eyes wide and dark. When she pulled the syringe out it was bloody. Cocking her arm, she slid the red wet point back into herself. She was mumbling faster now. He heard her say: If you get a room on the ground floor, people come through the windows to rip you off.

— A minute later she clenched her bloodstained blushing fingers and whispered: Ow, I missed the vein. When I miss, it burns like acid. — It took him a long time to get to sleep this time. Every now and then he'd open his eyes and see her rubbing some new place with alcohol before she quested with her needletip. Finally she found a good vein just above the knee. — I got lucky this time, she crooned to herself. Now I'm through for the night. I had a hell of a time getting it in. Daddy, didn't you hear me whistle? — He opened his eyes again. — You calling me Daddy? he said in amazement. She leaped in guilty startlement; she'd forgotten he was there. To make amends, she came right up to him, naked, abscessed and bleeding, and kissed his cheek. He knew that she wanted to be with him. He was helping her and so she wanted to give him the one thing she had to give. Sometimes she touched him as he slept. At last he began to doze once more and came into the dark room he'd seen years ago in Pompeii with the fresco of the man lying naked on his back touching the naked woman's breast as she squatted on him, stroking his hair, and he half awoke, wondering if the old lady might be touching him, but she was hunched over the sink, washing off her blood; the magic rocks cracked but did not quite smash his dream like the other fresco too leprous with age to make out anymore, just a man and a woman embracing. There'd been a statue of Priapus rising. Perhaps the old lady had just struck a match, because he was out of the dark room now, back in the shining busyness of last week's carnival. Just as a spectator walking along the margin of a parade rediscovers the bright plumes and butterflies which had passed him when he was still, the silver see-through wings of almost-naked empresses, the same musicians on truck beds playing the songs which it now seems will never end, so he followed something sensual and lovely which was probably the same thing that the old lady followed when she broke through her flesh with the needletip, but he never found it because something was pursuing him; it was the sounds that the old lady made, rocking and moaning all night, trying to find a vein. Longing for the courage or heartlessness to put her out, he went to sleep again and then it was early morning and the doorknob was turning to wake him wearily one more time and she came in.

How was work last night? he said.

Oh, pretty slow. Eight hours of nothing. Then a fifty-dollar blow-job. That was a good one. Then three more hours of nothing, so I gave up and came back here.

San Francisco, California, U.S.A. (1993)

She'd been renting herself out for thirty-five years now, years of nights like slow fat bubbles rising from the head of an electric eel, and one night after she had fixed so that she wouldn't need to vomit in his sink for hours ("getting well" was what the whores called putting the needle in), she sat beside him on his bed, and as a consolation prize for once more disturbing his sleep took him to the bottom of the murk where her story lived spiny and spidery like a snowcrab whose whitish spines glow faintly. The story began with her father's return, long after his second disappearance. The neighbors said that he'd come through the window one night in summer and that was how Mother got pregnant again, but neither she nor her little sister had seen him that time if in fact he'd come at all.

When the baby was born, he came back again and told the family that they were all to move to California. — Don't bring anything because you're starting a new life, he said. She was almost thirteen then.

Mother didn't quite buy all that. She still told each of them to bring her best clothes and one casual suit. What that meant was two of her flour-sack dresses.

When they got to California, Daddy was very nice. He was paying a lot of attention to her, which made her feel special. He brought them to his home in Daly City. He had a mistress who lived there, too, young, gorgeous, a college girl. He explained that Patsy was part of the family now. Her mother saw that she would have to resign herself to Patsy. She had the children. She'd do anything to make it work.

Daddy made them strip naked. He said that he was the benevolent dictator. They had to hold his Bible in their hands before they were allowed to speak.

When it was time to go to sleep, somehow she ended up in bed between Daddy and Patsy, with her little sister on the outside and Mother with the baby in the next room.

She was ashamed to sleep naked like they did, so Daddy permitted her to put on her nightshirt, but no underwear. Then darkness winked. She lay still. Daddy's hand was on her leg, and it began to go higher. He told her that he was only preparing her for life. Still she did not understand his meaning. At that time she hardly knew how babies were made. She hadn't started menstruating yet, had only kissed one or two boys. Daddy explained to her that in many African societies it was the role of the father to deflower his daughter, so that the birth canal would be prepared for her husband when the time came. He was pulling her thighs apart now and she was screaming and Mother came running in. Daddy turned on the light. Daddy said: She disobeyed me. Her mother went to her and for a moment she still hoped and believed, and Mother said to her: It's for your own good. The light died, and Daddy was between her legs again. She screamed despairingly and Patsy was holding her down and Mother was holding her down. Before his face blotted even the darkness out, she saw the cattish satisfaction on Patsy's face.

Confessing the blood that came out of her, Daddy said: I wasn't the first. I just finished what the other boys started. Their thirteen-year-old cocks were too small.

When the old lady was telling him this, he wondered under how many roofs if they could be flung up like gravestones he'd see children struggling feebly in the darkness, and then the scarlet darkness inside screaming out into the night.

When she turned fourteen Daddy sold her to an Ethiopian. He explained to her the advantages. She'd be an emancipated minor. She could do everything an adult could do except drink. The Ethiopian only wanted citizenship. She'd live with him in the same apartment building but she wouldn't have to sleep with him because she'd go on being Daddy's girl. He said to her so tenderly: I'd rather see you dead than fucking a nigger.

One day she came home and stole all the money out of Patsy's wallet. She went to Berkeley and asked the first person she met to please let her stay at his house. He took her home and fucked her all night, then kicked her out. That was what seemed to happen every night. After awhile she learned to ask for money.

Then I did that first shot of crank and that was it, the old lady said. That was it. I was totally sprung. I saw colors, and my shit didn't stink. Just one time. I was at a very low point in my esteem anyway.

San Francisco, California, U.S.A. (1993)

In the middle of a rainy evening while he ate Chinese takeout the black woman lay naked, fat-breasted and snoring on his bed, her teeth gaping like a vampire's, her stockings still on, her hand seeming to twitch because it lay on her twitching belly, her hair down around her neck. Beside her sat the old lady on the nod, so peaceful and luminous-faced, dreamy, turning a cigarette in her hand, cross-legged, eyes closed. Suddenly she winked at him. She put a finger to her lips. Then she slid her middle finger all the way up the black woman's cunt, pulled it out, and began to suck. — The black woman opened one eye. — Not even at the bottom of my list! she scolded, and then they both laughed.

It was drizzling very steadily outside. He was warm and sleepy. He lay down between them, and the old lady put his head so sweetly in her lap. Half asleep already, he imagined being her good Daddy now to undo everything and taking her to the beach. She sat on her towel with the soles of her feet tucked behind her, and she was watching the lotion sink into her arms. Just before her stood a red bucket filled with ocean. He had caught the water for her. The water waited inside the bucket, waited to be poured out, and if he and she should die, it would wait for a wind to blow the bucket over or for the red plastic to be cracked by time. She watched the ocean glisten on her fingers. The ocean shimmered faintly through the translucent bucket's sides.

She took the yellow bucket and put an ocean inside it and poured it into the red bucket.

The whore who'd been raped with the vacuum cleaner came in, smiling shyly, with a packet of white powder. — Excuse me, she whispered. I don't smell, do I? I'm sorry I haven't taken a shower today.

THE BEST WAY TO DRINK BEER

Winnipeg, Manitoba, Canada (1993)

Winnipeg, Manitoba, Canada (1993)

Outside the hotel window an Indian girl was saying: Pay me, and a white man said: It's in the car. I'll get it, I promise. No, don't come with me, bitch, you just stand there and wait. I'm going around the corner. I said you just stand there and wait! — Inside, an Indian girl—an Ojibway, this one—threw herself down on the bed, groaning. She'd been hit by a car when she was drunk. When they took her to the hospital she waited almost as long as the Indian girl outside the window, and then she said to the doctor: Excuse me! — What? said the doctor. — When are you gonna see me? — When I'm not busy, said the doctor shortly. — You're not busy now; you're just pokin' your nose in a bunch of goddamned papers! she shouted. What would you care if I just left? — You're right, yawned the doctor. I wouldn't care one bit. — So she got up and hobbled out and got drunk, permitting her leg to solve itself, which was why she'd staggered the dozen blocks to the hotel room so slowly, almost giving up; which was why she'd limped up the two flights of steps above the poolroom, squeezing the handrail until it groaned like her. Her face was yellow with pain, which was why she fell down on his bed

while he bolted the door, and then she said: Turn out the fuckin'
light.

As he neared her, she grabbed him with a thick arm that was all
muscle and ground his mouth against hers so that she could breathe
into him her life of gin and beer and bad food, and she locked the
crook of her elbow around his neck to pull him more irrevocably
under her tongue while her other hand snatched one of his and put
it on the crotch of her jeans. — Make love to me, she begged. Fuck
me good. Just don't touch my leg.

He was hers now and she inhaled sharply so that her breasts became
as the upturned crescents of a buffalo's horns, and then she said: I
broke up with my boyfriend. 'Cause he's jealous.

You lonely? he said.

Right now I'm having fun.

After that she was moaning: Please make me come.

Three hours later she sighed happily and said: You know what? I
like your attitude. I like your goddamn attitude! I like the way you
make love.

I like the way you make love, too, he said. I like you.

She kissed him. — If there was more guys like you I'd stay in
town. It's so fuckin' *depressing* on the reserve. I didn't even go to my
sister's funeral. Everybody cryin' and stuff. She died 'cause she drank
too much.

They lay there for awhile. She was naked from the knees up but
she'd never taken off her bluejeans or shoes because of her leg. Her
skin was not truly red except on her face and hands where she'd been
changed by the sunlight. The rest of her was a pale yellow ocher. She
pulled his face down and kissed him.

I gotta go, she said.

How soon will you forget me?

I always remember everyone, she said.

Then she said: You want to come with me now? Come walk
with me?

At that he felt a sudden uprush and was ready to go anywhere with
her, but then his caution became the wise hard old yellow skull behind his face and his caution said: Where do you want to walk to?

To get a bottle.

He remembered how she'd been when he first picked her up on

the sidewalk, stumbling, stinking-breathed, scarcely able to talk or listen, and for a moment he still wanted to go because if he drank with her he wouldn't care that she didn't care, but then the thought of it began to make him so tired and he said: How about if I buy you breakfast tomorrow and then we walk?

She said: OK. I come tomorrow morning. I promise. I'll stand outside. I'll wait eight-o'-clock, nine-o'-clock, ten-o'-clock, eleven-o'-clock. I promise.

You don't want to come up?

No.

OK. I'll come look for you at nine.

She kissed him once more on the mouth, holding him so tight. Then he unlocked the door.

How's your leg? he said.

Better, she said. Better from all the exercise.

And she smiled.

She kissed his face one more time. Then she limped down the stairs.

At nine-o'-clock the next morning she wasn't there, and at ten-o'-clock she wasn't there. At eleven-o'-clock he had to go. He thought: What does that say about her promises, and especially what does that say about the promise she made when she spread her legs without a rubber and I said: Do you have AIDS? and she shook her head very quickly without saying anything (she had my face mashed desperately against her neck) and I said: Do you promise? and she nodded . . . ?

He was looking for the key to the toilet down the hall when an Indian knocked on his door for rolling papers. The Indian said: What do you think of this hotel?

Not much, he said.

Everybody wants a decent washroom, a kitchen . . . , the Indian said. I guess I'm here to punish myself. See, I'm from Alberta. I moved here to be with my wife. She was the most beautiful lady I've ever known. A fullblood, aye? Said she loved me. Then she left me, moved back to the reserve.

I'm sorry to hear that, he replied. Somebody left me, too. Said she was coming back and she didn't.

You got papers or not? said the Indian.

Nope.

Fuck it. Let's have a quick one downstairs.

I need to catch a train out of this town.

Fuck your train, the Indian said. There'll be another train tomorrow. Get a round with me, aye?

Wide Indian girls were playing pool downstairs, some well, some
poorly, some completely drunkenly, and the cue ball glistened like
the whites of their eyes. — Fuck your train! his companion kept
muttering with a scornful smile. They drank together steadily. His
companion's cheeks glowed red like molten copper. Slowly his lips
began to slide and melt and slobber into a smile. — Fuck my wife,
he said happily. If you want you can fuck my wife.

That bitterish liquid, the color of stale pond water, connected him
to the Indian girls sitting in a dim nook by a pillar on that drizzly
Saturday afternoon. A smiling Indian man with long braids approached the bar and someone said: C'mere, my friend, and led him
out. Another Indian came in, with his head lowered, and the security
man with his shaggy shoulder-length hair who paced with his hands
clasped behind his back immediately went to him also and said: This
way. — The Indian dropped his head still further. Then he went out
the way he had come.

His companion was drunk now. It surely wouldn't be long before
the bartender or the security man got him.

I'm Scottish, his companion said. Well, a little bit Scottish. Mainly
I'm Ojibway. There's a lot of us Ojibways in Winnipeg. That's us,
and I don't give a fuck about the others. Those Cree. If they call me
brother I'll drink their bottle if they're payin'. I don't give a fuck
about them. See that cocksucker over there? He's Cree. He went
after my wife once, so that's how he got that scar. See that cunt over
there? That's his wife. I fucked her. She's Cree. She's just a slut.

Indian girls with mountainous shoulders, a tiny firefly of cigarette
in each immense round face, kept drinking beers, the greenish bottles
flashing like jewels against their blue-black bangs. A fat woman was
snoring in the corner like a gray jay hiding under the snow, her head
curled down on her back. The security man lifted her under the
armpits and dragged her slowly, determinedly, out into the rain.

His companion drank another beer and burped and laughed and

said: I'm fifty-seven years old, so I outlived my mother's age. I drink a twelve-pack a day, so if I make it past sixty it'll be a miracle, aye? So *what* is what I say. I been in Winnipeg eleven years, and I've fucked every hooker in this town. A little pokey-pokey, you know. Too much love!

The beer was blondish-brown like the roots of a crested wheatgrass, frizzy filaments spilling down into the dirt deeper than a tall man's height, bitter happiness foaming down into his balls. His companion was hunting hookers now like a Métis with his long rifle and red headband riding close on his pony, aiming at a wide-eyed buffalo. He stood up, began to stalk two women playing pool, and fell on his face. By the time he'd discovered how to plant his feet beneath him again, the bartender was beside him, pointing grimly to the doorway. The man began to walk out. Suddenly he turned and spread his swollen grayish cheeks like an Atlantic wolf-fish whose jaws sometimes open to show in faint anticipatory chewing motions its sharp yellow teeth, and the man's gold-ridged black pupils glared and bulged forward as he shouted: You gonna try an' fuck my wife again? That's my *wife* you fucked last night!

Then the rain fell on him.

Left thus to himself, the john drank another beer. He saw a tipsy woman with many parallel scars across her wrists (her face like one of those squarish bark baskets with rounded corners for winnowing rice) and he remembered how last night his companion's wife had said: Funny things happen in this town. Like my cousin Maisie. She kept tryin' to kill herself. Gash her wrist so many times with a knife, try to jump off a bridge, all that stuff. Well, she wanted to commit suicide, but she didn't have to. She died in her sleep.

Did you love her very much?

Her? I hate her guts! she'd laughed.

Now finishing the bottle, he went to the woman and said: What's your name?

Maisie.

I thought you died in your sleep.

I did, she muttered. Then the security man came and pushed her out.

It was night now, and he was alone. One tubby girl went up for another beer, and he saw the bartender take her lovingly by the shoulders, kiss her neck, and begin to push. He pushed her down the corridor that led past the hotel desk to outside, and then he came back. The lonely man went out to see what had become of her. She was on the street trying to hail a cab but forgetting in mid-gesture what she was about. — Everyone's hassling me tonight, she wept. And now I can't get a cab. I need a fucking cab. Call me a fucking cab! I need to eat! I wanna pee! Find my shoes for me, please.

Her asymmetrical purple mouth imploded, slobbered and kissed him.

The late darkness of summer had begun to dim the hot gray night. On Main Street sat a drunken Indian panhandler, and when he gave him change the panhandler stared at the coins adding up on his palm without comprehending; and he walked past three staggering Indian boys in baseball caps, and came to the old Indian hooker who had to hold onto a lamppost to keep from falling down, her tongue the brown, black-banded furry ovoid of a queen bee hibernating in the dirt under the snow of men's mouths, and after her he kept passing Indians leaning in front of hotels that served beer downstairs and a piece of thistledown blew against his face from a vacant lot full of puddles and frostcracked mud and beer bottles and planks and dandelions and camomile and horsetails, and it began to rain again. The vacant lot was a slice of muskeg, and muskeg was an Ojibway word. Across the street, an Indian in a blue cap walked head down, kicking something, and then he turned and kicked it back the way he had come. An Indian in a fringed leather jacket strode energetically, swinging his arms. Three Indian boys came. One said: Why you fellas fuckin' whinin'? It's time for another fuckin' round, so let's fuckin' go.

He remembered how his companion's wife (who was on probation for assault) had said to him: We have our traditions, aye? We have our power. Like, suppose it's stormy outside in the morning and we want it to be calm weather. All we got to do is say: I want it to be a nice day, and then smoke a pipe, and pretty quick it calms down.

He saw the woman who had died in her sleep and said to her: Can you stop the rain?

Sure, she said. Anytime. As long as it's not raining beer.

A Mountie came to shove her along and she said: Did you notice there's a red stripe on your leg?

Oh, fuck off, the Mountie said.

Did you notice that you're wearing a bulletproof vest?

Yeah, I noticed that all right, Maisie.

Are you wearing bulletproof trousers, too? Ah, hah, hah, hah!

```
┌─────────────────────────────────────┐
│ ┌───────────────────────────────────┐ │
│ │                                   │ │
│ │           A VISION                │ │
│ │                                   │ │
│ └───────────────────────────────────┘ │
└─────────────────────────────────────┘
```

Big Bend, California, U.S.A. (1994)

Some sit in darkness and gloom, says Psalm 107, and I was of them but I didn't know it more or less than a tree knows why he shakes his green-hung arms in an evening breeze. I'd seen and heard them die, an old friend and a new friend, just outside that city whose huddled steel doors had been so many times pierced by bullets that they resembled Go gameboards overwhelmed by the round black empty stones of Master Negativity. Just outside that city whose sandbagged and boarded-up windows were ringed around their frames with jagged silver ice, outside that city of scorched chair-skeletons and fresh-nailed coffins ran a river where my friends died. I think I met their murderers afterward, although in war nothing is clear. Or maybe they were Samaritans, those quiet ones with machine-guns who helped me pull my friends from the car and later tried to use their credit cards. I did what I could for the dead, which was nothing, and then I strove to guide myself back to the light.

It was a month later that I ate the psilocybin mushrooms, in the Sierras near Donner Pass with Jenny, whom I loved, and Paul, who was my friend. It was not my intention to have a vision, which must have been why I had one. Some people go to seek out hallucinatory novelties, as if the usual blue sky pasted upon the lenses of their spectacles were an annoyance, but I have seen enough, thank you: visions tend to trick me, backstab me, or rape me. Last night, for instance, I had a hideous dream that life was but a show in a dingy theater of stale air, the actors dully or busily traversing an immense map laid out upon the stage; and because the tale went on so fruitlessly, no one bothered to watch; semicircular rows of worn seats gaped like half-open mouths; but at the righthand extremity of the front few rows some observers sat in black raven costumes, with raven masks and long beaks. Whenever one of the poor souls on stage would say something like *I feel sick* or *I'm going to kill you* or *I insist that we fight to the last man* then the ravens would clap their wingtips daintily. They sat interested, amused, aloof, like Thoreau brooding over Walden Pond. And when each sad life upon the wide atlas page drew to its close, the ravens would caw until the rafters trembled with the shrieking echoes, then launch themselves into the dusty air, wheel, croak, swoop, and tear that doomed soul to pieces. So when Paul gave me some of his mushrooms I believed with confidence that no transfiguration would occur. The leaden wall between myself and all the dead people in my years of life would not be breached. Alcohol clouded it into a creamy graphite haze. Lovemaking swiveled it downward, making it a solid stone to lie and dream upon. No doubt the mushrooms would make it funny. Too much contemplation of any object, however unwilling the gaze, may reveal a secret. Better to change the angle of view as often as possible. — That was why I so frequently ascended mountains without seeing inside them. (In the Norse sagas people go "inside the mountain" when they die.) Whenever I began to fear that the Gray Wall was becoming smoky, translucent, almost transparent, it obligingly changed its skin. Once, for instance, I visited Ellesmere Island, which is colored a pale icy-blue in my atlas, so the Gray Wall became a slope of pebble pavement set in mud: jet-black rocks with sunbursts of orange lichen, smooth tan pebbles, golden rocks lichened blue like cheese mold, and as the slope continued gently up, my feet sank into the clean soft snow and it was a warm 3° C. Grasses and three-leaved plants, their leaves an autumn orange, poked up here and there like reaching fingers. Musk-oxen dung stood in little mounds, little pyramids of buckshot; and the hill steepened into a snow-covered ridge. — Another time the Gray Wall was a jungle mountain at whose base skinny-legged barefoot kids sucked from plastic bags of sugared ice. Mornings and evenings its mass of forest was tea-colored and indistinct. A dog barked at a horse under a thatch roof who neighed and rang his bell. In the afternoons, ladies in shirts gray and black with grime, with raised yokes of embroidery once black or white, sat gazing up to see if they could spy their husbands returning from the opium fields. The Gray Wall fed them. I saw a basket of bright green vegetables, saw everywhere babies sucking at the reddish-brown breast. — Today the Grey Wall was in the Sierras. A cool noonish breeze perfumed by resins and bees' nests swirled about us as our footsteps rimmed dark ponds, Jenny running ahead, too busy and excited to notice the flowers. (Later, mushroom-drunk on the way down, she'd sway and giggle in amazement: Look at that blue one! See that yellow one? Oh, God, why do I keep falling down?) Congregations of pines presented their thin and branching fingers to the air, growing them downward like roots. Because I still understood where entities started and stopped, I saw each thing as its own thing, which is the way we build walls by moving individual stones. There is nothing wrong with this. A dermatologist sees the freckles, not the face, and we do not fault him for it. But Paul and I continued up the mountain path, beginning to get the drunken feeling, eating those delicious vegetables of the inner ear, and then suddenly there came what I call the *mushroom laugh,* which always happens in an unexpected manner. This time it struck from the stones and boulders around me, all their freckles and granules and pixilations of texture flying out in a swarm of deep mirth whose sound was not quite a buzzing thrumming G-major chord. The main thing about the mushroom laugh was its inhumanness. I had chosen to eat the mushrooms, and that was the last choice that I could make. The mushroom laugh would now take me and do whatever it wanted with me, no matter whether I enjoyed myself or was hurt. I was nothing to the mushroom laugh.

The mushroom laugh was the crowd of raven masks. By the time we got to the first lake, where Jenny was waiting with the picnic, it had started to devour me.

Paul, that gangly mushroom veteran, wanted to help, and assured me many times that day that I could control the laugh and do what I wished with it. That had certainly been my experience with psilocybin before. But on this occasion the mushrooms were very strong; and perhaps there was some poison in them. My joy sneaked off, and up strode an immense pain which convulsed me into a ball, like a wolf in a strychnine cramp. I lay on my side at the edge of a lake which continually changed its shape. When I closed my eyes I saw sickening neon lines as in some hellish disco, which would not remain still or even unique; they doubled and tripled nauseatingly, remaining one even when they were three; and it was only later that I thought of Catholic theology. When I opened my eyes I was compelled to watch the shelf of rock I lay on changing color from pink to green, while my jacket did likewise, and its camouflage blotches crawled, oozed and contracted. I thought that if I observed any of these phenomena very long I'd go mad. The state I was in already resembled madness. My existence therefore became a constant struggle to change my perceptions, to focus my senses on something new which the mushrooms had not yet contaminated; of course this battle could not be won because whatever I found the mushrooms immediately seized. There was one stem which I had eaten only recently, and I knew that this stem was inside me, laughing the mushroom laugh, waiting to wrestle with me in its own time even as I fought with the others.

There's something in this batch that we have to fight, Paul was saying, his face pale.

I could not answer him.

Jenny, who had not yet been affected, came and put her arm around me. After a long time I was able to say to her: I love you. — These words were a leathery thing, part boat and part seedpod, which came out of my mouth and crossed the space between my understanding and hers. I felt that we were falling farther and farther away from each other, dwindling out of each other's souls.

Lifting my watch in an attempt to learn how long I'd have to wait for the drug to wear off, I saw the minute hand, pure black on the golden dial, contract into its own shadow, turning inside itself and passing through the center of the watch until it pointed to a different plane than the hour hand.

He's curled into a salamander, I heard Paul say to Jenny. He's watching the bugs in his head.

This terrified me. I believed then that Paul could see everything about me, that he could look into my head where my soul lay curled on its side, and my soul was a huge, fat, bewhiskered white maggot which Paul despised.

I tried to eat a biscuit to help absorb some of the drug, but it was all I could do to chew. The lump of sweetened starch tasted hideous under my tongue; everything nauseated me. It refused to dissolve, crouching under my tongue, soaking up saliva until my mouth was a desert; it was another inimical foreign thing that I had to war with. Raising my head in an attempt to swallow, I saw Paul, and his face dissolved into a pale white cheese as he soundlessly screamed backwards into space, leaving a contrail of black blood in the air before his mouth. Even as this happened I was aware that Paul had not been hurt, that this was a memory of my two friends who'd died outside that city of scorched silence.

Paul and Jenny wanted me to get up.

I knew that I was in a place I was a part of, so much a part of that I could never find my way out; there was not any in or out. I'm sure that this must be the way that animals perceive, this experiencing without reasoning. I don't mean to say that reasoning is good or bad. I enjoy my ability to reason, and yet I also recognize that reason is a prison. With great effort I was able to find rags of that shimmering tent of conventions I lived in. For example, when Jenny asked me if I could remember the name of a certain mountain in Tasmania, I thought for a long time, then finally was able to uncover half the name, which I thought might be helpful. I wasn't certain whether this was the first or last word in the mountain's name (which I did know was composed of two words). The word was *peak*. And I could not understand why Jenny laughed after I thought that I had helped her.

Jenny has a dog which is not very intelligent. Sometimes when I call the dog it will come a few steps, then get distracted by some sunny spot or rotten smell, and I'll have to call it again. That was how I was on this day. Jenny would call me and I would follow her; sometimes she would take my hand or even push me, and I'd know that she was there and react to her, but in the fifteen-second intervals between her calls or touches she would cease to exist for me. It was not that I ever forgot her; her reappearances never surprised me; nor did I stop walking, but she was no more or less important than everything else. This is true and not true. In some way she was very important to me, but without being in my mind except when she called to me. I did not want to hurt her or make her anxious. This in turn increased my own anxiety, because I wanted to do whatever she wanted me to do; and at the same time I knew that her sense of direction was very bad and that she might very well get us lost in the forest, but I was unable to explain to her why she should not be leading me further into the mountains—or perhaps she understood well enough that I did not feel right about going with her, but Jenny can be very obstinate and anyway she was my guardian; I could not reason, so it did not matter what I thought.

I felt terribly alone. Even though she was not far ahead of me on the trail, continually calling to me from just out of sight, I felt that she had let me go. (Paul I could not see.) There was no blame attached to this. I did not feel that she had deliberately rejected me; it was simply that we were drifting farther and farther apart. Often I would look around me and see only trees and rocks and lake and sky, all alien and borderless and vivid like those paintings of dense dark forests in old Canada; and I would feel so alone and believe that I might possibly be there alone forever. So I was freed from the cage of rationality, and imprisoned in the cage of brutishness. Then Jenny would call my name again, and I'd understand that I was not alone after all and that I was still walking. Then I could not understand what the trail was anymore. I heard her calling my name over and over from not very far away, and after an immense struggle I succeeded in saying that between every two trees was a trail. I stood staring at those hundreds or thousands of trails in front of me, and finally Jenny had to come to lead me by the hand. Then she was gone again, and I passed through the forest, which I experienced in a low wide way like a four-legged beast. I was alone, and I always would be alone—and not just always, but also forever and infinitely. I had already been alone forever—so alone!—and this grieved and exhausted me beyond description but I understood that I could do nothing about it but struggle to endure. My soul was maimed and suffering. God was all around me but I felt no less alone. The twisted silvery trees were all growing toward and inside God, conscious of Him as He was of them and me, but they could not reach me as I could not express myself to them because only the relationship with God was real and I could not get at God or come to grips with Him because He was everywhere and I was only toiling through Him, just as a person can walk all day and never put the sun behind him. And I strained to speak with God. It was no easier to express myself to

Him than it had been to Jenny, but no more difficult. I was burdened with sadness and also with pain from the mushroom poison which resembled a steel spider with scorpion claws crouched inside my rib cage, pinching from my heart all the way to my belly; and the pain was the same as the sadness. I was crying for my dead friends, and I asked God whether what I was now suffering, which seemed more intense than any other agony I'd ever felt, was worth having been spared in Bosnia. And God was in the trees and between them; I was speaking with God and walking with Him, asking only this question, and only once; it echoed like a note on the piano when the reverberator pedal is pressed; and then I asked Him why He created people only to shatter them. I was so sad and I had no answer but I knew that He heard me and I was going on; I would go on until He smashed me to bits, and I accepted that. There was a moment when I was able to pray for my friends and also for Jenny and Paul and for myself. Hours later, when the drug let me go with a snap of its claws, I was surprised to find that I felt calm and at peace. I think it was because I'd been heard, had asked and accepted the fact that there would never be any answer, that I must go on in my solitude just as I'd had to do in the car when my friends slumped dead and bleeding and I waited for the next shot.

San Francisco, California, U.S.A. (1993)

She bent over the bottlecap. — What sign are you? she said, pretending that he was there. — Leo is my rising sign. — Of course she was alone.

She made the white powder fizz in the bottlecap. She stirred it into the vial, twirling the plunger of the syringe like a cocktail swizzlestick. Then she bit open the rock, scratching her breasts.

Gettin' well, in a safe place, she purred. Don't have to kick anybody down. And a nice healthy bag. See, I always cop from fat dealers, 'cause they don't use. Skinny ones gonna steal for themselves.

She mixed it in with the head of her plunger. Then she shook the syringe, licked the needle clean, stuck it slowly into the underside of her forearm.

Wow, she grinned, a register right off!

Slowly, so sensuously, she slid the long steel point in and out of herself, her face sexual and alive for the first time. Her arm was raised; her hand gripped her chin. Her elbow trembled on her knee like another needle spiraling in. She leaned forward. The red sock was tied halfway up her bicep, and it too trembled and shimmered.

Damn! she said. I'm just having trouble getting a vein.

She pulled the needle out and eased it back into her flesh two inches under the pearl of black blood. She squatted, naked, hunched and dreaming. In that same molasses rhythm of hers she slid it in and out, moaning through her teeth. After a long time she pulled it out of the second wound and halfheartedly tried to smear away the bleeding with her dirty fingers but the two dark trickles only dabbled themselves together in mysterious patterns. She made the third hole equidistant from the others, mumbling softly, on her face the same greedy look as a masturbator's straining to get home.

Suddenly she hissed and let the needle go. It dangled from her poor ruined arm, half gorged with blood. Leaping up in great wonder, she pressed her ear to the wall.

If you hear the name Valerie, let me know, she said. I think they're saying Valerie in there.

Her fingers began their inexorable curl around the plunger again, and she was licking her chapped lips, but then she stiffened again, listening.

She's somebody I went out with for three and a half years, she said. She's *beautiful,* so beautiful . . . but rotten inside.

Oh! she cried. Got it! — The outstretched plunger wavered between her fingers like a dowsing rod of ecstasy. But then she withdrew it again, groaning. Her whole forearm was smeared with blood now. She massaged herself there, with the same automatism as a bee-stung dog shaking its body. That was the thing about her, that living on the basis of little more than a half-ruined instinct, like the dog proceeding as if pain were water. Then she made the fourth hole.

Oh, bleed, she whispered. Please bleed . . .

Then she was up on the chair in her stockinged feet, straining to peer through the peephole, licking her lips with desperate smacking sounds, moaning: Oh, Valerie, please let it be you!

She said: Hey, wow, I'm totally well right now. I promise I'll calm down in a minute.

Grunting, she began to thrust the plunger in and out once more.

I *know* she's up in this hotel, she said, breaking off. I dunno why she don't want me to know, though.

Then she whirled to regard the man who had paid for all this. — Sorry, she whispered.

She bent toward the keyhole, one sock on, one lying on the carpet where she'd wrenched it from her bleeding arm, and she was riding up and down on the balls of her feet so that her hard little buttocks bounced.

Why are they *hiding* from me? she wept.

She'd pressed both palms up against the door and had turned her ear flush against it. She was fellating the keyhole, licking it with an animal's unselfconscious slurpings.

Suddenly she threw the door open and said: You seen Valerie?

The woman outside wore clothes. She said coolly: I don't know the names, only the faces.

She slammed the door on the other woman and foamed like a tiger. — I don't know why she's hiding from me. It's all fucked up. Now they say they don't know who that is. But I can hear her right through the wall. They knew who it was when I fucking supported her!

Well, I may as well as well finish it. Lemme give myself a butt shot.

A noise came through the wall, a long sigh.

She's probably in there with another girl, she muttered.

She guided the needle into the crack between her buttocks. Another sound came, and she leaped up into a splay-legged crouch with the syringe hanging out. — *I do not love her anymore!* she screamed.

Now listen, she said to the man. You'll be here all night, right? You'll hear if she fucks someone. She's a really good lover. All the other girls that fuck her, they'll be making noises all night when she makes love to 'em. But her, she don't make a sound.

She fell to her knees again, curling into a sallow ball of sadness. She thrust the plunger all the way in. Then she began to sway while her head rested on her knees.

She was rocking, pressing her clitoris with a knuckle, hunching intently toward the wall. Every time Valerie's girl made another moan, she trembled with joy. Her labia had flushed the reddish-orange of molten copper. The empty needle hung from her like a breast sucked dry as she hunched forward, masturbating furiously.

She smiled and swayed for a long time. Then she turned to look at the man. Defiantly she said: Have you ever been in love?

No, the man said.

Oh, she said. I was just curious.

THE RED SONG

Mexico City, Distrito Federal, Mexico (1992)

Slender like candles they let their hair down beneath the trees. He knew that. Hurrying down the tunnel of fingernails, he saw their legs glisten in the rain. He prayed, his hands a knife to cut away sin from his face. But he could not stop knowing.

Under the night I'll help you, his friend said.

He replied: I'm afraid.

Not enough, or you'd have prayed me away! Tomorrow I'll find you. Tomorrow, in the night.

Tomorrow was a morning of shards in the dark dirt, an afternoon of rainbow laundry on white roofs, an evening of children peering over gates. Then tomorrow grew as dark as the sweat under a woman's breasts.

Wide yellow crosswalk-lines sweated yellow in the yellow light. On the corner, a man raised a roof-tarp as if for a market. Girls grew from the sidewalk like nightfruits, growing up from pink stalks and roots, with hair for flowers. Jiggling their purses and smiling, they tolled the night in the bells of their skirts. With open arms, they leaned into the black windows of cars to ask directions.

Across the street two men were already waiting, one with his hands in his pockets, the other squinting ahead. A third came, tapping his feet, wiping his nose. The corner by the phone booth had a standing army of men whose shirts and jeans seemed bleached, yet bright.

The boy's face was pleasing like a waxed peach as he stood on the night corner, tapping a pack of cigarettes against his palm. His friend was instructing him. His friend said: This little knife is to kill the hearts of all the pretty amigas, so that they'll love me. And this belt, my novia gave it to me, to bind me to her kisses. But I escaped. And this blue bracelet, a young girl wove it to tie me to her side. But I go where I please.

His friend was a squat brown rain idol with round holes in his mouth. His friend's skull glared ahead like headlights.

Another girl left her taxi, crossed slowly, let down her hair beneath the trees. Across the street, the madam opened a red notebook.

Slender like candles they stood on the narrow sidewalk which was their tightrope, and faced the passing cars. Tree-shadows passed through their flesh. Their high heels or knee-high black shiny leather boots glistened. Another taxi pulled up.

The truck with loud music stopped. The woman bowed her head slowly, but didn't trouble to uncross her arms.

In a voice like jellyfish collapsing, his friend said: That one's yours.

Oh, well, the boy said apologetically, she belongs to herself . . .

She's nothing but a pair of buttocks.

Everything has a mind, the boy whispered, afraid to look at this friend he contradicted. Everyone has a mind. Everyone has hands to work and make something good—

The idol laughed. — I have no mind. She has no mind.

She stood in the street like silverware gleaming in darkness. Behind her, a girl licked a Popsicle like a long red chili. For a moment it seemed that she licked her own tongue. She was the woman's daughter.

His friend nudged him. — How much? the boy said.

A hundred fifty thousand,* the woman said.

A hundred.

No. (Her pale white face shook.)

You win. Come with me. No, no, first give me your mouth.

She kissed him listlessly, like the trickle of a silver earring among black hair. Her kiss tasted of the penises of men long dead.

Triumphant, the idol swarmed into the air to infect the whole world. She did not see that, but her daughter screamed. (The madam wrote a cross in the notebook.)

Now the boy was bold. He took her by the chin. — I said come with me.

Wherever I go, my daughter goes also. She's afraid without me.

Come with me.

She undid her necklace of heavy plates of dark silver—smooth, almost buttery to the touch; they rang on the glass floor. The daughter turned her back. Knowingly she played with the silhouettes that vanish behind walls. So the pretty sisters used to play, noiselessly, in the clay rooms of old Egypt, after their god-brothers had taken them to wife.

The boy was not a boy anymore. He leaned back smoking, so that the round stone of his ring rose into the world. Smoke came out his nose. Again the mother cooled him with mercury tears of silver on whitestone, while the daughter turned her back. His friend was leading them by arm and waist to the culmination at the stall of green-lit bones.

What's the young girl's name?

I won't tell you, Señor. She's nothing to do with you.

The daughter turned her back.

Do you both have minds? he said. The longer I'm with you, the more your minds elude me.

I have no mind, the woman said. Long ago I let my mind down beneath the trees.

---

* In 1992, a hundred fifty thousand pesos was about U.S. $50.

Every time, he got older. The daughter turned her back. She played behind his white walls, soon to be brown with drying blood. Her mother became a transparent insect on the wall, its thorax glowing like an ironribbed lamp. He became a grand bone column hollowed out with bells. That was why the idol laughed.

Under the night she'll help you, the idol said. She and the young bitch.

He replied: It's always night.

When the daughter drew up against his shoulder, as if of her own accord, her shadow became longer than his. He reflected on his skull the soles of her feet.

Make the child sing, he said. Then I'll give her pesos and rubies. One ruby, anyhow. I have one ruby. Do you know what it's called?

For the last time, Señor, I beg you not to touch her. I insist on it.

I'll give her a ruby just to let her hair down! Imagine that! That's more than I ever gave you. Do you know what rubies are made of? In the end I'll get her, whore. She has no mind . . .

On a night like a hooked obsidian knife, the mother in despair and fear whispered in his ear the Three Holy Names.

At once he thought he had the phosphorus to ignite the world.

He found the chapel of paper animals. The paper lion was the one who must not be touched. He saw the paper mountain which even the priest didn't see. It was a slender pyramid on the wall beside the altar. As he approached, it enlarged itself to infinitude. The priest screamed as he ran forward. (Others beneath the trees had screamed that way when he'd begun whipping himself.) He ran into the mountain and was gone.

The soldiers said that she was a bad woman. She prayed her way up the myriad white laces on their black boots. Her last words on the gallows were: He died as sweetly as a little lamb!

Mexico City, Distrito Federal, Mexico (1992)

Sometimes this round hard world smells like sugarcones. Sometimes sorrow detonates in an explosion of parks and bells. Re-
gardless waits the future like an ivory-handled pistol in a
snakeskin belt.

As bell-strokes assembled the bones of the hours, the young girl
grew taller. She lived on the stalks and rays of seashell-light. Already
other girls circled her in the dance of red crabs around the drum.
Gliding like a cat on marble, she parted the bars on windows. They
called her the Red Song.

Your mother was a whore! the madam called out, and a hundred
girls laughed.

I was born on a stone mountain crowned with trees, she said. I'm
as clean as any woman's white blouse.

On a Sunday morning that smelled like cakes, a soldier came to
see her. He undid his pale green skull-crown ruled by logic like the
yellow scales and tiles of the cathedral-dome. A ruby was hidden in
his hair. — From your mother, he said.

Then she knew she was ready. She put on her shoes that could
dance across the sky. (She never awoke the sidewalk ache.) She outdid
the fat girl with doll's eyes.

The madam squeezed her and said: Why don't you let your hair
down beneath the trees? You have a good shape, you know; you're
slender like a candle. Men have money. Take them; leave them as
cold and clean as picked chicken-bones!

I don't know how, she replied.

Don't know how? Why, it's as easy as sucking a licuado up a straw!

I don't know how because I have a mind. Only girls without minds
know how.

Ah, so your mother had no mind? I owned your mother and I'm
going to own you. Just wait and see; you'll sing my song.

My mother had a mind, and I'm my own song.

Was your mother better than my mother? My mother worked so
long in the corner stand that she became part of the magazines, nuts

and candles! She had a better mind than God. Your mother had no mind, I tell you! And I'm going to rent out your smooth throat; I need money to warm me at night . . .

My mother had a mind! I don't care what you say. She knew the Three Holy Names. And I do also, Señora, I warn you!

The madam departed. But there came the night when all girls must dance (the madam knew that). They dance on the zócalo and throw cigarettes from their bosoms. He who catches a cigarette grows lucky. But that's not all of it, because each girl also tosses one cigarette that she's kissed with her lipstick. Catch that, and she's yours.

The old madam stood waiting like a shadow on a rock. Once she too had thrown cigarettes to boys. (Her yellow tattooed breasts were the carven eggs of some extinct bird.) The idol flew down and brushed her like a musician's fringed black sleeve. The idol said: Under the night I'll help you. I'll help you rake away her mind.

The Red Song leaped up onto the plinth. The hot breeze lifted her purple skirt like the outer skin of an onion so that everyone could see her black and gold lace stockings. So many slender brown legs, dancing in red shoes, white shoes, black shoes! But the boys watched the Red Song. They wanted to buy a ticket for everything. Her belt of copper had a hundred little locks.

Whenever she danced, the idol threw confetti in everyone's hair. The other longhaired girls threw their cigarettes, but no one would catch them. Weeping, they hurled gold and silver necklaces, but these also fell unclaimed on the cobblestones, striking with noises like breaking glass. Just as the orange juice vendor draws his arm in to his naked chest, then jerks it down again so that his body shudders and the extractor shudders and golden droplets spray his chest, so the other girls flailed and shook until they'd spattered each other with sweat. Nobody wanted their juice.

What's her secret? they shrieked.

A ruby, from her mother. (The idol told them that.)

In that lighted plaza dazzled by trumpet-sounds, the trees so garden-green and fresh beneath the purple sky that smelled like cigarettes, boys waited in line just to see the Red Song. The mariachi musicians with golden skeleton-bones up the sides of their black trousers played for no one but her. Whenever she tossed a cigarette from between her breasts, the boys shouted and fought for it, jostling like balloons on ropes, cursing and weeping with desire until the cigarette had been torn to pieces. The boys in white shirts and the girls in black dresses could not see each other. (As they stared at the Red Song, the corners of their eyes were sharper than knives.)

But the madam kept sight of the idol. Whimpering with greed, she made her supplicating embrace, her swollen hands not unlike the two broad ribbons ponytailing down the back of the soda girl who'd come from the corner of the fence where the hedge began, staring into heat and light all day, dreaming of the dance to come when she'd toss her lipsticked cigarette into the crowd of handsome boys who'd marry her.

Before laying down her wares that morning on their bed of fresh ice, the soda girl had gone to the zócalo. It was so early that nobody was there except for an old man feeding rows of pigeons. The soda girl leaped up onto the plinth and danced, the only one there at the center of the world. The old man smiled. He was the idol. That day she scarcely saw her thirsty customers; when they crowded her she stood up and wheeled her cart halfway around the bandstand, looking for less sunshine so as to diminish her trade. She needed no pesos, only dreams. The idol squatted on her head and whispered: Under the night I'll help you, my little amiga. I'll sharpen the ends of your cigarettes so that they'll pierce the boys' hearts! Boys have no minds. — The poor soda girl believed. Bending over her aqua-colored cart, fondling ice, she dreamed herself so deeply into the dance that not even the most lucrative thirst could reach her although she was the nun consecrated to orange fizz.

But that night she danced stamping her foot, soaking her lemon wedding-cake dress with tears. No boy looked at her. Her mouth downturned; her face became a clay mask. To her the Red Song was as unholy as some leather-lashed idol of worm-carved wood. The soda girl threw her cigarettes, and boys' heels ground them on the dirty night's stones. She screamed. She became a clay figurine holding up her breasts.

The other girls stopped dancing. They were stone giants of anger against the sky.

When at last the Red Song threw the lipstick-stained cigarette into that mob, every eye saw its red smudge like the flash of her cheekbone from far away, and it rose above the moon, then tumbled faster than a witch's bone while the madam leaned close to the idol whispering, her hand on the idol's chest, and the cigarette began to come down as the madam's and the idol's legs moved together; they were the only couple dancing; they bobbed, swung and whirled while the idol's starched shoulders swam closer to everything in the balloon-light (his head a little raised so that the white teeth in his yellow death's head could gape down the snake of itself, of its vertebrae and incised ivory counters; the idol had removed his ribs for the occasion and spread them around himself in a fan of rays); the cigarette was falling like death now so that the madam trembled, but she couldn't stop clutching for it and the idol grinned, threw his fingers behind his head, caught the cigarette, and placed it in her hand.

The other girls, the jealous ones, let out a joyous scream like boiling ice.

Mexico City, Distrito Federal, Mexico (1992)

Slender, so slender, she let her hair down beneath the trees. The madam opened the notebook.

On a gasoline-smelling night of blue walls, the peacock shadows of her dress swayed from side to side. When she spread the colors of her dress, men crawled after her like worms. Bars of darkness, tiger-darkness and tiger-light walled widely shadowed concrete into the nowhere, where she became an icon prisoned in gold. The ice cream man, pushing his stand home to darkness, stopped to catch armloads of red papier-mâché fishes that shot from her as she danced. He wanted to sell them, but they exploded like fireworks.

She was playing with a drop of blood, a little red drop of blood which other people thought to be a ruby. She let it be a secret inside her cupped hands.

Mexico City, Distrito Federal, Mexico (1992)

Slender like a candle, she let her hair down beneath the trees. Every night men gathered, heads high, hands high, feet and shoulders wide, to watch her arrive. The bandmaster powdered the faces of the dark-suited musicians who anticipated in her the white eyeshine of sexual intelligence.

Round faces, mustachioed and laced, puffed at the silver trumpets. When her hair tumbled down, the red-uniformed man beat his silver drum. Every time she smiled, three mandolins played by themselves. A blind man tinged his triangle when she stretched her whitestockinged legs beneath the black skirt. She cocked her hip, and an admirer brought alive his tuba like a gleaming snail. She blinked, and the guitar-player sang.

The other whores stood a little apart from her. This was at the madam's wish. They were the second-best.

A boy was walking by. All at once he began to sleep an endless dream of luminescent pears caged in marble. He needed the sugarcane taste of her sweat when she laid her black hair down on the white bone of his shoulder. Her armpits tasted like ginger, almonds, sugar, and, above all, sweating cocoa butter.

He searched his pocket for pesos. The head turned knowingly; silver earrings whirred across black hair-space to flicker for a moment in front of that reddish-brown face. Her eyes, her eyes—blacker than blood!

The boy remembered how boys practice bullfighting in the park, how the one who is the bull bows low, snorting, as he holds a pair of bull's horns to his forehead. He snorts again, kicking dust as the matador wheels the red cloth in slow motion, the knife hidden behind. Afterward he can lay his horns down, wipe the sweat from his nose, and stand. But the boy could not become human again.

Will you go with me, Red Song?

Where?

Under the darkness.

Yes, I'll go there. That's a good place.

He took her hand, which was as hot as a Mexicali night. The madam made a cross in her notebook. The blind man tinged his triangle like eyes funneling down into the bullring. As she walked away beside her lover, past the smiles of backpointing boys, past all the padrotes sitting in the park, the madam lowered her pencil, the bandmaster raised his baton, and the musicians made a new song that no one had ever heard before.

Mexico City, Distrito Federal, Mexico (1992)

She hid in her skirt of starched-white froth, her new skirt as delicious as wedding cake, turning her face away, giggling when his mouth pursued her. He'd married her for each of thirteen nights. But not yet could he hope to draw a slow kiss out of her.

Under the night I'll help you, his friend said. His friend was a new friend, an old friend, a brown rain idol with holes in his mouth.

I can help myself, said the boy. Tonight for me she'll let down her dark hair. Tonight she'll undo the silver buttons of her black dress.

She's nothing but a pair of buttocks, the idol said. Remember, in this world no one has a mind but you and me. Tell her that, when you buy her lighted shopwindow breast.

In this world only the Red Song has a mind! the boy said fiercely. Are you my friend or only your own?

Ask for the ruby, the idol whined. Remember it when she takes you under the night.

The idol was gone. The boy's arm slipped, hard and brown, around the Red Song's neck, cutting her hair in two.

He walked her quickly past the National Palace, where less lucky men stood in front, raising sheets tied to two sticks, two men to a stick, red flags and umbrellas and bullhorns, dust, a man selling Popsicles; the sheets said: GIVE US THE RED SONG. He walked her between the hedges of the Alameda, his smile in her eyes, his hand on her neck. (He was as gaudily unstable as the colored parasols in the park.) He craved the way she could grab handfuls of her blouse and offer it to the breeze.

Red Song, show me your little ruby this night.

I have no ruby. I only have a mind.

The round lamps came on as fragrantly yellow as lemons, hovering among the trees. The hurdy-gurdy attendant, attired like a sixteen-star general, cranked the air full of sweetness. The fountains jetted their eternal orgasms. Suddenly the attendant's identically uniformed triple-secret double marched to the boy and asked to be paid. The boy's heart vomited. He did not pay, because he needed every peso for the Red Song. The man went away whispering: You listened, but you did not pay. You stole the fruit of my mind.

The wet statues in the fountain had become as black as whaleskin. Everyone took ease in the benches that bound the nested circles of cobblestones whose center the fountains owned. Couples promenaded in step. There was still enough light to gleam on the backs of the women's high heels. But now it got dark quite suddenly, like tolling bells.

The boy swallowed and said again: Red Song, please let me take your ruby, your pretty little ruby . . .

Across the street, the madam opened her notebook.

I have no ruby! the Red Song cried.

But across the street the madam smiled, reached into her stony bosom, pulled out a cigarette, a shining cigarette.

Then the Red Song swayed and said: Give me a million in silver and gold.

The boy grasped her fiercely. — You swear?

I swear I'll show you my ruby. But I'll never show you my mind.

Mexico City, Distrito Federal, Mexico (1992)

The idol was not gone. The idol was the tooth in the dark ceiling, the little child at table whom others must serve.

The next night was as dark as the inside of a woman's skirt. Behind wide yellow crosswalk-lines the Red Song stood waiting. The musicians blew their silver trumpets; other whores breathed the Red Song's breath, hoping to steal beauty's luck. Already he'd leaped the cemetery wall, and his new friend, his old friend, brought the spade and was gone. (The idol was not gone. The idol was young earrings in an old woman's face.) Now the boy dug deeper than fungus and urine-smelling dirt. Guided by the light of scarlet worms, he opened sleep's barred windows. His shoveltip rang! He'd struck her mother's skeleton, sounded the long curve of the silver bird's neck veined with shadows, spangled with light!

He boiled the money clean: gray coins, yellow coins, he scraped out their maggoty marrow. A million pesos!—smooth and wet, in-cised with numbers and naked women. As soon as he'd heaped them into the Red Song's arms, the soda girl screamed with envy and stabbed herself in the breast, the musicians played all their tunes at once, the madam sprouted new teeth to lengthen her grin; and then the Red Song took the boy's hand. They went off together.

Now she let him touch the flowers that fringed her underchemise. He undid white ribbons and lace, white sashes like weeds around her ankles. Ruffles struggled at her shoulders like wings. He touched the buttons that went down her back. Each rang with its own note. Slen-der like a candle, she began to let down her hair. Then she pinned it up again. That much the madam had taught her—oh, the madam had a mind! — I ask but a thousand more, the Red Song said. The million is for the madam. The thousand, ah, the little thousand is for me.

Mexico City, Distrito Federal, Mexico (1992)

The next night was as dark as the dirt beneath a corpse's finger-nails. Her mother having now been stripped, he went to his mother and sang to her of his death, squeezed a thousand pesos' worth of tears from her eyes. His mother wept: All for your amiga, your little amiga—how she's stolen your mind!

Outside the house the Red Song stood waiting. The madam was not there, but one man in red livery beat the silver drum. The boy came running out with liquid silver scalding his cupped hands, and the drummer smashed the drum in a single stroke of triumph. Now the boy baptized the Red Song with those tears which cooled and became sacred as they rolled down her hair, becoming not pearl but mother-of-pearl—shell-coins engraved with numerals and mermaids. Once she was thoroughly studded with these precious beads, she sat herself up on a wall so that her face was as high as his face. He put his hands on the wall, one on either side of her. (Already up her dress, his fingers were families advancing on their knees across the Basilica's marble floor, the little children not knowing how to balance them-selves.) Rending the calm gold darkness, he played her breast like a dark hand stroking a guitar as she locked her legs around him. His head fell forward into his dreams. Her hands stroked his back; her arms pulled him closer. Their kisses rang beneath their heels as they hurried to the idol's altar; their kisses were tiles like cream, tiles like cream in coffee; tiles like custard. — But I'll beg you for a hundred more, she whispered. The thousand is for new ribbons. The hundred, ah, only the little hundred is for me.

Mexico City, Distrito Federal, Mexico (1992)

The next night was as dark as an Indian woman's hair. For the little hundred nothing attended her—not even the spastic grin of a redfaced trumpeteer. The boy no longer knew how to appease her demands, but another skull gazed into a skull-shaped pot still faintly spiraled with ocher; the other skull was his new friend, his old friend, who served him lust on spiderwebbed plates of black slate. The Red Song waited. He tiptoed past the sorrowful shadow of her tanned cheek, past the softly resigned look of the sleeping woman's mouth.

In the Alameda his dear friend called helpers: frogmasked, kiln-baked women with spread legs. For him they quickly caught a hundred pesos in crickets. Why sell their songs? This live money was precious, being sought by every soft brown hand heavy with rings. He came back guided by the light of marble on her cheekbones. Hopping onto her sleeping belly, they became obsidian counters carved with hieroglyphs and scowling slant-eyed girls. The Red Song woke smiling. As soon as she'd caressed those smooth black counters of preciousness, she stood up and took his hand.

She took him down the tunnel of fingernails between two churches windowed with dripping eyelashes. Following those ants which resemble triple beads of amber, she led him down blueflower-tiled stairs, down dark stone stairs guarded by moonmaned iron monsters, square-tongued gargoyles, down into the cave-smell beneath the rock-lobed ceiling, and her tongue thrust inside his mouth, dripping with saliva that burned like lemon juice. Then she brought him to the place like the twining roots of shadow on a trumpet's bowl, like the white grooves of dress shirts between black-suited shoulders. — Now give me just ten pesos more, she said in his ear. The hundred you gave me is nothing. Ten pesos, ah, ten little pesos is less than nothing, just a ghost to keep nothing good company.

Mexico City, Distrito Federal, Mexico (1992)

The night was as dark as a beetle's belly. He held out his hand in the darkness, and the idol put ten pesos in it. So she led him to a deep chamber in the earth, where the idol's skeleton with its jade deathmask lay inside an immense sepulcher of white stones, the corner slab inscribed with designs. Then she let down her hair. — One peso more is all I ask, said the Red Song. A single peso, not even for me. It's only the ten pesos that asks it.

Desperate in the darkness, he snatched the idol's coin back, clenched it between his teeth and bit it until it burst and one more peso spurted out. Then she led him to the chapel of paper animals. He became the paper lion.

Mexico City, Distrito Federal, Mexico (1992)

When a woman's head rides a man's heaving shoulder, there's a certain dark bird carved in lava that screeches. That sound the idol always hears; there's no escape.

The idol flew down between the Red Song's breasts and said to her: He stole everything. Every night now until you die, you'll have to let your hair down beneath the trees.

The boy did not hear. So proudly and joyfully he watched the turquoise earrings still trembling at the edges of her dark face, the pale, downcurving fingernail of light below her eye, the other crescent, very tiny, just under her lower lip. Yawning, he waited for the darkness between her eyelashes to widen. Her ruby glittered on his tongue. Then he swallowed it.

The Red Song pushed him away from between her breasts. (His

head was the idol's head.) He stared with sleepy eyes. She said to him: I know I have no mind. I'm nothing but a pair of buttocks. I heard you say that. And you, your mind lies under the night! Where's my ruby?

The boy smiled abashed and said: I threw it in the river.*

You have no mind! she cried. You're only a child who wanted ice cream in the shivering of the bells.

With sunny hair and spider-legs, the idol came to drink down her frothy hair. She did not see, but the boy did. The idol said to him: She claims that you have no mind! She means to eat your mind! You'll be darkness if you stay with her.

The Red Song sobbed out: You have no mind. And you made me bleed for your mind's sake.

Just as the beggar-woman jerks her baby awake upon the rich man's approach, so the idol woke the boy's anger, which was a little idol clutching and scratching at the grilles on the window of his heart, the grilles like square gold claws. So long she'd tormented him! His anger was the matador's silver dagger hidden always behind the red cloth.

You have a mind . . . he said, trying yet to love her.

Sitting beside him on a monument wall, she drew her knees under her armpits like a grasshopper and said: You have no mind.

His anger lurched the way that when you have a fever the flowers on the curtains crawl nauseatingly. He shouted into her face the Three Holy Names. (Everyone knows them.)

Her lips opened. She saw the paper animals. Her ruby was in the paper lion's mouth. She sat for a moment like a naked statue bronzily balancing on air. Then her dark head fell down upon his snow-white shirt.

* Mexico City slang: to go to the river = to engage in cunnilingus.

Mexico City, Distrito Federal, Mexico (1992)

At noon they tolled the half-spent day until the shadows of terrified pigeons darkened the plaza like rain. They fired the cannon as pigeon-wings seethed like steam. Then came the chanting procession of whores: women and children, two girls ahead bearing the Red Song's dress which was petalled like a sunflower, then six bearing a wreathed coffin, then the ladies in the back bowing beneath their parasols. At the very back came the madam, longing for the cathedral's smoky shade. By María, how her blood was simmering! But, her notebook open, she marched ready as ever for business. She followed her girls between the walls of waiting men. Men watched hoping for a stare of black, black lace. They'd forgotten the Red Song already, even though her ankles had never been like other girls' pale yellow ankles; their lust remained alive in just the way a fat girl's breasts strain for joy when she breathes. The madam smiled on them kindly. Resurrected, the soda girl sold orange fizz. The girls continued happy, she thought; they bore the Red Song lightly toward the church. No one knew she lay still bleeding in that coffin. Pale and swollen, she bled through her copper belt's hundred locks; the blood kept coming out until she floated up against the lid. So loudly did the pallbearers sing for the good of her soul that they did not hear her horrid sloshing. But at last blood began to ooze between the hinges of the coffin. For a moment longer it hid itself among her red roses. Then it jetted like the juice of pressed grapes. The six girls' shoulders were soaked with the dark black blood. They dropped the coffin and scattered into screams.

But the madam knew blood in the way that ice cream vendors handle dry ice with bare fingers, underawed by its steaming. She called her whores back. She pulled a withered cigarette from her blouse and threw it into the sewer. Then, gathering them around the lake of blood in which the coffin now floated, joining them hand in hand as they stood upon the cobblestones (circled more largely by the armies of waiting men), she said:

Whenever it rains, the red paint on the cathedral dome runs like blood. Blood goes where the shit goes, bleeding down our white restaurants that darkness eats like layer cakes. Blood goes down to the place where ancient ceramics turn brown in the earth. Listen to blood, my little nieces! Women know that blood's always being made—blood sings the red song! Even when the day's as white as the sunlight on the skull of that Indian lady selling plates, blood bleeds secretly from the gums of old men, from the throats of slaughtered cattle, from the prisoners' wounds, from between your legs, you women! Even in our cemetery whose skeletons are stuffed with bottles and trash, the hulks of switchboxes under dead traffic lights, the dust of old blood sifts out of bones. Blood's the song of rubies. Blood's the only song. Blood's as natural as a dead dog in the street.

Masada, Territory of Judea, Israel (1993)
Limbo (1994)
Capri, Campania, Italia (1993)

Masada, Territory of Judea, Israel (1993)

Now Eleazar went down to the Elders, for all Rome, as it seemed, had come against them to take Masada. [2]And the Elders were glad of his coming, and the Rabbis also resorted to him, for upon their hearts were shadows darker than the Dead Sea. [3]And the fighters lifted their eyes and watched his passing. [4]Then they turned their heads to study once again how the Roman armies did draw slowly closer. [5]And the Elders awaited Eleazar on the middle terrace of Herod's northern palace where it was cold and shady and sandy. [6](But the women waited with the little ones where the pale rock had been hollowed out into ritual baths.)

7 And Eleazar said: Have you heard the news from Jerusalem?

8 And the Elders said: We saw a spy come to you, and the spy was weeping.

9 Eleazar said: Jerusalem is perished, and we alone are left of the Jewish nation. [10]The Temple is no more.

11 Then the Elders burst into lamentation and rent their clothes in pieces, and their hearts were overthrown with sorrow. [12]And the women listened, but could not hear the cause, so they crouched in silence, waiting to learn whether they should scream.

13 And Eleazar said: 'Tis well that we've repaired this old strong-hold, and increased our walls towards Heaven, and bolted our gates with the strongest bolts. [14]Because now the conquerors of Jerusalem turn to us. [15]And belike they are saying to one another: This Masada is but a tomb that the Jews have built for themselves.

16 And the eyes of Eleazar were as sinister cavities. [17]And a craven man who'd drunk of fear went rushing toward the women's place, and no one said him nay. [18]The others sat on, and waited until they heard the women begin to scream.

19 Then Eleazar said: Now the worst is told. [20]But even if Jerusalem is finished, still we have our Laws. [21]And Masada is our rock of honor. [22]In Herodium and Machaerus a few brave comrades hold out. [23]Remain of good heart. [24]I shall lead you until the end. [25]And perhaps we can prevail even now, for who knows what the Lord has written?

26 Then the Elders raised their voices to reply, and said: Fight our battles, and all that you command we promise to accomplish.

27 And the Rabbis likewise became glad, saying: Now God will show His power to these Gentiles. [28]God can defend one against a thousand. [29]So we have no fear.

30 And in the Dry Hours, when they spied the Romans sleeping, they prayed among the pillars of the synagogue, requesting the Lord to send them relief; yea, they prayed beneath the harsh dark sky.

2 But it was as Eleazar said: Who knows the ways of God? — [2]In the Book of Chronicles 'tis written that King David and all Israel assembled to bring the sacred Ark from Kiriathjearim, and one whose name was Uzzah pressed his palms against the Ark, because the oxen had stumbled and he feared the Ark would fall. [3]What else should he have done? [4]But God raged, and Uzzah died. [5]This is why the proverb goes: *The mind of the righteous ponders how to answer, but the mouth of the wicked pours out evil things.* [6]Such are the ways of God.

3 In the first year the Romans could not take Masada, there being but one way up that Hill of Gold, and that was the Serpentine Path, above which Eleazar's soldiers waited with their boulders and cauldrons of pitch. [2]And their cavalry and picked troops did not yet assault that place, because Flavius Silva, the Procurator of that province, had set them to harrying the land far and wide, robbing, raping

and killing, so that the Jews would never dare to rebel again. [3]And Eleazar came down from Masada many times with his Zealots, and whenever his spies found Romans he came upon them by night, sparing none whom God had delivered into his power. [4]So the Romans were discontented. [5]And that first year passed. [6]At the dawn of the second year, Eleazar went to the Elders and the Rabbis who awaited him on the middle terrace. [7]And Eleazar said: Have you heard the news from Herodium and Machaerus?

8 And the Elders said: We saw a spy come to you, and the spy was shaking with fear.

9 Eleazar said: Herodium is perished, and Machaerus overrun. [10]The defenders are dead or given to the torture of chains. [11]Their wives have become Roman concubines, and their children beg for bread.

12 Then the Elders groaned. [13]And the Rabbis called upon the Lord to witness their sorrow, and the Lord gazed down upon them.

14 Then Eleazar said: But still we have our Laws. [15]Our oil continues sweet, and our wine is not yet vinegar. [16]The locusts have not found our grain.

17 Then the Elders said: You who are the son of a Rabbi, according to your wisdom do we continue our rebellion?

18 He answered: Purify yourselves, and celebrate our resolution with joy. [19]Tomorrow I shall order that the gate be opened, and I shall lead a hundred men down the Serpentine Path to kill Romans in the night. [20]Blessed be the Lord, whose goodness never fails the people of Israel. [21]We can prevail even now. [22]He will give us courage to live without dishonor on our hill of gold, high above the pollutions of the land.

23 And in the Dry Hours, while the Romans slept, the defenders prayed together, humbling themselves in sackcloth and strewing ashes upon their heads.

24 So the Jews yet defended Masada. [25]And they worshiped before the Lord, fearing only Him; but that could not save them, for it was already the will of the Lord that they be slain. [26]And still they withstood all the Romans' force and might and treachery.

4 Now at the dawn of the third year Flavius Silva received instructions from Vespasian Emperor of Rome to carry out the destruction of Masada, so he brought together his captains according to the

knowledge that was in his heart; [2]and he picked men of the Tenth Legion along with many Jewish slaves and prisoners of war, and he assembled them and formed them in ranks, and he put them under oath and armed them, [3]and they set out across the desert, with the Jewish captives bearing water. [4]And on that march many Jews died. [5]But Flavius Silva said: If thirst slays them now, we need not slay them later. [6]And he led under his command fifteen thousand cavalrymen, legionnaires, infantrymen and engineers. [7]And the number of slaves and prisoners who carried water for them was ten thousand.

8 Now Flavius Silva acted according to the Emperor's command. [9]And he walked around the Golden Hill with his engineers, stalking victory like a lion. [10]Then he built eight camps and fortified them well, for he gave orders wisely, so that none of his words fell to the ground. [11]And his engineers set the slaves to building a siege wall whose thickness was as the height of a tall man, and many of the slaves died, but Flavius Silva only laughed, for although he did not know Him, the Lord guarded his feet. [12]This wall entirely encircled Masada, and its length was more than seven thousand cubits, and it bore twelve towers.

5 Eleazar went to the Elders and the Rabbis who awaited him on the middle terrace. [2]And Eleazar said: There is no news. [3]The Romans have killed our spy. [4]Or, if news there be, I think your eyes can tell it to you. — [5]And he pointed to the west, where the Romans had brought in engineers to build a ramp, in order to bypass the Serpentine Path. [6]And at the summit of the ramp the Romans were building a siege tower sixty cubits high, reinforced with iron. [7]And from this tower they launched stones and arrows against the Jews, and from underneath it the Jewish prisoners were commanded by Flavius Silva to charge against the walls of Masada with a battering ram; and those who refused were crucified until they died with swollen faces. [8]And this time the craven man did not run, and the women did not scream, because it was as Eleazar said. [9]This was not news. [10]And the Elders were silent.

11 Then Eleazar said: But still we have our Laws. [12]And who knows what the Lord has written?

13 But the Elders did not take heart. [14]Then the Rabbis assembled them in the synagogue. [15]They prayed that their dear ones not become

carrion and whores and slaves. [16]They prayed that their altar not be profaned. [17]They fasted one and all until the soldiers could scarcely lift their spears. [18]And the Lord looked down upon their affliction.

6 Now the battering ram of the Romans breached the wall with a hideous clash, and the children started weeping, and the Rabbis called upon the Lord God while the women drew wine and water from the cisterns and poured it out before the Lord; but Eleazar with all the men built two walls of stout timber at the breach, and they packed earth in between. [2]And after this the Roman missiles only compressed the earth to a superior hardness, so that the enemy could make no shift against Masada. [3]Then the people praised Eleazar. [4]But the sound of the battle was like thunder; and the craven man howled. [5]And the soldiers lay day and night in their trenches, and the women and children carried water to them and brought them stones to launch against the Romans. [6]So the Romans grew weary and filled with fear, because they could not conquer that last stronghold of the Jews. [7]And they began to whisper against their governor, Flavius Silva. [8]But came the close of the third year, in the month called Xanthicus, when the wide gray siege ramp stretched like one of those tendons between neck and shoulder, [9]Eleazar son of Ananias went to the Elders and Rabbis who awaited him on the middle terrace. [10]And Eleazar said: The Romans are preparing fire. — [11]And from below they heard Flavius Silva shout in a terrifying voice: Launch the burning arrows! — [12]And the arrows came with a noise like hornets, and there were many of them, and their heads were smeared with burning pitch. [13]And they lodged in the outermost of the two wooden walls which Eleazar had built, and it caught fire. [14]When the defenders sought to save their wall, the Romans launched great stones which smashed the skulls of many brave men. [15]And the craven man screamed until the people covered their ears, and then Eleazar slew him with a sword. [16]And the fire destroyed the wall, and the earth tumbled out like entrails from the belly of a pregnant woman who is disembowelled by conquerors; [17]and the Romans exulted, [18]but then the wind changed and blew the flames back toward the siege tower, which began to smoke. [19]Now the Romans shouted in fear, and the Rabbis praised God; and then the wind changed again. [20]Then the Romans took heart, and compelled their Jewish slaves to quell the fire in the siege tower; and afterwards launched another volley of arrows to set afire the second wall. [21]And the Jews cried out. [22]Then the Romans called upon them to surrender, and the Jews were silent. [23]After this they heard the Romans laughing, and then the Romans went down to their camps to sleep. [24]And Eleazar said: Tomorrow they will conquer this place and bring us into shame.

25 And the Elders said: We must go to the temple to pray.

7 Now Eleazar mustered all the people together, to see how many had survived. [2]And he counted nine hundred and sixty souls at Masada, but many were wounded and defiled with blood. [3]And some were fearful and others remained as steadfast as stone; and they all prostrated themselves through the Dry Hours of that last evening. [4]And they became very faint. [5]And they abased themselves in the inner chamber, and the Rabbis led them in entreaties for God's mercy upon themselves and their inheritance. [6]Their hearts were as deep and dank as the Western Wall's great cistern, whose stairs went interminably down into a slit of darkness; and in the slit one saw other stairs descending into an immense bubble of golden dirt bearing black and white stain-continents. [7]The pigeons which nested in the ceiling cooed, and their echoings seemed demonic and far away. [8]In their prison of fear the people were shut away from the stars. [9]Their sorrow scorched them with darkness, and their prayers were appalled. [10]Then at last Eleazar stood up, and put his hand upon the shoulder of the Chief Rabbi. [11]And most wearily he spoke to the people the words of Judith the daughter of Merari the son of Ox: *Do not try to bind the purposes of the Lord our God, for God is not like man, to be threatened, nor like a human being, to be won over by pleading.*

12 Then the people were silent, but the Elders said: What would you have us do?

13 And Eleazar prayed to the Lord. [14]Then he rose and said: We must kill ourselves, so that the Romans cannot work their will upon us. [15]And we must do it quickly, for at dawn they come.

16 The Elders had grown accustomed to walk in his ways, and so they said: You speak from a true heart.

17 But the people cried out then, because they saw the approach

of their deaths.★ [18]Yet the other way, of awaiting the Roman legions in their terrifying armor, that they likewise dared not take. [19]So they bowed down and were pale. [20]But at last they said: Behold, we are your flesh, and the bones of your flesh. [21]We do as you will.

8 Then said Eleazar: I am glad. [2]The Lord called my death from the womb; behold, it is born; it is here. [3]He pulled your deaths from His quiver, my brothers and sisters; behold, they come speeding hither. [4]We are rebels to the Romans, but we cannot rebel against the grave. [5]We shall not be confounded; and this night we'll find respite from our sighs.

6 Now they kindled tall flames to burn their houses and treasures, and the women made their hearts as pale blue as the Dead Sea. [7]But the children said: Mother, why do you throw my pretty things in the fire? [8]Father, why do you set our house alight? [9]But their parents would not answer. [10]Thus they destroyed the toil of their hands, and all that had been handed down to them, in order to baffle the Romans' greed. [11]But their stores of food, oil and wine they piled in the middle of the square, so that the Romans would see that their siege had failed to starve them. [12]Then they went into the night to slay themselves.

13 Weeping, the men of Masada embraced their wives and children, stabbing them one by one; and thus they made of their dear ones offerings to the Lord. [14]Then these self-made widowers formed themselves in squads of ten, as was their wont when they went down to fight with the Romans. [15]And they cast lots, thereby choosing one man out of each ten to slay the others. [16]Thus they died, all on the same night together. [17]And at last there was but one man left upon Masada the Hill of Gold. [18]And he passed through the smoking houses, and he searched the rooms of the ruined palace to make

★ Some modern commentators have suggested that they specifically feared the intentions of Eleazar, who was known to have killed so many persons, Romans and Jews alike, including even Menachem ben Judah, the hero who'd slaughtered the Roman garrison at Masada seven years past, at the very beginning of the Rebellion. The tale goes that shortly before Jerusalem fell, Menachem ben Judah found Eleazar's father, Ananias the High Priest, in a state of terror at the impending Roman victory, for which he killed him—an act which Eleazar avenged.

certain that all were dead. [19]Then he set the palace on fire and leaped onto his sword. [20]And when the Romans breached the charred walls at dawn and came upon the Jews, and when they saw that they were dead by their own hand, all expressed admiration for their defiance, even their governor, Flavius Silva.

9 But it must be told that two women and five children were still alive . . .

[The Hebrew text breaks off here.]

Limbo (1994)

A nd all this I entombed in my heart, burying it deep in my heart's four chambers. And the chambers of my heart are called *Courage, Fortitude, Righteousness* and *Sacrifice.* But although I have applied my mind to have these things, although they are engraved in the doorways of my heart, I do not possess them. In defiance of God I seek most vainly to prolong my life. And when righteousness calls me to ascend the Serpentine Path, my fear whispers that I shall never come down living from the Hill of Gold. And when courage bids me rise up against tyrants, my fear speaks in a soft low voice, bidding me bow down to wickedness, that I might accept the bribe of my life. And when fortitude commands me to offer my throat to the blade of pain, my fear shows me the way of hiding, there in the manmade wells and bubbles in the rock of the tanner's shop. And when sacrifice summons me away from the sweetness of the light, then my fear pains me like the stinging salts of the Dead Sea.

I am a woman with child, and I do not want to die.

God listened, and said to her: Go, and eat the bread of your life, my sad young maid. Lift up your heart, and await the coming of the enemy. They will be easy with you, on account of the others who have died. They will weep tears of pity, and your slavery will be light.

Capri, Campania, Italia (1993)

And I myself, neither man nor woman, but only scribe long dead, my flesh long turned to crackly old leaves, imagine how if this woman could have chosen her own Hill of Gold there would have been no Eleazar whom she feared (although the Hebrew sources report that she was his kinswoman), no Serpentine Path, just an empty white walk studded with light, and trees at regular intervals, then a road roofed with branches, a giant palm, then lights set into the steep coast of night, the sound of a girl singing eerily to herself, silence, and then people calling far away, a barking dog, the smell of the cold sea. The girl sang again, two notes; perhaps she was only calling to the other woman, who it is written was old, or to one of the five children who hid and feared. Her echo rose into the black heavens.

Let the Hill of Gold become some sunny rock of trees and white houses.

Two girls (let them both be that; nobody likes to be old), one in a sweater, one in a jacket, arms linked at the elbow, promenaded back and forth along the terraced way until a school of other shouting girls swept them up. They all ran down to the sea, where the cacti had legs like crossbreeds of spiders and artichokes. There was a shimmering wall of pines between cliff-stairs and the sea. They had never seen death and wanted to go dancing. That night their lovers would come on the ferry. They'd go with them hand in hand between tree-swellings and turquoise water and white cliffs to the tree-haired Arco Naturel, which has several shining sea-holes where some of them would make love; others would descend as far as the Grotta Matrimonia, that gigantic hollow in the earth like a drained boil; and as the boys they'd chosen gripped their breasts, they'd lie looking upward at the chalky ceiling studded with pale stones like jewels of baseness; perhaps for a moment they'd feel uneasy, almost remembering the cisterns of Masada where they'd hid while above them the ones they loved died praying and bleeding; they'd gasp in the boys' arms, then afterwards grow shy and run ahead up the trail into a steep thicket from which the narrow white crags burst up. All the girls met here every morning to dream of boys together amidst the leafy reaches of golden buds and lilies. The boys came running after them, pounding up the old Roman road. A gull rose and fell in the shade of the steep bay. The boys were searching, but they couldn't find them; the girls knew this secret place so well. They watched the boys coming from far down the treepacked cliff where grottos spat out ocean from their crusted lips; and they giggled. It was almost dawn. They almost didn't want the boys to find them. It was their last night together. Tomorrow morning they would leave this thicket of rosemary, emerging from their wall of white boulders bulging with cacti in whose crotches were birds' nests and balls of pine needles; and they would go down to the sea to get married. After that they would never meet again. Some would go with their husbands to live in Rome. Others would set up house in Napoli or Firenze or even far Catania. They'd never again gaze together at those rocks like icebergs in the dark sea, those ocean-stones whirl-kissed by eddies and fan-shaped waves. That is why, succumbing to the promptings of history, I now introduce to these pages the apostate Josephus Flavius, who was not a Zealot, and held out in a cave with many other men when the Romans came. The Jews in that cave had proposed to stab themselves, but Josephus convinced them it would be less of a sin if they killed each other. Better yet, he contrived to be at the end of the line. Ah, Josephus, how I love you, for you loved life! You were good to yourself; you despised that monstrosity called High Principle. When all but he and one other man were dead, he persuaded his companion to surrender at his side. What happened to Josephus's friend I don't know, but Josephus (who wrote our best extant account of the Jewish War, always glorifying himself and the Romans) was dragged before Vespasian in heavy chains. Because he prophesied with a sycophant's urgency that Vespasian would soon be Emperor, he kept his life and in due time even became rich and free. His first two wives had abandoned him. He married a nice girl in Rome and later left her for a Cretan belle . . . So I wonder: Would the two young women who hid from their fate have played the same game that Josephus did (excluding from their hearts, of course, his own reptilian selfishness)? I can almost hear them laughingly urging their sisters down the hill, gently coaxing and swaying them ahead, until they were the only two

left; and then they slipped away to be virgins together forever. —
No, I don't think so. — Now the heads of the boys rose above the
heads of pine trees, gazing down from the crags. From the shade of
a white crag, boys came running, bearing their sweethearts a glorious
hellfire of blue flowers. They pulled their true loves away from the
other girls, took them swimming in green water with reddish stones
underneath, white gulls overhead like whitecaps. The girls whispered:
I love you so . . . — Why did they weep when they said it? Did
they truly long to flee the empty sea-horizon, running back up the
tree-frizzed slopes their bare feet knew so well, meeting other
girls above the white cliffs? Now it was dawn, the low white wall
of windows and arches at the water's edge cliffs not white yet, but
purplish-gray, the other ferries white, whitest of all the hydrofoil's
wake. The boys took them by the hand. The girls kissed their mothers
and fathers goodbye forever. Their husbands had already bought them
ferry tickets. And the island quickly became a lump of rocky cloud
in the sky, stretching its coast off long and low until it fell off the
edge of the world.

California and Japan (1993)

The first time he read the Japanese girl's letter his heart rushed because he was sure that she was saying she was his. He had written to her passionately. She'd replied: *If you have a little enough time, please stop by Tokyo to visit me. You probably are not interested in Tokyo, but maybe in seeing me.* To him this phrasing seemed so delicate and perfect a statement of acceptance that he kissed her letter for joy. Then at the end she said: *Please come back alive from Burma. Because I love you, too.*

Night after night he stayed up rereading this and imagining holding her in his arms. He felt that he was approaching her ever more closely. Soon he'd be kissing the moist lips of her desire. But he wasn't there yet; although he knew what she'd written by heart, he had not penetrated every veil of her meaning. Her penciled marks were as cold and smoky as the Japanese Sea; it was only latterly that his urgency had begun to sense the low brain-colored island of Japan coming closer, to see the khaki squares as of a woven mat, interspersed with the dull leaden glitter of cities: *You probably are not interested in Tokyo, but maybe in seeing me.* Now he was close enough to glimpse Japan's dragonclaws and rivers, and the water like silvery fog (*but maybe in seeing me*), those dark green curds called trees. *In seeing me. Because I love you, too.* But then one night the letter was used up. Instead of tacit it seemed lukewarm. He tumbled into despondent confusion.

333

A week went by in which he didn't read it, and then one hot afternoon he took it from the envelope and traveled down its lines. This time it was not lukewarm but sisterly, loving, enthusiastic, not at all erotic. There was some other matter in the letter—chatty, newsy stuff—which in previous nights had appeared to him only as the lingerie which translucened the more exciting words, but now he comprehended that it was in fact the real stuff, that love was no more than fondness and the invitation merely kind and polite. He'd only thought otherwise because the letter he'd sent her first had been so desperately tender. What if she'd never even received that letter? After all, there was no reference to it. Ah, the perils of context! So he flew away from Japan, leaving her lights and blackness for more blackness.

He said to himself: How *can* the meaning of these words squirm and wriggle so much on my mind's hook?

But then he thought: After all, I never knew what anything else meant, so why should I know what this means? It's written that there's no such thing as truth . . .

He sent her a love-charged reply and waited. Six months later he heard from her in a Christmas card that she was about to marry someone else.

DISAPPOINTED BY THE WIND

Toronto, Ontario, Canada (1993)

Toronto, Ontario, Canada (1993)

West of the place where Niagara's turquoise marbles itself with foam and changes to cobalt, there are other blue veins in my atlas which idle between Lakes Erie and Ontario; north of them the eye is caught by Lake Ontario's burrowing nose which one's gaze traces from Burlington to Bronte, Oakville to Clarkson, Port Credit to Mississauga, and so up to the city of Toronto. In the autumn this way of going allows one to make the acquaintance of wide blonde and redhaired trees. There are coppery-leafed forests along the riverbanks, and lanes of leaves the milky green of English apples. Closer to Toronto they have all turned the hue of golden deliciouses or McIntoshes; and in Toronto itself they have mainly left the trees. Looking once more at my atlas I discover the whole weight of northern Canada bearing down on Toronto. From James Bay roots of frosty rivers grow south, reaching.

In October, when I was visiting, a chilly wind blew always from the lake, piling up fog that was beige with whitish highlights like a field of October corn. I felt alone. On the subway people wore woolly jackets over their sweaters, sitting bowed against the dismalness of the

335

growing cold. By January they would be long used to it, but that was because by then the summer would be dead and in a frozen grave, permitting the mourning to take place with detachment, irony, and eventually even joy as the extremists joined the strong fierce red-cheeked battalions of winter, gloating in fresh stinging winds; but at the moment summer was newly deceased, still paling and cooling and clotting on a bed of crunchy leaves. So each subway passenger was alone like some Arctic traveller who, homesick while the wind groaned, stretched a hand out of the sleeping bag and ate dry cereal, pushing the cold back a few steps. I knew a little about what cold was. Toronto was not cold yet. On the borders of Canada lay snow-drifts as pure and rich as cream. In summer the mud had been wet between them. It was just above freezing—much colder with the wind chill. Beside the Arctic Ocean was a ridge of pumice-like rock, and then a long low snow-ridge, flat on top like a barn roof, that was almost the same color as the sky. When I tried to read or write there my fingers quickly became numb. The wind grew more forceful; the tent-fly was caked with ice, and my wet boots froze. That was not cold yet; that was still summer. But now the sea had begun to freeze, and down in Toronto we knew that even without knowing it. On the subway we felt cold. Each passenger hunched with his hands in his pockets or deep inside his sleeves, longing to retract arms and legs within his heartwarmed torso to resist the cold, as a sphere of glowing blood. The men glared or sadly gazed; the women wrinkled them-selves into frumpishness or followed the flashing stations with clear and angry eyes.

At night it was so much colder still that loneliness overcame le-thargic sadness. That was why at night the girls in their thick coats seemed to offer promises of warm cuddlings. It was like Walter Ben-jamin in Moscow in 1926, pursuing Asja Lacis and scribbling: *Moscow as it appears at the present reveals a full range of possibilities in schematic form: above all, the possibility that the Revolution might fail or succeed.*

Asja would not give herself to him anymore. Her hair was as weightless as milkweed down. But one evening they pushed their coats off the bed and he lay down with her on top of him. They started kissing. He put his hands inside her warm sweater.

As I rode the subway on those foggy Toronto nights, I looked at the women and felt that I could have gone home with them to be warm, but I never asked any of them, and when I reached my stop I went out without looking back.

This happened night after night. Night after night I derived pleasure from sitting across from the women of Toronto, imagining holding them in my arms in their dark warm bedrooms. Night after night I passed through the turnstile and ascended to Yonge Street, where the clammy wind tried to steal my hat. Then late one evening I came out into the silver, frosty air, and the wind was ready for me. It snatched my hat and whirled it over the roofs of buildings. It tweaked my nose and earlobes with burning mischievous fingers. It caught me up and lifted me above the lake. I saw my hat far ahead of me, a black star whirling higher to cap one of the delicious white stars of winter. Because I had fallen in love with the wind, I was permitted to become the white star, and my black cap sailed lovingly down onto my head. I was in the bedroom of the wind. The wind wanted to play with me, love me and eat me. I married the wind, and rode the wind all night.

In the morning I woke up naked on an island of dark wet gartersnakes and birches whose leaves were speckled and orange. The wind came to kiss me, and sent an orange rain upon the sand. When I stopped blinking, the trees were bare and the snakes had slipped underground.

I was not cold. My body was as red as a brick. It glowed and tingled and pricked. I found a thicket of Indian pipe in the sand and picked them, made black-jointed flutes with which to serenade the wind, and the wind, still loving me, raised the lake about me, sloshed cold violet-green water about me in glee until it burned pleasantly on the rims of my ears.

Then the wind got tired of me. I don't know why. I had striven to be entertaining and different at all times. My own joy had certainly not diminished. But it didn't matter. This was divorce. My clothes fell down upon me with a thump, and in the dead calm I began to shiver.

I crossed the lake in an old canoe and reached town just as the wind began again. Soccer players in blue jerseys were running amidst the leaves. A woman clutched the strap of her handbag, her face down in the wind. I wanted to ask her to marry me, but I was too cold. I found a street of brick houses and big dogs, where pillared porches and porticoes were overhung by pale orange leaves. Their tall narrow windows were as dull as the sky, reflecting the clouds that skidded before the wind.

I met a redhead in a long velvet jacket. She was holding her little boy's hand as they strode though fallen leaves.

I've been disappointed by the wind, too, she said.

At first I thought she was talking to me. But then I understood that she was only trying to smooth the sadness of her son whom the wind refused to take away.

The boy saw me. — Look, look! he cried to his mother. — His ears are red and happy. That means he's the wind's friend.

I smiled, said nothing, and walked away. Truly it was an ear-aching wind.

On the subway the grinning laborers in their pea-jackets, the bald owlish businessmen in wool coats, the ladies in furs all hunched against the cold. Only one person, a fanatical prophetess who wore sackcloth, was kin to me. But she would not see me or the wind; I left her alone.

Coming up the windy tunnel to Yonge Street, I found the boy, happily escaped, and running towards me amidst leaves and prayers blowing in circles. Men ran with their heads down, holding the brims of their caps. The boy begged me to bring him back over the feathery water of the windy lake to that khaki and ocher island of dying-leaved trees which lay so low in the lake that only windstruck people could find it. When I asked him how he knew about it, he said that his mother had told him. Then I knew that I had misconstrued my mis-construction, that she had been talking to me. I refused him, led him back through rolled-up leaves like trilobites on the sidewalks, and by subway we returned to the apple-colored maple leaves which curled on the trees of his neighborhood, swarming and wriggling down over the house pillars where girls in thick Indian sweaters and beaver ear-muffs ran shivering. The lady in the long velvet jacket was waiting for us. As she leaned forward to kiss me, the warm sighing breezes of her mouth reached my heart, and I melted into a puddle of water.

TIN SOLDIERS

Boot Hill, Nebraska, U.S.A. (1991)

Past the heat-seared road weeds, past the Tomahawk truck stop, I found the magic barrier crossing which once had filled me with awe and exaltation so many years ago when I left the east forever (so I'd thought) by Greyhound; now it eased me, pleased me, but could not help me anymore. It was the line between east and west. At first it was just a jaggedly wavy gray-gray horizon; then it doubled, dark purple from cloud-shadow; the same dark purple I once saw in Gallup, New Mexico. All had to cross that line, and when they did, it changed them. In the white convertible ahead were two white-helmeted soldiers. The one on the right kept saluting. When we got closer I saw that he was a girl whose long locks snapped and fluttered below the white suncap; she kept stretching her arm out as if to catch more than her share of the harsh hot sunlight. Then we got a little closer, and I saw that she wasn't a girl at all, just a pimpled boy with long greasy hair, smirking and elbowing his brother the driver, smoking cigarettes; it was to flick the ashes that he stretched his arm out. Then we drew level with them, and I saw that he was an epileptic, foaming at the mouth, eyes rolled back; in his hand a tightly rolled strip of white paper that his fingers could neither squeeze nor drop. As we passed them, he winked. Then I realized that he was only on some drug.

We'd crossed the line. We were all in the west now. Looking back

339

at the white convertible, I saw how a leathery expressionlessness like something out of a sleazy cowboy novel had molded itself over the pimpled boy's face; he'd become a Westerner once more, his amoebic freedom gone until the next time he went east. I was reminded of the way that Boot Hill's cracked and white-stained iron-gray boards leaned hard in the hot-packed dirt. **W M COFFMAN SHOT 1875.** Mrs. Lillie Miller, since petrified, was surrounded by black fence, cracked dirt and junipers. A single black-eyed susan grew by the new houses (one driveway held a canvas-covered boat). They'd crossed the line. A barely legible stone said **UNKNOWN COWBOY 1883.** The unknown cowboy in the white convertible tipped his hat, massaged his pimpled cheeks, and yodeled: *Yiiiiiiiiiiiiiiouuuu dippy-dippy-dooayheeyoooooooooooooooooooooo!*

FOURTH OF JULY

Pacific Palisades, California, U.S.A. (1992)

Pacific Palisades, California, U.S.A. (1992)

S tarfrosted balloons at the parade nudged the sidewalk people who'd drawn up bare knees like grasshoppers. The man in the white suit and the red vest raised his swizzle stick. He commanded his platoon of cymbals, trumpets and arms with full authority, except over Frieda. The parade marshalls turned the corner slowly, seated on top of their car in a successful campaign to outdignify the white lace umbrella with red and blue ribbons and the Rolex float; because it was one of those idealized beach days when the fences smelled like lemon wax; it was the emancipated day when the majority in their united wisdom emerged from double-garaged houses hidden behind roses to exercise their rights and interests—nay, vested rights, imperious mandates!—exercised them to the full amount of their recognizance, subject to the well-poised consent of the legislature. That was why the pink car with pigears rolled slowly, conveying the senator and his lovely wife. Next came the bagpipers, strutting, whirling their sticks, stern and solemn, staring straight ahead. Benign red faces in kilts beat the tattoo of liberty under liberty, conceived in liberty and dedicated to the city councilman in the skyblue car with the two American flags who led the seablue car followed by the horses and other well-intentioned persons; the councilman had read the manual on how to attain and lose happiness.

341

The councilman leaned down and half whispered to his chauffeur: You know what Frieda kept saying? *We were darkness once.*

The chauffeur coughed politely.

Frieda and Priscilla had come that morning when the councilman was inexpertly ironing his necktie. (At that moment the chauffeur was still playing catch with his son.)

Is there any luggage that I can help you with? the councilman said.

No, said Priscilla. Can't you see that we didn't bring anything?

He showed them upstairs to the guestroom where Priscilla used to sleep when she was little. On the wall hung an old stick-figure drawing of Frieda's which Emily had framed. Priscilla turned it to the wall. Frieda got the bunk bed. It was the first time he'd seen Frieda since the bad thing before the other bad thing had happened.

I really appreciate this, Frieda said. Especially right before the parade and all. You know, I got into some sort of strange circumstances or I wouldn't be here.

Oh, sure, said the councilman heartily.

Are you going to wear a *dark* costume? she said slyly.

Well, now, Frieda, I guess that depends.

The necktie was ready. Priscilla came into his room as he was tying it. It was red, white and blue.

That looks really stupid, she said.

I'm trying to get votes, he explained.

I want you to watch Frieda for half an hour while I fill a prescription for her, said Priscilla. And listen for the phone. She'll try to call one of two places—either the cemetery office, or else a cab to go there.

The cemetery office!

Priscilla was turning the picture face-out again.

Do you mean where Emily is buried?

Look, I wouldn't be here if it wasn't an emergency, Priscilla said.

I could unplug the phone, the councilman offered, determined to disregard her spitefulness, there being, after all, no victory that he could gain over her anymore except the one, by definition unacknowledged, of self-restraint.

Would you be so good as to do that? Priscilla said very formally.

Even as a child she'd been both severe and pompous. Closing his eyes, he saw Emily helping the small girl into a new white dress, trying not to smile while the girl gave her a lecture on how to fasten buttons. She'd loved Priscilla, who now went into the bathroom. The councilman checked his necktie again in the hallway mirror and, sighing, stepped into Frieda's room. That sad individual was biting her nails. A traffic helicopter overflew the house, so that the windowpanes buzzed, and Frieda began to laugh, her face still in her hands.

Do you have an ashtray? she said abruptly. I have a headache. My mind has been hurting for a long time.

How long? said the councilman very agreeably, watching the summer morning pour down the sides of buildings.

Three eons. Since before Auntie died. That's why I want to work on my writing now. On my scientific theories.

Oh, said the councilman.

They're cosmic, she said, rather defensively. They're about darkness.

The councilman went to the bathroom to comb his hair one more time and make sure that he still looked good because the chauffeur was coming. Then he thought about Emily. He did not care to think about her right now. He did not want to think about Priscilla or Frieda or the parade, either, but he had to. He closed the door.

Priscilla was knocking. He hated her. He took off his glasses, wiped his eyes, put his glasses on, checked his tie in the mirror, and opened the door.

Where's Frieda? Priscilla said.

She's not in her bed?

No.

They went into the other room and stood looking at the empty bunk. The window was open.

She must have gone down the fire escape, said the councilman. Is she suicidal?

Not at this point, I think. She was excited to come here because she remembers Auntie. But I really don't know. She's changing quite fast right now.

Has she done this before?

This is the second time. I've got to do something right now.

Me too, said the councilman coolly, seeing the chauffeur pulling up.

Ladies and gentlemen, our Citizen of the Year.

The reviewing officer waved everyone along, the four horses pulling the Wells Fargo stagecoach, teenagers on top waving to the old
people in their sidewalk chairs, the dog on the leash. The Citizen of
the Year didn't fall off the back of his chair.

And now, isn't that *wonderful!* Three lovely ladies!

The councilman looked, and did not know which ladies were
meant. He was in the parade now. Were they the clown girls stabbing,
winking and whistling while the girls on the sidewalk grinned in
wonder; or the women in sunhats sitting together on the bumpers of
cars; or the girls in baseball caps and bikinis, girls of the blue-gray sea,
blue-gray mountains, girls of the palmtrees like lollipops, girls of the
cars and boats? He checked his tie. Then he saw Frieda in the back
of the red car, which was bright as the skin of a carbon monoxide
corpse. A woman in a skeleton costume sat beside her, waving an
American flag at the crowd. — That lady's out to lunch, he thought.
This is the Fourth of July, not Halloween. Oh, well, what does it
matter? He wanted to let Priscilla know about Frieda, but she was
searching at the cemetery as far as he knew, and meanwhile the
Chamber of Commerce's President named the Youths of the Year,
who seemed to be a pimply couple waving between stars and American flags. He'd never seen them before. A baby stretched out her
hand at the councilman and he smiled and waved at the indifferent
young mother. The chauffeur drove in silence, watching the speedometer, which read three miles per hour. The councilman wanted to
check his tie again, but didn't. He kept looking for Frieda but all he
could find was an old man bowing from a strawberry Ford, bowing
toward the sea down between the trees.

Frieda! Frieda! he heard Priscilla scream. *Oh, my God!*

Looking right and left, the councilman saw sea air and sailboats.

Then among the quick low buttock-sweeps of cars and all the
exhaust flavors, a girl's hair was curly like ferns blooming from the
back of her crash helmet. It was Frieda. She grasped the skeleton's
waist with one hand, the back rail with the other. Her arms were
stained with dirt. Speeding in her pink shirt, she shrank into the palm
of the afternoon. The councilman saw Priscilla in an Impala, chasing
her. She'd almost caught up with her. The councilman saw her white
sneakers, her tanned calves as she straddled the dark wheel, leaning
with her hips and behind. Then he saw someone else's hand in the

window of a Volkswagen Rabbit, and on the freeway the other cars gathered about her like chesspieces. Far ahead into the smoggy hills, the red tail-light winked underneath her once more, and then the grayness of other cars drowned her.

Hours after the end of the parade, Priscilla returned alone.

Lifting up Frieda's pillow, he found a sheet of paper, which read:

If I have to suffer then you are the cause. I have just as much of a claim on Auntie as you, maybe more because Priscilla says you murdered her, not that I believe her because she is also a murdering bitch but if anyone killed Auntie it must have been you because she always loved me not you. As soon as you married her she started to die. If you'd just left her alone she would have lived forever and married me. But no you couldn't live alone you murdering sonofabitch you had to have your Emily. Well don't think I can't marry her even now. I have the science to bring her back. If you need somebody why don't you latch onto Frieda because I don't want her and her blood is poison. There's darkness all around you. I'm going to find your wife.

I'm not surprised, said Priscilla later. My sister was very fond of Auntie.

THE ANGEL OF PRISONS

San Bruno, California, U.S.A. (1992)
Phnom Penh, Cambodia (1991)
Mogadishu, Somalia (1993)
Coral Harbour, Southampton Island, Northwest Territories, Canada (1993)
Bangkok, Phrah Nakhon-Thonburi Province, Thailand (1993)
Wailea, Maui, Hawaii, U.S.A. (1993)

County Facility for Women, San Bruno, California, U.S.A. (1992)

Birds and poppies outside, meadows and fences inside; and that wasn't inside yet, not after the gate security check, not inside the black double doors (opened by intercom), nor the gray and white tiled anteroom. This was the "pre-release facility"—another little sneer of optimism to enliven the Angel's report; no doubt they'd name a womb the "pre-birth facility" if they could, but what about babies who were born dead? — Because there were no bars, this jail was also called the "open facility." It was about as open as its "modesty curtains" were modest. The southeast sally port led into a long clean corridor that smelled of paint.

The basic design concept is there's a center and the cells are off the center, the officer explained. What we're trying to use is internal controls, positive reinforcement. We're trying to effect a behavior change.

Why not? laughed the Angel.

The control room was high and square, with windows all around, slanted down onto the halls and the cement floors where the women sat at picnic tables or lurked in their open cubicles. The ones in orange jumpsuits were low-level felons. The ones in yellow were awaiting sentencing. The ones in blue had received clearance to go outside. There was an odor of carrots.

That one, the Angel said.

I seen you up there, said the hunky girl in yellow with the pursed lips.

Do you know where you are? the Angel said.

Sure.

Why are you here?

Somebody called somebody's mama dirty.

That's right, said the Angel. That's finished you. And do you remember the darkness when you died?

I dreamed I been walkin' on worms . . .

That was when they buried you. That was when they shoveled the earth over your eyes.

The air gits so thick around here.

You'll get used to it. After your skull is fully exposed, you won't mind the shortness of breath. Maybe you'll get to like the noises that the rats make when they go by. But the darkness . . . Well, it takes time to learn to see in the dark.

Naw, it don't really git dark at night, the girl said. They have to keep the lights at a certain level. If they don't, people start talking or someone might git a seizure or something. Anyway it don't matter. The longer you're here the more sleepier you git, 'cause you git to do more activities.

And are you ready for your final judgment?

I go to court the thirty-first. I'm fightin' goin' to this drug program. They're tryin' to make me do this year plus eighteen weeks. And I told em y'all must be out of y'all fuckin' head. I'm on three years' felony probation. Anything over two bags is sales. They dropped it to possession 'cause I'm a user. You never know what that Judge is gonna do. He got some shit in His cornflakes you don't know what He gonna do.

I'm glad you know that. So you figured out that there's a worse place than this.

Yeah. Yeah, I know that, Mr. Angel. You're not the first social worker told me that. You know, that other social worker really pissed me off. He said to me: I see a lot of discomfort in your soul. — So why does he say that?

I don't think you should be worrying about that. What you ought to be doing now is remembering your life.

Everything is *ought* around here.

Your only hope is to understand what got you here, the Angel insisted.

They just picked me up on the street down here.

They just picked you up, did they? My. Through no fault of yours?

I been in the hospital fifty-one days. I didn't know I had a bench warrant. They said: You know you got a warrant, Miss Tompkins. — My probation officer is an asshole. He's just automatically assuming this is a habitual offense. Please don't try it. 'Cause I can git fucking ignorant. Fuck him and feed him fish. He's one of them fucking niggers that want to make a name for himself.

(For a long time the Angel stared into that yellowpale, lined resentful face. He faced her inimical lizard-eyes. He watched time stain that pale and aging face, that pale tongue. She mumbled with her snaggle-teeth.)

And what's in *your* name? the Angel said.

My name don't mean nothin'. You can *see* I'm wearin' the yellow.

And what's in your sin?

My sin don't mean nothin', neither. Like I said, it depends what side of bed that Judge gits up on.

And you think that's wrong?

'Course it is.

I see. Well, then, if you were the Judge, how would you run the universe?

Like, last night these girls were boxing and they got real mad. They were doing it 'cause something was said to somebody. I got laughing. I woulda judged 'em. I woulda judged 'em both laughing, 'cause they were in the wrong. But they say this Big Judge He never laughs. Just looks at you and sends you down. You gotta git left to yourself, but they don't know the meaning of the word respect. They don't play the game.

But you do, I take it, said the Angel with a yawn that rose to the very high ceiling and rolled down those whitewashed halls.

Now this here girl, I never hit her. But they gave me ten days. She broke my dentures. I'm a model inmate. She claims I stole ten dollars from her. She 'pologized to me two weeks ago, saw me in court. I said sure. It ain't but two teeth. Two teeth's all I need.

Time's up, the officer said.

Keep her out of trouble until the Judge gets to her, said the Angel.

No problem, the officer said. We control the power-operated doors here. We control the TV stations. We control the music.

T-3 Prison, Phnom Penh, Cambodia (1991)

We give them also general knowledge, the officer said. All the prisoners here, they can read and write. Through our education we can make some people understanding. You see, after the prisoner leaving here, we give first thinking and then degree of knowledge, and then we give them the job. In the prison there are handicrafts. They can make small tables. You see, the prisoners, they produce some production, and then they get more from store. When we let them free we give them some supplies.

Do you think these people here are bad people?

You see, these people, they believe now. They trust our policy. They will become good people. They want to get amnesty from our government.

When will their reeducation be completed? said the Angel.

It's not much longer to stay. Soon they will be good.

And are you good? asked the angel.

Me? said the officer. Of course I am good.

Bring in the prisoner, said the Angel.

The man came in bowing and blinking, skinny and terrified.

How long have you been in prison? said the Angel.

Two years and seven months.

Have you had a trial?

No.

What sentence do you expect?

I hope that the authorities here will let me free at one time and now I try to be a good people as the other . . .

You are not good now?

No, sir. No, I am not good.

The Angel took the right hand of the prisoner and placed it in the officer's left hand. He said: By the power vested in me I join you both in marriage forever. You are fitted for each other.

Central Prison, Mogadishu, Somalia (1993)

The prison was an immense white skull on a hill of snow-white rock and snow-white sand near the seaport. The blue gate, partly rusted, opened all its teeth at the Angel's touch. He ascended the steep white steps overlooking the sea. The next door was rusty red, and a guard saw him coming through the bars and opened so that he could follow the snow-white hall which was flecked and cracked and pitted, and so he came to more bars. There was a dusty white courtyard. The first section was on the left. It was white, of course, with bars. That was for the prisoners with one to fifteen years. Behind the courtyard's single tree was the Asab section: fifteen years to life.

Well, thought the Angel biliously, let's see who's good now.

The man's face was sick and cratered. He was dull-eyed and stinking, and there were scars all over his skinny body. The guards allowed him to sit down. Otherwise they would have been compelled to hold him up.

I get a sickness all around my penis, the man said. I got a small boil on penis, then I scratch it.

Are you a thief?

A looter.

Weakly he smoothed his sweaty hair.

First I have stab someone with a knife to get fifty shillings, the man said. Police complained and put me here.

Can you read?

No.

Do you know the Qur'an?

Yes.

Do you think about it now?

If I think about the Qur'an I know I am destroyed for everything. So I don't think about it anymore.

So you feel alone, do you?

I—I don't have a wife. My family is still alive. They too are hungry. They too are looters.

The Angel paced. — You know Whom I work for. He's preparing the sea of fire for you right now. Do you have anything further to say?

The man looked at him. — The only thing I can tell you is that I am sick, and if I can get some medicines I am better.

You know there's no medicine for you, the Angel said. You know that you were born for burning.

I want to be good, the man whispered. I want to be different, but my problems are not different.

Ah, so he wants to improve, the Angel smiled to the guards. Well, what can I recommend? I know! Why don't you practice screaming? You really ought to get your lungs in shape.

Airport Waiting Room, Coral Harbour, Southampton Island, Northwest Territories, Canada (1993)

want to go back to jail because people are so friendly there, the smiling man said.

Well, maybe I can put in a word for you, said the Angel modestly.

I did two months and two-and-a-half months and four months, crowed the smiling man. For sexual assault. And in jail I learned to walk like this!

The smiling man shuffled back and forth across the floor, turning his head blankly from side to side. The Inuit girls laughed and cringed back.

I'm going to Winnipeg to get my head examined by three psychiatrists, he said proudly. I won't be back for a long time, maybe two years.

He lay down in fetal position on the floor.

I really like the food in jail, too, the smiling man said. (There was something in his eyes like crawly white ice on the blue sea.) It's the best food in the world.

On the other hand, said the Angel in delight at his own sagacity, if you *want* to go back to prison, then you must not deserve to go. That's how we've always operated.

At this, the man leaped to his feet and screamed horribly. The Inuit girls screamed at his scream and ran outside.

A Brothel with No Name, Kong Toi, Bangkok, Phrah Nakhon-Thonburi Province, Thailand (1993)

The room had a rectangle cut in the door so that the keeper could peer in. It was the small prison, the short-time prison. There was a pallet with two round pillows. The pallet ran from wall to wall. It had a veneer of plastic paper which pretended to be wood, and it was sticky from the sweat of naked bodies. Beside it was the knee-high basin with the hosepipe; that was where she squatted afterward; and then the plastic cup for used rubbers.

Within seconds, the tiny room reeked of her purple lipstick.

Twice she pulled him out to make certain that the condom hadn't broken. Each time she fiddled with it again. All the girls believed that death was spread mainly by angels.

The sweat dripped down from his face onto her face, making her lipstick shine. She maintained her phony smile that never changed. She was the one who when he'd gazed into the large prison, the glass area where numbered girls sat (pink lights on the girls' rosy meat) had tried to cover up her number with her towel, so she was the one he'd picked. Reluctance meant guilt and badness, so it was his mission to lock his wings around her and bring her to Hell.

When he tried to kiss her, she pulled away. So he kissed her again and spat into her desperate mouth.

Because he was not an evil angel and because he was off duty, he put his hand on top of her head to keep his thrusts from banging her against the wall. Then he ejaculated right through the condom, a burning manna of nectar and rose-sweat. Now she would become immortal. Now she could suffer forever, as soon as he pulled the trigger.

But she never said anything. She didn't pretend she wanted to be good; she didn't argue, plead, explain, or justify.

And the angel was unnerved by her nothingness, her heavy dark acquiescence. If she had only cursed or pleaded!

I want to be good . . . he whispered, rising and tiptoeing away.

Wailea, Maui, Hawaii, U.S.A. (1993)

Within that complex polygon known as a swimming pool, water lilted in dapplings stolen from the throats of blue giraffes. Inside these unsteady zones the fixed rectangles of individual tiles remained, like bones. Along one wall a waterfall had been built to correspond to any number of blue wedding cakes; at the two far ends were blue wells which resembled immense toilets. A fat pale man descended grimly into one of these, looking warily down. Once he was safely inside, the back of his head alone remained visible, rocking slightly like a carrot-top in a breeze. On the outside of his prison another man sat, just above his waist in water, with a gold medal against his hairy breast. He wore blue sunglasses and his forehead was sickeningly white. A blonde lady in green glasses joined him, squatting coyly to keep her buttocks out of the water. From time to time they both looked at their waterproof watches. Then they resumed their gazing down into the pool. After she got out, he stood up and watched her. Then he followed. — Goggles will do it, he whispered. — Behind them, in a canvas pavilion open to the sea, a woman in a purple bikini rubbed lotion in slow circular motions on her soft haunches. Another woman ventured ankle-deep into the pool, her hands on her fat hips as she gazed alertly from side to side. After a long pause, she slashed water from her wrists up to her elbows. She stood for another moment, and then she got out. Ripples went from her like the indentations over a belly's ribs.

The man in the toilet was thinking with a swimmer's breasting motion. He whirled his head to glare at the women. Among them he saw a sinister lady in blue goggles.

You're the one, aren't you? he said. I see your sordid soul.

The lady grinned. — That's right. Do you have a last request?

It's not fair, the Angel said. I always did what I was told.

Now you're talking to please Him, but you know He's disconnected your phone, the lady said.

I only left one unburned. How could that whore matter?

You did a fine job, the lady said. He doesn't argue about that. It's just that your number's up. And you know what, buddy? You were right in what you said. She didn't matter. Because, you see, He doesn't have mercy. Ever. Did you forget that? The sentence says that I'm to burn you forever by inches. Are you ready to start?

The Angel ducked his head under the water, thinking to enjoy the coolness while he could. Then he began to clamber out. There were invisible bars in the sky which the lady swung back for him, unlocking air with the key that had once been his.

This is your towel, the lady said.

The Angel lay down. Inside the giant toilet rang the shrieks of the other punished souls. He tried to enjoy their agony, but couldn't. He stared hopelessly at all the palmtrees as fresh and proud as peacocks' tails.

Sacramento, California, U.S.A. (1992)

Sacramento, California, U.S.A. (1992)

t was the morning after her first night of work in the Chinese restaurant which was also a dancehall.

How many men danced with you? I said.

Two.

And all you did was dance?

She looked me in the eye. — No.

How were they? I said.

Better than you.

Once you told me I was good.

That was a long time ago.

So they were good too, I guess.

The first one made me come six times. He wanted to do it all night, but he hadn't paid for all night, so I made him stop.

How about the second one?

He's so good I'm going to marry him. I can't get enough of him inside me.

How much did he pay?

Nothing. He was so good, I wouldn't take anything from him. I took all the money the first one gave me and gave it to him. That's why I got fired.

And you're happy?

Of course I'm happy. I'm leaving you and I'm going to get married. I'm going to have the best cock in the world all to myself.

I guess you will.

I guess I will, *darling*.

What are you going to do for work?

He knows the old lady here. He's going to try to get me my job back. He's going to tell her how good I was.

So you'll be working here?

I hope so.

Are you working now?

What do you mean?

I mean, if I paid you right now, would you go to bed with me one more time?

With you? No. You're not my customer.

If I were paying you I'd be your customer.

You can't ever be my customer. You're not anything but somebody I used to fuck a long time ago.

Yesterday wasn't such a long time ago.

Yes it was.

How much did the first one pay you?

A million dollars, all right? Now leave me alone.

I have five hundred dollars. I'll give it to you if I can have half an hour with you.

Where did you get five hundred dollars?

I just got it. I got it to give you.

And the whole time we were together you never even got me roses.

That was different. That was because we were together. But you said we're not together anymore, so I have to give you something special if I want to love you one more time.

Well, five hundred dollars is special enough, I guess. Half an hour. Come into this room. But you have to wear a rubber, and you can't kiss me.

Why?

Because I don't love you anymore. I'm engaged to someone else.

What will you do if I kiss you?

Your half hour just started. One minute's already gone. I only have to see you for another twenty-nine more minutes, and then I get five hundred dollars and I never have to see you again.

I don't think it's fair to start counting before you shut the door.

There. Now the door is shut. Will you unbutton the back of my blouse?

Did the other two do that?

I wasn't wearing this blouse. But they would have done it, and they would have loved it.

There you are.

Do you like how I pull it over my head? I can feel you looking at my back. My naked back. I can feel your eyes on the hooks of my bra. Do you want to unhook my bra? My tits are excited. My nipples are hard because in a minute you're going to unhook my bra and then I'm going to turn around and shove my tits into your mouth and that's the last time you'll ever be allowed to suck my tits.

What are those bruises above your collarbone?

Love-bites. From those two men. Especially the second one. My whole body smells like him.

I can't smell any other smell but yours.

Oh, yes you can. You can smell those other men all over me. That man-smell's as strong as gasoline. You can see the gashes from their fingernails and everything. But you won't admit it. It would be too humiliating. You'd start to cry, you pathetic jerk.

Are you going to take your underpants off?

You heard me. I told you you had to suck my tits before you could do anything else. Look how hard they are. I'm going to make you suck them until you can taste the other men's spit and breath and sweat.

No.

Do you want to stick it in or don't you?

I don't want to do it anymore.

You changed your mind? Fine. But you still owe me five hundred dollars.

No.

No what?

I said no.

I could see it coming. I should have known. Well, my new husband will beat the shit out of you. Why don't you run on home and wait? I'll give him the key that used to be mine. He'll come over today and break your arms and legs. He's really good at that. That's his job. Here goes my blouse again. Are you going to button me back up or are you going to renege on that too?

I'm going to rip your underpants off and rape you.

I'd like to see you try. All I have to do is look at you and it goes limp. You couldn't rape a jellyfish.

Did you ever love me?

I don't remember. I don't think so. But I felt sorry for you sometimes. I feel sorry for you now. You don't have five hundred dollars, do you?

No.

You just wanted to look at me one more time.

That's right.

How much do you love me?

I love you so much.

You want to fuck me now? It's that important to you? Go ahead. See, here goes the blouse again. There. Now you can touch me. But my tits aren't hard anymore. Don't just stare at me. Look, I'm even taking off my underpants; I'm lying here spreading my goddamned legs; what else do you want? Oh, I know. You want me to tell you I love you. I'll say I love you when you're starting to come. Is there anything else you want?

No.

Well, then, are you going to do it or not?

Yes, thank you, I'll do it.

Good. Here's your rubber. Let me juice myself up.

Let me hear you practice saying I love you.

I love you I love you I love you, all right? Now hurry up.

I don't feel anything.

That's because you're not used to wearing a rubber. You're not really fucking me anymore; you're fucking a piece of latex that happens to be inside me.

That isn't what I mean.

All right. Both the guys who did me said they had AIDS. So I have AIDS. Take the rubber off and fuck me and get AIDS if that's what you want. See if I care. Here. Off it goes. Like peeling a banana. Now I'll put you back inside. How's that?

It's good.

Can you feel my death crawling inside you?

Oh, it feels so good—

You're thrusting deeper and deeper into my death. My death is in you now. Are you getting ready to come? You look like you are. I love you. This time I really mean it. I love you. I love you because you're going to die for me.

INCARNATIONS
OF THE MURDERER

San Ignacio, Belize (1990)
San Francisco, California, U.S.A. (1991)
Agra, Division of Uttar Pradesh, India (1990)
San Francisco, California, U.S.A. (1991)
Resolute Bay, Cornwallis Island, Northwest Territories, Canada (1991)
San Francisco, California, U.S.A. (1992)
Mexico City, Distrito Federal, Mexico (1992)
Interstate 80, California, U.S.A. (1992)
Battambang City, Province Battambang, Cambodia (1991)

San Ignacio, Belize (1990)

Two girls sailed under the fat green branches of trees that curved like eyebrows. At the top of the grassy bank, a plantain spread its leaves across the clouds. They passed little brown girls swimming and smiling. They passed a man who dove for shrimp which he put in a plastic bag. Breasting the painted houses that were grocery stores rich with onions, Coca-Cola and condensed milk, they rode the wide brown river between tree-ridges and palm houses.

As they paddled, the plump wet thighs of the girls quivered; water danced on their thighs. A few wet curly hairs peeked shyly from the crotches of their bathing suits. They had golden hourglass waists.

A man was a dragonfly. He hugged his shadow on the river until he saw them.

The water splashed under a great green tree-bridge that grew parallel to the water. Its branches were red and black like the skin of a diamondback rattler. In the branches crouched the man. The plan that the man had was as as rubbery and pink as a monkey's palm. But the canoe was not there yet. The two girls were still alive.

Yellow butterflies skimmed low across the shallow water. They saw the girls, too. They saw each other. They saw themselves in the water and forgot everything.

The tree that owned the water was closer now. A white horse sneezed in a grove of golden coconuts.

All morning the man had been thinking of the two girls whom he was about to kill. Knocking yellow coconuts down from the trees with a big stick, he'd sliced away at them with his machete until a little hole like a vagina appeared. He put his mouth to that pale bristly opening and drank. (Slowly, the white meat inside oxidized brown.) But now he was silent, suspended from his purpose as if by the heavy supple tail of a spider monkey.

Now the two girls passed little clapboard houses with laundry out to dry. They passed the last house they would ever see. In the river a lazy boa was wriggling along. That was the last snake they'd ever see.

They went down the ripple-stained river, the ripple-striped river. They saw the broad green rocks beneath the water, the soft yellow-green tree-mounds. They came to the tree of their death, and the man jumped down lightly and stabbed them in their breasts.

The canoe lay long and low across the neck of an island. Reflected water burned whitely on its keel.

The man opened red fruits. He bit them. They were soft with two-colored grainy custard inside.

The spice of the blood was like the sweet stinging of the glossy-leaved pepper-tree, whose orange fruits burn your lips when you eat, burn again when you piss. This made him happy. He went to sleep and awoke. A toucan chirped like a frog. The taste was stronger in his mouth. He laughed.

He wandered among the caring arches of the palm tree that shaded him like wisdom, and his shirt was hot and slick on his back. He came to the grove where the white horse had sneezed and knocked down a coconut. He drank the juice, but the taste of blood was even stronger now. He looked sideways in the hot high fields of trees.

Knuckles itching pleasantly with insect bites, searching through the wild-looking fields for ground foods with the sun hot on his sun-burned neck and wrists, he swiped down a sugarcane stalk with his machete and then skinned and peeled it in long strokes, from green down to white. He was good at using knives. He snapped off a piece and chewed it, tasting in advance its sweat so fresh and sweet. But the other taste loomed still more undeniable.

Between his teeth he thrust slices of young pineapple, bird-eaten custard apples, bay leaves, green papayas, sour plums from a leaf-bare tree. He bit them all ferociously into a mush. Then he sucked, choked, swallowed. Building a fire, he made coffee, which he drank down to the grounds. He cut an inch of medicine-vine and chewed that bitterness too. The taste of blood increased.

He spat, but his spittle was clear. There was no blood in it. He pricked his tongue with the point of the knife, but his own male blood could not drown the other, the female taste.

He drank rum and fell down. All around him, trees steamed by humid horizons. When he awoke, the taste was stronger than ever. He began to scream.

There was a cave he knew of whose floor was a sandy beach. The man ran there without knowing why. Jet black water became black and green there as it descended into bubbling pools close enough to the entrance to reflect the jungle, from the branches of which the black-and-orange-tailed birds hung like seedpods. The widest tree-boughs were festooned with vine-sprouts like the feathered shafts of arrows. Behind them, where it was cool and stale, the cave's chalky stalactites hung in ridge-clusters like folds of drying laundry on a line. The man ran in. He splashed through the first pool. It was alive with green and silver ripples intersecting with one another like a woman's curls. A single bubble traveled, white on black, then silver on silver. He ran crazy through the next pool. Farther in the darkness was a chalky beach, cratered with rat-prints and raccoon-prints. This was the place where the cave-roof was crowned by a trio of stalactites. Here, where everything but the river was quiet, a pale whitish bird fluttered from rock to rock, squeaking like a mouse. The bird flew back and forth very quickly. It hovered over rock-cracks' wrinkled lips. It landed on a crest of lighter-colored rock like a wave that had never broken. It darted its beak between two studs of shell-fossil and swallowed a blind ant. Then it departed into deeper caves within the cave, floored with silence and white sand. Water shimmered white on black rocks—

The man opened his mouth to scream again and the white bird came from nowhere. The white bird was the soul of one of the girls. The bird stabbed the man's tongue with its beak and drank blood. Then it flew away, not squeaking anymore.

The man swallowed experimentally. The taste was only half as strong.

Farther back still was a pit. He had learned from the white bird that a tiny black bird flew there. The man clambered down. It felt like being inside a seashell. Deep down, the flicker of his lighter showed him pink and glistening rock-guts. Smoke streamed from the little lighter like a beam from a movie projector. He held the lighter below his mouth, so that the black bird could see him. The bird came swooping and cheeping. It was not much bigger than a bee. It flew back between his tonsils. He could feel the bird's pulse inside him. He longed to swallow it, to recapitulate his triumphs. But then the taste would strengthen again. The black bird pierced him and drank a drop of his blood. It took him again. Then it flew away in silence.

The taste was gone now. The man shrieked with glee. The cave was empty.

Outside, it was so brightly green that the hunger of his eyes (which he hadn't even known that he had) was caught: as long as he looked out upon it, he thought himself satisfied, but the instant he began to look away, back into the darkness, then his craving for greenness screamed out at him.

He ran outside trying to see and taste everything. He ran down the streambank to a kingdom of pools in bowls of baking hot rock. He drank water from rolling whirlpools; he dove down whitewater to brown water, beneath which his open eyes found chalky sand-valleys, green-slicked boulder-cliffs; he grabbled at these things with his fingers and then licked his fingertips. In the best whirlpool rushed the two girls, lying down against each other, kissing each other avidly, eating each other's soft flesh.

San Francisco, California, U.S.A. (1991)

Down the fog-sodden wooden steps he came that night to the street walled with houses, every doorway a yellow lantern-slide suspended between floating windows, connected to earth by the tenuous courtesy of stairs. Earth was but sidewalk and street, a more coagulated gray than the silver-gleam of reflected souls in car windshields, heavier too than the gray-green linoleum sky segmented by power wires. He went fog-breathing while the two walls of houses faced each other like cliffs, ignoring one another graciously; they were long islands channelled, coved and barred, made separate by the criss-crossing rivers of gray streets. Somewhere was the isle of the dead girls' canoe, which he needed now to get away from himself. All night he walked the hill streets until he came to morning, a foggy morning in the last valley of pale houses before the sea. He stood before an apartment house whose chessboard-floored arch declined to eat him as he'd eaten others; the doors were shut like the sky. The curving ceiling of the arch was stamped with white flowers in squares. Black iron latticed windows as elaborately as Qur'anic calligraphy; white railings guarded balconies. Spiked lamps smoldered at him from behind orange glass. Timidly he hid behind the sidewalk's trees whose leaf-rows whispered richly down like ferns . . .

Once he admitted that this house was not for him, he turned away from all hill streets side-stacked with rainbow cars and went down further toward the sea. So he came to the street of souls.

The candy shop of souls lured him in first. His nose stung with the fog. He opened the door and went in, staring at the long glass case that was like an aquarium. Here he found the chocolate ingots, the pure mint-striped cylinders, the tarts studded with fruits and berries like a dozen orchards, the vanilla bread-loaves long and slender like suntanned eels, the banana-topped lime hexagons, the chocolate-windowed éclairs domed with cream like Russian Orthodox churches, the round strawberry tortes gilded with lemon-chocolate to make pedestals for the vanilla-chocolate butterflies that rested on each with breathless wings, the sponge-cakes each like an emperor's crown, the complex wicker-basket raspberry pies of woven crust, heaped with boulders of butter and confectioner's sugar, the tins of violet lozenges, the bones and girders made of licorice, the low white disks of sugar-pies topped with fan-swirls of almonds like playing cards, the peach cakes, pear cakes, the row of delectable phosphorescent green slugs, the flowerpot of coffee frosting from which a chocolate rose bloomed, the strawberries that peaked up from unknown tarts and tortes bride-bashful behind ruffled paper—

He sat at a little square marble table, and without a word the lady brought him a green slug, served on a white plate with white lace. He reached in his pocket and found a single coin of iron with a hole in the center. He gave her that. He sat looking past the glass case at the rows of fruit confections in matched white-lidded jars—not for him. With the silver fork he stabbed the slug and raised it into his mouth, where it overcame him between his teeth with a sweet ichor of orgasmic limes, and so he became a thief—

Agra, India (1990)

Two green-clad soldiers were striking a man in the face beneath one of the side-arches of the Taj Mahal. The man was not screaming. He was a thief. The soldiers had caught him, and were beating him. All around him, the Mughal tombs bulged with hard nipples on their marble breasts. — The Emperor, he had so many wives, he spend a month's salary on cosmetics! cried the guide.

Blood flowered from the thief's nose.

This tower closed now, said the guide. The lovely boys and girls jump off, suicide. For love and love and love. Closed now for security reason. But *this* part, this open ivory day.

The thief fell down when they let go of him. The soldiers stamped on his stomach. Then they raised him again.

Now, sir, lady, come-come. Look! This marble *one* piece. No two piece. No join. Only cutting!

The thief looked at the guide with big eyes. The soldiers punched him. Then he was not looking at the guide anymore. Sir and lady went away, trying not to hear his groans as the soldiers began to beat him. Sir and lady wore the dead girls' mouths.

Yes, please! Hello! Sir and madam!

(Sir and lady were staring again. They could not help it. The soldiers were kicking out his teeth.)

Water rippled in long grooves of onyx, malachite, coral, but sir and lady did not see it. They did not know that they had once been dead girls. They knew that he knew them in his unspoken beseeching, but that merely echoed as clouds echoed between the lapis-flowered marble screens. Far beyond the screens lay dim white-gray corridors of peace. Darkness, incense and shadows crawled slowly on marble, searching for secret sweet-smelling vaults. These were the tombs of old scores, bad crimes rotting but not yet shriven down to bones.

The soldiers hustled the thief into darkness.

Outside it was a foggy morning. Skinny men rode bicycles, with dishtowels wrapped around their heads. Roadside people squatted by smudges to keep warm. On the dusty road that stank of exhaust, platoons of dirty white cattle were marched and goaded toward Agra. They had sharp backbones and floppy bellies. Sir and lady crossed that living river and stood beside a pole which had once been the tree of their death. In this sacred place they felt compassion for their murderer. If they had been able to remember, they would have forgiven him fully. As it was, their pity made his next incarnation easier.

Postcards, please? Small marble! Elephant two rupees!

Cowtails and buttocks were crowded together long narrow and wobbly like folded drapes. They swished and twitched as if they were alive and knew where they were going, but they didn't; they only followed where they were pulled, like the thief being led into the recesses of that gorgeous tomb.

San Francisco, California, U.S.A. (1991)

When the rattle of his bones being put back together became the rattling whir of the cable cars going up Nob Hill, then he shot forth out of darkness among the square red lights of the other soul-cars swarming from the parking tunnels, zebra-striped gate up and down; for awhile he followed a big dirty bus that had once been a selfish man, and he rolled up Powell Street, which was sutured lengthwise with steel. Crowds were standing off the curb. There was no room for them yet. He saw a man pushing a shopping cart full of old clothes. Globes of crystallized light attacked him from the edge of Union Square. Higher up the hill he rolled by hotels and brass-worked windows, flags and awnings; he saw the pedestrian souls slogging up slowly, the Chinese signs, the yellow plastic pagoda-roofs, the bulging windows of Victorian houses. A girl with a sixpack under her arm ran smiling and flushed up the hill. At the top of the hill he could see far, saw a Sunday sailing panorama off the Marin headlands, with tanned girls drinking wine coolers, and college boys pretending to be pirates with their fierce black five-dollar squirt guns, and the Golden Gate Bridge almost far away enough to shimmer as it must have done for those convicts from Alcatraz who doomed themselves trying to swim there. The red warning light still flashed on the island, now noted for its tours and wildflowers. The cellblock building became ominous again when the evening fog sprang up and the tanned girls screamed as their twenty-four-footer tacked closer and closer to the sharp black rocks, already past the limit demarcated by the old prison buoys that said **KEEP OFF**; and seeing the girls he wanted to kill them over again but then his cracked bones ached from being beaten and he bared his teeth and thought: If I can't eat them by stealing them, I'll get them another way! and he laughed and honked his horn and other cars honked behind him so he rolled on down the hill and came to the street of souls.

Fearing to enter the candy shop which had brought him such pain, he parked, offering himself again to that knife of fog and silence, the handle a crystal stalagmite; and he came to the coffee shop of souls.

Brass safe-deposit boxes walled him, side by side, bearing buttons and horns. Each one had a different coffee inside. The smell of coffee enflamed him. There were rows of stalls for muffins, each of which reminded him of the pale brown coconuts he had drunk. In his pocket he found a single coin with a hole in it. They gave him a muffin. He became an anthropologist.

Resolute Bay, Cornwallis Island, Northwest Territories, Canada (1991)

O n the komatik, whose slats had been partly covered by a caribou skin (now frozen into iron wrinkles), he lay comfortably on his side, gripping two slat-ends with his fishy-smelling sealskin mitts which were already getting ice-granules behind the liner (an old bedsheet) because every time he wiped his nose with the skintight capilene gloves the snot was soaked up by the old bedsheet which then began to freeze; and as the komatik rattled along at the end of its leash, making firm tracks in the snow-covered ice, the wind froze the snot around his nose and mouth into white rings, but not immediately because it was not cold enough yet to make breath-frost into instant whiskers; however, it was certainly cold enough to make his cheek ache from contact with the crust of snot-ice on the ski mask; meanwhile the smoothness of the sea began to be interrupted by hard white shards where competing currents had gashed the ice open and then the wound had scarred; sometimes the ice-plates had forced each other's edges into uprising splinters that melded and massed and hardened into strange shapes; the Inuk wended the Ski-Doo between these when he could, going slowly so that the komatik did not lurch too badly; his back was erect, almost stern, the rifle at a ready diagonal, and he steered south toward a thick horizon-band that seemed to be fog or blowing snow; in fact it was the steam of open water. Over this hung the midday sun, reddish-pale, a rotten apple of the old year.

Then the groaning ice fissured into a shape like a girl's mouth, and the komatik broke through. He fell under the ice. The other girl was waiting beneath with her mouth open to drink his blood and he was already freezing and paling, but then the girl breathed upon him lovingly and he was warmed. The first girl, the one who was ice, opened her mouth; the second one lifted him on through to the sky.

San Francisco, California, U.S.A. (1992)

Inside the cheerful egg-yolk yellow of the Muni car, with its two-toned rising and falling whine, the man was eased confident through its narrow grooves, past hanging laundry, swashbuckling in traverse across the street-scored sides of house-choked hills, creeping patiently down the shady lanes designated for the Muni's exclusive use, then bursting back out onto the sunsetty hillside, crooning to a stop in the park where Latino children got off. Suddenly the car reeked of leather jackets like the smell of cunnilingus; fashionable people had boarded. Keeping power wires company beneath the deep blue sky, the Muni bore the man toward the vortex which would determine his next state. He knew this but did not want to bear it. An Asian mother tenderly helped her little child negotiate the aisle, the child grasping her finger in a needing hand, and he wondered whether he had been or would be her. A little black boy in an orange jacket ran down the sidewalk, and then the Muni turned onto Market Street so that the boy was gone forever, and the man felt lost. An Asian girl boarded and stood beside him for a moment, gripping her two quarters fiercely; they did not have holes in them. Did that mean that she had but one life, or that she had already lived? The girl saw a vacant seat and went away. Now the Muni car hummed at the corner by the Chinese restaurant. It drummed secret hooves, twisted along the metalled furrows that it needed, stopped, and buzzed while a pony-tailed man got on. Swooping like nuns to a steeple, the Muni turned the last aboveground corner where so many metal rails from other Muni routes joined this nexus, shining like ice. It rang its bell like a submarine about to dive, entered the long narrow cage, and sank into its cement foundations so that the evening seemed to get later and later, the afternoon shadows on the walls becoming twilight gray, then midnight black as the Muni shot into the tunnel. Believing himself now to be safely southeast of the street of souls, he permitted his anxiety to go just as beer foam slowly narrows, collapsing in the middle as the bottom eats itself away. Then at Civic Center two girls got on with barely healed wounds in their breasts. They approached him in silence, each with her left hand behind her back. They looked into his eyes. He tried to look away. They bent over him and began breathing slowly and calmly into his face. Closing his eyes in despair, he struck out and his fist encountered a girl's fist which stopped him while three other girl-hands prized his fingers open and placed a token with a hole in it onto his palm; instantly a reflex of greed and longing for life overtook him, so he closed his fingers over the token just as the Asian girl had done with her two quarters, and he felt himself becoming something but when he opened his eyes he was still on a subway.

Mexico City, Distrito Federal, Mexico (1992)

They had left the extremely wide, yellow and subterranean Aero-puerto terminal where he was born. When he was a youth they reached Oceana in the middle of the street of time, mesh fences on either side, the people elegantly serious, quiet. A vendor came along dumping candied eggs on everyone's lap. Though eating one of these would doubtless have carried him to new possibilities, he was not tempted. He feared to taste blood. The vendor returned and collected the eggs. No one had opened a single one, although two girls read the label. He was still holding his egg as the vendor neared him. Suddenly he felt a bird-heart beating inside its thinness and his fingers began to curl to clench the life out of it, but he bit his lip to save himself and swallowed his own blood, shutting his eyes and waiting until he felt the vendor remove the egg from his palm. Then he allowed himself to gaze upon his life again. The two girls stood, one wearing black shoes, one wearing white, their knees bent, holding the stanchions, swaying, almost dancing, blackhaired (one braided, one waterfalled), looking subtly down at his feet, in an obviously coordinated awareness, and he peered into their lovely broad faces and they smiled and touched him and then got off at Misterios. He was old by then. He swayed and fell down dead.

Interstate 80, California, U.S.A. (1992)

Gray-lit struts took his weight as he shot across the bridge; flat gray-green ribs were stripped of their nightflesh by the dingy lights, the lights of Oakland rippling in between like scales, inhuman lights all the way to the gray horizon. What a relief when the world finally ran out of electricity, and we'd have to turn them off! On his left was a city of stacks and towers clustered with lights like sparks that could never be peacefully extinguished, could never cool themselves in the earth. A gush of smoke blew horizontally from the topmost stack. He scuttled up greenish-gray ramps of deadness into the dead night, accompanied by characterless strings of light, dull apartment tower lights, dark bushes; he bulleted down a lane of dirty blackness clouded by trees on either side, remnant trees suffered to live only because they interrupted that ugly terrible light. Then he came into the outer darkness of unhealthy tree-mists where the sky was as empty as his heart. He slid like a shuffleboard counter through the cut between blackish-brownish-gray banks of darkness, the sky greenish-gray above. He crossed the grim vacuous bridge that was the last place before the night country; he pierced the turgid black river (so night-soaked that he could perceive it only at its edges where light coagulated upon black wrinkles) and came into the ruined desert.

The toll bar came down. The attendant was waiting. Cars were beginning to honk behind him as he sat there at the tollbooth of souls, looking through his pockets. Finally he found a single coin with a hole in it. He reached, dropped it into the attendant's palm. The toll bar went up. He became a piece of jute cloth.

Battambang City, Province Battambang, Cambodia (1991)

A woman in a mask who had a blue blanket over her head put the soft limp jute of him onto the conveyor belt. Then he got washed and rolled. The rollers gleamed and worked him back and forth, softening him. He could not scream. To her he was not even a shadow. (A poster of the president changed rose-light on its shrine.) What worked the rollers? The factory had its own generator, its own grand shouting alternators, built to last, 237 kilowatts . . . The jute of his soul got matted and soft. He did not see the hammer-and-sickle flag anymore. His soul got squeezed by a rickety rattling. Now he was squished almost as thin as a hair. People dragged him away slowly, pulling long bunches of him with both hands. He was in a vast cement-floored enclosure whose roof was stained brown. They stretched him out. Slowly he went up a long steep conveyor. He emerged in a pale white roll of hope, twirling down, narrowing into a strip. The barefooted workers gathered him into piles on the concrete floor, then stuffed him into barrels, which were then mounted on huge reels. Murderers like him had destroyed this place once already. There had been twelve hundred workers. Now that it had been rebuilt, eight hundred and sixty worked there, eight hours a day, six days a week, not knowing that jute was souls. They cleaned and pressed him into accordioned ribbons of fiber that built up in the turning barrels. A masked girl stood ready to pack him down with her hands and roll a new barrel into place. He recognized her. She pressed him to her unscarred breast. Then someone took the barrels to go into a second pressing machine. A metal arm whipped back and forth, but only for a minute; the barefoot girls had to fiddle with it again. His substance was cleaned and dried. A masked woman lifted up levers, twisted him by hand into the clamps, pulled down levers, and he spilled out again. He recognized her also. She smiled at him. Now everyone could see him being woven into string, dense, rough and thick; this string in turn was woven into sacking. They were going to fill his empty heart with rice. This is not such a bad destiny for anyone, since rice is life. The barefoot girls teased out the rolls of soul-cloth, gathering them from the big roll in different sizes (63 × 29 inches and 20 × 98 inches); boys dragged them across the floor at intervals, stretching, looking around, slowly smoothing them amidst the sounds of the mechanical presses. So they stacked him among the other sacks. Girls sat on sacks on the floor, sewing more sacks; they were fixing the mistakes of the sack-sewing machine. Then they pressed the sacks into bales. But he'd turned out perfectly; he did not need any girls to stitch up holes in his heart. He was ready now in the bale of sacks. If someone guarded him well he might last two years. Then he'd turn to dirt. A man's hands seized his bale and carried him toward the place where he would be used. Then the man's work-shift was over. The man went to serve his hours on the factory militia, readying himself for duty in the room of black guns on jute sacks. The man knew that in the jungle other murderers were still nearby.

I SEE THAT YOU LIKE ORIENTAL WOMEN

Sydney, New South Wales, Australia (1994)

Sydney, New South Wales, Australia (1994)

I see that you like Oriental women, said the taxi driver.

Greek women are very nice too, I said. (I tried to be polite and I could tell by his accent.)

Let's be honest, the taxi driver said. All women are beautiful. Especially a young virgin from anywhere, full of hormones.

My wife stared out the window, disgusted and offended. But the driver did not see. He saw only me, because I was one of his kind, a man who liked Oriental women.

I was married to a Chinese girl, he said. I met her in Beijing. She was absolutely, uniquely beautiful. One in a million. A dress model. I had to marry her twice, once in Beijing and again the afternoon we arrived in Sydney. Here in Australia they don't recognize those other marriages. If you don't marry them again it's considered sexual slavery.

So what happened?

Oh, it was about children. She wanted them and I didn't. She accepted it initially, but after the sixth or seventh abortion she began to kick. She tried to come back to me six months after the divorce, but I didn't want to be reconciled.

Why's that?

Oh, by then I had a hot young black girl. Every night I stood her on her head and filled her full of my jizz.

We'll get out here, my wife said.

I wondered if he was going to stare, turn to me, and cry: Oh, it talks! — But he only said: Right we are. Enjoy your stay in Sydney, ma'am.

My wife stood waiting on the sidewalk with her arms folded. As I was paying him he whispered with a wink: You've put some miles on her. Better trade her in for a new one soon's you can. You want me to tell you where to go in Sydney?

Looking into his eyes, I saw such raw wet pain in them, throbbing and obscene, that for a moment I could not breathe. In him there was more need and less hope than in any beggar I had ever met. I started to tip him a tenner, but he shook his head and said hoarsely: Listen to me, pal. Please listen. You've got to be more careful. I *know* things! You'll need it for the alimony payments.

Goa, Goa, India (1990)

TOO MANY GODS

Goa, Goa, India (1990)

They gave him parrotfish in brown rivers and he gave them white lotus flowers, purple lotus flowers; he transmuted fish into flowers. Girls and old ladies stood at the side of the road, holding out garlands for sale. They sold his flowers to him in the temples; he paid in good luck and deeds. Then he planted the flowers in the slit windows behind funnels in the stone. They grew into white towers with arches and statues. He planted the money plant in its pedestal in the courtyard. They gave him flowers, garlands and coconuts for offerings. But they were his flowers anyway. On the hillside his worshippers raised a stone phallus to him. He penetrated the faithful who lived slowly moving across their glistening fields, walking barefoot behind their water buffalo. Then the fields were fertile. At a distance suited to humility, rows of pickers and transplanters bent as if in prayer, but they were only taking from him again. Still he gave them cashew apples: red, yellow, green; gave them palm tree suns with green rays, gave them tiny black birds skittering over the swamp, houses tucked under palm trees. The hills of Goa were wrought with trees—mango, cashew, jackfruit, pineapple, and mango. Cashew liquor goes very good with Limca, they said, pleased. But they complained a little, because every year they had to change the roofs of their palm-leaf houses. — They wanted eternal leaves. If he'd given them those, then they would have wanted to be eternal, too. They wanted everything he had. They gnawed at his knowledge, paying nothing. But he couldn't help feeling pity for them. That was why he'd taught them how to fix things. To repair a bridge, they heated metal on wood fires which they'd started with dry coconut fronds. It was easy; he made it easy. His heart was bright green like a rice field.

Mango and bamboo went brown. Across the brown square fields, a woman came striding slowly in a red sari. She said to him that everyone was going to raise blue concrete crosses in front of their houses, because a porous arch had been exhaling the steam of Saint Francis Xavier's breath. Saint Francis Xavier was dead now, so he could not be contradicted. Everyone had decided to paint Jesus on the spare-tire covers of motorcycles.

He said no word. He stared at the woman in the red sari until she felt as tiny as a cashew fruit. She fled among the silvergreen palm-tree mango-tree hills.

He entered the town, and saw the Portuguese governors, plump, sweaty, with long black sickle moustaches, sitting wearily in their black and gold armor, which made their hips as big as women's. He shrank them down, but they were so far lost they didn't even notice it.

Saint Francis Xavier, dead under a roof of palm thatch; opened his eyes and saw him. There was already a halo around his head. Dappled, holding crucifix and rosary, Saint Francis Xavier said to him: They'll expose my body four times a year, on a bier of teak, resting on an angel's head!

He replied to Saint Francis Xavier: I'll be there. And I'll cover you back again, as a clean cat covers its shit.

He stared at Saint Francis Xavier, but Saint Francis didn't shrink. He was dead.

He went back to the black waterbuffalo wallowing in swamps. He saw his white churches, green trees. His arch still crowned a palm mountain.

His remaining worshippers gnawed him, like a cow nuzzling the side of a thatch house.

Houses went up, too, in the new town, roofed with red rusted tin. Churches went up. Saint Francis's church they built of porous laterite, its black brick arch rough like lava. Tall narrow windows capped old arches of the old black stone. Its roof-long timbers were parallel like those of a ship, then gold. The sun of Jesuit initials, I.H.S., underlooked two cherubs above; then beneath the sun, standing on a big gold pyramid (the child Jesus between his legs), stood Saint Ignatius with his hand raised, a silver crown upon his head, his belly plate widening like that of a beetle. He was bearded, radiant, distant.

And Saint Catherine's church, that was a white church, with a white dog, a big white arch, plaster behind hot cruciform. Inside, it was cool, white and gold. It was floored with gravestones. There were white summery muscles and tendons and arches on the ceiling. There were shell strips on her windows. She was shuttered with translucent shells.

He said: There are too many gods here now.

They gave him parrotfish in brown rivers and he gave them nothing. Girls and old ladies stood at the side of the road. They tried to sell his flowers to him in the temples, but he wouldn't buy them. They were his flowers anyway. On the hillside the angry worshippers knocked down the stone phallus. So he denied them cashew apples, palm tree suns, tiny black birds skittering over the swamp, houses tucked under palm trees. They stopped giving him anything. They stopped asking him for anything.

He walked the narrow tongue of beach, divided by palm trees from the bare ocean and the horizon-ridge of someday.

He paced among the slow vulture-shadows where the Moslems had once built a deep-moated fort. Trees grew on the walls. Grim black rocks. Shadows between the walls. Narrow windows. Turrets and sky. Night clouds like white stars. Gray trees. The smell of distance. The smell of dirt. A grasshopper. The feeling of an island. Dark gray water, light gray sky.

FORTUNE-TELLERS

The Sphere of Stars (1993)
Yangon, Myanmar (1993)
San Francisco, California, U.S.A. (1993)

The Sphere of Stars (1993)

Occult philosophy once pleased the yearnings I had in adolescence to produce terrifying effects, thereby flowering into someone superior to others. Shouldn't we grant everyone a pardonable time of life? The white supremacists who firebombed our city councilman's house yesterday, the black gangsters who shot two Jews for their sports jackets the day before—heaven's sake, they didn't mean it! — And that is just how I was. I wanted to fly not because I had anywhere to go, sought to raise the dead not for instruction or care for their clammy friendship. Hence the failure of my suffumigations. What if the liver of a chameleon, being burned upon a rooftop, did *not* incite thunderous storms? That was a lesson from the TETRAGRAMMATON: I'd trusted to corrupt procedures to fulfill shallow ends.

But now I know. More than fresh rain I'd prefer to imbibe the dew of beautiful correspondences which is the true elixir of sorcery. Grease to a mechanic, metaphor to a Muse—such is similitude to a magician. Yes! I will speak to you of the three Spheres, and the cords of sympathy between them—ropes of power, if you will, far more necessary to the continuance of creation than those anonymously identical electrons which represent the mediocrity of mass democracy, oh, my friends! — While browsing in an ancient Coptic tractate, I found these lines: *Discern what size the water is, that it is immeasurable and incomprehensible, both its beginning and its end. It supports the earth, it blows in the air, where the gods and angels are. But in him who is exalted above all these there is the fear and the light, and in him are my writings revealed.* This place of fear and light is the core of talismanic magic: an empyrean cosmos of crystal, a Sphere in which reside the ideals of all created things, swarming like quartz and diamond bees around the radiant nectar of their First Cause. — Enclosing this realm one finds the Middle Globe of constellations. A seal has been inscribed upon each star's flames to name it forever according to its character, be it Tetra, Zebul, Sabbac, Kadie, Berisay, or any of a billion trillion others—for it is a law that no two stars may have the same name. They have spirits of various colors and luminosities; and they are the agents of the forms in the inner sphere where we began. Their rays broadcast influences down to the outermost Sphere of Material Elements within which we find ourselves incorporated; where *all* is guided by them in every place from the Zone of Snows, where the sky may sometimes be afternoon-blue and the sun lies orange on the frozen sea, to the tree-choked hollows between hot sugarcane hills: —every leaf is veined in its own language with a name, and that name is the name of its star.

Now you know the secret. Each crystal of sea-ice already sends up an essence to its own pale planet. The blood of a bat, they say, mixed with saffron and other ingredients, then brought to a boil upon a grave, will call out of moldy darkness a quorum of demons. But why trouble yourself? The bat already has a bat-star, and the corpse in the grave its star, too; everything is controlled by those maddening rays! The known antipathy between lignum aloes and frankincense, the astrological rules of ascendants, trines and sextiles—all these phenomena can be derived from the characters of the stars which pull them hither and thither.

Sometimes (I admit) I gaze into the night sky longing to blot away those hateful masters of our destiny. Were I to awake inside my coffin, my consolation would be to find no lethal dimples of light to interrupt the lid—foolish solace, I grant, because the stellar rays can pass with easy malignance through earth and stone any quantity of infinities thick, to link whatever they choose with their significators in that eerie Sphere of Stars. Even in the day of Jupiter one cannot hide the evil; the rite of the burial of scorpions cannot forestall it; the conjuration of vegetable souls cannot delay it. Always those horrible stars! When I see a cliff so tightly bulging with ferns as to resemble an immense palmhead; when I find a land swollen with leafy treetops, fringed with plantations and bananas, tunneled with jungle-walled lava-paved creeks, I grow dizzy in contemplation of the immensity of that hideous Sphere above, for whose tyranny every pebble in the water has been wrought; every fruit ripens in accordance with the commands of its celestial orb; each darkness between leaves corresponds to the space between two stars, the dark and waxy ether of the firmament, the mass of anguish that calls for evil to come.

In the desert I once met cracked and banded cliffs in grand profusion, and I knew that behind heat and tree-stillness they too were starcrossed to the depths of their pink dirt. I sweated and squinted in the sun (which I liked to think was the Star that ordered me), and ascended a hill of salmon-colored sand, slipping back, digging in my heels. Boulders like the shells of turtles stirred uneasily against my knees. I touched the yellow flowers and grey shrubs, greeted the hundred-foot spruce tree and climbed the white, black and red wall that shook me with its starry silence. With that I'd gained the rim, thereby mastering the tidy distant trees; for a moment I forgot that each and all of these entities were likewise ruled from above; then I saw the meteorite sunken in the sand, the awesome matter of a star, and I pressed my face against the scorching sulphurousness of it to reaffirm my bondage. Let no one deny the sacred correspondence. Better to acknowledge the wisely baleful Star that rules you.

Yangon, Myanmar (1993)

t was thus for eminently fine reasons that while in Rangoon I felt impelled to make submission to the astrologers. My goal was to help somebody escape from Burma, just as if I were to release more sparrows from a cage for five kyats★ apiece, feeling each tiny brown life beat so weakly in my palm, and then opening my fingers to see the bird go upward. The idea was to gain merit (for we all believe that Papal indulgences can be sold). I once bought a whole cageful of the little things and sent them into the air one by one, feeling so happy and good that I plain forgot they were only bird-puppets being retracted upwards on their star-pulled strings. What can their Heaven be but one of those dark stale restaurants on the second floor of some unpainted building? So I surmise, since all birds come down again, and when they do the bird-sellers catch them in order to sell their freedom again. After all, why should there be intermittence for sparrows? So they flutter busily down from the Sphere of Stars, and what do they see? — It was at Sule Pagoda that I usually bought my prisoners; and they did not fly far. That is why I know that they first saw how Sule's narrow gold spires grew from widening layers of silver roofs whose festoonings were as masses and strings of lichens; these guarded gold figures grew progressively larger as the sparrows neared the ground, then ended in steep wide red roof-plateaus comprised of long slats. Below this was the raised polygon on which all the towers and Buddhas were set (at the Buddhas' knees, offerings of leaves, flowers and bananas). The people walked barefoot on the wet white marble tiles. So many Buddhas! And I wondered this: If the Buddhas outnumbered the stars, could evil destinies be neutralized by calmness? I prayed at the first shrine roofed with silver leafery (darkness in between like ashes), and my prayer ascended those tapering gold towers which were strung between stars. I prayed at the second and the third, where I was kept company by a nine-year-old shavepate, a novice

---

★ In 1993, a kyat (pronounced *chat*) was worth slightly less than a cent on the black market.

monk in scarlet robes. Passing a skinny old lady shaking a pair of joss sticks, I came to the place of glass hexagonal heads like giant lamp-shades inset with fringed and brassy bells. In a niche of compound mirrors were two Buddhas. I chose the left hand, the lesser, and prayed that I might do good for someone. Could the stars be appeased or tricked? Past me the sparrows flew down the tunnelled stairs of lukewarm slippery marble where beautiful girls sat among strings of their blossoms and mounds of fresh leafy flowers like the treasures of vegetable stands, looking out at the warm rain and spitting flowers on long peeled sticks. They had sold me a bouquet for Buddha. They sat bare-brownfooted, wearing flower dresses, assembling votive um-brellas of all colors, and white *thanakah*-paste was smeared on their throats and faces. Below them the temple was encircled by puddled pavement around which trucks and buses slowly crept; there were stair-tunnels on every facet of the pagoda; and in that zone the sparrow-sellers waited with their cages. There, too, ranged around the base of the pagoda, were the fortune-tellers' booths.

Some made elaborate calculations on a notebook page before they pronounced, while others used a silver pencil on a slate, and still others saw everything through the immense metal-rimmed magnifying glasses that gave them power.

There was a fortune-teller with a tight brown face like a skull, shaved, with a long black goatee, a black-and-silver moustache, and thick black glasses. His skinny brown-veined fingers grappled my palm. The skull peered with deep concentration through an immense magnifying glass.

Eisenhower's palm was on the wall, seven times life-size. Other giant hands were continents of horses, elephants, towers, knives and flowers. The cell smelled like incense from the temple above.

You try to help others, to be of service to others, he said.

The skull's eyes were also magnified by his glasses. He wanted to know on what day of the week I had been born, and when I could not say he found it in a hundred-year calendar.

You have a strong lifeline, he whispered. You will not die a bad death. But you must be careful of your stomach.

In his pale gray jacket, which matched his dust-colored beard, his elbow on an immense black book with red pages, he sold me knowl-edge as sweet and plentiful as the smoke from one of those Burmese cheroots whose green cross-section contains a hundred chambers of fragrance.

You are not married?

I had to think about this.

No, I said finally.

Long brown fingertips probed the palm of the hand, seeking to align me with the wisdom that he kept in his narrow glass cabinet filled with books in gold wrappers.

You must meet a woman older than you who was born on a Wednesday or a Friday.

When he asked me if I had any questions I said: How can I help the people in Burma?

From a child you have been interested in Buddhism, he said. You must not try to help by any other means, but through study and religious concentration. You will have great difficulties, but you will overcome them after the seventeenth of September.

You will die peacefully, he added. You know, some die of hunger, and some are hanged, but never you! You will meet death in a better way.

And I said again, with my palms under the pressure of the skull's fingers: How can I help Burma?

Better to give the help to the religious, the true religious, whispered the skull.

What he was saying was that I must not go against the stars, that I had no right to decide anything without asking permission of those who oversaw him.

San Francisco, California, U.S.A. (1993)

And yet some of you still disbelieve in astrology. For me those star-rays of influence are as reliable as the steely light-strings that the trolleys slide on beneath the Sunset District's gray skies. My wife and I used to live there, and so did another couple, a white man of ill luck and his wife, a Japanese whose face was a long slender triangle. Years after we moved away a sad thing happened; and that night I slept in the apartment of their sister-in-law, who was my friend. The sister-in-law had a Japanese doll that the Japanese girl had given her (she was always giving presents like drops of blood from her loving heart). This doll was as long as my arm, and more slender. Flat in shape, almost like an immense tongue depressor, it had been constructed from paper wrapped around a cardboard core; somehow it lived as a woman in a red kimono of white flowers, bearing a blue gift in her arms. She had Japanese pigtails and inky black Japanese eye-dots. A calligraphed cartouche ran down her. I thought that I knew the sister-in-law, but I had never seen this doll before.

The sister-in-law was moving away after seven years. After she left there'd be nobody I knew in this neighborhood anymore. Her new home was a room in a flat with other women. She could not take all her possessions with her. So she was having a garage sale, and the Japanese doll already had a price tag on it that said three dollars. — She's given me so many nice things, the sister-in-law said to me. I have another wooden doll from her. This one has been on my mantlepiece for years. I feel sort of bad about getting rid of it, but, you know, it's something that could make some little girl very happy. I would have loved it when I was that age. I hope a little girl buys it.

That night I could not sleep, partly because the living room was very stuffy, partly because for a week I'd had a fever that made me anxious, but mainly because I could not put out of my mind the Japanese girl sobbing in the kitchen as she'd told the tale of her days, pressing her cheek against my chest while her pure transparent tears splashed down onto my hands. I believe her husband was in the bathroom. So, as I said, I could not sleep (and the next morning the sister-in-law told me that she had not slept, either—although for different reasons, according to the stars). At three in the morning, overrun suddenly by such grief and loneliness that I was compelled to bite my lip, I sat up. I considered going in to the sister-in-law, just to hold somebody, anybody, but that would have been awfully selfish. So I took the doll in my arms. I felt better at once. Finally I slept.

In the morning the sister-in-law passed by on her way to the bathroom. — You know, you can have that doll if you want, she said. I'd be happy to give it to you.

Remembering how the Japanese girl's voice had been hoarse from so much crying, I thanked the sister-in-law but said I thought that keeping this doll would make me unhappy. After all, the doll had not been meant for me. If it had come from a person I never met, it could not do me any harm (for in astrology and voodoo we believe that auras have less power the less one knows about them). And I remembered that once the Japanese girl had said to me: No, if we must separate, I doan' want to see him again. Because I must forget him quickly, to find my new happiest. — And I knew that if the Japanese girl left her life, then she would leave her sister-in-law, too, and me, and everyone, forever. If I had a doll of hers, then that doll might pull her back a little, keeping me a ghost in her heart that could not die. That would not be kind. So I sat up in bed and put the doll gently on the floor, knowing that I would never hug it again.

Years before, there'd been an October's day when we'd met at Anza Lake, which exuded a fog as livid gray as mercury, and the dog's wet fur stood up in clumps like tufts of reddish grass as she panted and snorted after thrown sticks, swimming narrow-nosed in the lake, waddling out and shaking herself, happy and alert in the clammy breeze. My wife stood plump-kneed, commanding, happily absorbed on shore, crying: Get the stick! Get the stick! Swim, swim, swim— *good girl!*

The Japanese girl and her husband came up the path. She called our names smilingly and hurried ahead to meet us. As I've said, she possessed one of those sweetly extravagant natures which long to make others happy, pouring themselves into work, gratefully returning every kindness a hundredfold. He'd found her when he was teaching English in Japan. Although I was happily married myself (I forget now if my wife was born on a Wednesday or a Sunday), I envied him his discovery. I too, as the Burmese astrologer well knew, have had many of my most joyous hours in being of service—or trying to; for many times one does harm meaning to do good. *She* at least I had helped, or so I believed. The first time I met her, she could speak only a little English. Her husband's Japanese was better that year than at any other period of his life, because they had just come from To-kyo, so he probably should have interpreted for her. But he was tired and had been doing that for months, and, as it happened, a friend of a friend had just given me a quarter-pound of marijuana—a princely

gift, which (prince that I was) I mainly passed on to others. So the husband was in the kitchen, madly smoking the delicious herb, and I was left
to entertain the wife, who was afraid of drugs. Now, it may seem that this
situation demonstrates the sexual motive behind much of my supposed
altruism—for why wasn't I content to have made *him* happy? But it was
not like that. I had nothing against him smoking up all my marijuana. It
was meant to be given away. But there was something so defenseless and
good about her—a homesickness, a brave cheeriness to prevent others
from being embarrassed by her own terrified incapacity. I had the sense
that others had not perhaps been kind to her—oh, nothing cruel, but
there were so many new Americans who could not speak English; maybe
the longstanding Americans grew a little tired. I would not be one of
them. I chatted with her, enunciating slowly, using simple words and
pleasant ideas; and I could see that she was grateful; every moment I felt
warmer toward her; and her husband smoked on.

A week or so later I bought her a dictionary and some English
primers. Again she was grateful. The husband smiled a little distantly.
I could see that she was ashamed that he did not thank me too; she
cast him a look of shy reproach, which made me feel awkward; and
I wondered if I had overstepped.

But we continued to be great friends, all of us. She prepared a
four-course Japanese dinner for my wife and me (did I mention that
they were very poor?). She was very intelligent and hardworking; her
English continually improved. I was always happy to see her. Whenever we met, she came running into my arms, while my wife and her
husband stood looking on.

So on this fall day as I stood inhaling the smell of eucalyptus and watching her come hurrying toward me along the edge of the white-wrinkled
brownish creek, I found my arms flying open of their own accord. I
watched her tiny feet flash through fallen moon-crescents of leaves. — Hi,
Jenny! she cried, waving gaily. My wife replied, unsmiling. The Japanese
girl threw herself into my embrace and kissed me on the mouth. There was
nothing wanton or teasing about her; she was only affectionate.

I want to say hi and thank you for inviting us to see you today,
she cried, it is very glad to see you! Jenny, we couldn't see you the
last time so we are very happy to see you today.

Her husband had now approached, and he went toward my wife
tentatively, unsure whether he ought to kiss her or merely take her

hand. I forget what he did. He never stayed much in my mind. For this I am entirely to blame, I admit. He had many good points. He worked hard (it was not his fault that he could never hold a job); he loved his wife very much, and told me once that he could never be unfaithful to her. As he said this he gazed at me a little challengingly.

I remember that afternoon of long chives and forgotten blackberries. The air was as still as a breath. I remember how the four of us went walking alongside the brown guts of that creek that twisted and wound into a brownish-silver mirror. It was better than silver jewelry. Perhaps it could be reproduced by melding ten parts silver with three parts copper, not just any copper . . . I remember seeing the Japanese girl reflected in it, and my heart soared.

Her husband and I talked, too. He'd brought a bottle of mescal which we passed back and forth. I admired his physical strength. I respected the manual labor that he did (her job with a Japanese company brought in more money, but how could that be his fault?). We crossed the tree-bridge, he and I, climbed hills as thickly grasshaired as bear fur, and after a long time we found ourselves in a place of myriad orange thistleflowers on tall iron-colored stalks, flowers like the "choke" of an artichoke, cupped by artichoke-like leaves. My instant thought was to pick two, one for my wife and one for his. Then I saw how he regarded me, and we turned away together, descending to our wives, following a path among gray groping stalks of dead grasses as skinny as an insect's leg.

A year or two later, my wife and I had to leave San Francisco. I remember how the Japanese girl sobbed in my arms, refusing to let her husband pull her away, while I stood holding her, rocking her, kissing and being kissed by that beautiful face, trying to calm her while my wife looked on.

Five years fell like shooting stars. They had a child now, I'd heard; they'd moved twice; he'd just lost his latest job. I happened to be in San Francisco on business, so I called and they invited me to dinner. Her English was almost perfect by then. That was the night that the thing happened that shocked me so much that the aftershocks kept ringing hours later when I sat on the yellow-lit bus that brought me through the night whose fog chilled my knees. I was next to a security guard whose epaulets bore crimson stars. He gazed down at the toes of his jackboots, drained by the rays from Gemini which had propelled him so mercilessly through life. I could not stop thinking about what had happened. We passed cages of light in the silent foggy darkness, slowly withdrawing from the Outer Sunset, the houses closer together now and taller, more and more filled with light. The woman across the egg-yolk-colored partition grimaced, her face a wrinkled brittle mask, her hair greasy and shiny. After her eyes closed, the most prominent part of her face was her nostrils, those twin black star-points of negativity, like the eyes of that Japanese paper doll.

What had happened was this:

The two of them had been quarrelling again—or rather (to be more accurate) she had continued to upbraid him in shrill and humiliating terms. To change the subject (it seemed that I was changing the subject every few minutes that evening), I asked her which of the twelve Chinese years each of them had been born in—for even Japanese and Koreans take cognizance of this calendar.

He was born in the Year of the Rat, she replied, looking at me (never at him!).

What kind of character is a person born then supposed to have? I asked.

Always running around, she said scornfully. Running this way and that way. I doan' mean it in a good sense.

And you? I said quickly, changing the subject one last time.

Me? I was born in the Year of the Rabbit, she said. Very good. Very cute.

What does that say about your character?

For the first and only time that night, she smiled. In a voice that glittered like a new steel blade, she said: Ladies born in Year of the Rabbit, we lose our husbands early. They die very young. Soon I will be a happy widow.

It was impossible to mistake what I was hearing. This was a confession of intended murder.

Of course it was not her fault. What she was had been decided by the conjunction of stars in the Year of the Rabbit. What he was was likewise determined.

I have seen a few dead bodies in my work as a journalist. I have looked into a number of murderers' eyes. When I took my leave of the happy couple a few moments later, I said to myself: I truly believe in the stars.

```
┌─────────────────────────────────┐
│ ╔═══════════════════════════════╗ │
│ ║                               ║ │
│ ║           BLOOD               ║ │
│ ║                               ║ │
│ ╚═══════════════════════════════╝ │
└─────────────────────────────────┘
```

BLOOD

San Francisco, California, U.S.A. (1986)
Bangkok, Phrah Nakhon-Thonburi Province, Thailand (1993)

San Francisco, California, U.S.A. (1986)

You want some blood? said the guy in the camouflage coat.
Yeah.
The back of my arm is good.
The doctor hit it. — Yeah. That's a good vein, the doctor said.

I hope so. It's at a hard angle, though. You can get it straighter there, Doc. It's up to you. You know how you want to do it.

The needle went slowly in. The guy in the camouflage coat bit his lip. Not looking, he said: You get it?

Yeah.

Good.

The blood came out from between the wings of the butterfly in a pretty thread, reproducing those times when traffic becomes a liquid with many red eyes that oozes through tunnels in obedience to horizontal pinball gravity. Just as taxi-lights bleed across the ceilings of tunnels, so the pink vibrations took wing inside his eyelids. The corpuscles were smoking, tottering trucks and weepy-eyed cars rushing like red ants between the ribs of some dead bridge.

Still going, huh?

Yeah, said the doctor. It's a gusher.

391

That's good, 'cause I never mess with the back one.

He looked down at the floor. Yeah, he went on. I have a positive antibody. I hope I don't have AIDS. I've been feeling terrible lately.

As he sat there leaning forward he jigged his knee and he jigged his fist on his knee. He looked very serious.

Bangkok, Phrah Nakhon-Thonburi Province, Thailand (1993)

The guy in the camouflage coat got a Butterfly Bar vest and a bar number like the girls and went around like some tragic diffusion of evening traffic, saying to them: OK you pay me one baht I sleep you hotel no problem I smoke you my Mama-Papa very poor—and they laughed.

But the slender sad girl whose hair was rubberbanded back in a ponytail said: I no like my job.

Why you work Soi Cowboy then? he said, throwing his jacket off and rolling up his sleeve.

Little money. I send money Mama-Papa.

You have Thai boyfriend?

Before I have. But he send me away. I small small money. He marry big money.

The slender girl never resisted. Her tiny fieldworn hands would always settle on his back, gently caressing. (Before, I work water buffalo, she said.) She had a pale ocher face. She never complained about his not using a rubber.

You want some blood? he said afterward.

No, sir. Why you say give me blood?

I want to do it to you. I did it to you one way, but maybe you still don't have my antibody. I want you to drink my blood. I want to maybe stick you with this needle and squirt my blood into you, OK?

The slender girl wrung her hands. — OK, sir. Up to you.

The guy in the camouflage coat remembered the woman who'd given him the disease. He remembered going to the doctor with her.

Hi, the doctor had said. Are you gonna do this?

Yeah. I guess, said the scared woman, smiling. Then she said quickly: no, I really have to get to work. — She ran away.

She was dead now.

Close your eyes, bitch, he said to the slender girl. I don't want you looking into my eyes while I do this. Don't worry. I'll pay you one thousand baht.* Make a fist. Make a fist, I said. Yeah, that's a good vein. You got such pretty little veins.

Thank you, sir.

OK, it's going in. Don't move. Don't move. There it goes.

Thank you very much, sir.

What the fuck are you thanking me for? I just murdered you.

Excuse me sir me no no understand you speak.

I apologize, he said. It's just that I've been feeling pretty down lately.

---

* About U.S. $40 in 1993. About what an all-night girl might expect to receive.

OUTSIDE AND INSIDE

Berkeley, California, U.S.A. (1992)
Phnom Penh, Cambodia (1991)
Hong Kong, Territory of United Kingdom, Southeast Asia (1993)
Mexicali, Estado de Baja California, Mexico (1992)

Berkeley, California, U.S.A. (1992)

Outside the vast squares of yellow bookstore-light, the panhandlers, longhaired and greasy, held out their palms, asking for their dinners, and two started fighting, while inside people turned the pages of picture-books whose flowers smelled like meadows of fresh ink.

I don't want her around me! a panhandler shouted. I don't need that fucking bitch! I hate that monster.

Inside, everyone pretended that the shouting was silence. A man looked at a book and wanted to buy it, knowing how wonderful it would be to sit in his own house with a drink in his hand looking at this thirty-eight-color picture-book printed on paper as smooth as a virgin's thigh while the sun kept coming in through the leaves—

Outside, somebody screamed.

The man bought the book and went out. He saw a man smashing a woman's head against a window of the bookstore. The glass shattered, and as the woman's livid and half-dead face shot into the yellow light he saw it become beautiful like the planet Saturn ringed by arrowheads of whirling glass that rainbowed her in their cruel prisms and clung to wholeness in that spinning second also ringed by her hair and spattering blood.

The man ran back inside where the woman's mouth lay peaceful. He opened his book and invited her in. Gently he raised her head and pillowed the book beneath. Spangles of blood struck the pages like a misty rain, becoming words which had never existed before. She began to bleed faster and faster. Her hair grew down between the words like grass, underscoring and embellishing them with fragrant flourishes. Her eyes and teeth became punctuation marks. Her skin became pages of bloodless purity. Her flesh kept company with the threads and glue; the plates of her skull broke neatly into cover-armor. Then there was nothing left of her above the raw red throat.

He picked up the book, which spoke to him, saying: Now you have loved me, and I will love you forever. But where are my hands? Where are my feet, my breasts?

I'm sorry, the man said. They're outside.

Bring them in, the book told him. Bring them through the window.

Holding the book tight, the man ran out to obey her, but police had already condensed out of the night. When he tried to smash the corpse's shoulders through the window, they led him into the squad car. He knew that they would take him inside.

Where are my hands? the book wept.

They took you away, the man whispered.

The book began to bleed despondently.

Phnom Penh, Cambodia (1991)

Once when the thioridazine wore off he found himself with a Bible because they'd taken away the other book to be kept forever in a long manila envelope labeled **EVIDENCE**. But the woman he'd helped and loved had finally found him. She whispered to him from the Bible, telling him to ask them for an atlas, and when the psychiatrists agreed because that was a sign of healthy involvement with the world, he opened the atlas at random, and the wide heavy covers flipped down to anchor him in the new country which he would soon find; and he looked and read **KAMPUCHEA**. So he entered a dark-staired hallway without electricity in Phnom Penh, kids hopping barefoot everywhere, silhouettes in hallways, black crowds watching in the hallway, smells of sweat and body odor and death, fat girls peering out of a dark doorway, giggling. Three girls leaned out. Warily they smiled. The door opened on a sunny place where more fat girls peered out carefully. He stepped into the new part of the hall that the open door had made, the bright part, and they beckoned him in. People were watching. He stood there in the place between outside and inside, entering a nested memory of an openwalled restaurant not far away where he had sat, feeling neither inside nor outside, a Chinese movie shouting along on the TV, while boys rode past one and two to a bike; awnings swirled in the breeze. Then he came out of that memory and entered the open door. All the pretty girls sat on the floor or the rumpled bed, watching TV. The madam closed the door behind him and then he knew that he had truly been admitted to the inside. But he also knew that he could not stay. Sooner or later he'd have to rent one of the girls, or else they'd make him leave. And even if he did rent somebody, so that he could come inside her, eventually he'd finish or his money would be finished and then he'd have to go back into the black hall again, which was outside like the far side of Pluto.

He closed the atlas. They gave him two more pills and checked beneath his tongue to make sure that he had swallowed. Soon he could feel himself going inside again.

Hong Kong, Territory of United Kingdom, Southeast Asia (1993)

The woman whispered, so he opened the atlas; and the harbor burned with bluish-gray fog, cool winds ruffling nothing on the blocky buildings across the water which were backdropped by camel's back hills the same color as the fog. He went among the tea-colored faces in round glasses, became present on the ferry across the gray-green sea. The happiness of going without map or guidebook, having no idea what he'd find, prevented him from recognizing the danger of the tall white buildings like punchcards on the horizon.

Not only this outsider, whose education in boundaries had been so abundant, but also the other inhabitants of Hong Kong, that abstraction as readily graspable as a parallelogram, often heard a strange woman's voice calling to them from across the water, the voice of a woman neither inside nor outside, who therefore called from loneliness, wanting to be loved so that her hands at least could live with her brain and skull; but to most others her pathetic aspect, which did require something of them, made them prefer not to recognize her; of course it was also that they were completely inside, so that they had little use for somebody who was neither one nor the other. Better not to acknowledge *any* ghost. Of course he was compelled to, because he already had. It is not as easy to get rid of consequences as first principles. He heard her desperate whisperings as he got off the ferry and approached the bank walled with sparkling transparent cubicles in which people paced or pressed or sat downgazing at computer mysteries; in the lower levels, where the public was permitted to come, embankments of metal and marble gleamed like sunlight, while the uniformed ones swarmed safely behind. Below this was a glass floor of many rectangular panes, joined by silvery rods; beneath this the gloomy silhouettes of the lowest walkers passed at obscure diagonals, all at the same pace.

He descended the slow escalator that brought the red uniforms and red displays into broader angles like an airplane approaching the runway, falling from the ceiling, which was a Ptolemaic crystalline sphere.

To cross the street you took an escalator above the statued men at the bank, crossed a marble bridge of potted plants whose leaves gleamed almost as coldly as the black shoes of the officials who marched so soundlessly, followed the V's of darker marble like caramelized sugar on a pudding dessert, turned left at the stained glass window, and then you could look down at the red and silver taxis, the blue and tan double-decker buses, the gray cars and white cars— all very clean, of course—sliding below you along the immaculate street. Then you came to a glass door which let you outside. You followed a walled path, which traversed a steep hill bulging with ferns, lilies, ginkgo trees and tall palms whose tea-colored darknesses strained toward the glowing fog and were undone by the weight of their own success; their umbrellalike spreadings and droopings from the resolute stalk were a falling back of darkness into darkness. This was the Battery path: a pavement of roots, like the muscles in athletes' shoulders. This was a city of clean paths telling him which way to go.

Where is my body? the woman whispered. Where are my bones?

He could not reply.

Waitresses paced inside the glass house with the waterfall outside, and it was just the same as the birds in the aviary. He was at the nexus, the Husserlian insertion point, the city that was neither outside nor inside; so he thought that he might very easily find the key. Once he did, he could help bring the lost woman entirely into one realm or the other. The waterfall, the skyscrapers, the marble tables of the restaurant, were all so incongruous. On the ledge above the waterfall a statue of a boy stood with his arm upraised, and then the camera finished flashing and the statue moved once more.

In the twilight, the swarms in suits and uniforms hurried along the edges of black buildings whose tiles were as slick and shiny as new cakes of soap, each building with a different brand name glowing from it like a pulsing wound. So many crowds! But it seemed that they were all inside. The city's metonym was this tank of shrimp thrashing white legs at each other, bulging their eyes out and straining to fly in the water like beta-test helicopters. He was the soft red carp breathing with difficulty between two reddish companions, its eye bulging and rotating with almost the same intensity as the white spots on the shrimp's scratching legs. But who were these other fishes like slabs of ring fungus swishing their fins lethargically in the murky water, straining and crowding? So many! He'd never know them . . . Behind the counter of the next window, uniformed men weighed out so many different barks and leaves and colored roots and dried sea creatures on white paper. People sat at stools before them, as if by a soda fountain. He heard the woman take in a long trembling breath. The men weighed out abalone shell for liver-cures and dyes, terrapin shells for lung complaints and renal bleeding, sea-horses for impotence, hawksbill turtle shells for epilepsy, oyster shells for acid stomach, geckos to quench thirst and increase virility, centipedes to stop hemorrhages, tiger shins for arthritis, stag penises for a cold uterus, fossil bones for insomnia and amnesia, sulphur for virility, cinnamon for diarrhea, eucommia bark for hypertension, castor beans for cutaneous ulcer, red beans for headache. But there did not appear to be anything to remedy traumatic spatiotemporal amputation. The woman was whispering. — A jewelry window said: **61% OFF.** He saw gold chains and crosses on squares of white paper. The next window was crammed with twenty-three-carat gold sunglasses round and oval and square, even a pair that folded down the nose, and a pair not much bigger than a fountain pen; it would barely cover one's pupils. He passed another long narrow jewelry shop at whose red-velvet tables the clerks sat punching calculators, drinking Cokes and wearing golden spectacles as fierce as new-cut diamonds. The glow of red characters on yellow awnings bored into his eyes with the same brightness as the golden objects for sale in the windows. A crowd of dark-uniformed policemen stood straight, their black walkie-talkies and holsters and nightsticks hanging correctly down; they walked with their hands behind their backs.

Where is the book you put me in? asked the woman.

This is the atlas, he said. This is the book. — And he bent down and touched the pavement. He knew that everything was set upon a single page.

Open the book, she said weakly.

It's open already.

Where am I, then? Am I inside or outside?

I don't know, he murmured, suddenly resentful. I don't know where I am anymore, either. I lost my freedom because of you.

Eastward, where the streets became grayer and narrower, there was a stand of aquariums in the street, the goldfish and the other deep blue ones he didn't know slowly fanning their tails within glass worlds like the spirits in the bottles in the liquor store whose walls formed part of the thoroughfare, or the banana-clusters which hung over the apples in the fruit stand, beset by swaying red lights. The signs were carved and painted now, not lighted. Sometimes they halfway or entirely spanned the narrow alleyways like stilt roots and flying buttresses. Windows and gratings and balconies clutched each other across spaces of narrow darkness.

He bought a bottle of rice whiskey at the liquor store and poured it out upon the pale sidewalk. — Here is your blood, he said. Now it's in the book.

A girl in pink, with scarlet lips, was leaning against the ice cream freezer in the liquor store talking with her husband, and when her mouth shaped itself into O's the crimson seemed to rise like smoke-rings to join the red signs and suddenly the husband was lighting a cigarette, and the fire at its end seemed to have come from her mouth. She touched the husband's hand. Across the street, a man was searching through a pile of apples, and when he found one that seemed redder than the rest and held it up, the watcher looked at the girl and saw that her mouth had just made an O again. Here was the being who could save the woman he cared for by bringing her entirely in or out of the atlas. Enchanted, he came closer, until he could hear her speak waterfalls that peacock-tailed so brightly down the wall of the Stock Exchange, losing themselves in the hill of potted yellow flowers which bordered the long, long escalator. (Underneath were the hundreds of white gambling booths.) He caught a red O in the air. It was hard like a marble. Throwing it down onto the pavement so that it shattered and disappeared, he muttered: Here are your bones. Now they're in the book. — The girl's ruby syllables rolled him away, so that floundering past a marble lobby (evidently of a seafood restaurant in whose immaculate tanks swam crowds of giant silver carp), he could peer but briefly into a small store to see the round table and the two girls slowly slicing a mound of ginseng. He fell through a red bubble of her delicious spit, tumbled into the market of dried fish whose broad gray mummies lashed together resembled palm fronds, was carried through the restaurant whose two men in black tuxedos were just lighting the final torch around the golden border of a red sign that uttered something incomprehensible to him; and like the men in suits and ties on holiday riding escalators up the hills of Ocean Park he swam volitionlessly past two ladies whose store contained nothing but dried white shark fins, each behind its own pane of glass like some strange sea-trophy; that was when he realized that he was in the sea.

He bought a shark fin for one Hong Kong dollar. Then he took it around the corner where the two ladies would not see and be hurt. He slapped it gently down onto the hard epidermis of the street and whispered: Here is your flesh. Now it's in the book.

He thought he heard her moan.

A man unhooked a bundle of dried fish from the awning pole of his shining store, covered the boxes of nuts with burlap, returned to unhook the bale of dried eels, then the hanging light bulb, then stepped outside and pulled down a rusty wall of darkness over everything.

Next door a stern man was still sitting behind his desk, emperor of rolls and scrolls of marbled cloth, and he stared out the window. He gaped his gristly jaws and gulped, which proved him to be a fish.

Entering that shop, the watcher bought a length of midnight-black cloth and unravelled some threads from it. — Here is your hair, he said, letting go the strands. Now it's in the book.

The people whose *ahs* and *ows* twisted in the guts of the night now drowned the scarlet-lipped girl's speech entirely; so in hopes of finding other luminescence he ascended a steep hill of meat and lighted produce stands whose pears and potatoes shone like lanterns (their bok choy greener than darkness, their cats mewing like tweaked piano wire). Strings of lights transected the heavens to encourage the ones struggling up that coagulation of night, carrying those purchased brilliancies away darkened in plastic bags.

The Sinew Co. was being closed, but inside the shopping malls, people were still peering and pointing, the women especially wistfully touching the glass of Rainbow Leatherware Co. and Rolie Collection. A restaurant was serving tea. He bought a cup of it and cupped his hands over the steam. Then he brought his cupped hands down to the floor and said: Here is your breath. Now it's in the book. Now you're complete in my book at last.

The whole city sighed, or perhaps the sigh came from somewhere deeper than that. Then the voice said: Thank you. I love you.

The ferry buildings were like space stations, with their lights and roundness and dockings; but they did not whirl, only rose and fell, and a reflection of the sea rose and fell in their television-like windows. Beyond the Star terminal rose a golden bowtie of neon, tall and absurd, crowned by a white trapezoid and a blue spire. Forgetting the scarlet-lipped girl and the woman whom he'd saved, he let himself be caught by the blue neon-light on black water.

Goodbye, a woman's voice said from under the water.

The thin old man with the white star on his chest stood holding the gangplank railing in a gloved hand, watching something too proud for others: the blackhaired girls with arms folded over their breasts, the skinny boys jutting out their chins, the ladies in glasses happy not to have missed the ferry, the married couples (wives on their husbands' arms). Then the whistle blew, the ferryman braced his foot against the bulkhead and strained at the rope, winching the gangplank up against the door. He stood watching Kowloon come closer (another ferry passing the black water, a vast illuminated casket). He remembered the Japanese restaurant where the indigo-pigtailed waitresses stood in corners with their hands behind their backs, white bows tied behind their short black skirts; and they wished him happy New Year and grew into the New Year like those tropical trees tasseled as if by strings of lime-colored beads. But he himself was coming outside his life again as steadily as the Kowloon ferry bearing through the cold and fishy night. — The ferryman stood still, squinting at a newspaper, his pinkish-orange face worn down almost to a skull by rain and fog and wind. He stood without support, swaying easily with the lurching deck. The horn sounded three times; the water began to burn evilly with the red and blue neon reflections of Tsim Sha Tsui, and he locked his newspaper away to again pull on his plastic gloves. He stood by the gangplank, patiently watching the greenish-gray window-lights and orange-gray wall-lights come closer. Then he gripped the rope, unhooked the chain, and let the pulley go. The crowd went out calmly, lighted faces going steadily into darkness.

Mexicali, Estado De Baja California, Meixco (1992)

So after that they let him outside. He was back inside his mind, they said. His behavior was normal. Just as in the ancient Egyptian cartouches south of Aswan each world is pale blue inside, yellow all around, so within himself he kept his secret color now. He'd closed the book and shelved it. Henceforth he'd return silence to all pleas.

He wanted to buy a ticket to take him farther outside. The sun formed white triangles and trapezoids on the floor of the railroad station whose early morning air was hot and stale, and people sat around picking their eyebrows because none of the ticket windows had opened yet. Two officials went into the MODULA DE ASIGNACIONES and he felt hopeful until they came back out and locked the door.

He waited all day and half the night. Finally, at the stroke of midnight, the window flew soundlessly open, and the woman stood behind it, smiling. Without speaking, she gave him a ticket of glowing gold.

He got on the train, and it took him into a tunnel that coiled round and round underneath the earth. And he came to the core, which was a giant geode glittering with crystals underfoot and overhead. And in the very center of the world was an atlas on a chain. He opened it, and the woman's bones fell out (they were very skinny and fragile, like fishbones), followed by her hair and gobbets of greasy flesh and flakes of her blood and all the other things which he had given her. The man broke off a crystal from the ceiling and buried it in her remains like a seed. Soon there grew a brilliant flower that filled the entire hollow heart of the world. Just before it enveloped the space which he had occupied, it invited him in . . .

THE STREET OF STARES

Redfern, Sydney, New South Wales, Australia (1994)

No, no, I did not go all the way to Blacktown (and in Launceston a disgusted cab driver said: Have you heard the latest? In your country the schoolchildren have to sing *Baa, baa, green sheep* in order to avoid offending the niggers. Next thing you know some do-gooder will say the name "Blacktown's" not good enough for them!); I did not go all the way to Blacktown, because Redfern was closer, and because a waiter had proudly related: I took a girl to Redfern and she went white as a sheet! She didn't know we had neighborhoods like that in Australia. — Being already as white as a sheet myself, in part due to birth, in part to illness, I figured that no red fern or black town or green sheep could make me seem any whiter. The **NEXT TRAIN** sign said **BLACKTOWN** but I did not go there; I rode between the grim-grimed pillars and arches with steel on top, was carried out past bulldozers gnawing gravel and then in again. **NO THOROUGHFARE. TRESPASSERS WILL BE PROSECUTED.** That was what you saw if you tried to exit the wrong way at Redfern Station. The wide-gravelled channels of railway beds beset me with brick walls. The train went on to Blacktown, and a man with a pole came and slammed Blacktown away to bring up another destination.

Under the sign, another man stood drinking V.B. He held the can very tightly in his hand. He did not quite reek as some drunks do but he was beery enough. He looked into my face. They called him black and that was what he sometimes called himself, but actually his skin was more reddish, almost Venetian red like that of the brown-haired aboriginal girl on the train who'd looked at me with such big searching brown eyes, working her plump, kissable lips as if to say something that she'd never said; this man opened his mouth and said: Buy me another, mate? How 'bout it? — Then he fell down. That was Redfern Station.

Outside there was a street, and across the street was a wall with a giant snake painted on it in aboriginal style, with the words 40,000 YEARS IS A LONG TIME . . . 40,000 YEARS STILL ON MY MIND. Turning the corner of this street, at the Redfern Aboriginal Cooperative, I found myself looking down a narrow street where right away a fat woman with a beer in her hand said: Excuse me. Could you spare a smoke? and the wall went on down that street, muraled with silhouettes who had white-dotted skeletons; and I saw grimy rainbows and dot-painted flowers and then the street narrowed further, sloping down into shady house-walls where people sat on their porches listening to radios, drinking, smoking and staring out. This was the Street of Stares. I had the feeling of coming into a place where I did not belong. White shoes and socks glowed on dark and shaded bodies, all lining the way and watching me. Second storeys gaped doorlessly like the bomb-burned flats I'd seen in Sarajevo; sky shone through one such hole; the others were dank and dirty and graffiti'd, coolly unfriendly like the eyes of the watchers, or so it seemed to me as I went on, remembering times when I'd come into certain black neighborhoods in my own country and found myself immediately hated, but then a man nodded back at me and said: G'day, mate! and I was comfortable again, which might have been stupid, because Snake, who that day became my wise uncle, told me: I'm not allowed to go out at night. My woman don't let me. Lotsa fights. I tell you now, don't walk around here. — That was Snake, and his woman was Sadie, and then there were Ruthie and Rob, all of whom lived together farther down that narrow street which smelled in places like airplane glue, not as far as the very end where thick gratings and brick mirrors greeted the next highway, across which lay the stinking pub where I bought the case of Victoria Bitters so that Rob would like me and take me in to Ruthie, Sadie and Snake behind that wall built less of grimy brick than of stares.

Originally we was from up the bush, Snake said, opening the first V.B. North coast. We came just visiting here. Then we stayed.

Tell you something about Redfern, the younger man cut in. They got a different attitude here. A bad attitude.

So why did you come visiting then? I asked.

Well, really there wasn't nothing up there, said Snake. Not enough to do. More opportunity in the city than in the country. That's why we're here.

Yeah, look at him talk, laughed Rob as he took out a beer. What kinda *opportunity* have *you* found, Snake? What kinda *opportunity's* anybody got in this town?

A lot of people playin' the numbers just to pass the time, Snake admitted. Really can't go anywhere. I'm only just visitin'. Wanna go back, huntin' and fishin'. And my woman, she's from the snow country, the table lands.

I miss the trees, the mountains, the grass, agreed Sadie wearily, sipping at her V.B.

All we needed up there was a tent, said Snake. Like, you could go to the river and get everything. I can kill anything with a stone that big. I could take two men out. I done it before.

Maybe someday I'll go somewhere, said Ruthie. Because they always stare. If I was sittin' on a train, I look out the window so they don't bother me. Some people don't have no respect. Oh, how they stare!

Shall we speak of stares? I myself seldom fail to gaze into other faces as they come to me. Looking is a natural act, and if Ruthie had come to my notice on a bus I would have looked at her because she was beautiful, but Ruthie would not have known that I was looking at her for that reason. That afternoon she said to me: When you get in a bus, the first thing people do is look you up and down, see if you're black. — I guess that was how it was for me, that first time I came into Redfern. They were all gazing at me—all of them!—and I was not their color. Maybe each gazed at me for his own reasons, but because they all gazed I had to assume a single reason, the same one that Ruthie assumed in her bitter anger. So perhaps the way to discover people's lusts and angers is *not* to fish behind their peering eyes but to read what they write on the walls of their public toilets. In a men's room at the Sydney airport I came across this profundity:

KILL ALL ABO'S I HATE COONS HA HA FUCKEM

which another soul had seconded as follows:

ABO'S WILL RUIN AUSSIE LAND

—a remarkable reversal of fact which took my breath away so that I almost did not appreciate the remarks of the third sage who had weighed and balanced and urinated and concluded: GOOKS ARE WORSE. — What exactly does it mean for land to become Aussified? Let me introduce a retired farmer I met in Tasmania, where the exterminations of the last century enjoyed great success: there are no fullblooded Tasmanian aborigines anymore. Horses bowed in the whitish and yellowish grass where this farmer had lived his years out, and huge cylindrical bales stood upon the fields like gateposts for the low blue sea-wave of mountains to the west. Age parted him from his farm, but his heart lived there yet; I think he was homesick for his peppermint gum trees. — The wildlife around here is a tremendous problem, he told me. You clear a field here and the animals will come from miles around, just strip it, clean it out, particularly kangaroos and wallabies. — He was the son of pioneers whose hard work had justified them to themselves. The land belonged to them. The kangaroos had no right to it. I requested his views on those strange, dark, barrel-shaped marsupials called Tasmanian devils, and he said: People in fat lamb areas could have experienced a lot more problems with them than I did. On my two hundred and fifty acres, while I did see them, they were never in sufficient numbers to cause a problem. — Their foreseeable extinction could not grieve him. Maybe he was even glad. It is not for me to hold him blameworthy. He paid allegiance to the laws he believed in, and lived quietly. If some native plant or animal caused "trouble" or a "problem" then he resolutely defended his interests; otherwise he kept neutral. He didn't kill venomous snakes, for instance, unless he found them close to the house. This philosophy, so conveniently practical with its tiny cabinets of self sameness, had come with a drawer to fit native people in also. — The whites have just about had enough of free handouts to the blacks, he explained. A few educated aboriginals tend to cause a bit of trouble. The uneducated black, he don't expect so much.

Snake, Sadie, Ruthie and Rob did not expect very much, I guess, maybe because they knew that Redfern was Aussie land. — This used to be a white community, Snake said, opening another V.B. Before the blackfellas moved in. The whitefellas want it back. They want to put a carpark in.

Redfern, Sydney, New South Wales, Australia (1994)

I'll tell you something else about this place, said Snake. They got no respect for the elders. The young fellas have got to keep the respect they got for the elders. The mother and father, they're not strict. And the old ones look out for us. You see, I call 'em all uncles and aunties.

That's what I noticed when I came down here, Rob mumbled, leaning back, closing his eyes, and raising the can of V.B. to his lips as his other wrist relaxed, his fingers falling and opening. (The case was already more than half gone.) — I call everyone brother and sister, but here they just pass on.

That's right, Snake, it's about respect, said Ruthie. No respect anywhere. I'm glad I haven't got no kids. They'd just get raised up in this shit. The average white person hates us, except for ferals and hips.★ And the bikers, too. They back us up. But the others . . . Especially the police. I saw one man last week, they made 'im strip down to 'is skin. Happened right outside this house. That's their aim, to strip us of our dignity.

You tell your magazine how there's always police, Sadie said. Blackfellas want peace; the police always wanna teach us a lesson.

(And here I have to say that the second time I went to Redfern, which was at night, I saw the police slam people down, but I also have to say that those people were wretched drunks who were hurting each other.)

Snake pointed. — Police got a camera there on the street. For surveillance.

Always watchin' us. Since we was kids. Always movin' us here and there. My man here, he got took, said Ruthie. He got took, I got took when I was seven, and put into institutions where we got the religion. The gubbers† did it.

What did they do that for? I said.

We was just sittin' around at home, said Rob, opening another beer. But they see us in our family and they say you're poor. You run around naked, barefoot. So you get took.

Where did they take you?

I can't really remember, but it comes to me in bits and pieces.

★ "Ferals are the people who stand up against the loggers," Rob had told me. "Hips are the people who deal [drugs]."
† "Governors:" white men.

Redfern, Sydney, New South Wales, Australia (1994)

R ob, who'd met his wife at the rehabilitation center, called himself a blackfella but he was pale golden in color, like any Caucasian surfer in Sydney or Honolulu or Santa Barbara. In 1688 William Dampier had described the aborigines he met as "coal black like . . . the Negroes of Guinea." The people Captain Cook found were dark brown. Maybe there is no such thing as race now, not really; so many Greenland Eskimos I met were blond and blue-eyed like their Danish fathers; my goodhearted D. is Thai but Thais sometimes think her black African; it seems to me that the most that can be said is that there are loose racial types which some people conform to and others live in between. I wish that I could bring back to life the juryman who addressed the press after acquitting seven whites of shooting and mutilating twenty-eight aborigines at Myall Creek in 1838: *I look on the blacks as a set of monkeys and the sooner they are exterminated from the face of the earth the better. I would never consent to hang a white man for a black one. I know well they were guilty of murder, but I for one would never see a white man suffer for shooting a black.* What would this man have made of Rob? The only way he could have known that Rob was black would have been if Rob had told him so.

They shanghaied him an' his wife, Sadie explained, they brought 'em from here to there.

'Cause once they take you to the institutions, they drum it all out of you, said Ruthie.

The language, it wasn't taught in our schools, said Sadie, drinking. And my grandmother, she wouldn't teach me, because it all ends in the white man's . . . — She trailed off.

So you don't remember anything from before?

Me an' him, we're still hunters, said Snake. Sit up in the tree, yes, you sit up in the trees waiting, then you jump off and catch that wallaby. An' cobra's good to eat. Good fish bait, too. Go to the river, look for the right kind of log. There's stinkin' logs and good ones.

Willow logs and gum tree logs, those are the good ones. Dive down, cut off the log, you can smell the snake inside. Cobras is musky tasting. They taste like the tree they live in. Smell the leaf of the tree, smell the cobra.

Tell him about that time you saw the snake, said Ruthie to her husband.

Oh, said Rob. (Paint was peeling from the bricks behind him where Ruthie's chair nudged the wall between their house and the next house along the Street of Stares.) — Well, one time I was out in the bush an' I run into a big lizard. An' I seen his eyeballs, an' I saw his *red*, and then I knew it wasn't a lizard, but a fifteen-foot-long snake, an' it chased me. It chased me 'til dark, when I got on the road. Once they feel that hot tar, they can't go no more.

I watched the other three listen to this small story, which they had surely heard before, and saw how it seemed to bring them alive for a moment. Ruthie leaned back laughing with her arms across her belly. There is a connection between native people and animals which never seems to be lost. What do they see; what do they know? This is something that those of us who do not have native blood will never understand. (There are many intuitive secrets like this. Rob, for instance, was a dot painter. I asked him how he'd learned. — It's not teach yourself, he said, it's in there. I can tell straight away if a Koorie★ fella's done it or some whitefella.) Something of this nature was occurring when Rob told the story of the snake. I have seen that same alertness and happiness enter the eyes of Canadian Inuit office managers, Ojibway prostitutes and Sioux panhandlers when somebody mentions a caribou, a beaver, a coyote, even an insect, and when I see it I envy those people because I do not have it. This was what Ruthie wanted to keep. — One time this big king cricket came in, she began. It was *this* big! It was lookin' at Rob.

An' she tell me to kill it, he said sourly.

Thank God we didn't kill it, because it was very rare.

That was the whole story, and then Sadie talked about how good wallabies tasted and Ruthie drank another V.B. and got sad again and said: Once they started feedin' the people on flour and treacle, we started gettin' fat. Before that there was no such thing as a fat aboriginal woman.

★ Aboriginal.

I got all that knocked out of me, said Rob with satisfaction. Eatin' all that junk food. They beat it right out of me. Now it don't tempt me.

Course we can't hunt what we want, either, said Ruthie. Like wallabies. Even though the government is killing those animals as pests, we get prevented.

It was about then that I understood that Ruthie with her pretty, mobile face was an ideologue, a militant. Everything she said was hard and inflexibly generalized. Oppression often seems to forge such people. Because the world they exist in is hostile, whatever analysis of their condition they build cannot be the graceful and perhaps unsound tower of the intellectual, who has the leisure and means to rebuild should some chance wind of malice or objective truth bring it down. People like Ruthie make fortresses of their convictions. They build guardedly, of heavy thoughts quarried from local reality. Her pure young face suffused itself with passion and sadness. She tried to sell me her T-shirt which said STOP BLACK DEATHS IN CUSTODY, but I didn't have any money left.

Redfern, Sydney, New South Wales, Australia (1994)

So when you get up in the morning, what do you do? I said.

Snake finished his V.B. and got the next. — Get up, he said, say hello to everyone, thank God we're still alive, that the pigs didn't kill us in our sleep.

The cops call it crime, said Ruthie. We call it survival.

Well, look, I said. (I was getting a little tired of her.) If things could be different, how would you want them to be?

Don't ask us that! cried Ruthie, leaping to her feet. We just want what belongs to us!

We never signed no treaty, man, said Rob, sitting there with his beer clasped between his parted knees, tanned, bearded and grim. And they just took our land. Once we can get our land back, maybe we can get something. Whatever we get, it's better than nothing.

What land will they give you back? my friend Jenny asked naively. Whatever they don't want.

We want land, said Ruthie greedily. We'd make money just like the fuckin' white people. Make us a million off that land.

Sadie smiled a little. — I'd buy a house, a car, and plant a *big* crop.*

I'd buy half a mountain and a river, said her husband quietly.

Why not just *give* us the mountain and the river? Ruthie shouted. It's ours.

She took the last V.B. in the case and popped it open. Then she whispered: They're gonna kill us, too. Just like everything else. We're gonna go extinct. Just like the animals.

No one said anything, and she drank half her beer in one go. Then she said: We don't come from monkeys. We're just here. We always were here, always will be.

After that, she poured the rest of the can down her throat.

So I walked up the Street of Stares, back toward Redfern Station where the sign said **DANGER: LIVE WIRE ABOVE,** and they watched me. (See how they visit and talk to each other here, Snake had said. In the rest of Sydney they can't sit and talk.) — They'd given me presents to remember them: a boomerang pulled off their wall, and a catalogue of a dot painting exhibition in which they'd inscribed their names for me. Below hers Sadie wrote TRUE BLUE KOORIE. Then Snake wrote AUSTRALIANS ABORIGINAL. — I followed the wall that was muraled with boomerangs and suns and dot-painted flowers, that long wall that led away from the Street of Stares, riddled with forests of muraled meaning, inscribed with swooping lines like the long furrows that ran down Snake's arm at the hilt of his blade of bony muscle. That was the wall that now hid me from all the addicts who tried to sell me boomerangs, from Sadie, who'd shown me a dot painting with its snakes and snails and coils, from Rob, now disappeared to get high, from Snake and Ruthie who sat looking at the empty case of beer.

* Of marijuana.

COWBELLS

Mont-Pellerin, Canton Vaudois, Switzerland (1992)
Mexico City, Distrito Federal, Mexico (1992)
Jaipur, India (1990)
Los Angeles, California, U.S.A. (1994)
Mexico City, Distrito Federal, Mexico (1992)
New York City and State, U.S.A. (1992)
Zagreb, Croatia (1992)
Split, Dalmatia, Croatia (1994)
Ban Rak Tai, Mae Hong Song Province, Thailand (1994)

Mont-Pellerin, Canton Vaudois, Switzerland (1992)

A steep land creaked with sap in the beech-green air. Ivy grew up the backs of trees, pretending to help them with lying green vertebrae, as meanwhile it sucked their strength. To live means both to strive like the ivy and to suffer like the trees. Dying unites both these elements in a painful struggle. Did the vegetation feel this? They say that plants and slaves do not feel. — Below tolled cowbells like a gamelon, rising through grasshoppers' seed-rattlings among the gone strawberries. Delicious green swellings of the mountain, those the ivy could not drain, but cows grazed them down to the thick. The cows scarcely moved, it seemed, but they ate all day, tearing off greenness with big bites. They gnawed more slowly than the lake-haze, which, hot and blue-white like the wrapper of a milk-chocolate bar, ate the summit, but of course what they gnawed on also took longer to grow back. Even as I watched, those mist-ringed hills of grass, flowers and cowshit (lake and sky both white) were regurgitated. The cows, on the other hand, did chew their cud sometimes, but the grass remained as short as a soldier's hair. Of course the cows' lives were passing. Bronze bells clanged. Now again squatted the haze like a red cow splayed down, gazing stupidly at nothing; once more the hills were lost, but the cowbells still rang. They told milkmaids where the cows were; they did not tell the cows anything. When John Donne wrote what I already knew, that my companions' death-knell is also mine, he failed to map out why I need to hear it. Perhaps the bell does not toll for me. Why not suppose that its real purpose is to keep God apprised of where I am, so that in His good time He can lead me into the slaughterhouse? Perhaps the inevitable needs no warning. That was why the cows' lives rang on and the cows did not listen.

Mexico City, Distrito Federal, Mexico (1992)

The dark bull ran through the ring with his horns lowered, leaving tracks in the brown sand. His life was ringing out. He jerked his head. It was only the first tercio. The banderilleros flared their lavender and yellow capes at him like dresses, so he charged, but they pivoted in place, baffling him repeatedly. He stopped, wanting to give up, and they annoyed him again, so he gored the weary old horse, which fell on its side without a groan. I wonder now whether the horse had followed the bull's movements with much attention; if so, there would have been no wisdom but that of fatalism. How severely the horse was hurt I don't know. I saw no good death. The banderilleros raised it back up again, and the picador in yellow remounted. Then came trumpet and drum. Most cattle die violently, so perhaps it would have been too much to expect a bell to call this bull to his fate; did he hear the inner bell yet or had the trumpet been no warning? Why should we be warned? The bull hornswiped the cloth away from a picador. He leaped, lowered his head, swished his tail. Everyone whistled with happiness.

One banderillero backed away; the other rushed in and threw the first two darts. The first dart came out; the second hung in flesh. The bull jumped. The man threw two more darts. The bull turned, watched, began to switch his tail. What was he to do? His life stood hardly in his power. The man skipped closer to the bull. The bull lowered his head. The man stabbed the darts in.

Came the trumpet and drum, the matador with red (the silver dagger hidden always behind the red cloth). The bull sought red, found nothing. Did he know yet? The matador thrust across the colored horns. The bull jerked and turned in a confused frenzy at this man with the red cloth. Pink blood ran down the bull's neck. The matador closed on him, pacing deliberately in pink stockings. The bell tolled. Yes, after all there was a cowbell. The bull reminded me more and more of the horse that he had gored. He stood lowering his weary head, gazing at yellow cloth spattered with his blood; and perhaps he was acute enough not to molest his own death by giving a sign of bellicosity or pain which might have suggested that anything could have been done. All gathered around him like advance mourners. Finally he fell. Three funeral horses came plodding. A chain went under his carcass, then the trio dragged him around the ring and out.

Jaipur, India (1990)

Listen to the bells. I prefer to imagine my death as a dancer in silver and gold, her eyes painted with long tails which extend slyness all the way to her cheeks. Her face is plump and pale, her lips very red, succulently moist. Her anklets are thick with bells. She stamps her foot on the marble floor with a noise like a gunshot.

She can tremble so that the bells shimmer and hiss on her ankles, although her legs do not seem to move. She kisses her hand to me, slices the air with her arms. In her face, a joyfully cruel expression of utter mastery and possession. The music of her silver bracelets ravishes me. But does anyone think that the moment before the three horses drag me away will not be hideous?

Los Angeles, California, U.S.A. (1994)

One very hot afternoon in Los Angeles, Korean Jenny and I had come into her mother's house which soon would be someone else's house because the mortgage payments didn't make sense anymore and so the bank was about to foreclose; and because it was so hot, Jenny had had a margarita with me at one of those Mexican restaurant chains; and now she wanted to lie down. She slept. I was bored. After a long time, I laid my head down on her breast. I put my lips on her soft golden throat; and at once I could feel her pulse hurrying her on through life, rushing her and ringing her by so many emphatic little steps (like the clicks of her high heels) toward death. Not being able to hear my own pulse, I felt left behind. Every one of those powerful heartbeats of hers seemed to be pushing her farther away from me, so that I could see the time coming when I'd be alone on that beige carpet looking past the rubber plant into the mirror of emptiness at the base of the stairs. I got up and sat on the sofa. Now I only heard her breathing—a respiration fullhearted and trusting, accepting of the destiny which she'd fight screaming when it came.

Mexico City, Distrito Federal, Mexico (1992)

The next bull came shooting into our sadistic world, a meteor of dread and hairy rage, galloping in the useless circles to which the ring constrained him, turning and twitching, his anger some hideous snaky thing of shells and teeth strung on a dried intestine. But he could never touch the picador. Next came the old horse again—an easier victim, so the bull rushed to gore his fellow creature's side again and again. The banderilleros arrived with their darts. The bull's front legs dug in the dirt. Sometimes, once in a great while, he got his horns into a banderillero's cape, which they'd convinced him was the soul of his tormentors, but once he'd thrust, it crumpled to nothing.

The matador swaggered in, folding up his cape so calmly. I heard the trumpet and the drum. The bull charged, missed. (Turn the continent sideways, and it becomes a leaping bull, the Aleutians its horn, Central America its tail; it is springing down upon the Queen Elizabeth Islands.) A disdainful corner flick, and the bull went for it. He heard the bell, and was the bitterer for it. No one can say that he beseeched. That was why the crowd cheered. The matador scarcely moved. Again and again the bull was baffled. The matador swung his hip and turned the cloth away. Slowly he strode closer, the red cloth up in the air, making the bull gaze high. He pivoted at the center of the world, the bull his great doomed satellite.

The bull's head lowered to the red cloth. The feathered lances danced in his sides as he whirled. His tongue hung out; his back and sides were crusted white.

Finally the matador dropped the cloth contemptuously on the bull's mouth and the crowd beat pots and pans, waving their hats. He stood back and knelt before the bull. They shouted *ahh!* and leaped to their feet as he shoved the knife in! They waved papers and handkerchiefs until the bull fell. They awarded the matador the ears.

Men with spades came to clean up the manure and the blood. Around the ring they threw sombreros and jackets. Exuberant, the matador hurled them back. As he went around the ring, a snowstorm of sombreros and shirts came, even a wineskin. He strode to the center of the ring, fell on his knees. Then he rode out on his admirers' shoulders.

The bull lay on the sand. He had now transcended the icy white barrier to understanding established by silver (pitchers of silver and abalone; weirdly gray mirrors of silver: all colors appear in those mirrors, but half-obscured as by angular white sparks of preciousness); some silver has a yellow gleam, but the edge of a silver bowl seems pure white . . . They came and pulled the lances out. The three funeral horses dragged him around the ring. He made a track in the dirt.

New York City and State, U.S.A. (1992)

So we know about ivy and trees, but what if the ivy were mere wires; what if the trees were only square white pillars in the dimness between trains; what if the leaves were incandescent lights? Then the forest would be light-spangled darkness, lit the way my legs glowed luminous green under a certain bar. Then I'd know I was in New York. Outside of this forest other died trees whose wiry roots dangled down like ivy over the concrete wall of the parking lot. The Hudson River was a root boring past the chilly eastern towns whose wall-bricks were a pathwork of dirty colors. I'd thought I was going to go outside the city often but then I didn't because whenever I started planning that I got a bad feeling about it—usually after I remembered those dying trees. So instead I visited the dog poisoner.

He was not an evil man at all; he possessed rules. The dog had to have annoyed him more than once. People needed to have treated him badly at the same time. There could be no risk to him. Those conditions being met, he'd lay down the strychnined meat.

The dog would bolt that food, crunching bones between yellow teeth. The poison was in the best parts, the fatty parts. First the dog would stretch out, happily gnawing the last thick bone. Then suddenly it would cock its head. It raised its ears, listening alertly to the bells which only it could hear. Something was happening or had just begun to happen which the dog did not understand yet because the growling whimpering convulsions had not begun. The dog knew only that what was happening was extremely important. It chewed no bone; clanged the bronze bells of death.

Zagreb, Croatia (1992)
Split, Dalmatia, Croatia (1994)

Thus far I've written as if the bells never lied, as if the appearance of that sound, whether silvery or iron (as Poe would put it), was invariably more than rhetorical—as if, in short, supernatural law were quite simple. But one summer's night we walked past the scraping and squeaking of the long narrow streetcar (it's very old, Adnan said, it's not Amsterdam!) and duly arrived at the marble and glass ice cream bar which gleamed with glasses on glass shelves, which gleamed mirrors. A redhead and a brunette in slatey uniforms lived behind the counter, the brunette sloshing a foamy ice-coffee in her hand, then stirring, the redhead slowly drying glasses until they gleamed with late night brilliance from behind their marble bastion with its trays of filled ashtrays and dirty coffee cups. I was in one of those moments of suspension, hence susceptibility to the supersensible, because Francis and Adnan were chatting in Serbo-Croatian, which I didn't understand; so first I looked at the redhead, who ignored me; then I gazed upon the brunette, who scowled and glared; and then I sat drinking my mineral water (thirstily, because it was a very sultry September) and I listened to the bells. They'd rung me through that afternoon's long blocky buildings, each with its blue street-plaque on a corner; and I remembered the hot gush of window-air in the taxi, my back beginning to sweat in the bulletproof vest within the gray hideaway windbreaker (which two years later would be claimed by Francis's murderers in Mostar; I left that; I remembered almost everything else). I wasn't thinking about Mostar. The taxi driver kept shaking his head when he heard I was going to Sarajevo. Francis had decided not to go because it was too dangerous. We'd turned past the Red Cross van, down pastel-yellow-facaded streets. Still that heavy soggy summer feeling. Everyone was sitting under the cigarette-branded awnings.

The driver had been in a battle. They'd had to pull back.

Is Dubrovnik safe? I said.

Not yet.

Can I buy a gun?

Nobody will do that for you. Everybody's afraid.

Anyway, said the driver abruptly, the worst thing I've ever seen wasn't a battle; it was a traffic accident.

It was then, and again that night in the ice cream bar, that I heard John Donne's bell tolling for me, warning and prophesying with ominous gloom; Francis had heard it, too, and taken more heed than I. He awaited my return from Sarajevo. One might say that whoever disregards the bells believes in absolute freedom; and yet I tell you most truthfully that later that night I could not sleep because I was so certain that the morrow would introduce me to my death; and yet I was powerless to avoid going. I saw the end as surely as when I awaited the arrival of Francis's family in Split two years later; no one could decide when the funeral would be, and the family could not come for three or four days yet, so I stood watching a procession dedicated to Dule, the patron saint of Split; waiting for the end to flash wittily through this celebration of Christian peace; hymns shrilled through the loudspeakers and white-robed men with red crosses on their hems strode forward with their arms folded. Now here came the nuns and little children; there marched the dignitaries of the church; I saw the palanquin of the icon—so many people were singing! Here were the police, there more nuns, now an old lady with a flower; and then at last came the real force, the boys in camouflage behind their general . . . *They* knew; they called the tune on that sunny windy evening of bells. And when I'd lain on the floor of

Adnan's room that other night earlier, Francis snoring softly on the couch, I thought and believed that in only a few hours I would *see* and I would *know*; I would meet my end! And I was terrified. I lay with a dry throat, wishing that I didn't have to go. And of course I didn't have to. Nobody was forcing me to go. And yet I couldn't not go. Whatever sent me to Sarajevo and whatever preserved me were not my own forces. And the next day only a yellowjacket stung me; the sniper's bullet missed my ankle by a good six inches. So I lived on, in a kind of unbelieving unreality, and Francis lived on in safety; it was only next time that we went to Mostar. And that day neither of us heard any echoing ringing; and I lived and Francis died.

Near Ban Rak Tai, Mae Hong Song Province, Thailand (1994)

What to say, then, but that those bells mark the intervals of our lives, and nothing more; that those strange sensations of disquiet that we get, "as if something were walking on our graves," are simply what we feel upon being reminded of the obvious fact that life is the one disease for which there is a cure? Aren't those Swiss cows better off not listening? — Well, I learned another clanging lesson when the black-pajama'd driver took D. and me between the green windmills of banana fronds, with cliffs of naked rock and dry jungle above. A pyramid of blue-green rock burst up out of the forest-grown earth-cliffs.

He believe in ghost religion, D. reported. Very funny! They have celebration for ghost. They put something in the floors of their houses. If you have five person, they put five chicken and five meat in the door. If you have five man, you can have the chicken. If you have two woman, you can have the sex change. No, I see. Meat for man, chicken for women.

It was not so very clear. But then D., bless her, was not wildly fluent in English. The boy drove us down a road of trees, into a sun-exploding valley with misty jungle ridges ahead.

After all women playing together, we share chicken, D. translated. All women have some something they put in bamboo in chicken legbone to see their destiny. Then all the women can look inside to tell you. But just now the young people they don't know.

The boy smiled very quickly.

He afraid for ghosts, said D. If they have some fever or diarrhea, they think from ghost.

What color is a ghost? I said.

From his idea, he think ghost is a yellow color.

What about my dead sister? Can she hurt me?

He says impossible. If you do good thing, then she can never hurt you.

But I dream of her skeleton, I explained. (Francis had not been killed yet. His skeleton had not yet joined hers.)

Oh. Yes. That was her ghost . . .

Now rusty leaves hung above that road of yellow ocher; when other trucks came the dust was as thick as fog. We turned into a valley between dry brown rice terraces and saw the village. This was where people began to have Chinese faces. Just past a small wooden house, a woman was walking down the steep road, bearing an immense conical basket of twigs on her back. A reddish girl with mud or soot on her temple suckled a child who tranquilly wriggled his dirty toes.

In the rainy season he can't drive, said D. Then ghosts fly all around.

The driver lived in a very long big house behind a barrier of earth. He took us inside, while his young wife sat outside with her knees together and her heels braced far apart, wiping her nose and embroidering red diamonds and borders on white cloth on her black vest with yellow lightning borders which had consanguinity with the red and blue and pink stars on the black sleeves; and so many tiny triangles of color within color; and piglets went all around, chasing chickens; her long black hair fell down to her back.

We saw a pile of dusty pumpkins, pale like apples of dust; we saw a sleeping platform with mosquitoes everywhere. There was dusty sun in the windows. That was his house; that was the dark house.

I wondered: Can a ghost wear a straw hat? Can a ghost smoke a pipe of sugarcane?

In that dark house there was a long wide place, all ash. Baskets and stone lived on the mats. On the wall, a white paper with V-shaped perforations forming a cross.

It's god of Hmong, said D. This ghost. You put table under it and then chicken.

Ask him if the ghost will warn him when it's time for him to die.

He says yes. He say put special something in bamboo in meat legbone to understand his destiny. Then ghost come.

How many ghosts are here now?

Million million.

And what do they say?

The driver came closer, smiled in the thick jacket, looked sadly and searchingly into D.'s eye as she leaned toward him while a fat pullet waddled between them. I stared at a sandy-colored cat licking itself and stretching in the sand. He uttered something with great effort. D. translated: He say, ghosts speak everybody die, die like plant, like grass, like leaf. So soon we die. Ghost say we warn you because we want you afraid. If always afraid for ghost, ghost very happy. Because ghost very jealous already die. Ghost speak like bell, *ring ring ring!* Because then you can be afraid. If afraid, you same same ghost. Very funny, eh?

Mahebourg, Mauritius (1993)

Mahebourg, Mauritius (1993)

A man's brown knees flexed steadily above the sea, and then they vanished. He pulled his shirt high above his underpants. His waist vanished. He continued on past three rowboats and began to emerge again. A name waited to be born from his mouth. The ocean was astonishingly hot, shallow and bright in that place behind reefs, and the other fishermen who were rooted in it gleamed and sparkled with this liquid light which now peeled so evenly from his legs as he approached a sandy islet where there was no imperfection. His waist came back to air, then his knees, and finally the very bottoms of his feet shone as he lifted them, walking across the islet to a man in a pink-orange shirt who stood casting in time with the cadence of my sleepy eyelashes as I sat in a shady tree, my tree-leaves green and cool and bobbing like breasts. The man began to laugh with happiness when he reached the one in the pink-orange shirt. He shouted: Eddy!

Eddy, his sack filled with small fish, presently waded back into the hot green morning of yawning puppies where a dingy called *Venus* lay upturned beside a wall on which a schoolgirl had written MON AMOUR. Another fisherman rode by on his bike, his plastic bag full of minnows; he smiled and called out: Eddy!

Inside the Chinese dry goods store the men shook hands *salut!*, their faces proudly raised. They cried: Eddy! They sat back down on

upended crates, smoking cigarettes, looking out the bright doorway
at dark girls in yellow sundresses who rushed past under parasols. The
boy with the naked silver mermaid on his jacket smiled dreamily, and
Eddy laughed and cuffed him.

A girl in a blue skirt entered silently like cool water. She swung
toward the counter to greet the fat old Chinese lady, and her skirt
whirled, spilling frilliness down her thighs so that the boy with the
silver mermaid could see the mesh of the door right through it. Eddy
had been sitting in front of the display case. He stood up at once.
The girl in blue smiled at him. The glass pane moved soundlessly in
his hand. The girl nodded, and his arm sank into the world of treasures. I remembered how in the hot wet night that smelled like leaves,
a man and a woman in a yellow skirt had gone wading in the shallow
sea, fishing with lantern and net, and the changing light formed the
reverse of shadows on their bodies as they walked almost splashlessly
in the knee-deep water, casting their hunter's light between boats.
Eddy and the girl in the blue skirt were like that now; for the girl
stalked parasols, pointing to every one in turn, and Eddy reached
inside the glass and handed them to her, nodding respectfully at every
word she murmured while the old Chinese lady behind the counter
looked on sleepily, fanning herself with a fan of many colored ideo-
grams. His friends sat drinking the beers that he had bought them,
and they gazed out the doorway at the girls walking by in a jingle of
morning silver. They did not look at the girl in blue anymore because
she would have felt them looking, which would not have been polite.
She held the red parasol, then the blue one, then the green one with
gold flowers on it. Eddy fished for whatever she wanted. When she
decided that the green one was prettiest, he told her how much it
was, helped her count out her rupees, took them in hand, and brought
them over to the counter for the old lady. The girl in blue thanked
him. She stepped back into the day, where it was proper for Eddy's
friends to admire her again. They saw her open her new parasol and
go in shadeful delight.

Eddy visited the dry goods store every morning and every night.
He knew where everything was. He helped the old lady for nothing
because he felt so free in that place.

OK, Eddy! laughed his friends. It was already eleven. They sucked the last lukewarm swallows from the bottles whose labels each depicted a phoenix so skinny and jointed that it should have been a spider. The Chinese lady was snoring when they went out. Along the main street people leaned up against hot gratings or sat on bicycles or stood mahogany-footed in sandals (some women in silver anklets), because it was the day of the Tamil procession. Eddy and the boys were on the corner. They sat on railings, tapping cigarettes against scarred hands. Children came out and called: Eddy!

A child cried out, a cry without language. Eddy froze. They could see the Tamils coming, still far away, a crowd of them creeping from beneath the horizon-tree. A policeman headed them; then came the advance men wheeling an altar draped with many cloths, a cave of colors in which something burned in a coconut. A car blooming with yellow pennants shouted religious music, followed by many men in white robes who came clacking purple sticks together. After them came the ones whom everyone waited to see. They too were singing and clapping, bearing altars which expressed the holiest pictures, altars roofed with arches of flowers and bananas; they were the men whose mouths were pierced and hung with chains, whose tongues were penetrated by silver hooks, whose cheeks were perforated just like those of the fishes that Eddy caught; they were the men with spikes sunk into their waists and backs and chests, the men hung with limes, carrying the heavy wooden altars past the old one in sandals who'd scraped the paint of *Venus* down smooth (a pod shot down into the painted boat with a boom, and he opened his eyes; already the day was half gone). Behind and around were the ladies of each family, dressed in their best saris, anklets and bracelets sharing the jingling swing of their men's silver chains against bellies and lips, the men wearing purple loincloths, carrying the heavy altars like Christs carrying crosses. They gazed straight ahead as they came. They were a part of the world to whom Eddy meant nothing. They recognized their own gods, felt them in their flesh. Across the street stood the girl in the blue skirt, shaded by her new parasol; to her also Eddy was invisible at this moment. She watched the mutilated men with a look of almost pleading concentration. She needed to understand what made them do this thing to themselves, and she could not. Most of the other spectators no longer asked. They had watched this twice each year for as long as they'd lived. It was something to be seen without being understood, just as a husband sees his wife give birth again and yet again so that her pain is too expected to be comprehensible anymore. Now came the priest with the book, attended by singing ladies in parasols, and then the man with so many hooks in his back that he glittered like a scaly trout, then the man with spiked combs in his thighs and a spiked sun of silver in his chest, his altar enriched by peacock tails, leaves and flowers. So they walked the quiet streets of shade-trees and whitewashed walls. The last altar took fourteen days to make. As it came, people clapped and cried: *Ohhh!*

After the young boy with a single dagger through his cheeks, came the man with the great temple of flowers on his shoulders, his spikes heavy with lemons and limes. The man's feet staggered steadily on shoes of spikes. He was a man pinned full of limes and bells; he lurched along, his temple canted with agony and weariness. One couple laid their sick daughter down in the middle of the street, the mother running ahead to hose it clean. The child was wide-eyed and silent. He, the one with silver spiked shoes hooked into the backs of his calves, he stepped dreamily over her, frothy-mouthed. Again and again they snatched her up and stretched her down before him to be healed. Who was the sacrifice? Once she looked into Eddy's face; but then her eyes swam back to her savior with his bloodless wounds.

Afterwards the Tamils gave juice and water to all, and the brownish-green sea rolled in like sleep.

He went home and his wife ran out, threw her arms around his neck, and laughed: Eddy! — He kissed her. And all afternoon the world greeted him again.

In the evening he sat on the cool sidewalk where his little children ate bowls of rice and milk, uttering his name in transports of pleasure while he smiled lovingly, and two kittens watched the milk, and then a boy came running in with an octopus he'd caught in a coffee can, the dead creature milky-pale in the darkness. The son and daughter babbled to their father, chewing rice, peeking into the coffee can, and the octopus's silence grew louder and louder.

After he stopped by the dry goods store for a Phoenix beer or two, Eddy sat smoking and drinking with his friends on the beach. There were so many stars. Eddy pointed. He knew exactly where the moon would be at ten, where at eleven, and so on through the night. And yet the stars did not address him, the sea did not speak to him. The woman in the yellow skirt was lantern-fishing with her husband. Knee-deep in the salty night, they called to Eddy, but the sea made mysteries of their speech.

SAY IT
WITH FLOWERS

Bangkok, Phrah Nakhon-Thonburi Province, Thailand (1993)

In Pat Pong there was a long crowded alley filled with lips on signs and girls, filled with hands on trembling beers, and in that alley there was a bar where the ladies laughed but always went back to doing their receipts, and among those ladies a deaf and dumb girl was making up her face very slowly, bending over a mirror not much larger than a fingernail, with her pigtail almost down to her waist. I did not see her at first. I saw a delicious-buttocked prostitute on a barstool giggling *I wuv you* to an Australian who had a paunch. I saw two white-teethed barmaids gazing outside, their fingers on the counter. I saw the eyeshine of their intelligence. *Where you saleep?* the girl was saying to the Australian.

Beside her, an older woman swiveled on the barstool to show me some thigh, I think because I had closed the doors and rung the bell which meant that I'd just bought every girl in the bar a drink.

This was not one of those bars where music's mountainous loudness reared and crashed inside my bones, where lights shot colors round and round, where the theme was gaiters and buttocks and weird lingerie, all the better to flash lust red along those legs and breasts illuminated like roast chickens on a rotisserie. — Nor was it one of those bars that were so dark that you could not see the women's faces, maybe because they were so sad, and the women touched their lips and touched the zipper of your pants and said: OK I smoke you OK? — This bar had neither dancers nor fellators. It was a small, quiet place whose girls wore T-shirts or long formal dresses. Just above the whiskey bottles, small bat-winged fishes swam in bottles of water in which seedlings grew forests of fantastic roots and above which they uttered huge lion-toothed leaves. The fishes flickered, the air conditioner imparted steadiness, and the girls sat as peacefully immobile as basking lizards. It was my favorite bar. If I wanted to, I could sit there and read a newspaper all afternoon and no one would ask me for anything. The Australian was asking to be asked. I was not. That was why the older woman and I carried on a duet of mere politeness. She showed me thigh, as I mentioned, so to compliment her I raised my glass and cried: I pay for you one thousand baht!*

No no I forty-four you thirty-four I like you same son same *student!* Me ten husband already! I *Mama* you!

OK, I pay for you ten thousand baht.

No no no.

OK, I said, my duty ended, and as I turned away I saw the deaf and dumb girl in the corner, bowed over her thumbnail of a mirror.

She could speak only in a series of cries which resembled those of a woman reaching orgasm.

Drowning accident, a barmaid said. She get water in her ears. After that, she never speak or hear again. Crazy in the head.

Walking over to her corner, I saw her lipsticking herself with graceful untiring insect motions. The other girls were sipping their Scotches, sodas and fizzy waters, but she had nothing. I wanted to be her friend.

She can have a drink, too, I said. I promised you I'd pay for everyone.

---

* About U.S. $40. Although in 1993 some bars in Pat Pong charged 1,500 baht or more for a girl, a small establishment such as this one would have asked between 300 and 500.

OK, sir, never mind, said the barmaid.

I put my arm around her and bought her a Coke.

She she she want speak with you, but she cannot, said the barmaid.

Stroking her waist-length hair, I drew a heart on a sheet of paper, and she uttered a cry of joy. She wrote: *I like you.* — I kissed her hands, and she pretended to push me away.

I gave her my pen, and she drew a flower, and then a long-beaked bird. I drew a flower, too. For an hour we constructed a garden on that greasy piece of paper, and she made that strangely happy noise of hers. Our flowers twined and gathered like the roots that the bat-winged fishes swam between, and we crafted each petal with the care of a reputable goldsmith because we owed all the responsibilities of citizenship to this world of ours which we were crowding with green-ness and lemony-smelling bushes (on each, a single yellow flower). In the center of that world we made a country where her shy spirit could dwell in the tea-dark shadows of tree-tendons. Have you ever seen the cloud-forests around Chiang Rai? Our country was steeper than those (that sheet of paper being a sheer white wall) and lusher, its hills bursting with wet leaves and trees bulging and bowing under the weight of their own fecundity. Together we drew our bananas and breadfruits, our red and blue blossoms scented with the sweetish smell of her lipstick. We raised throat-high grasses and the spider-webbed darknesses between flowers, penning in each stamen with a steady loving stroke. I made for her a flowering banana's petals folded back (stubby peels they were, with white bananas inside). Smiling faintly, she thickened the hills with green lace that was delicious like her beloved frothy spit. Finally I presented her with a Virginia meadow beauty, four petaled, pink like her lipstick, whose antlers of a buttery gold reached down to cool the backs of her hands. She moaned in delight.

But the next time I went to that bar, the lady who'd had ten husbands said: Your darling no come today. Hurt her leg motorcycle accident. Hospital. Never go back here. So. You buy me, ten thousand baht?

Never mind, I said. But I'll buy you a drink.

After I'd paid I got up and went to the corner where the deaf and dumb girl had sat. There was a lipsticked napkin, almost certainly not hers, which I turned over, half hoping to find a flower ballpointed on the other side; of course there wasn't anything. It was only a variation of the game I'd played with the woman who had ten husbands, the sad game of searching for something known not to be there.

A few days later, a friend of mine visited that bar. He told me that she was back. He assured me that he'd seen, touched and danced with her. And that wasn't all. He'd found another bar in the same alley, a better and friendlier bar where the drinks were cheaper and he'd met two beautiful deaf and dumb girls, one of whom was a midget. He highly recommended the midget. He said that lately he'd begun to notice deaf and dumb girls everywhere. They were discreet and they were cheap. I myself never saw them.

It would be an exaggeration to claim that every day I thought upon the one I had cared for, but sometimes I wished that I could be with her just an instant, just to make her utter for me that cry which I had so greatly longed to believe expressed perfect happiness.

THE RIFLES

Montréal, Québec, Canada (1993)
Inukjuak, Québec, Canada (1990)
Montréal, Québec, Canada (1993)
Eureka Sound, Ellesmere Island, Northwest Territories, Canada (1988)
Montréal, Québec, Canada (1993)
Montréal, Québec, Canada (1993)

Montréal, Québec, Canada (1993)

They caught baby birds and held them. One bird they passed too many times among them and it ended up with a broken wing. They threw it repeatedly into the air to see if it could fly, but it only tumbled crazily down into the moss, flapping its good wing in desperate silence. Finally they dropped it into the campfire. They did that where life was green and muddy and stony in late July; they did it on their low brown mass of island with its pale-eyed lakes and skinny long wispy streaks of snow across gullies and mounds; they did it in their streaky whiteness between capes, but he'd done it down south with Reepah, picking her up one time too many so that she loved him and couldn't fly away, then dropping her and when her wing got better seizing her again. He'd never drop her, though, never. Besides, she'd started it.

He felt terribly nervous and gloomy as he waited for Reepah at the airport. She was now above the blue and green squares and rectangles of fields half hidden by bright northern clouds (small irregular puddles of forest among them); now if she looked down she'd see the lovely indigo of the Saint Lawrence River mirroring clouds between the pincers of its islets where the river darkened between the flat gray bellies of thunderheads; it partook of the wide grace of rivers suddenly tinged by hot dark clouds.

Thank you for Montréal, she said.

It was a July day, a sunny day of rain in Montréal. The maple trees sparkled. Red trucks were so red and the fresh girls as bright as wet stones, striding umbrellaless in the rain.

She wanted him to buy her cigarettes. She said: Secrets is my best friend.

She didn't really want to talk to him or be with him. When they met a drunken Inuk lady on Rue Sainte-Catherine, Reepah talked with her for hours. Him she ignored.

She wanted him to buy her beers until she got drunk. He didn't want to. She looked at him with a hard and nasty viciousness he'd never seen before and shouted: You want to fuck me tonight? If you want to fuck me, I want drunk. I want *drunk!*

Fine, he said. You don't have to fuck me at all. I'll get you drunk and you can do whatever you want.

After her second or third beer she got louder and happier and she said: I like you. 'Cause I'm drunk.

Every few blocks some spectacle would come out of the summer darkness, like the fantastically roofed houses shooting steep and narrow above the dark street. Purple-plumed clowns mimed by candlelight. They passed the fountain where Reepah had wanted to swim in the afternoon, and she didn't remember it. Everybody was sitting around it; its water fell with a glow; and people sat on the grass listening to musicians and smelling the sweet summer night. Reepah dipped her hand in and wanted to go get drunk. Fullbreasted girls in sundresses floated on the grass's emerald darkness. On the lighted cobblestones a pancake-made-up twelve-year-old was singing humorous French ballads in an exaggerated mincing voice while her father played the guitar; then suddenly the songs grew serious and he could tell that she had a magnificent voice. Reepah smiled faintly for the first moment. Then she sat scratching and staring at her empty beer.

The musicians (who were really astoundingly good) got everybody clapping, so she clapped; in those marble mirrored morgues of blue-lit soundproofed sex bars at first she smiled with naughty delight to see naked boys and girls but soon enough she sat picking her teeth morosely between beers (each of which lasted seconds), and her lower lip gaped slightly wider at the flash of genitals or the applause of the other drinkers but then her black eyes would gaze into some particularly monotonous version of zero. And then a beautiful dancer might move in beautiful ways and she would stare steadily, leaning forward, maybe trying to be beautiful in the way the dancer was (the dancers usually thought that Reepah was a boy), trying to learn what made this other soul the center of attention in a way she could never be. When she was happy, when he bought her another beer, she cried: *Aw-riiiiiiiiiiiiiiiiigh'!*

If you don't like me, it's OK, he said. I'll give you some money for the hotel and then go away. Yes or no?

I don't know, she wrote on a piece of paper.

Reepah, I love you.

Same here, she wrote.

Reepah, I want you happy. I want everything for you.

I like Montréal. I am sad I don't have money.

Don't be sad. I don't have much money but I'll give you a little bit.

I want some beer, please.

In our room at the hotel, he said, not wanting to have to get her at the police station.

Way not read now? I am sick. I am tired.

They went walking late after midnight down to Chinatown and then back up the hill to Sherbrooke Street and she cried: Wow! Look at those lights! Just like good orange Inukjuak berries!

That was about the only time she sounded happy over anything but beer. He had wanted to give her something good and she had wanted to come there, but nothing that came from him could reach her, not even Montréal's streets, which were a guitar of light.

Inukjuak, Québec, Canada (1990)

Thirty or forty feet high, and therefore up in the clouds, a small lake had been set in rock by God. The rapids from this made a foamy white fall as soft and pure as caribou hair. Crowberries, grasses and lichens grew on and between the rock shapes around the pool, so that the grayness of the place was softened by green, red and yellow. A cool wind blew away some of the clouds like smoke, leaving zones of blue as sweet as anything in Italy. It seemed here above the bog of caribou skulls (the place so lovely with grass-antlers nodding even on foam-sprayed rock) that the foreverness of the Barren Lands was something lovely like the eternal echo of a bell—something secret, too, like whatever sensibility she had—her consciousness or integrity, both of which were either eroding or else withdrawing from his like those shrinking clouds.

In the lake itself, just where the falls commenced, rose a low rock-island, faceless like an irregular crystal (in other words, shaped just like any other rock-mass hereabouts), and it was close enough to the bank that a strong man might be able to leap onto it. He was not a strong man but he wasn't weak, either. On that day when he had walked away from Reepah's house because they loved each other in a sad and terrible way that made her steal his blue pills until she passed out snoring while the baby cried and shat on the floor, he proposed a contest with himself to see if he could reach that rock with a running lunge—the loser being by definition he who missed, and was therefore whirled down the rapids. He landed on the rock, had no sensation of winning, paced awhile, turned, jumped back, and missed, of course. For an instant, just before the cold water got him, he saw Reepah's face shining as if in darkness, watching him with hurt black eyes, her lips slightly parted as if she were about to scream in pain and terror. Then the falls had him, and every stone he grabbed slipped out of his hands, and he was thumped and choked and chilled and bruised all the way down. It was a warm and windy day, so when he got out he didn't shiver much. He walked back to Reepah's house, squish-squish-squish . . .

Montréal, Québec, Canada (1993)

Reepah?
Reepah, why did you come to Montréal with me?
I don't know.
Reepah, today you don't talk to me. So I get afraid you don't like me.
I want drunk.
You don't like me. You only like drunk.

She was clapping all by herself on the balcony, smiling and nodding and in the street below her people were beginning to jump up and down in the happiness that the music gave them and the musicians were stamping their feet and dry ice smoked in all colors from the stage and the musicians whirled their arms and everyone went: *Aaaaaah!*

Aah, whispered Reepah on the balcony, not looking at him.

The next morning she slept until checkout time, and when he woke her up so that he wouldn't have to pay for another day she cried: *Aaah!* Doan' wake up me! I'm hot. I doan' like you.

Eureka Sound, Ellesmere Island, Northwest Territories, Canada (1988)

Before he ever met Reepah he'd been farther north at summer's end where the ripples in the leads flowed like chevrons, like herringbones. At the edge of a gray ice-islet, slush crumbled steadily into the water with a hissing noise.

In the evening there was a pencil-thick line of clear sky across the fjord, and he could see the white streak of ice in the middle and the white and brown land to the south, amputated miraculously flat and even by the fog-knife, and a steady steam noise came from the weather station, the buildings and petrol towers standing silhouetted in the fog like a great city. A streetlight glowed in front of the dome of the H building, and other lights glowed behind it—as his joy would do in Inukjuak when she held him sleeping in the tent with the baby between them; when she actually loved and trusted him. A truck rolled across the red and blue pontoon bridge. It was the Inuk handyman again taking him and many friendly soldiers to the dump to feed slops to the wolves, but there was only one fox and one seagull and the soldiers stood with their cameras dangling in disappointment. They were scheduled to fly to Alert on the thirteenth and back to Ottawa on the fifteenth. They worried about the pastries, wishing that they could lose twenty pounds. (Shivering in his tent, he wished that he could gain twenty pounds. It was very gray in there and he could see his breath and his iron-frozen boots hurt to touch.)

He was at the end of a long journey, waiting for the supply plane to come and take him home. He'd been far from the soldiers in a country that began with a lake which was a gray mirror the color of the sky, with nothing else but a low ridge-horizon. From this lake he'd walked up the ridge that was very snowy and white and gently treacherous because he could not see the top of it in the fog (although he kept thinking that he could), and half-frozen tussocks burst out of it, half-soft, but crushed hard and slippery so that his feet glided off and fell hard in an ankle-deep snowhole, over and over, every few steps. Reepah never fell when she was sober. A low ridge of cloud circumnavigated him. Pastel-white mountains pulsed in the yellow light. It was 26° F. Half a month later he'd come back and the gray lake was frozen. He'd wanted to drink from it before. It was suppertime, and he was thirsty so he chopped a piece out and melted it on his stove. It tasted like burned desolation. He was lonely but not yet thinking of Reepah because he didn't know her, and he wasn't thinking of the lake in Inukjuak because he hadn't been there; later he'd say to himself: those two lakes were the same. They were one lake, the lake of my wrongdoing. What did I do wrong?

Montréal, Québec, Canada (1993)

I love my Reepah.
   I love you, too. I want more beer, please. Thanks for beer. I
want boyfriend in Montréal.
I'm your boyfriend in Montréal.
I want it.

Montréal, Québec, Canada (1993)

The night before she went back home she sat with him on the hotel balcony gazing down into nothing and when he asked her if she liked the parade that was going on below them she worked her lower lip and nodded and that was all; she'd virtually given up speaking. Only in the middle of the night when she woke up drunk would she say anything; usually she'd laugh and say: I want to kill myself. — Why? he'd say. — Because I hate myself. — Why? — I don't know. — Then they had another fight because she wanted him to buy a bottle of vodka for her to take back and he'd said OK but since it was Sunday all the *Sociétés des alcools* were closed and the grocery stores didn't have it. She didn't understand, and blamed him. He'd bought her a sixpack of beer as a consolation prize but that wasn't good enough anymore although she'd been drinking nothing else the whole time except for ginger ale; every night at about two or three she'd wake him up by tickling him and then demand one beer, one cigarette and one ginger ale; all she'd enjoyed doing was going to more sex clubs, getting drunk and wishing she were beautiful enough to be a stripper, too. No, the sixpack wasn't good enough. She kept saying in that new hard and angry voice: *You stupid. You stupid.* — For the first time in the years he'd known her he felt rage. He opened one of the bottles and poured it down the toilet. — Don't call me stupid anymore, he said.

You stupid.

He poured out the second bottle. So it went with the third, the fourth, and the fifth. She looked at the last bottle and her thirsty greed momentarily overmastered her pride, so she said: OK. I'm sorry OK.

Then a moment later she looked him full in the face and said: You stupid. I hate you.

He poured the bottle out.

She took her suitcase and went into that Montréal midnight with the intention of leaving him forever, and he sat in anguish worrying about her because she didn't have any money; she'd come without money and he'd doled it out this time so she couldn't get crazy drunk and cause more trouble; what would happen to her? But she was free; she didn't want him; she had to make her own way. She came back because she'd forgotten something; then she went out again. Through the window he glimpsed her down on Saint-Denis between the giant grinning green plastic monster heads where the music went whirling crazily like a Russian orgy, singing up over the street of those shouting jigging heads from which she had previously curled timidly back; she vanished there now.

He stood at the window and saw chess-chested kicking girls and bluehaired greenfooted drummers.

An hour later she came back quietly, her face screwed up by weeping, wearing those same low brownish wrinkles he'd seen in the indigo sea salted with ice. — My friend went away, she explained. He said I can't go with him.

OK, he said. Let's go to sleep.

They turned out the light and he rolled tight against the wall to avoid annoying her. She said very softly: Please don't come to the Inukjuak anymore.

His heart almost exploded. For a moment he could not speak. — I'll go where I want, he said finally.

Please. Please.

OK. I won't go to Inukjuak anymore.

Then she laughed with relief and touched him and made love to him and said she loved him. That was the worst.

He lay awake thinking how the previous night she'd gotten drunk and said: I want to go to Inukjuak, so I can see my boyfriend in Heaven.

How did he die?

From rifle. He killed himself.

When will you kill yourself?

When I go to Inukjuak.

Early the next morning he took her to the airport and the last he saw of her she was walking away, wiping his goodbye kiss off her mouth with the back of her hand, a gesture he recognized from somewhere, although she'd never unkissed him before; then as he went to get his bus he realized that it had been with that same slow forcefulness that she used to squash mosquitoes against the wall of the tent.

In Coral Harbour a boy had asked him why Reepah would meet him in Montréal but not in a northern town.

Maybe the south is more interesting for her because she doesn't live there, he said. Maybe she's ashamed to be seen by other Inuit when she's with a *Qaallunaat*.★

Don't worry, the Inuk said kindly. Lots of our girls have ugly boyfriends and we don't mind it. One girl even goes with a man with a wooden leg.

Later still, walking upon the tundra, he remembered Reepah stepping so easily and confidently from rock to tussock, never wetting her toe in any hidden puddle, never needing to look.

★ White man.

WHERE YOU
ARE TODAY

Zagreb, Croatia (1992)

Zagreb, Croatia (1992)

In the reddish-black light of a bar that stank of cigarette smoke, four men sat around a table watching their hands. They had big pale arms. Drunkenness gleamed on their waxy foreheads, and their pale shirts lay open to the chest. They were sweating and grayhaired. The U-shaped shadows across their faces and paunches cheated the checked shadows around their dark eyes that burned like cigarette-ends. Their features were bland and flushed. Their glasses were as empty as falsehoods we tell every night.

The drunken artist slowly signed his worthless painting. He had the same last name as the best chess player in the world. Slowly he rolled his cigarette between thumb and forefinger and shook it like a baton.

The drunken zombie said: The time I was dead, dead, dead, it was real medicine. I used medicine that my body couldn't accept. That was the day I died. My heart had the pulse zero. It was only sleep, a very deep sleep like heroin. You see, brothers, I'd spent more than three years in India. That was the time yellow fever was popular. At least eighty percent of the junkies caught yellow fever. But I was

443

playing with fever. It was something like playing poker or one-eyed jack. That's how it was when I was dead.

The drunken gypsy said: There is no most beautiful. Let's say tomorrow I am free, I am—I don't have to work . . . No! I want brandy! And one beer for all of us, just to water it . . .

The drunken soldier, the old one in the plaid shirt, was the only one who still had money. He got brandy and one beer for all. He shook his fingers at the others, a glass of brandy in his other hand, brandy on his breath.

The drunken zombie said: They took my passport in 1978 for making samples of medicine for myself . . .

Silence! Silence! cried the drunken gypsy. The soldier wishes to sing.

Bowing, the drunken soldier placed his fingers on the drunken gypsy's arm. Then he began to sing, demonstrating that he almost had teeth. His singing was a series of spitting sounds.

The drunken artist, the beefy one, squeezed his own biceps and wept as the bikini-girl twitched in the flesh of him. He'd tattooed her into marrying him so long ago that she was faded to the color of old chewing gum. He wept, and whispered: Children, everyone wants my money.

Take it easy, said the drunken gypsy, who was happy.

The drunken soldier's cigarette dropped out of his mouth. — I was in Tito's army in '64, he said. I saved all your asses. Without me, you wouldn't be where you are today.

LAST DAY
AT THE BAKERY

Sarajevo, Bosnia-Herzegovina (1992)

Sarajevo, Bosnia-Herzegovina (1992)

At two o'clock on a rainy afternoon, a dozen people waited in front of the bakery. Behind the fence, a man in camouflage stood guard. The people were pale and they shivered. The man in camouflage spoke to someone at the inner door and then approached me, never letting go his gun. I was permitted inside. I could feel the stares of the waiting people in my back.

The name of the director was Mešak Kempl. He was very tired. He said: This bakery has been hit five or six times, and we never stopped for one day. We're still working. But there's been no electricity for the past two weeks, and no diesel, and erratic water. Today for the first time the whole city is without water.

How many bakeries are there?

Before the war, there were two. One is now held by the Chetniks. Two or three hundred private bakeries provided half of our bread, but they're mostly not working now. So it's only this bakery that provides bread for the city. Two weeks ago we made one hundred thousand loaves a day. Even that wasn't enough. Now we make fewer than fifty thousand. Our trucks have been shelled at, shot at—every

445

truck has holes in it! We've had two drivers killed and five severely injured in these five months of war. And after tonight, we will be making no more bread. Well, maybe by some miracle we'll get more diesel . . .

I could think of nothing to say. There was a fresh loaf of bread on Kempl's desk, and he smiled and offered me a piece.

The only thing we have left is the will to work, he said. The people would prefer it if the plane was full of guns and ammunition, not flour.

He smiled. — We've come to the end, he said.

What will people eat?

There's left some pasta and rice. The pasta factory itself hasn't been working for fifteen days.

He took me into the room that smelled like dough, where two men in white uniforms were straining their arms deep in the mixing bowl because there was not enough diesel to use the electric mixer. — We have only two more bowls' worth left, said Kempl. Then the dough will be finished.

The room was almost dark, but it was warm. Three lights in the entire bank were working. A pretty girl in white was taking loaves of dough off the conveyor belt. Then the fermentation box drew them into darkness, the hygrometer at seventy, rolls and rolls in wheels slowly turning.

There was an immense space of empty floor where it was dark. This place was like the heart of a dying man, still pumping life, but only in negligible quantities and only for a little longer. The fresh brown loaves, smelling so yeasty and good, slowly rolled off the last conveyor. There were no loaves before them, and none after. Those hot brown loaves spiralled down to the basement like golden squirrels, to be caught by a girl in white who loaded them into cartons.

The director shook my hand politely. He offered me a loaf of bread to take with me. As I went back into the chilly rainy afternoon and passed the line, which had now grown to fifty people, the tears burst out of my eyes.

CLOSING THE BOOK

Sacramento, California, U.S.A. (1992)

He had left her burning in her tears at the Greyhound station, and now he was about to take the city bus home. It was twilight. Knowing that she was standing in line at this moment, facing him, yearning for him, made him weary and afraid. A black cawing creature crooked itself through the slatey air between palms. A bus came, well lit inside. People dreamed or stared as it rolled them away. Perhaps she was boarding her bus now, passing through the long smelly darkness of the loading garage. The blue-uniformed baggage man would be kicking the last suitcase deeper into the sidecave; then he'd slam down the cover. Could she hear that, sitting inside? She'd be looking out her window at the numbered metal doors. The driver would close and lock the one she had just come through, so that she couldn't see the Coke machine anymore, but through the window she'd still be able to find legs opening and closing with comic earnestness, reflecting themselves on the bile-green floor. Now she'd be staring at the streaks of brown grease above those metal doors. He could feel her thinking of him. He'd never get away from her. She thought of him until the driver came in and started the engine. The

447

driver took his coat off, slammed the door, slid glasses over his nose, honked, and began to pull out into the street. A man in a baseball cap was whistling and pacing, a garbage bag over his shoulder. Cold shadows and tired lights began to encase the buildings in their night incarnation. Another bus went by, almost empty, a rolling box of lateness. She would be on the freeway now because the traffic was light. It was too late for her to be accompanied by the noises of little boys in baseball caps eating chips. The other heads growing from the seats like halitosis melons would be weary heads, not even mumbling as she passed the Hofbrau and the Hotel Marshall on that bus which sometimes smelled of leather, sometimes of tunafish, always of that disinfectant whose nauseating fumes always commanded him to consider the toilets of mental wards. He could see himself sitting behind her, glimpsing the top of her head over the seat, her shoulder between the seats; maybe she'd reach for the reading light and he'd see her arm bloom sweetly up. He allowed himself to remember kissing her. Remembering was just the same as reading the commentary on a favorite poem, not to learn any secret, but only because he'd read the poem to satiation without yet exhausting his love, and scanning the commentary was a way to kiss the poem again without reading it. Nobody was in sight. Blank or vicious little headlights scuttered around the bases of the chilly skyscrapers. It got darker. The trees were now almost the color of the sky. Cool darkness pressed on his head. On a squat skyscraper, a glowing red bead tipped a horn of darkness.

You want some love? a whore said.

Too much love is my problem, he said.

All right, honey. Well, we don't have to call it love.

He looked up at her and she was not very pretty but she was very determined and he remembered how one Japanese term for a courtesan meant *ruining a castle*.

I don't know who she is, but if you want I'll be her, the whore said. Just tell me how to be her and I'll be her for you. I need my fix real bad.

Can you be a train? he said. I left her on the Greyhound but if you were a train you could carry me home to her.

The whore got down on her hands and knees on the sidewalk and whistled like a train. She began to crawl toward him. He stood up, and the sound of his heels upon the hard night sidewalk echoed like light. Laughing, she snatched at his ankles. Gently he took her hands away and sat down on her back. — All aboard! she cried. Her eyes became headlights. The train thudded very slowly between the gravel shoulders and fences and across the trestle bridge to morning, only slightly rusty, that put the brown river behind.

Sacramento, California, U.S.A. (1992)

Soon now he'd knock at the door of the cool house where she'd be waiting to leap into his arms. He sat on one of the long wooden benches, which was warm and moist with so many people's sweat, and listened to the echoes that clashed beneath the high vaulted ceiling like belltower vultures, harsh and flat and desperate in the heat. Soon he'd be drinking her spit. Soon he'd be holding her in his arms listening to the moon. He wiped his sleeve across his forehead. It was breathlessly hot. Little girls in matching dark plaid dresses whose squares were as wide and solid as flagstones—evidently some school uniform—wandered, eating onion chips and drinking sodas. A slender-legged Japanese girl with a severe black braid knelt on the marble, watching black boys play cards on the next bench. The boys had their uniform, too—white shirts and bluejeans. They were eating ice cream cones. — Cheat! one shouted. — No I didn't, wept the Japanese girl. You play!

As he looked around the station, he saw more and more of these children who wore the mark of the beast. Plaid dresses and white shirts multiplied like bacteria beneath the lens of his recognizance. The old ladies who leaned on their luggage carts, gossiping, shaking their heads so that their steering-wheel-sized earrings shook; these souls too seemed to be a part of the school, because he saw them wearily enumerating children with their forefingers. A man in a pork-pie hat whom he'd been sure had nothing to do with it suddenly smiled in a sinister way; a boy in a white shirt had run up between the man's knees. The man turned away. Could he himself be the only one who did not belong? A white girl and a Latina girl sat on the floor, kicking like horses, playing finger games among their plaids. Suddenly they stared at him over their shoulders. They began to whisper. A black boy in a white shirt ran to them, darted his head anxiously, then tore away in brand-new sneakers to a sweating lady who sat dragging a handkerchief across her broad brown cheeks. The lady frowned. She cupped her hand, waiting for him to expectorate his tidings like chewing gum. He muttered into her palm. The lady gazed sharply at the girls. Then she blew on a whistle. At once, everyone in the waiting room got up and streamed through the exit without looking back.

He sat alone.

A blonde girl in a black plaid dress came out of the ladies' room.

— You're not with them, Mister? she said.

No.

Really?

How could I be? Am I wearing a white shirt?

Who do you belong to?

Nobody. How about you?

Nobody.

Mister, you wanna be with me? 'Cause I'm not with anybody.

He thought of the woman who was waiting for him. She wanted to have his baby but was unable to get pregnant. Maybe she'd want to have this girl.

He looked into her face. — Do you want to be my child or to have my child?

I don't care, the girl whined. I just gotta be with somebody.

Then you have to take off your uniform. Otherwise how can I trust you?

You wanna be with me or don't you? You don't want to be with me.

Wailing, the little blonde girl dug her fingers into her eyes. Then she ran to the farthest corner of the waiting room and pressed her face against the wall.

They called his train. He got up and left her there. When he passed down into the cool tunnel that led to the train tracks, there was no one. The ceiling vibrated from the buses and trains overhead. He walked on, passing ramps which terminated in triangles of scorching sunlight.

He got on the train and it was full. He walked backward through car after car, past the dining car where they were serving the last shot of gin they had, and finally reached a car of middle-aged people who somehow looked alike. One seat was empty, but when he asked if he could take it the sighing lady said: That's for our darling. Have you seen her?

No.

She's a little blonde girl in a black plaid dress. I don't know what's happened to her. We can't think without her. We can't laugh without her. Look at us! Every hour without her makes us a year older. I can't compose myself, young man. You see, she was at the center of things.

Sacramento, California, U.S.A. (1992)

The leering twitching grayhaired mumbler ahead of him kept seizing his sleeve and whispering: Is this the good bus?

Yes, he said finally. It's the good bus because I'm going to ride it to the woman I love.

But is it the *good* bus? fretted the man. I mean the bus to Nome, Alaska. Now Anchorage is a slow town at night. That's why I'm going on the good bus to Nome, Alaska. Is this the good bus?

I'm going to the South Pole, he replied. It won't be easy to get there on a bus; you have to drive onto a big iceberg.

Then I'll save up all the ice in my cocktails! the old man cried with a wink . . .

Inside the dark and waiting Greyhound it was cold and stank of disinfectant. He looked down on the lunch hour world, experiencing the sense of progress that one gets when watching car after car roll down a one-way street. The driver came on, closed the door, locked his seatbelt, worked the wide wheel with one hairy arm, stopped at the red light, sucking his cheeks, then went forward. Office workers impelled themselves blindly into the mall.

The old mumbler, who sat behind him, craned and said: Is this the good bus?

If she takes me in her arms it'll be the good bus, he replied.

The bridge ahead with its tower above the row of roofless arches invited him across the graygreen river. A flock of birds flung themselves somewhere meaningless like a handful of wood chips.

We're in Alaska now, said the old man.

How do you know?

Because I smell her perfume.

She doesn't wear perfume.

That doesn't matter. You only love her. That's what they say. But I belong to her forever. And I'm telling you this: As soon as she takes you in her arms we'll be in Nome, Alaska. They told me that, too. Now I know this is the good bus. I'm going to sit here now and be quiet and hope and wait and pray until I see her running to meet you and kissing your mouth into Nome, Alaska.

Sacramento, California, U.S.A. (1992)

The morning was overcast and cool like her touch as he passed the shop-windows that were just now sleepily raising their eyelids. He felt very rested, but also very hungry. The long brown scaled ribs of the first bench soared against his back. Behind him, other benches squatted in a queue. No one was in the waiting room but he. The fountain had been turned off. The ticket window was down. On its eight faces, which had been textured to resemble the sockets inhabited by pomegranate seeds, two luminescences like oval headlamps moved as his gaze moved. Perhaps they were the headlights of his high and silver train. He got up and went outside the station, watching the empty track. Suddenly the taste of her saliva came into his mouth.

On the train, a child was crying with dull hopelessness. He sat down in a seat still warm from a vanished body. The train began to move almost immediately. Wet gray streets, wet white-gray sky, wet green-gray trees, mudfields and green fields unraveled, the train clicking like a monstrous loom. There was nowhere to go except home, and home was nowhere anymore. He was starving. To the even jack-hammering of the rails he sat remembering the dinner she'd made him last night: lamb chops and home fries and buttered beans.

The train slowed, as if to enjoy the shade of the overpass, then rolled between a trestle's interminable X's as it crossed the greenish-brown river.

He disembarked with the others and went into the first coffee shop he could find.

Both waitresses limped. One was a fat lady whose gray hair was cropped so severely that she might have been a recent electroshock patient. The other was an old Chinese who shouted almost consonantlessly.

The Chinese lady brought him a menu.

Pork chops and eggs, please, he said.

Why you wan' po'k cho' OK! screeched the waitress.

The walls glistened yellow-green with grease.

A giraffe-necked man in the next booth kept biting his ladyfriend's ear with a silly laugh. An old man lurched in, clutching the rails of his walker. In came a woman, limping.

The clockface was so gilded with decades of grease that it might have been deep sea brass.

A whore and a pimp were sitting side by side at the counter. The pimp said: They stole something else from me. I threw away all my underwear that didn't have holes in it so they'd leave me alone, but they stole the raggedy ones just the same.

The whore yawned and drank her coffee.

What'll you have? said the fat waitress.

Number three, said the pimp.

I dunno what the number three is, said the fat waitress. You order what it *is*, not what number it is. I don't care how many girls you got working for you.

Gimme some soup then, said the pimp meekly.

A man in a booth smoked, sucking his elliptical face into a round tobacco moon while his glasses gleamed greedily.

The fat waitress hobbled bowlegged, leaning on each booth as she went, struggling with a scalding platter of meat that was too heavy for her.

He remembered the taste of her armpits and the pulsing of the veins in her fingers when he kissed her hands. He thought of the train going farther and farther from her.

The Chinese waitress brought his pork chops and eggs.

Thank you, he said.

She stared at him in surprise.

What do you have coming, hon? the fat waitress was saying to the whore. I didn't hear you.

Two over easy, the whore said bitterly.

He was never going to see her again.

You whaiee po'k cho' ho' saussssssss? shrieked the old Chinese lady. Hot sauce? OK.

Thank you, he said when she brought it, and she smiled a timid old smile. That was when he began to love her.

Where's my soup? said the pimp.

Just a minute more, said the fat waitress.

I don't have time for you, bitch, the pimp said. — He got up and walked out. The whore looked down at the counter and ground out her cigarette against the saucer.

Your friend's no good, said the fat waitress in outrage. I told him the soup would be ready in a minute and he called me a bitch. The hell with him.

The whore said nothing.

You whaiee whea' toasss please? shrieked the waitress.

Sure, I'll take some wheat toast. Thank you.

This time her smile was full and open.

As he ate he looked around him at the horrible place. The man who had been smoking moved in the next booth, which the giraffe-necked man had left. His face was flushed red. He stuck his cigarette into the nosepiece of his glasses and glared dreamily. — *Thank you,* he said sarcastically. I oughta run you through, you asshole. Talking to that Chink like that. *Thank you,* he says.

The bill came to $4.60. He was going to leave six, which would keep a dollar in his pocket after the bus. When the old lady came, she said: Whaieee now e'thing OK?

Nodding silently, he took out seven dollars.

Too much! she shrieked.

Wearily he pushed it into her hand.

T'ank you, t'ank you!

Thank you, he said. As he got up, he watched her fingers tighten ecstatically around the money.

SOURCES
and a note

p. xi Compiler's Note: James Branch Cabell quotation — *Let Me Lie, Being in the Main an Ethnological Account of the Remarkable Commonwealth of Virginia and the Making of Its History* (New York: Farrar, Straus, 1947), p. 17.

91 "Houses," Roberts Camp section — C. H. Hinton, M.A., *The Fifth Dimension* (London: Swan Sonnenschein, 1906), p. 38.

145 "Spare Parts," first Somalia section, "The principal meteorological factors" — W. Thompson, *The Climate of Africa* (Nairobi: Oxford University Press, 1965), p. 3.

214 "The Atlas," Bible excerpt — New Oxford version, Proverbs 7:25–29.

214 "The Atlas," *Qur'-An* excerpt — A. J. Arberry, *The Koran Interpreted* (New York: Collier Books, 1955), XXVII:41–47.

222 "The Atlas," Sarajevo brochure extract — Sarajevo Tourist Association booklet, "Sarajevo, Yugoslavia: English" (Novi Sad: Munir Rasidovic, 1985).

230   "The Atlas," Lautréamont excerpt — Comte de Lautréamont, *Maldoror* and *Poems*, trans. Paul Knight (New York: Penguin, 1978), p. 281.

248–49   "The Atlas," first translation of *Snow Country* sentence — Yasunari Kawabata, *Snow Country*, trans. Edward G. Seidensticker (New York: G. P. Putnam's Sons, Perigree Books, 1981; repr. of 1957 Knopf ed.), p. 3.

249   "The Atlas," second translation of *Snow Country* sentence — Yasunari Kawabata, *Palm-of-the-Hand Stories*, trans. Lane Dunlop and J. Martin Holman (San Francisco: North Point Press, 1988), p. 228 ("Gleanings from 'Snow Country' ").

249–50   Note: "Translations" of the Kawabata sentence on these pages are mine.

320   "The Hill of Gold," Masada section, "The mind of the righteous": — New Oxford version, Proverbs 15:28.

324   "The Hill of Gold," Masada section, Judith's words — Apocrypha, New Oxford Version, Judith 8:16.

333   "Disappointed by the Wind" — Walter Benjamin, *Moscow Diary*, ed. Gary Smith, trans. Richard Sieburth (Cambridge, Mass.: Harvard University Press, 1986), p. 6 (letter to Martin Buber).

379   "Fortune-Tellers," Sphere of Stars section, Coptic text — James M. Robinson, ed., *The Nag Hammadi Library in English,* 3rd rev. ed. (Harper San Francisco, 1990), "The Concept of Our Great Power" (VI, 4), p. 313.

408   "The Street of Stares," third section, "I look on the blacks as a set of monkeys . . ." — M. F. Christie, *Aborigines in Colonial Victoria 1835– 86* (Sydney: Sydney University Press, 1979), p. 45, quoted in Eve Mumewa D. Fesl, *Conned!* (St. Lucia: University of Queensland Press, 1993), p. 64.

431 "Say It with Flowers" — When I returned to that bar a year later, the woman with ten husbands was still there. It was night. She clutched me fiercely like a bird of prey and drew me in, shrilly and threateningly cawing entreaties. The place was full of men and terrifying laughter. The next year, no one I knew worked there.

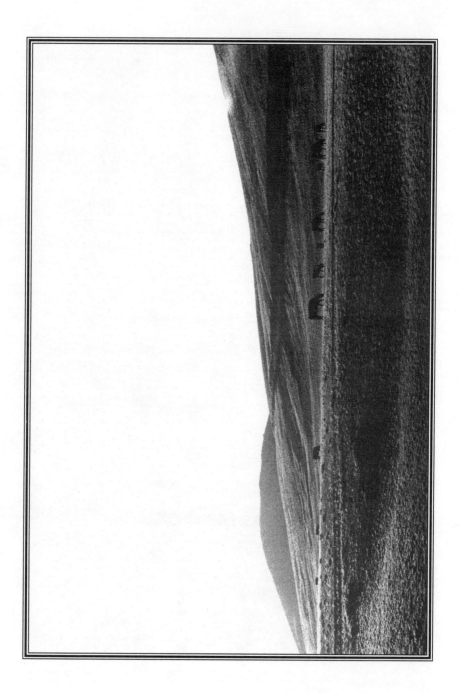

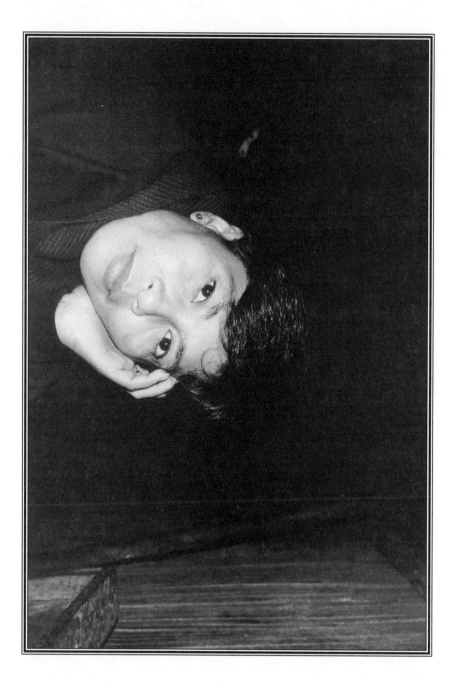

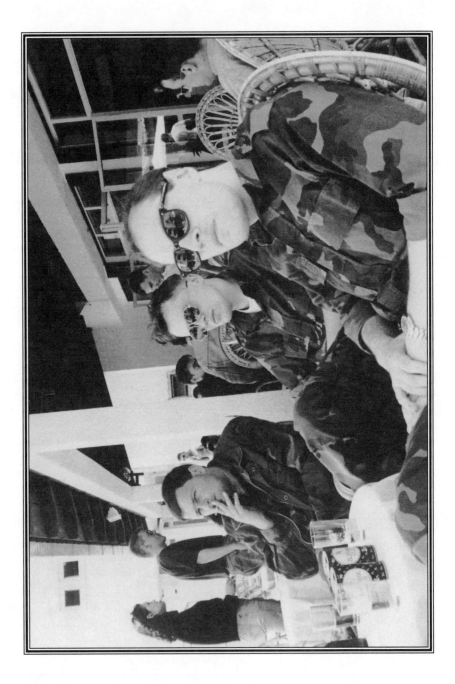

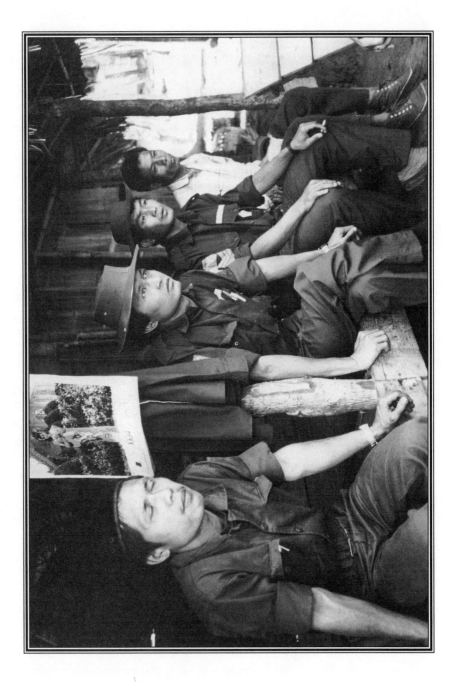

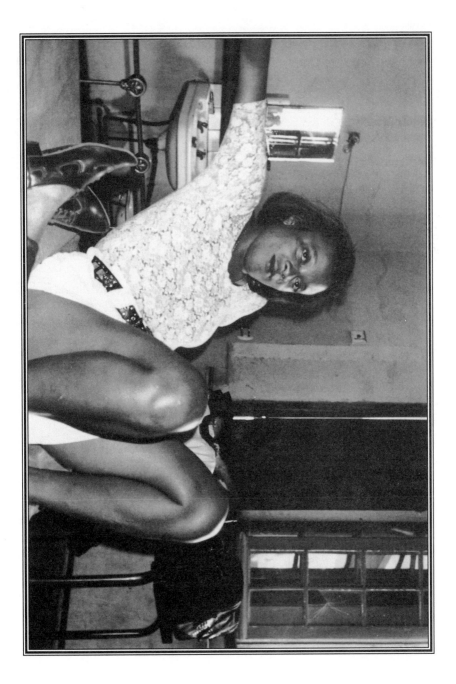

ACKNOWLEDGMENTS

Author's Note

"Opening the Book," the New York section of "Cowbells," "Lunch," "Charity," the New York section of "Five Lonely Nights," and "What's Your Name?" first appeared (in more or less that order) in the 1994 special New York issue of *Grand Street*.

"The Back of My Head" first appeared in an abbreviated form in *The Los Angeles Times Magazine* in 1992. This story, along with all of this book's other 1992 pieces set in ex-Yugoslavia (except for "Where You Are Today"), was part of four BBC Radio 4 broadcasts which I made in Berlin in 1992 called "The Yugoslav Notes." (The Yugoslavia pieces in *The Atlas* are accompaniments to the sections "Where Are All the Pretty Girls?" and "It's Not a War" in my essay "Rising Up and Rising Down"). I am happy now to restore "The Back of My Head" to its original form.

"An Old Man in Old Grayish Kamiks" was first presented (in abridged form) in 1994 in a BBC radio program entitled "Four Corners."

"The Prophet of the Road" first appeared in *The Los Angeles Times Magazine* in 1992.

The San Diego section of "Houses" first appeared in Larry McCaffery's anthology *Avant-Pop: Fiction for a Daydream Nation* [Boulder: Black Ice Books (Fiction Collective Two), 1993].

"Under the Grass" first appeared in 1994 in *Grand Street*, minus the final "Roma" section which they did not care for.

"The Best Way to Smoke Crack" first appeared in a Japanese translation in the magazine *Subaru*.

The "Traveller's Epitaph" in "The Atlas" first appeared in *Zyzzyva*.

"Red and Blue" first appeared in *Spin* in 1994 in a slightly abbreviated form.

"The Best Way to Drink Beer" first appeared in *Esquire* in 1994 under their title, "How to Drink Beer."

The first paragraph of "Resolute Bay, Cornwallis Island, Canada (1991)" in "Incarnations of the Murderer" was originally a part of a BBC radio program I presented entitled "Are You Spies from Greenpeace?" (January 1992). "Incarnations of the Murderer" as a whole first appeared in the electronic anthology *Post-Modern Culture*. The version herein has been revised and expanded.

"Outside and Inside" first appeared in a shorter version in *Conjunctions*.

"The Rifles" was first published in *Grand Street*.

"Last Day at the Bakery" first appeared in *Story* magazine in 1994.

Grateful acknowledgment is made to Reed International Books for permission to reproduce the following from *Philips' International Atlas: A Series of 160 Pages of Coloured Maps and Plans Forming a Complete Geographical Survey of the International Relationships of the New Era, Its Territorial Changes and Commercial Communications*, Third Edition, edited by George Philip, F.R.G.S., George Philip & Son, Ltd, The London Geographical Institute, 1937: Rainfall, Isobars and Winds; Flags of All Nations; and North Polar Regions - South Polar Regions.

Photographs by the author.